SACRA

Sa

08/18

Everybody loves the compelling suspense novels of

LAURA GRIFFIN

UNFORGIVABLE

"Another top-level romantic suspense . . . Strong characters, a tight and complex mystery plot, and nonstop action make *Unforgivable* an unforgettable read." —*Romantic Times*

"The science is fascinating, the sex is sizzling, and the story is top-notch, making this clever, breakneck tale hard to put down." —*Publishers Weekly*

"The perfect mix of suspense and romance." —*Booklist*

"Razor-sharp suspense, sizzling-hot romance! *Unforgivable* has 'keeper shelf' written all over it."

—Cindy Gerard, *New York Times* bestselling author of
the Black Ops Inc. series

UNSPEAKABLE

"A tight suspense with the sexiest of heroes and a protagonist seriously worth rooting for." —*Romantic Times* (4½ stars)

"A page-turner until the last page, it's a fabulous read."

—Fresh Fiction

UNTRACEABLE

Winner of the 2010 Daphne du Maurier Award for Best Romantic Suspense

"Taut drama and constant action . . . Griffin keeps the suspense high and the pace quick. A perfect combination of forensic science, mystery, romance, and action makes this series one to watch." —*Publishers Weekly* (starred review)

"Top-notch romantic suspense! Fast pace, tight plotting, terrific mystery, sharp dialogue, fabulous characters . . . unforgettable."

—*New York Times* bestselling author Allison Brennan

"The characters are top-notch, and their gradual romance—entrenched in mystery and suspense—leaves readers sighing contentedly." —*Romantic Times* (4½ stars)

WHISPER OF WARNING

2010 RITA Winner for Best Romantic Suspense

"A perfectly woven and tense mystery with a sweet and compelling love story." —*Romantic Times*

"Irresistible characters and a plot thick with danger . . . sexy and suspenseful ." —Romance Junkies

"Action, danger, and passion . . . a compellingly gripping story." —SingleTitles

THREAD OF FEAR

"Suspense and romance—right down to the last page. What more could you ask for?" —Publishers Weekly Online

"Catapults you from bone-chilling to heartwarming to too hot to handle. Laura Griffin's talent is fresh and daring."
—*The Winter Haven* (FL) *News Chief*

"A tantalizing suspense-filled thriller. Enjoy, but lock your doors." —Romance Reviews Today

ONE WRONG STEP

"Starts with a bang and never lets up on the pace . . . The twists and turns of the story leave the Le Mans racetrack in the dust." —*The Winter Haven* (FL) *News Chief*

"Enjoyable, fast-paced romantic suspense."
—Publishers Weekly Online

ONE LAST BREATH

"Compelling characters, unexpected twists, and a gripping story." —Bestselling romantic suspense author Roxanne St. Claire

"Heart-stopping intrigue and red-hot love scenes . . . *One Last Breath* rocks!" —*The Winter Haven* (FL) *News Chief*

"An action-packed tale filled with passion and revenge."
—*Romantic Times*

"Fully fleshed characters, dry humor, and tight plotting make a fun read." —*Publishers Weekly*

"Mixes suspense and snappy humor with wonderful results."
—*Affaire de Coeur*

All of Laura Griffin's titles are also available as eBooks

Also by Laura Griffin

LAURA GRIFFIN

SNAPPED

POCKET STAR BOOKS
NEW YORK LONDON TORONTO SYDNEY NEW DELHI

The sale of this book without its cover is unauthorized. If you purchased this book without a cover, you should be aware that it was reported to the publisher as "unsold and destroyed." Neither the author nor the publisher has received payment for the sale of this "stripped book."

 Pocket Star Books
A Division of Simon & Schuster, Inc.
1230 Avenue of the Americas
New York, NY 10020

This book is a work of fiction. Names, characters, places, and incidents either are products of the author's imagination or are used fictitiously. Any resemblance to actual events or locales or persons, living or dead, is entirely coincidental.

Copyright © 2011 by Laura Griffin

All rights reserved, including the right to reproduce this book or portions thereof in any form whatsoever. For information address Pocket Books Subsidiary Rights Department,
1230 Avenue of the Americas, New York, NY 10020

First Pocket Star Books paperback edition September 2011

POCKET STAR BOOKS and colophon are registered trademarks of Simon & Schuster, Inc.

For information about special discounts for bulk purchases, please contact Simon & Schuster Special Sales at 1-866-506-1949 or business@simonandschuster.com.

The Simon & Schuster Speakers Bureau can bring authors to your live event. For more information or to book an event contact the Simon & Schuster Speakers Bureau at 1-866-248-3049 or visit our website at www.simonspeakers.com.

Cover design by Lisa Litwack

Manufactured in the United States of America

10 9 8 7

ISBN 978-1-4516-1736-8
ISBN 978-1-4516-1741-2 (ebook)

For Meredith

ACKNOWLEDGMENTS

It's always a team effort, and I'd like to thank everyone at Pocket for bringing this book to life, including Abby Zidle, Lisa Litwack, Ayelet Gruenspecht, Renee Huff, Parisa Zolfaghari, and many others who work behind the scenes. You guys rock! Also, a special thanks to my agent, Kevan Lyon, as well as the law enforcement and forensic experts who helped me on the research end: Ruben Vasquez, Luke Causey, Kathy Bennett, Mark Wright, Jessica Dawson, and Pat Whalen. Any mistakes here are all mine.

On a personal note, I owe a special thank-you to my mother, who was in Austin that fateful day when so many innocent people lost their lives. Thanks, Mom, for sharing your story and helping to inspire this one.

SNAPPED

SNAPPED

CHAPTER 1

Parking on campus was a bitch and so was Sophie. Or at least, she was in a bitchy mood. She was hot, hungry, and doomed to spend the better part of her lunch hour waiting in line at the registrar's office.

But then she spotted it—a gleaming, perfect, gorgeously empty parking space not fifty feet in front of her. The green flag indicating time still left on the parking meter was the cherry on top of her lunchtime sundae.

"Thank you," she sighed as she rolled past the spot, shifted into reverse, and flipped her turn indicator. She had just started to ease back when an old-model VW zipped up behind her.

"Hey!" Sophie pounded her horn as the Bug driver whipped into her spot while pretending not to see her. She might as well have been invisible.

"*Un*believable!" Sophie jabbed at the window button and leaned out to yell at him. "Yo, Fahrvergnügen! That's *my* spot!"

A horn blared behind her and she glanced around. Now she was holding up traffic. She shifted into drive and muttered curses as she scoured the busy streets for another scrap of real estate large enough to accommodate her Tahoe. Of course there wasn't one. She glanced at her watch. Damn it, she was going to be late getting back to work, and she'd long since used up her tardy passes. With a final curse, she pulled into an overpriced parking garage three blocks downhill from her destination. After squeezing into a spot, she jumped out and dashed for the exit, pressing numbers on her cell phone as she went.

"Mia? Hey, it's me." She stepped onto the sidewalk and blinked up at the blindingly bright sunlight.

"What's up, Soph? I've got my hands full."

"Shoot, forget it, then."

"What?"

"I'm at the university," Sophie said. "I was going to ask you to cover the phones for a few minutes if I'm not back by one."

"I'll get down there if I can, but—"

"Don't worry, I'll get Diane to do it." Diane was the assistant evidence clerk at the Delphi Center, where Sophie worked, but she wasn't exactly known for her cheery disposition. "She owes me a favor, anyway. We're still on for margaritas with Kelsey, right? Six o'clock?"

"Schmitt's," Mia confirmed. "See you there."

Sophie dropped the phone in her bag and continued uphill. The sun blazed down. Her blouse grew damp. Her tortured feet were a testament to the folly of buying Victoria's Secret sandals on clearance. After waiting for a break in traffic, she darted across the street and felt the heat coming up off the asphalt in waves. Jeez, it was *hot*. Thank goodness she was signing up for a night course.

At last she reached the grassy quadrangle and enjoyed

a few patches of shade as she neared the registrar's office. Students streamed up and down the sidewalks, talking with friends and reading text messages. Sophie gazed wistfully at their cutoff shorts and tank tops. Once upon a time she, too, had lived in grunge wear. She didn't miss the clothes so much as that time in her life, when she'd had nothing more to do than go to keg parties on weekends and cut class to hang out with her boyfriend. Now both those pursuits seemed worse than trivial— they seemed wasteful. How could a few short years make such a difference in her outlook?

She marveled at the irony—here she was plunking down her hard-earned money to attend a class she would have happily ditched just a few years ago. The perfect revenge for her I-told-you-so parents, only they'd never get the chance to say that because she had no intention of telling them she was back in school. This was her private mission, and if she failed to accomplish it, no one would ever have to know she'd tried.

Sophie navigated the busy sidewalks, longing for a pair of Birkenstocks instead of heels. She glanced again at her watch and *knew,* without a doubt, she was going to be late.

Crack.

She halted in her tracks.

People shrieked behind her, and she whirled around. Her gaze landed on someone sprawled across the sidewalk. A man. Sophie stared in shock at the jacket, the tie, and the bloody pulp that should have been his head.

Crack.

Someone's shooting! The words screamed through her

brain as she scanned her surroundings. She was in an open field. She was a clear target.

More shrieks as she bolted for the trees. A staccato of bullets. Clumps of grass burst up at her and she fell back, landing hard on her butt. Before her eyes, a woman collapsed to the ground, clutching her throat. A child in pigtails howled. Crab-walking backward, Sophie glanced around frantically. What was happening? Where was it coming from? Screams echoed around her as people ducked and dove for cover.

She rolled to her knees and lunged for the nearest solid object—a cement block at the base of a statue. She crouched behind it, gasping for breath, every nerve in her body zinging with terror.

Where is he?

More gunfire. More screaming. Sophie cupped her hands over her head and tried to make herself small.

"She *lent* it to you? That's the best you got?" San Marcos Police Detective Allison Doyle scowled down at the pimply-faced perpetrator and waited. It didn't take long.

"She didn't say that *exactly.*"

"What did she say, *exactly*?"

"Well, it was more like understood, you know?" The kid slouched against the door to his dorm room. "Like I could use it long as I wanted, so long as I returned it."

"I see." Allison nodded over his shoulder, at the array of loot spread out on his single bed: four iPods, two BlackBerrys, and an iPad not even out of the box—which constituted the reason for her little visit to this room that smelled like gym socks and God knew what else.

"What about the iPods?" Allison asked. "You borrow them, too?"

A girl burst into the hallway. "Someone's shooting! Oh my God, people are *dead*!"

Allison yanked out her Glock and rushed down the hall. "Who's shooting? Where?"

"The quad! Someone's *killing* people!"

"Go into your rooms and lock your doors. Now! Stay away from the windows."

Allison raced across the lobby and out the glass door. It was like stepping into an oven. She took an instant to orient herself, then took off for the university quadrangle just as her radio crackled to life.

"Attention all units! Active shooter on campus! South quadrangle!" The usually calm dispatcher sounded shrill, and Allison felt the first twinge of panic. "Reports of casualties. All units respond!"

Allison jerked the radio from her belt. "Doyle responding." *Jesus Christ.* "Where is the shooter? Over."

For a moment, silence. Then a distant wail of sirens on the other side of town. Allison sprinted across University Avenue and did a double take. Cars were stopped in the middle of the road, doors flung open. The engines were running, but the cars were empty.

"Shooter's location is unknown," the dispatcher said. "I repeat, unknown."

Jonah Macon stared at the dilapidated house where absolutely nothing had happened for the past seven hours. He hated surveillance work, and not just the boredom of it. His six-foot-four-inch frame wasn't designed to be crammed into the back of a van for days on end.

"If I drink another cup of this coffee, my piss is gonna turn black."

Jonah shot Sean Byrne a look of disgust but didn't respond.

"Nice image," Jonah's partner Ric quipped, tossing his Styrofoam cup into an empty Krispy Kreme box. Ric Santos had volunteered to bring breakfast this morning, and the doughnut shop was just around the corner from his girlfriend's place.

So here they all were—bored, caffeinated, and jacked up on sugar that needed to be burned off. Jonah leaned back in his seat and popped his knuckles as he stared at the video monitor.

"Seriously, how late can he sleep?" Sean asked. "I'm about to bust in there and drag his skinny ass out here myself."

"Movement at the door," Jonah said, and everyone snapped to attention.

A man stepped onto the porch, finally breaking the monotony. Jonah's team had been in the van since before dawn, waiting for their subject to kiss his girlfriend good-bye and lead them to the crib where they were ninety-nine percent sure their murder suspect was holed up. Sure enough, they watched onscreen as their subject got some good-bye tongue action before tromping down the rickety front-porch steps.

"Think he's stepping out for a paper?" Sean asked sarcastically.

"I'm not sure he can read." Ric eased out of the bucket seat in back and slid behind the wheel while Jonah reached for his radio to give the guys in the car down the block a heads-up.

The phone at Jonah's hip buzzed. Then Ric's phone buzzed. Then a snippet of rap music emanated from Sean's pocket.

Everyone exchanged grim looks as they took out their phones. Jonah answered first.

"Macon."

"Get to campus, ASAP! Where's the SWAT van?"

"Perkin has it," Jonah told his lieutenant. "He's up in Austin at a training op—"

"Someone's shooting people all over the quad! Get over there and suit up. Grab everyone you can."

Jonah braced himself against the side of the van as Ric peeled away from the curb. From the look on his partner's face, Jonah knew he was getting similar instructions.

"What's your setup?" Lieutenant Reynolds demanded.

Jonah was already leaning over the backseat to do a quick inventory of the cargo space. "Two shotguns, a rifle, and a couple of flash bangs." His pulse started to pound. "How many shooters?"

"We don't know."

"What kind of weapon?"

"We don't know that, either. We don't know shit! All I got is a bunch of hysterical 911 calls, someone's gunning down people on the lawn. Some kid just got shot off his bike. ETA?"

Jonah glanced through the tinted windows as a blur of storefronts raced past. "Two minutes, tops."

"Okay, then you're it, Macon. I'm fifteen minutes out. You guys got any Kevlar?"

"Three vests and a flak jacket."

"Take all of it. And call me when you get there."

• • •

Crack.

Another burst of cement on the nearby sidewalk. Sophie huddled tighter and looked back at the howling little girl.

"Get *down!*" Sophie shouted.

From the pavement, an arm reached up and tugged weakly at the girl's shorts. The arm was attached to a hugely pregnant woman who was lying in an ever-expanding pool of her own blood.

Dear Lord. Someone had to get them out of here, but there was no one. The campus that had been crawling with students just moments ago was now a ghost town. Sophie darted her gaze around. Where was the shooter? She eased up slowly and peered around the base of the bronze statue.

Crack.

An agonized scream behind her. Sophie recoiled. She peeked beneath her quivering elbow and saw a man hunched at the base of a flagpole, clutching his bloody ankle.

Sophie's gaze was drawn to the corpse behind her, now baking on the sidewalk. At the edge of the grass, another man lay sprawled across the ground, a backpack beside him. A student. Sophie's heart jackhammered against her rib cage as she watched the flies already buzzing around him.

This can't be happening.

The crying intensified. Sophie glanced again at the child, who was hunched over her mother, sobbing uncontrollably. She had to be only two, maybe three years old. The woman twisted onto her side, probably trying to shield the girl with her body. They were behind a large oak tree, thank goodness. But if the child moved too much—

Crack.

Glass shattered on a building nearby.

Crack. Crack. Crack. One by one, the second-story windows exploded. She thought of those shooting games at carnivals where the targets were little yellow ducks.

Sirens grew louder as Sophie scoured the rooflines for any sort of movement or muzzle flash. She went from building to building all around the quadrangle, searching the red tile roofs and the highest row of windows.

Her gaze came to rest on the white limestone monolith that sat atop the hill, overlooking the entire campus like a giant Sphinx. And suddenly she knew. The gunman was on top of the library.

And from there he could see everything.

CHAPTER 2

Bo McCoy sprinted up the steps to his fraternity house and shoved through the front door. A couple of guys playing Ping-Pong shouted at him, but he couldn't hear them over the music blaring from someone's stereo. He took the stairs two at a time, then tore down the hallway. He slipped on a puddle outside the bathroom, but scrambled to his feet and kept going, not stopping until he was standing in front of his closet and staring up at the long plastic case. He yanked it down, then grabbed a box of bullets from the top shelf and shoved it in the back pocket of his jeans. The fluorescent orange hunting cap on the shelf caught his eye. It was a hundred degrees out, but he grabbed it anyway just for luck and stuffed it down the front of his pants. He raced out of his room and down the stairs.

"Hey, McCoy, where's the fire?" one his brothers called from the doorway as Bo leaped down the porch steps and sprinted across the lawn.

Bo ignored him and raced toward the quad.

The hastily designated command post was the lobby of the psychology building on the south side of the quadrangle. The east facade was made of glass, unfortunately. But as an advantage, it had a clear view of the entire quad, plus protected accessibility through an underground maintenance tunnel that connected it to several other buildings. Jonah stood in the lobby now, juggling calls from two different bosses—Reynolds, his police lieutenant, and Cosgrove, his SWAT commander. Cosgrove and most of Jonah's SWAT teammates were at this very moment hauling ass down here from Austin.

"We've got officers setting up barricades at all entrances to campus," Reynolds was telling him over his cell phone. "Campus security evacuated the buildings facing the quad and the rest are in lockdown. Still no confirmation on our guy's location."

"We got a location on the shooter?" Jonah yelled across the room at Ric, who was on his radio.

"Dispatch just took a 911 call," Ric shouted back. "From a woman pinned down at the base of a statue. She says the shooter's on top of the library."

Jonah rushed to the window and looked out. "Shit! He's got the high ground."

Jonah hoped to hell the caller was mistaken, but he doubted it. The library was the highest point for miles. If Jonah had wanted to set up a position, he'd have picked the exact same spot.

A cold ball formed in the pit of his stomach. Who were they dealing with here?

Jonah got back on with his SWAT chief. "An eyewitness says he's shooting from the library roof. That's six stories high."

"Set up an inner perimeter. How many men you got?"

Jonah glanced around the lobby. He had one SWAT

guy from the sheriff's department who'd just happened to be at the campus health center when the all-call came through. Brian was in plainclothes and armed only with a Sig. His wife—a nurse—was busy treating a student who'd hobbled into the lobby with a bloody foot.

"We got two SWAT including me," Jonah said. "Plus I've got two SMPD detectives—"

"Make that three."

Jonah turned to see Allison Doyle coming out of a stairwell. Her cheeks were flushed as though she'd run all the way here.

"When was the last shot?" Cosgrove asked.

"Eight minutes ago," Jonah said. Was he finished? Had he offed himself?

"I'm twenty minutes away," Cosgrove said. "We got a police chopper coming down from Austin, but they're not off the ground yet."

Jonah stepped closer to the window and surveyed the situation. On the other side of the quad, a line of students crouched behind a concrete planter. An injured girl was slumped against a brick water fountain, hidden from view of the library and holding a bleeding arm. Farther south, a pair of legs poked out from behind a bike rack. Jonah couldn't tell whether the person was alive or dead.

"Macon? What's the status?"

Crack.

Everyone turned at once to look out the window.

"We can't wait," Jonah said. "We need to take him down now."

His commander hesitated. It would be less risky to hold off until they had everyone assembled and could do this by the book. But by then how many more kids might die?

"I'd rather have this guy shooting at us than picking off innocent people," Jonah said.

"Okay, do it."

Jonah got off the phone, took a deep breath, and turned to face the four cops awaiting his orders.

"Ric and Brian, you're on entry with me." He nodded at Sean, who was the best marksman of the bunch, besides himself. "Sean, give Brian your vest. I need you at the top of that building with the rifle." He pointed at the highest building besides the library, which was just across the quad. "Use the underground tunnel to get there."

Allison stepped forward. She swiped a lock of dark hair from her face and gave him a look that dared him to blow her off. Allison worked property crimes. She was green as grass, but she had a badge.

He handed her some binoculars. "See the big ugly building just north of here?"

"The architecture building."

"Whatever. Get to the top of it and get on your radio," he said. "We're going to need some eyes."

The elevator doors parted and Allison rushed out, nearly crashing into a kid in an orange hunting cap.

"Hey!" She grabbed him by the shirt when she spotted the gun case. "Where you going with that?"

"The balcony," he squeaked. "On the corner of the building."

Allison took a moment to decide. This could be their

shooter, for all she knew. But her gut told her it was just some kid looking to be a hero. She jerked the gun case away from him and released his arm. "Show me."

He led her briskly down a corridor to a large conference room with a balcony facing north. Prime view of the library.

They weren't the first to notice it, either. A man was set up there already, peering through a rifle scope. He was seated in a plastic office chair with the barrel of his gun resting atop a beanbag on the balcony wall.

Allison rushed outside.

"SMPD. I'm going to have to confiscate your weapon."

He turned and squinted at her from beneath the brim of his camo cap. He wore jeans, a faded T-shirt, and worn shit-kickers. He turned and spat tobacco juice on the concrete.

"Reckon you're gonna have to shoot me first." He turned and leaned back over his gun.

Shit. She hadn't counted on the vigilante element. This town was full of gun owners.

Allison's heart thudded as she wrestled with what to do. She'd spent most of her career busting petty thieves and drug addicts. But what she did today mattered. A lot. And she didn't know if she was ready for it.

She made a snap decision. If they couldn't take out the shooter, maybe they could at least distract him and buy everyone some time.

Her gaze moved to the library. "You got a good look?"

"Just waiting for my shot."

Allison set the gun case on the ground and popped the latches. Inside was a Remington 700, like the one she'd been trained on, only newer.

She glanced over her shoulder at the boy. "What's your name?"

"Bo McCoy."

"I take it you've been hunting, Bo?"

"Yes, ma'am."

"That's good." She unhooked the binoculars from around her neck and shoved them at him. "I need you to be my spotter."

Their footsteps sounded like rolling thunder as they pounded through the tunnel. In contrast to the fierce heat outside, the air beneath the campus was cool and damp. Fluorescent light fixtures dotted the walls, but visibility was poor and Jonah had to pay attention to keep from bumping his head on the low-hanging pipes.

A campus security guard led the way through the maze. As Jonah jogged through the bowels of the university, he sorted through what little information he had and tried to come up with a plan. First and foremost, he needed intel. He desperately hoped his team's eyes were in place by the time the entry group reached the library.

They rounded a corner and the guard trotted over to an elevator bank.

"Hold up. We need info." Jonah glanced around and knew he'd never get a good signal down here.

"Up," Ric said, and headed for the door to a stairwell. They took the steps two at a time. At the top, a sign on the closed door said MAIN LEVEL, and Ric and Jonah exchanged looks.

"Cover me," Jonah said, then took the lead as they went in low, guns drawn, using the rhythm they'd developed through years of working together. He swept his gaze left, right, front, back. Jonah had braced himself for blood and carnage, but all he saw was a vacated library.

The place was eerily silent—no hushed voices, no clacking keyboards, no scrape of chairs on the white marble floor. Books lay open. Laptops and backpacks sat abandoned. Jonah stood still for a moment, trying to think over the ringing in his ears—the faint buzzing noise that had started during that very first phone call.

You're it, Macon.

He hustled to the window and did some quick recon. The library sat on high ground. Even from this first-floor vantage point, the campus was spread out before him like a picnic. The surreal part was the stillness. Not a flutter of movement as everyone remained hidden behind whatever cover they'd managed to find. The six people sprawled across the lawn were either dead or pretending to be, and Jonah's gut tightened with fury at the sight.

He radioed his lieutenant on the secure frequency they'd established.

"Macon here. We're in the library, ground level. What you got?"

"He's still on the roof. Sean spotted him."

"He get a shot off?"

"Missed. Doyle got hold of a rifle. She's trying to get a bead on him, too, but he's keeping out of sight."

"How many gunmen?"

"By all accounts, one, but that's unconfirmed."

Jonah ran his hand over his face and it came away wet. Jesus, he was soaked.

Ric nudged him and handed over some binoculars.

"Bronze statue," he whispered, nodding his head toward the window.

Jonah jerked the binoculars to his face and scoured the scene. One of the bodies on the quad shifted, and Jonah's pulse jumped. Kid was alive, though how much longer he could stay that way was anybody's guess. He swept his gaze south down the grass until he spied the bronze statue where the 911 caller had been. She was still there. Heeled sandals, bare legs, skirt. Jonah saw a flash of blond hair as she peeked around the concrete base and lifted her gaze upward.

Sophie Barrett.

"Holy God," Jonah muttered.

Crack.

Everyone looked up at the ceiling.

"He's starting up again, Macon. I'm going to call off our sniper fire. Your team's clear to move."

Sophie pressed her forehead against the searing-hot concrete and tucked her knees in tighter. She turned her head and cast another worried look at the woman behind the tree. She was dead now—Sophie was almost sure of it. Her fingertips were tinged blue, and she hadn't moved in the past fifteen minutes. The little girl was tucked beside her in the fetal position, sucking her thumb and staring blankly across the grass.

Where was the ambulance? Even the sirens had stopped. All she heard now were fire alarms from the direction of the dorms and the distant sound of bullhorns shouting commands. Sweat trickled down Sophie's neck and arms. She licked her chapped lips and tried not to think about her parched throat.

Or the flies hovering over the bodies behind her.

The little girl sat up and started glancing around. *Don't look,* Sophie wanted to say, but the girl kept looking. Her gaze came to rest on her mother. Sophie heard a hiccup.

"Sweetie, lay down." Sophie motioned for her to put her head down. "Lie still next to Mommy."

The girl turned and stared at her. Her pigtails were askew and her eyes looked glassy.

A snippet of music rang out. Sophie grabbed her phone off the ground and checked the screen.

Jonah Macon.

"Oh my God, where are you?"

"Help's coming," he said. "I need you to stay put."

"We need a paramedic here! I'm on the south quadrangle. There's a woman—" Sophie glanced at the girl and lowered her voice. "Jonah, she's not moving anymore. We need an ambulance!"

"They're coming. Just don't move, whatever you do."

"Can't someone do something? He's on top of the library!" Sophie sucked in a breath as the little girl clambered to her feet. She was still behind the tree, but one step in either direction, and she'd be a target. "Get *down*!" Sophie motioned frantically, but the girl wasn't looking.

"Sophie, are you listening? Stay behind that statue. Do *not* move, do you hear me?"

The girl looked down at her mother and started to cry. She took a step backward. Then another.

"No!" Sophie scrambled to her feet and lunged.

Crack.

Jonah's heart skipped a beat.

"Macon, heads up!"

Jonah glanced up from his phone as Ric stopped on the landing above him. His stern expression yanked Jonah back to the mission.

They'd hit a locked door marked EMPLOYEES ONLY. Jonah stuffed the phone in his pocket and raced up to enter the four-digit pass code that had been given to him by the security guard downstairs. The guard hadn't offered to come up here without a vest, and no one had twisted his arm.

Jonah made eye contact with Ric and Brian before punching the code's last digit. They nodded. A faint *snick* and Jonah turned the knob. Slowly, he pulled back the heavy metal door. One by one, they slipped inside and eased the door shut behind them.

In contrast to the clean, bright stairwell they'd come from, this one was dim and dirty. Jonah had expected a barricade, maybe a booby trap. But the stairs were clear and the three men climbed them swiftly and soundlessly, Jonah in the lead. His pulse was racing. He pictured Sophie hunched behind that statue, and it raced even faster. He pictured her gleaming yellow hair and wondered if the motherfucker on the roof had used it for a target. Jonah pushed the thought away. He focused on the mission. Two more half-flights, eight steps each, and then he'd round the corner. He counted off each step, knowing the next time he passed through here, he might be in a body bag.

He reached the landing. He signaled his teammates. He readied his shotgun and turned the corner.

The last half-flight was empty. The stairs were bathed in sunlight from a rectangular window that looked out on the roof. Jonah reached the top step and signaled his team. He nodded at the brick that had been used to prop open the door a few inches. Jonah had the pass code for this door, too, but he didn't need it because of that brick. It sat there like an invitation, beckoning him outside.

And in that moment, Jonah knew this guy's plan was suicide by cop. Really, he'd known it all along. This guy wanted to go out in a blaze of glory. The only question was, how many people would he take with him?

The ringing was back in his ears, only louder now. The world seemed brighter, sharper than it ever had. His body tingled. His shotgun felt weightless in his hands.

You're it, Macon.

By their predetermined plan, Brian reached around and rested a palm on the door. They exchanged looks. Three, two, one—

The door swung open and Jonah burst into the white-hot sunlight.

CHAPTER 3

The roof was empty.

Jonah swept left, right, then stepped away from the door to look up and behind him, at the top of the structure that housed the stairwell. He did a second scan of the low concrete wall that rimmed the main roof. Nothing. Meanwhile, Ric and Brian had eased toward the outside corners of the stairwell structure.

Voices, low and crackly.

Jonah searched for the source and spied the small black radio tucked up against the south wall. Beside it, a gray duffel and a box of ammo.

But no sniper.

Either he'd leapt off the roof or he was behind them on the north side of the building.

Pop!

A puff of dust kicked up on the south wall as someone fired from below.

Pop! Pop!

Different weapons, coming from different directions. Jonah didn't have time to worry about friendly fire.

He signaled for Brian to round the west corner of the stairwell building, he and Ric would round the east. It was a plan they'd thrown together on the way up those lower flights of stairs, and Jonah could think of about twenty flaws in it, but it was the best they had.

Silently, Jonah led the way. In his peripheral vision he saw shell casings glinting in the midday sun. There were dozens, maybe hundreds.

He wiped sweat from his brow. His T-shirt and jeans were saturated with sweat, but he was glad for the Kevlar and his Nikes, which gave him stealth. He sensed Ric behind him, trading signals with Brian so they could time their assault. Their shooter or shooters could be waiting around the corner in ambush.

Ric's hand appeared at Jonah's side, signaling: *Three, two, one.*

Jonah swung around the corner. Nothing. On the west side, a faint scuff. If the shooter didn't know they were up here, Brian's boots had just given them away.

Now, now, now! a voice in his head ordered. Jonah surged forward, turned the next corner.

A flash of movement at the top of a ladder.

"Roof!" Ric shouted the same instant Jonah lifted his shotgun. Footsteps pounded on the top of the stairwell building.

"One shooter!" Brian yelled as both Ric and Jonah doubled back to the south.

A smack against the pavement as the man jumped to the rooftop. They reached the corner at the same instant Jonah saw the gunman. Sun reflected off his pale bald head as he shoved a pistol in his mouth.

Bang. He dropped.

And where he'd been standing was just bright blue sky.

Allison peered through the rifle scope and waited, heart galloping. Was that pistol fire? What was happening up there?

A flutter of movement near the ledge, and gunshots echoed around the quadrangle like popcorn.

"Hold your fire!" she yelled into her radio, on the off chance the shots were coming from police. But she suspected it was more vigilantes trying to pick off the gunman.

"Shooter down." Jonah's words came over the radio, and Allison's shoulders slumped with relief. She rested her forehead on the borrowed rifle.

"We're going to sweep the roof," he continued in an edgy voice. Had he taken out the shooter? What had happened up there? "Looks like a lone perpetrator, but we need to confirm."

"Do a floor-by-floor of the library." The order was issued by a voice she didn't recognize, probably the SWAT commander. "All officers, hold your fire. I repeat, hold your fire. And get those kids to stop shooting, too."

Allison sat up straighter and blinked the sweat from her eyes. She gazed at the library, feeling a sense of numbness combined with caution.

No movement, which was good. Jonah's team was keeping low and away from the edge. She just hoped they were right, that the gunman was by himself.

She glanced at the man beside her, who still had his rifle pointed at the roof. "You hear that?"

"Yep."

Allison stood and peered over the balcony at the grassy quad. Half a dozen students—either dead or injured—lay sprawled in the sun, while others cowered behind trees and trash cans and even flowerpots. Everything was so still, it could have been a photograph. Her gaze drifted back to the motionless bodies.

"Is it over?"

She turned to look at Bo McCoy, who held the binoculars she'd given him in his slender young hands.

"We don't know," she said, even though in her heart, she did know. It *wasn't* over—not yet. And for some families, it never would be.

"Stay here until you get the all-clear." She handed back the rifle. "And don't shoot anything," she ordered. "We've got cops up there."

She rushed back to the ground floor, using the stairwell because her shell-shocked brain forgot about the elevator until she was halfway down. As she entered the ultra-modern lobby of the architecture building, she heard the nasal sound of a bullhorn outside.

"I repeat, all is clear. The gunman is down."

For a moment, there was no reaction. But as she stepped from the air-conditioned building into the sweltering heat, the freeze-frame shifted into motion once again. People emerged from behind bushes, statues, even lampposts. Someone dropped from a tree. They poured out of buildings and crowded onto the sidewalks. Everyone gazed up at the library while some pointed, and the swell of anxious voices competed with the ever-increasing wail of sirens.

Allison hurried through the crowd to a place where she'd seen a victim go down. The boy was on his side, clutching a bleeding arm. His fingers were crimson and his face was white and slick with sweat.

"Help's coming." Allison grabbed something someone handed her—a wadded T-shirt—and pressed it against the wound. The boy moaned, but at least he was conscious. Another T-shirt appeared, and she added to the makeshift bandage.

"What's your name?" she asked.

He mumbled something she didn't catch.

"You hear the ambulance? That's for you. Just sit tight, okay? Anything hurt besides this arm?"

He squeezed his eyes shut and shook his head, and Allison glanced up. All around her was a forest of legs. Students, faculty, staff. But where were the medics?

"Help is coming," she promised, then jumped to her feet as she spotted an EMT.

"Hey! Over here!" She waved him over and then backed away as he and a partner knelt down and went to work.

Allison rejoined the crowd and searched for more injured. But it was now impossible to see the wounded through the thick soup of people. Some were shouting, some were weeping. Some staggered around, wide-eyed and dazed. An alarming number of men, young and old, held deer rifles pointed at the sky, and Allison hoped like hell this really was the act of a lone gunman. Any accomplice would have no trouble disappearing into the mob.

Jonah pushed his way through the throng of bodies.

"Allison!"

She couldn't hear him. Not surprising given the noise.

Between the sirens and the helicopters, Jonah could hardly hear himself think. He squeezed past a barricade blocking off the inner part of campus. Someone grabbed his arm, then noticed his Kevlar vest and let go.

He caught up to her near the command center. Behind her, the entire quadrangle had been cordoned off with yellow crime-scene tape.

"Allison, wait up." He snagged her arm and turned her around.

"I thought you were on the roof." She glanced up at it. Choppers hovered above the library like hornets, and a white tent had been erected over the corpse to keep news cams from filming as the crime-scene techs did their jobs.

Allison gave him a worried look. "I hear it was pretty intense up there. You okay?"

"That woman behind the statue. Have you seen her?" Jonah held his breath.

"The statue?"

"She called 911. She was pinned down behind the bronze horse sculpture, right over there."

Recognition flickered. "You mean the blonde? Tall?"

"Where is she?"

"They took her away in an ambulance."

His chest squeezed. "She was wounded?"

"She looked okay to me. She was on her feet. Her kid was bleeding, though."

Jonah stared at her.

"Doyle! I need you on crowd control!" Reynolds motioned her over to a parking area behind the psych building, where some campus health workers were dealing with minor injuries. Jonah's boss saw him and frowned. "What are you still doing here? I thought you had a debriefing."

"I'm on my way."

But his boss was already stomping over. Reynolds was big, barrel-chested, and the silver bristles of his flattop contrasted with his ruddy skin.

He motioned Jonah away from the crowd. "Get to that briefing, give your statement, and go home. Keep it short and to the point." He aimed a meaty finger at him. "And take off that vest. I don't want reporters picking you out. We got every news channel in the country headed down here."

Jonah gritted his teeth. A mass murderer had just shot up the college and his lieutenant was worried about reporters.

"I'm on my way." Jonah turned to leave.

"Keep it tight," Reynolds called after him. "Less is more, Macon. Don't forget that."

The emergency room at County Hospital could have been in a war zone. Rows of gurneys filled with injured students lined the wall. People sat on the floor and slouched in corners, holding makeshift bandages and awaiting attention from harried nurses and med students. Sophie hadn't seen a doctor yet, and she assumed they were all in back tending to critical patients. Waiting-room chairs had been stacked and shoved against a wall in order to make room for the steady stream of gurneys coming in from ambulances. Load after load came off with bleeding arms, shattered wrists, injured feet. Several people had facial cuts from flying glass. Sophie reached up and touched her eyebrow, wondering how bad her injury was. She'd taken a hefty chunk of bark to the temple when the tree she'd been running for got hit with a bullet.

The child in her lap squirmed, and Sophie gazed down at her. Every attempt to elicit a name had been met with silence, and Sophie didn't know what to do, so for now she was going to wait here, holding an ice pack against the girl's forehead and hoping she didn't have a concussion. The girl had a big blue goose egg from when Sophie had tackled her to the ground and she'd hit a tree root. She also had a split lip. The blood there had dried, and Sophie had managed to clean it with some wet tissues, but it looked as though it needed stitches.

"Would you like to play a game?" Sophie shifted her on her lap so she could look down at her face. "It's called the name game. I'll start. My name is Sophie. Kind of like sofa. What's *your* name?"

The girl turned away and burrowed her head against Sophie's dirt-streaked blouse.

Her throat tightened with frustration. She was terrible with kids. She'd never been one of those nurturing types who oozed mommy vibes, and yet here she was in this overcrowded waiting room with a child who refused to turn loose of her.

"How's your head feel?" Sophie rearranged the ice pack, which was almost melted.

No answer, just more squirming. Sophie scanned the ER doors. They were automatic, but they stood permanently open now as a steady stream of people rushed in and out. Despite the signs posted around, there was a cell phone clutched in almost every hand,

and people were babbling away frantically. Everyone was looking for someone—a daughter, a boyfriend, a sorority sister. Sophie had positioned herself strategically by the entrance, and almost everyone glanced at her. But their gazes didn't linger, and she knew they hadn't come here searching for this brown-haired little girl.

"Let's go for a walk." Sophie tried to ease the girl off her legs, but she clung tighter. "Come on. Just a short one."

Sophie scooped her onto her hip and managed to elbow her way through the mob of people swarming a table where a list of names was being maintained by a besieged staffer. It was worse than a bar after a football game, and Sophie didn't have her usual tricks available to get someone's attention. She resorted to rudeness and elbowed a skinny guy right out of her way.

"E*xcuse* me," she said, and the woman looked up from her handwritten list. "This child is missing her mother." Sophie winced at the words, but it couldn't be helped. "They were separated on campus, and I need to know if her mom came through here—"

"Name?"

"I don't know."

"You're not family?"

"No. Look, her mother's pregnant. She was injured. She was taken away in a separate ambulance and—"

Someone jostled her out of the way, and she tripped backward, almost dropping the girl. Sophie turned and snarled, and when she looked back, the woman was bombarded with other questions.

Sophie scooted away from the crush of people. Her chair was already taken. She found a tiny bit of space beside a ficus plant and leaned against the wall there as she pulled out her phone to make another round of calls.

Once again, no answer at San Marcos PD, probably because every parent of every kid at this college was trying to get through. She scrolled through her call list and tried the sheriff's office again, and again, nothing. She tried the local CPS office, but was once again routed through a message system and dumped on someone's voice mail.

Sophie adjusted the girl on her hip and reached deep for some patience. She left her name and yet another urgent message, along with her phone number.

The girl looked up at her as she clicked off, and Sophie forced a smile.

"Is your head feeling better?"

An ambulance screamed right up to the door, drowning out the question. The girl burrowed her face against Sophie's neck until the siren finally ceased.

"Hey, you!" Sophie caught the sleeve of a man in scrubs as he hurried past.

He looked at her like a deer in the headlights.

"I need a nurse here. This girl needs medical attention, and I also have to find her parents."

He glanced over his shoulder at the exam rooms swarming with people.

"Her mother was badly injured," Sophie said. "She's short, brown hair, about eight months pregnant. Is she back there, do you know?"

"Uh, I really don't—"

"Check. *Please.* This child doesn't have a parent here. I don't even know her name."

He stepped back, and Sophie caught his hand. "Wait." She plucked a pen from the pocket of his scrubs and shifted the girl onto her hip. "I'm going to write down my cell number." He had hairy arms, so she wrote on the back of his hand. "My name's Sophie," she said, desperately trying to make a personal connection. "Find out if there's a pregnant woman back there and call me." She gave him a meaningful look. "Her injuries looked very serious, so she may be in surgery." *Or the morgue.* "But I at least need her name. I've got to get in touch with this child's family."

"I'll do what I can." He glanced down at his hand and jogged off, and Sophie slumped against the wall. She felt faint, queasy. The room was hot and airless, packed with too many anxious bodies. Sophie closed her eyes. The girl's skinny arms tightened around her neck, and she felt a fresh wave of panic. She had no idea what to do next, so she started humming the first thing that popped into her head. It was an old gospel song about flying away, which was exactly what she wanted to do right now.

The girl's arms gradually relaxed, so Sophie kept humming. She glanced down at the scraped little legs wrapped around her waist. She smoothed a hand over the girl's hair and picked a leaf from one of her pigtails. The girl's head drooped, and Sophie continued to hum softly. She turned toward the door leading to the back where the guy with her phone number on his hand had disappeared.

A man stood there, staring at her. He was oddly motionless amid the chaos of the ER. Sophie shifted so he could see the girl in her arms, and his entire face flooded with relief. He pushed his way through the crowd.

"Becca!" His voice caught on the word, and the little head jerked up from Sophie's shoulder.

"Daddy!" She launched herself out of Sophie's arms and into the man's, and he squeezed her to his chest. Sophie stepped back to give them room. Over his daughter's shoulder, the man met Sophie's gaze. The pained look in his bloodshot eyes spoke volumes, and Sophie knew that Becca's mother was dead.

Jonah pulled into the apartment complex and glanced up at Sophie's window. Looked like she was awake, which was both good and bad. Good, because he wouldn't have to turn around and go home, and bad, because what he needed to do right now was turn around and go home.

Home was where he should be. It was late, he was beyond tired, and he wasn't fit company for anything other than a bottle of Jim Beam. But he'd been thinking about Sophie all day, and somewhere along the way he'd convinced himself that this detour was a good idea.

He parked his dinged pickup and hiked up the stairs to her apartment. The place looked just as dumpy as he remembered it, only someone had gotten around to pouring some chlorine into the pint-size swimming pool. Must be new management.

Through the paper-thin walls, Jonah heard newscasts blaring as he made his way down the row of doors. Sounded like everyone in town was tuned into the same story. He reached Sophie's unit and rapped on the door. He waited. And waited. He rapped again.

Jonah's pulse spiked when she answered. He didn't know what he'd expected. It was after ten. Maybe he'd thought she'd be weeping into her pillow, or talking on the phone, or watching TV. He hadn't expected her to be naked.

"You always answer the door like that?"

She had only a bath towel wrapped around her and she hitched it up higher. "Are you off for the night, or is this a police visit?"

"I'm off."

She stepped back to let him in, and he frowned down at her as he crossed the threshold.

"You didn't even ask who it was."

"You have a distinctive knock." She tossed a look at him over her bare shoulder as she walked to the back of the apartment.

Jonah's feet remained firmly planted in her living room.

The bathroom door was ajar and he saw a sliver of her reflection in the mirror as she leaned over the sink.

"You just getting off?" she asked.

"Yep."

"Long day."

"Yep."

"There's beer in the fridge."

"I'm good, thanks."

She finished doing some makeup stuff to her eyes and closed the door. He heard drawers opening and closing, then a hair dryer.

Jonah took a moment to look at her setup. It was just as he remembered it from the one other time he'd been in here: small TV, inexpensive prints on the walls, worn but comfortable furniture. Everything was simple and affordable, with the notable exception of her stereo. It was sleek and new and perched on a six-foot bookshelf, along with her extensive collection of CDs. She had a purple iPod plugged in at the moment and was listening to something low and bluesy. Once upon a time, Sophie had been an aspiring singer, but he didn't know if that was still the case.

Jonah glanced down the hallway. The bathroom door was open all the way now, and he guessed she'd slipped into the bedroom. What that particular part of her apartment looked like, he had no idea.

The last time he'd seen Sophie—before he'd seen her cowering at the base of that statue—he'd just closed a homicide case. It was a serial killer, and she'd been on his list of targets. She should have lost her life, but instead she'd walked away with some cuts and bruises.

And a boatload of emotional problems.

Jonah had been knee-deep in the case. He'd processed the scene. He'd taken her official statement. And his thoughts about her then had been just as inappropriate as they were right now. He probably would have acted on them, too, if he hadn't been hit with a shit ton of work. When he'd finally come up for air, Sophie Barrett had moved on with her life, and Jonah had forgotten about her troubled gray eyes and her endless legs and the sly way she smiled when she got the upper hand in a conversation.

The bedroom door opened and she strode back into the living room wearing faded jeans, a snug-fitting Dallas Cowboys T-shirt, and leather sandals. There was nothing at all remarkable about the outfit, except the way she wore it.

"So. What brings you here?" She tossed a leather

purse on the couch and folded her arms over her chest as she looked up at him.

"Just thought I'd check in on you. What happened to your face?"

"Caught some tree bark."

"Looks like it needs stitches."

"It needs a Band-Aid. What are you really here for?"

She tilted her head to the side, and he realized he'd been kidding himself earlier. He wasn't here to check on her. His reasons were much less noble. In some corner of his mind, he'd thought he'd just knock on her door and she'd let him inside and make him forget about everything else.

When he didn't answer, she grabbed her purse off the sofa and dug out her keys. "I'm going out with some people from work. You know a few of them. Want to come?"

Sophie was the receptionist at a forensic lab, and Jonah knew a lot of her friends from past investigations. They were okay people, but he didn't feel like being around them tonight.

"No. Thanks. I'll get out of your way."

"You can walk me down."

She led him to the door and locked up, and he checked her out again while her back was turned. Her hair smelled good. She was wearing the same heeled sandals he'd seen earlier. She was almost six feet tall but he'd never seen her in anything besides heels.

"You get your car back okay?" he asked, shifting back into cop mode as they headed downstairs.

"It took a while. The campus is still closed. I had

to wait around for a security escort just to get into the garage where I parked. Guess they're still searching for evidence?" She turned to look at him.

"Yeah."

"So, have you identified him?"

"Not yet."

They crossed the lot and stopped beside her shiny black Tahoe. Jonah knew it was no coincidence that she'd parked it near the one security light in the entire parking lot. She was safety-conscious—had good reason to be.

She gazed up at him with somber eyes. "Thank you," she said.

"For what?"

"What you did today. It was very brave."

He shrugged. "It's my job."

"A job is answering phones. Flipping burgers. Not confronting a homicidal maniac. That takes courage."

"Kind of like dodging bullets to save some kid you don't know?"

"You saw that?"

"I was in a stairwell," he said. "I heard about it."

She looked at him for a long moment. Then she went up on her toes, and he tensed as he realized what she was doing. Her lips were soft and cool. They moved against his gently, teasing, until lust overcame his shock and he pulled her hard against him, and damned if she didn't taste as hot and sweet as he'd always imagined—times a thousand. He wanted to take her back upstairs. He wanted to pull her into that bedroom and let her blow his mind.

And he was a manipulative bastard for coming here

tonight. Her hand slid up his chest, and he caught it.

She opened her eyes and eased back.

"What was that for?" he asked, and it came out like an accusation.

"I don't know. My way of saying thank you?"

"You don't have to thank me."

"No?" She lifted an eyebrow. "Isn't that why you came here? To get thanked?"

He stepped back.

She unlocked her car and tossed her purse inside. "Don't look so guilty. Everyone has different ways of dealing with trauma. Some people need alcohol. Or pills. Or sex. It's a coping mechanism."

He crossed his arms, annoyed at being analyzed, mostly because she was right. "And what's your coping mechanism?"

"Me, I need people. I need friends from work and a noisy bar without a single television." She slipped behind the wheel, then gazed up at him and sighed. "And I'll probably have a margarita or three to forget about this god-awful day. Sure you don't want to come?"

"I'll pass."

"'Night, then. Don't stay up too late thinking about your case. It'll be there in the morning."

"Yeah, sure."

But as he watched her drive away, he knew he was going to go home to his bottle of bourbon and think about not much else.

The man watched the Tahoe turn onto Main Street and speed through a yellow light. It was 10:35. She was in a hurry. She'd wasted too much time with her visitor, and now whoever she was meeting would be getting impatient. He rolled to a stop at the intersection and followed the SUV with his gaze as it turned into a crowded parking lot.

The light turned green, and he drove past the cafés and boutiques and textbook exchanges that lined the street. When he reached the beer garden, he glanced into the parking lot but didn't make the turn. Instead, he circled the block and pulled into a lot beside a restaurant across from the bar. From there he had an unobstructed view of the entrance.

From there he watched her.

As she reached the door a woman with auburn hair stepped out. The two hugged for a long moment and then stepped back, dabbing away tears.

So much for that brave face back at the apartment.

He watched the women enter the bar and gritted his teeth. Plate number KRG 624. Sophia Elise Barrett.

Sophia.

She was a loose end. A potential problem. A mistake. Only one, but it was enough.

It was one too many.

CHAPTER 4

San Marcos was a quiet college town nestled on the banks of a river, and on clear nights some of the bars and restaurants opened their windows to catch the breeze off the water.

The doors to Schmitt's beer garden were open tonight, but Sophie wasn't focused on the weather. She sat at the end of a long, sticky table, picking salt from her margarita glass and trying not to listen to the conversations swirling around her. Although this was one of the few watering holes in town without a television, it wasn't immune to the disaster. People sat at tables and at the bar, swapping stories about where they'd been when it happened and people they knew who had been injured. About half the customers were following the story on their cell phones.

"I was at the Arby's drive-through," one of Sophie's coworkers was saying. "Sounded like firecrackers. Didn't think anything of it until I passed about three police cars on my way back to work."

"I was in the lab," someone chimed in. "We watched the whole thing on YouTube. You see that kid on the bike?"

"Anderson Cooper had him on earlier."

"Thought he was dead."

"Nah, just an elbow, I think. They had a camera in his hospital room."

Sophie looked away and forced herself to take another sip. It tasted like nothing. She might as well have been drinking ice water.

"That woman that died, she was married to my T.A."

"Nielsen?"

"Kincaid. I had him for biochem. He's a good guy."

"So, what's the body count?"

Sophie's shoulders tensed.

"Four, last I heard. Eric Emrick and Professor Graham, plus Kincaid's wife. And, you know, the shooter."

"Shit."

"Yeah."

Sophie plunked down her glass. "It's five."

They glanced over.

"Jodi Kincaid was pregnant, so really it's five. I watched her bleed out." *And didn't do a damn thing to help her.*

People around the table looked at her, then shifted their glances away uncomfortably. Sure, they'd welcomed her when she'd first shown up, but now her sullen mood was putting a damper on the lively conversation.

She turned away and pretended to be checking out some guys at the bar.

"You okay?"

Sophie glanced at Kelsey, who was watching her with a worried look.

"I should have stayed home," she said. "I guess . . . I

don't know. I didn't want to be alone tonight, but this really sucks."

I should have stayed home with Jonah. As soon as the thought entered her head, she shoved it out again.

"We could go to Mia's," Kelsey suggested. "She and Ric are there. She didn't want to leave him on his own tonight after everything that happened, but maybe we could go over and, you know, just hang out."

"No." The last thing Sophie wanted to do was trade stories with Ric. He'd been on the takedown team, which meant he'd seen the man kill himself. He probably didn't want to rehash his day any more than she did. "They probably want to be alone," she added, picking up her drink. "When Mia called earlier—"

Crack.

Sophie jumped in her chair and dropped the glass. She glanced over her shoulder at the back room, where someone was playing pool.

Someone with a very nice break.

Sophie righted her glass and glanced at Kelsey. "Sorry." She grabbed some cocktail napkins and started mopping up the mess.

"Maybe this was a bad idea." Kelsey swiped some napkins from nearby drinks and helped her. "This place is so noisy."

"No, really, it's good," Sophie said. Margarita slush was everywhere, and for some reason her eyes started to burn. "I don't want to be home tonight."

"Are you sure?"

"Absolutely."

They piled soggy napkins on the end of the table and Sophie handed her empty glass to a passing waitress.

"Get you another one?"

"Um . . ." She glanced at the waitress, then the bar. "I'll just take a beer. Whatever you have."

The woman gave her a bemused look, but Sophie was too rattled to care. It would probably taste like water, anyway.

Sophie took a deep breath and forced a smile. She'd talked Kelsey into coming here, and it wasn't fair to ruin her evening, too. Usually their roles were reversed and it was Sophie prodding Kelsey to get out and have some fun. As a forensic anthropologist, Kelsey was typically the one who dealt with death all day and needed a distraction at night.

"So." Sophie groped for something to say as her friend eyed her with concern. "How are *you* doing? I never heard about your trip to California. How's—" She stopped midsentence as a familiar man walked into the bar. Tom Rollins from Channel 3. Sophie recognized his too-white teeth from the six o'clock news. Damn, was he here for business or pleasure? His gaze scanned the bar, and then he turned to say something to the man standing behind him—probably his cameraman, although he wasn't carrying a camera at the moment. But their movements had purpose, and she could tell this was a business outing.

Sophie stood up and grabbed her purse. Insensitive coworkers she could handle. Frayed nerves she could handle. What she couldn't handle tonight was a reporter, particularly one who knew about her past.

"On second thought," she told Kelsey, "I think I'll head out."

Kelsey got to her feet, looking more worried than

ever. "Want me to follow you home? Or you can come over?"

"No, I'm fine. Really. I think I just need some rest." Oh, crap. Rollins had spotted her and had that spark of recognition on his face. Sophie quickly turned away. "Cancel my beer, would you?" She gave Kelsey a quick hug. "Don't worry about me. I'll see you tomorrow."

The most experienced cops in the department were tapped to join the task force, and Allison had no idea why she'd been invited to the party.

She stepped inside the conference room, which smelled of reheated coffee, and immediately noticed the lack of female faces around the table. Men were in abundance, though: three SMDP detectives from the Crimes Against Persons squad, two sheriff's deputies, and practically all of the top brass from her department. She also noted the suit at the end of the table—probably an administrator from the university. Allison picked an empty chair and sat down beside the head of campus security, whom she'd met several times during the course of her theft investigations. She was glad to see him here. The sooner the finger-pointing got over with, the better.

Everyone settled in with their Styrofoam cups and listened as Lieutenant Reynolds gave a rundown of yesterday's events, as if everyone at the table hadn't heard the same litany of facts relayed on the endless cable-news loop.

Allison watched Jonah's face as the lieutenant talked. He and the other two detectives had a grim, greenish look about them that confirmed where they'd spent the morning. According to the grapevine, they'd been in Austin at six A.M., watching the Travis County ME perform autopsies on yesterday's victims.

It had to have been horrible, especially the pregnant woman. As dull as property crimes could be, at least Allison had never had to sit in on something like *that*.

Reynolds ended his narrative in typical cop-speak: "Macon and his team confronted him on the south side of the roof, at which time the suspect placed a nine-millimeter pistol in his mouth and pulled the trigger."

"Are we done calling him a suspect yet?" Ric crossed his arms impatiently. "The GSR tests checked out and we've got his prints all over both weapons."

"We definitely have our guy," the chief said. "The question is, who is he?" He turned a pointed look at the crime-scene techs across the table from Allison.

"I was here all night," Minh responded. The CSI specialized in fingerprint identification, and Allison had worked with him before on burglary and auto theft cases. "I examined both the Sig nine-mil and the Remington, lifted prints. Each one of the prints recovered from the weapons matches the body. No problem there."

At the word *problem*, the detectives leaned forward slightly. Allison noticed Reynolds and the chief did not. Whatever this news was, they'd already heard it.

"I ran everything through AFIS," Minh said. "Nothing in the database. I put a call in to Quantico, trying to make sure I'm not missing something. Our digital imaging equipment's a little outdated, to tell you the truth. The feds haven't gotten back to me, so as of right now, we have no ID."

Chairs creaked as people leaned back. There was a collective sigh of frustration.

"I know the dactyloscopist at the Delphi Center."

All eyes swung toward Allison, and she realized she'd just done the very thing she'd meant to avoid doing at this first task force meeting—drawn attention to herself.

She cleared her throat. "He's helped me out in the past with some burglary cases." Skeptical looks all around as she reminded everyone she worked property crimes. "Anyway, he's got the best equipment available and access to a bunch of different fingerprint databases. It might be worth a try."

Allison looked at Reynolds and knew he was thinking about his budget. The man was tight as a tick and probably didn't like the idea of hiring outside experts when they had a CSI trained in fingerprint work. It was one of the few aspects of the case they should have been able to handle in-house, but clearly Minh was in over his head.

"Do it," Chief Noonan said. "And let's take them a DNA sample while we're at it. There's bound to be a record of this guy somewhere. He shoots up twenty-eight people, he's got to have a sheet."

"Not necessarily."

Now it was Jonah's turn in the hot seat.

"Fact, I'd be surprised if he did. Sir."

"Why's that?" The chief looked annoyed.

"Not all rampage shooters have a criminal history," Jonah said.

"Oh, are you a profiler now?"

Jonah straightened in his chair, but continued to look confident. "Just stating a fact. He could be a law-abiding citizen who went through some sort of setback—lost his job, his girlfriend, ran into financial problems, whatever—and then he snapped. No reason to assume he's been arrested and printed before."

"Send it to Delphi, anyway," the chief said, "and do it fast. Doyle, call your friend. I'll follow up with the director."

Allison was glad to see Chief Noonan pulling out the big guns. The Delphi Center was one of the world's top crime labs and it was right in their backyard. But it was private, which meant expensive. Still, the media fallout from this thing threatened to be catastrophic. Less than twenty-four hours in, and the town was crawling with reporters from all over the country. Students were giving interviews on the street. Angry mothers who'd come to yank their kids out of summer school were on CNN venting about gun control and campus security. It wasn't surprising the chief wanted to get a handle on this thing right away.

And no matter how many task forces they put together and how many high-tech labs they hired to run evidence, it was pretty hard to look competent when they couldn't even come up with the *name* of the man who had gunned down twenty-eight people.

"What about military databases?" Ric suggested. "Guy could have sniper training, maybe he's a Marine or something."

"If he is, he's not much of a marksman," Jonah said. "Twenty-five wounded and only three kills?"

"It's worth pursuing," Reynolds said. "Look into that angle. And we also need more on the guns. What does the Delphi Center say about restoring those serial numbers?"

"Their ballistics guy left me a message," Jonah answered. "He hit some kind of snag but thinks he'll have something later today, definitely by tomorrow."

The chief looked irritated. "What about the slugs? You get anything useful at autopsy?"

"Each victim took one hit," Ric reported. "Two head shots and a neck. The bullets went to Delphi—same tracer who has the guns. He's the best around."

"Yeah, well, sounds like he's slow," Reynolds said. "You two go rattle some cages up there. We need that ID." He opened a file and pulled out a piece of paper, which he slid across the table to Allison. "Meantime, we'll try the old-fashioned way. We had a forensic artist at the morgue this morning. She came up with a composite drawing for us."

Allison gazed down at the picture, which still smelled like fixative. It was done in colored chalk on gray paper and looked as lifelike as a photograph. How had someone drawn this from a corpse, particularly one with the back of his skull blown out? She studied the image, transfixed by the bald man and his icy blue gaze. What sort of thoughts had been going through his mind as he squinted through his scope and took aim at a pregnant woman?

"Doyle? You with me?"

"Sir?" She glanced up at Reynolds.

"I said you're our liaison with the campus on this thing. You're here because you've got all the contacts over there, and we're hoping you'll get some cooperation. I want you to shop this picture around, see if you can get a name. Talk to every security guard, every maintenance worker, every resident adviser you can find. This guy was able to access the roof, which tells me he has some kind of inside connection."

"We don't think he's an employee," the campus security chief said defensively. "I combed through our last five years' worth of personnel records myself. But it's hard to tell for sure because of the shaved head. Maybe that's a disguise. Or maybe he worked for us in the distant past."

"Either way," Reynolds said, "he gained access to that roof somehow, which means he knows his way around, which means someone should know him." He looked at Allison. "Maybe you'll get an ID off the picture before we get a hit with the prints or the guns. Use your contacts over there—anyone and everyone you can think of who might have seen this guy."

Chief Noonan gathered up his files and tapped them against the conference table, signaling an end to the meeting.

"That's it, people," Noonan said. "We need an ID, and we need it fast. I've got angry parents ringing our phones off the hook. I've got lawyers threatening lawsuits against the town and the school. I've got news crews on every corner yapping about the Summer School Massacre." He stood up and looked straight at Allison. "And I've got a press conference at four o'clock. Don't make me go in there empty-handed."

Jonah hiked up the steps to the Delphi Center and took a moment to look around. The brown, freeze-dried lawn he remembered from January had been replaced by a carpet of lush green, and the building's marble columns gleamed in the noon sun. If you forgot about the fact that the lab sat in the middle of a body farm, it wasn't a bad place to work, really.

"You been back here since winter?" Jonah asked Ric as they walked in. Compared to the ninety-plus temperature outside, the lobby felt like a meat locker.

"Not officially. I've dropped by to see Mia a few times."

Mia Voss was Ric's girlfriend. She also happened to be one of the top DNA tracers at the lab. Strained budgets and local politics prevented SMPD from calling on her for all but the most important cases—their evidence usually went to the state crime lab in Austin, where it languished for months or years before being tested. The sad fact was, most police departments didn't have the money to make use of all the fancy technology available now. Even when DNA was available from a bloody murder weapon, a rape kit, it typically gathered dust in some evidence room until the case was headed to trial, if it ever went.

But nothing about this case was typical, starting with the fact that every aspect of it was being picked apart on CNN.

Jonah approached the reception desk, where detectives usually encountered a dazzling smile that made the drive out here worth it. But Sophie wasn't around today, and Jonah's half-hour road trip was rewarded with a sour look.

"IDs?" a woman asked, holding out a hand.

The sound of hammering drifted from down the hall as they flashed their credentials and waited for her to enter them into the system. Jonah made a point to befriend gatekeepers—even grumpy ones—so he gave her a smile.

"A little remodeling?"

She rolled her eyes. "New evidence room. They're doubling the storage space."

"Sounds nice."

"I've had a headache all morning."

She handed over visitors' badges, and they went their separate ways—Ric to the evidence room and then up to fingerprinting, while Jonah paid a visit to ballistics down in the basement.

As the elevator made its grumbling descent, he thought about Sophie. He'd been looking forward to seeing her here, but it was probably good she was off. She needed the rest, and he definitely needed to focus. He had a clear objective in front of him, and if there was one thing Sophie had a talent for, it was distracting him. He followed a long, windowless hallway to the firearms lab, where he found Delphi's head ballistics expert shooting a handgun into a steel tank. Jonah tapped his knuckles on the glass window and Scott Black walked over to let him in.

"I was just about to call you."

Jonah nodded at the nickel-plated pistol in his hand. "Nice piece."

"A little flashy for me. Belongs to a gangbanger out of Houston."

"You get those numbers yet?"

"Made some headway on that Remington. Come take a look."

Scott led him to a long counter where the rifle was sitting atop a piece of butcher paper. The barrel looked wet.

"Is that oil?" Jonah asked.

"I'm using the magnaflux method. You know it?"

"No."

"Basically, the idea is that when a gun is pressure-stamped with a serial number, the metal is indented with the number, but the material underneath the number also undergoes a change. So, you can file off the numbers, but it's still possible to restore them." Scott pointed to the very faint numbers on the left side of the barrel. "In this case, I applied a magnetic force to the gun, then sprayed it with an oil that has iron particles suspended in it. The particles collect in the places where the metal is disordered, which reveals the number. We got a pretty good read here. Our guy's running the number through some databases right now."

"What about the handgun?"

"That's a little trickier." Scott leaned against the counter. "The first method didn't work. Looks like your shooter, or someone, really got after those serial numbers. Most people just file until the numbers aren't visible, but in this case, someone shaved off a lot of metal."

"Think it's a hot gun?"

"Could be. I can probably still get the numbers for you, but I'm going to have to move to a method that's what we call 'destructive.' Chemical etching. You guys done collecting prints and taking pictures of it?"

"We have what we need," Jonah said.

"Then I recommend this procedure, but I'm going to need official approval."

"You got it."

Making this ID was top priority, and Jonah was

authorized to do damn near anything to get the shooter's name. He signed off on the test and headed upstairs to see Mia.

As the Delphi Center's crown jewel, the DNA section occupied a lofty place on the building's top floor. The glass corridor leading to Mia's office offered sweeping views of the Texas Hill Country. It was a nice place to work. Beat the hell out of Jonah's cubicle. Still, he would never trade places with a lab rat, even a crime-fighting one. He got way too much satisfaction from slapping on the cuffs.

Mia stepped out of her office and spotted him. "Oh, hey." She smiled. "I heard you guys were here."

She was in her typical lab coat, which Jonah was pretty sure she wore to balance out her ponytail and freckles. But even the coat and the official-looking clipboard in her hand didn't make her look a day over thirty.

"Ric's downstairs," he told her.

"He just called." She checked her watch. "I'd go down and say hi, but I'm late for a staff meeting. Walk with me?"

They retraced his steps toward the conference room near the elevator.

"If you talked to Ric, then you know a blood sample just came in that's about to get bumped to the front of your line," Jonah said.

"The university shooter." Mia shook her head. "I still can't believe it. I'm just sick that you guys were up there with him." She gave Jonah a grim look. "Thank you for taking him out."

"He took himself out."

"Well, you helped. Anyway, I'm surprised his prints didn't come back."

"Could be this is his first rodeo."

"I'll get to the sample as soon as possible. But if he's never been arrested, odds are slim we'll get a hit with the Offender Index."

"I was thinking he could be in the Forensic Index," Jonah said. "Maybe we can link him to an old crime scene, then I'll call up the detective somewhere and see if they've got a suspect list. If someone's local or has a connection to the college, it could lead to an ID."

"Good thought." Mia stopped in front of the conference room. "I'll start on it right after this meeting."

"Actually—"

"Aha." She pulled the clipboard to her chest. "Now I see why I'm getting the personal visit. You want me to drop everything now."

"This is important," he said, without a scrap of regret about torpedoing her day.

But Mia looked unmoved. "They're all important."

Jonah turned and gazed out the window. He nodded beyond the rolling green hills, in the direction of Austin. "You heard of the Charles Whitman shooting back in '66? One of the first mass murders in U.S. history—the original school shooting."

She nodded. "He killed seventeen people."

"Before he climbed to the top of that clock tower, he paid a visit to his mother and bashed her skull in. Then he went home and stabbed his wife through the heart while she slept in their bed." Jonah paused to let his words sink in. "The sooner we get an ID on this guy, the sooner we get a handle on what we're dealing with."

Mia cast an anxious look at the conference room, where it sounded as though her meeting had already started. "Point taken," she said as the elevator dinged and some lab-coated people stepped off. "Here, I'll ride down with you."

Mia went to retrieve the blood sample, and Jonah returned to the reception desk. Ric wasn't there yet, and Sophie's fill-in was busy playing solitaire on her computer.

Jonah noticed the purple iPod at her elbow. He'd seen it last night. He wandered over to one of the lobby's side doors and peered through the glass at the cluster of picnic tables beneath a leafy pecan tree. Ninety degrees in the shade today. Not much of a picnic spot, although somebody seemed to think so.

Jonah muttered a curse. He pushed open the door and went out to see Sophie.

CHAPTER 5

Sophie focused on the picturesque landscape and thought once again that she really should take up yoga. Maybe if she learned to breathe better and twist herself into a pretzel, she'd have another tool in the arsenal she used to battle her tension headaches. She took another chomp of the Hershey bar she'd bought for lunch. She'd tried aspirin, classical music, and now chocolate, but nothing seemed to be able to get rid of the pounding that had been dogging her since eight A.M.

"Thought you were off today."

She turned to see Jonah stepping into the shade of her pecan tree.

"Why would you think that?" Sophie adjusted her blouse and took inventory of her appearance. She was having a decent hair day, but her skin was dewy with sweat. And she didn't kid herself about what a night of tossing and turning had done to her eyes.

"Little Miss Sunshine's taken over your desk." Jonah stepped closer. For an instant his gaze darted to her cleavage. "I figured you called in sick."

Sophie stuffed the rest of the candy bar in her purse

and swung her legs over the picnic bench, taking care not to flash him. "That's Diane. She covers my lunch shift." She glanced at the door behind him. "You here alone?"

"Ric and I drove out to deliver evidence."

Sophie's stomach knotted at the reminder of the case. As if she'd managed to forget it for a single minute since she'd woken up this morning.

"Mind?" He nodded at the bench.

"No."

He took a seat beside her and leaned his elbows back on the table. "Hot out here for a picnic."

She cast another glance at the building. She should get back, but she was dreading it. She distracted herself by checking out the man next to her. Jonah was huge—six-four, probably 230. A solid 230, not the doughy kind. Today he wore his typical detective's uniform of button-down shirt and dark slacks with his badge pinned to his hip, just beside his gun.

Sophie looked away. Every time she got around Jonah, she felt a warm wave of security. Maybe it was his size. Maybe it was the badge and gun, although she knew plenty of other cops, and none of them had this effect on her. She needed to tread carefully here. Security went hand in hand with dependence, and dependence on a man was not on her agenda.

Jonah nudged her elbow. "So, I meant to ask you. What were you doing on campus yesterday?"

She gazed out over the hills. "Oh, you know. Just passing through."

She felt him watching her.

"I'll find out," he said. "You may as well tell me."

He *would* find out. He was a thorough detective, liked to pin down the details.

She sighed. "I was enrolling in a class, all right? What's the big deal?"

"I don't know. You tell me."

She looked at the hills again. "I've been taking some public relations courses."

"Why is that a secret?"

"It's not, I just . . . I don't know. I haven't really told anyone."

"PR, huh? You looking to go corporate?"

She had a different goal in mind, but she didn't feel like discussing it with him at the moment. She didn't feel like discussing any of this.

"I thought you liked working here."

"I do."

He looked at her expectantly.

"I just don't want to answer phones all my life. Not exactly a dream job."

"I thought your dream was to be a singer and this receptionist thing was just paying the bills."

Sophie looked away. That was *definitely* something she didn't want to discuss today. Her dreams of being a professional musician had ended the night she'd been attacked in a parking lot just before a gig. The incident had caused a seismic shift in her life, one she didn't really care to chat about on her lunch break.

She checked her watch. "I need to get back to my desk."

They stood up. She tossed an empty soft drink can in the trash, and Jonah fell into step beside her on the path to the building.

She glanced up at him. "Any breaks in the case this morning?"

"Not exactly." Now it was his turn to sound defensive.

"You still don't know who he is," she stated.

"We're expecting Mia to help with that."

"You're resorting to *DNA*?" She stopped and gaped at him. "What about his fingerprints, his guns, his wallet?"

He gazed down at her with a guarded look, and she realized he'd tried all those things, obviously.

"DNA could take days. *Weeks*." A bubble of panic rose in her throat, and she didn't know why. "Isn't there some faster way to find out his name?"

He watched her carefully with those hazel eyes, which were much too observant. "Why's it so important to you?"

"Of course it's important! Don't you want to know who he *is*?"

"Was. And yeah, I do, because it's my case. What's it to you, though?"

She started to say something, then stopped. She wasn't sure why she needed a name for the man who'd put her in his crosshairs yesterday. But she did. She *needed* it.

"I don't know." She blew out a sigh. "I want to understand, that's all. I need to make sense of it."

"Some things don't make sense, Sophie. Some things just happen."

She looked up at him and felt her throat tighten. He was right, she knew. Knowing the killer's name and his background and seeing his life dissected on the news wouldn't change anything. It wouldn't bring twenty-year-old Eric Emrick back to life, or that professor, or give Becca Kincaid back her mother.

Jonah opened the door, and a cool gust of air washed over them. Sophie stepped inside, ending the conversation before her emotions came spilling out. Her headache was back in full force now, chocolate bar be damned. She strode to her desk, which Diane had abandoned promptly at one o'clock per her usual routine. The bleating phone was drowned out by the high-pitched saw down the hall, but the vertical row of flashing lights told Sophie she had half a dozen callers demanding her attention.

She snatched up the headset, took a deep breath, and closed her eyes. *Calm. Friendly. Efficient.* Her voice was many people's first impression of the Delphi Center, and she liked them to picture her sitting serenely in the lobby, directing incoming communications. When she did her job right, callers to the lab didn't have to know about absentee employees, or upheaval from construction projects, or petty office politics—all of which could undermine the center's credibility. Image was important.

Sophie waited for a break in the noise before fielding the calls, one by one. Jonah stood at her elbow, observing her every move.

"You've got a knack for that," he said when she finished. "If I tried to do it, I'd probably hang up on half of them and piss off the rest."

She smiled. "I've been told I give good phone."

His just looked at her, and another call came in.

"So, did you need something?" she asked. "Because I have to get back to work—"

Pop.

Sophie flinched and glanced anxiously down the hall. The nail gun continued, and she bit her lip.

Jonah followed her gaze toward the construction

noise. Then he looked back at her. "You know, no one's going to think less of you if you take some time off."

"Why would I take some time off?"

"You had a pretty crappy day yesterday."

She tipped her head to the side. "And what sort of day did you have?"

His jaw tightened and he looked irritated. Good. She didn't need a sympathy pass any more than he did. *She* wasn't the one stuck in some hospital with a bandage around her head or a shattered elbow or a leg she could never walk on again.

"Look, Sophie . . ." He glanced at the elevator bank, probably looking for Ric, before settling his attention on her. The buzz saw started up again, and for a moment they stared at each other. When the noise abated, she waited for whatever words of advice he was going to dole out next.

"You want to have dinner later?"

She couldn't keep the surprise off her face. The saw screamed again, saving her from having to respond.

He wanted to have *dinner*? She wasn't sure what to do with that. Men hit on her all the time—one of the side effects of a job that required her to be friendly with the public all day long. A lot of guys interpreted her ready smile as a neon sign that said, *Ask me out, I'm easy.* Cops were the worst, because they tended to have big egos and didn't need much encouraging. But she sensed there was something else behind Jonah's invitation.

Then again, maybe the kiss had been the neon sign. Duh.

"We ready?"

They both turned to see Ric standing there. His

gaze went from Jonah to her, then back to Jonah again. Sharp detective that he was, he seemed to realize he'd interrupted something.

"Give us a sec," Jonah said.

Ric pulled off the visitor's badge clipped to his pocket and put it on the reception counter. "We're due at TCMEO in thirty," he told Jonah, before nodding good-bye to Sophie and heading for the door.

TCMEO was the Travis County Medical Examiner's Office. Sophie knew because she paid attention and had picked up on all the clever little codes people used around here.

Jonah was on his way to an autopsy, and she felt a pull of sympathy for him.

He handed over his visitor's badge. He was frowning now, and she realized her silence was becoming rude.

She also realized it was Thursday.

"It's just dinner," Jonah said. "It'll probably be late, too, because I've got about a hundred things to do before I knock off today. I can call you when I get off, or—"

"No."

His eyebrows went up.

"I mean, *thanks* and everything, but I can't. Not tonight."

He waited for an explanation, and for some reason she gave him one.

"I have a date already."

This seemed to surprise him even more, and she felt a surge of annoyance.

"Well." He tapped his knuckles on the counter. "Good enough. Guess I'll see you around, then." He glanced at the door where Ric was waiting on the other side of the glass, then back at her. "Take care of yourself, Sophie."

"Thanks." She gave him her trademark smile, one hundred percent phony. "You take care, too."

John Doe's postmortem was already under way when Jonah and Ric arrived. The deputy medical examiner was hunched over the grayish body, poking a gloved finger around the mouth.

"Stippling above the lips," Dr. Froehler said to his assistant. "Fouling visible as well." The deputy ME gazed down at the burn marks left by gases that spewed from the pistol just after the trigger was pulled. He was obviously building support for the manner of death he planned to put in his report: suicide.

Jonah reached for the jar of Vicks sitting on the counter just inside the door. He swiped some gel under his nose to help with the smell before handing the jar to Ric.

"I hate this place," Ric muttered.

"Yeah, me, too."

Jonah stepped up to the steel table, giving himself the same vantage point he'd had this morning when he'd been in here with Jodi Kincaid and then Eric Emrick. Walter Graham had been autopsied in the suite next door, and Ric had stood in for that one.

Three autopsies in one day. It was a career record, one Jonah hoped never to repeat.

"Detectives." Froehler glanced up and nodded.

"Doc." Ric replaced the lid on the gel and plunked it on the counter. "The boss knock off early today?"

The deputy ME sniffed, which Jonah took for an affirmative. It was common knowledge that Froehler was the workhorse around here, while the head ME was more of a figurehead. Even so, the man had dragged himself out of bed this morning to perform two of the four autopsies. Jonah figured he'd taken note of all the news coverage and decided he needed to look hands-on.

"Still no ID," Jonah informed the doctor. "Any tattoos or scars that might help us out?"

"None."

Jonah glanced at the series of X-rays lined up on the light box across the room. "How about prosthetics? Unusual dental work?"

"His bones and his teeth look normal."

Jonah and Ric exchanged looks. By the tone of his answer, they could tell something *didn't* look normal. But knowing Froehler, they'd have to wait around to hear what it was. This doctor was meticulous—sometimes frustratingly so—and he didn't venture his opinion without evidence to back it up.

"What about personal effects?" Ric asked. "Anything we missed in his pockets?"

"Just the Timex wristwatch that was handed over this morning."

"His clothes are over there," Froehler's assistant added. "I didn't find anything."

Jonah glanced at a table across the room, where some clothes had been spread out. Black Hanes T-shirt, size medium; blue jeans, size 32 X 30; socks; underwear; and a pair of size-nine Altamas in desert brown.

The boots were favored by military guys, and they— more than the shooter's skill with a gun—had convinced Jonah that running the fingerprints through a military database might not be a total waste of time.

"How about track marks?" Ric persisted. "Evidence of drug use?"

Froehler straightened his wire-rimmed glasses but didn't look up. "We'll know when we get the tox screen."

Jonah gritted his teeth. His fuse was short today, and it wasn't just because he'd gotten up at the butt crack of dawn to come up here and watch two innocent people get sliced open. "Is there *anything* you can tell us yet? We need an ID here."

Froehler stopped what he was doing and gave him an appraising look. "There is one thing." He moved to the side of the body and lifted the left arm, which was lax now that rigor mortis had passed. "It's possible he's recently divorced."

Jonah stepped closer and frowned down at the hand. No wedding band, but sure enough, there was a faint white line around the ring finger.

"I'll be damned," Ric said. "I didn't notice the tan mark yesterday."

"Also note the callus," Froehler said, separating the last two fingers to show them the marks where a ring had rubbed against the skin.

Ric looked at Jonah. "So maybe his wife dumped him and he had a meltdown."

Jonah stepped back and leaned against the counter. As motives went, it was one of the oldest around. Still, he didn't like rushing to conclusions. Plenty of men's marriages broke up and they didn't all start shooting up campuses.

Jonah's thoughts went back to the setting, the methodology, the victims. Given the planning that went into the attack, he felt sure the university was significant in some way. Maybe his ex was taking classes there or worked there. They wouldn't know until they got an ID.

Froehler ducked around the hanging scale and selected a scalpel off a cart filled with shiny instruments. Jonah braced himself for the Y-incision, just as Ric's phone started to buzz.

Lucky bastard.

Ric checked the number and glanced at Jonah. "It's Sean. Maybe we got something back from Delphi."

He stepped out to take the call, and Jonah watched him through the window to the autopsy room. After a few minutes of listening, Ric waved him over.

But not before Jonah was hit by a wave of foul odors.

"We got a match on those prints," Ric said as Jonah stepped into the hallway. "James Himmel, thirty-seven, of Columbus, Georgia."

"That's near Fort Benning. He ex-military?"

"Army had his prints on file."

"So, what's he doing down here?"

"No idea," Ric said. "He's not on staff or enrolled at the college. Sean's running his credit cards right now, seeing if anything local pops up."

"He married?"

"We're checking."

Jonah imagined some young woman moving down to Texas to start over after a bad breakup. Then he imagined her dead in a bedroom somewhere, like Charles Whitman's wife.

If there was a secondary crime scene, they needed to find it soon.

"Detectives, you'll want to see this."

Jonah turned around to see Froehler's assistant poking

his head from the door. They both hesitated. Whatever it was couldn't be more pressing than this latest intel.

"You go," Ric said. "I'll get started on some calls."

"I'll explain to Froehler, meet you out front in ten."

Jonah returned to the steel table, giving the doctor exactly two minutes to show him something important. A pair of bloody shears lay on the cart beside him. Christ, he'd opened the chest already.

Froehler looked up at Jonah. "I thought I saw it on X-ray and I just confirmed it."

"Confirmed what?"

"Tumors." Froehler nodded at the gaping chest cavity. "This man's eaten up with cancer."

CHAPTER 6

Gretchen emptied the packet of orange powder into the saucepan and stirred with one hand while reaching for the refrigerator door with the other.

She scanned the shelves. No milk, damn it. She grabbed a tub of margarine instead and made a mental note to add milk to her grocery list—the one that never seemed to get fulfilled.

"Is it dinner yet?"

She shot a glance into the living room, where the twins sat cross-legged on the carpet, surrounded by Legos.

"Almost." She scooped out some margarine and added a dollop to the mac-n-cheese. "Did you girls drink milk today at Mrs. Garcia's?"

"Yes," they answered in unison.

Gretchen felt a touch of relief. They might be skimping at home, but at least she could count on Mrs. Garcia. The woman took care of six kids during the day, and her fridge was always stocked with milk and fruit. That and quesadillas had been staples of the twins' diet since school let out.

Gretchen spooned pasta onto plates, then cut up a hot dog.

"Ready," she said, ferrying the meals to the table. She returned to the kitchen and filled two cups with water as the girls sat down.

"So." She sank into a chair. Families that ate together stayed together. Or was it prayed together? Either way, she made an effort to sit with her kids for at least a few minutes every evening. "Tell me what you did today."

By some tacit agreement, Angela did the talking tonight. "Played freeze tag, watched SpongeBob, and folded clothes."

"Whose clothes?"

They both shrugged.

Gretchen watched her girls shovel macaroni into their mouths. Their appetites amazed her. It was probably another growth spurt, one that was going to strain her bank account.

"Mrs. Garcia's clothes?" she asked.

"No. Boy clothes."

"*Man* clothes," Amy corrected.

Gretchen considered that. Mrs. Garcia lived alone, so either she was taking in people's laundry or she'd gotten herself a boyfriend. The woman was sixty-four and on the frumpy side, so Gretchen guessed this was another one of her businesses. She wasn't sure she approved of her six-year-old daughters being used as un-hired help, but she couldn't really complain. Affordable babysitters were scarce, and Gretchen couldn't have any disruptions at work.

"Can I have more hot dog?" Amy asked, popping a chunk into her mouth.

"Use your fork, honey. And no, we're out."

Two pairs of solemn blue eyes looked up at her. They didn't say anything, which was worse than complaining. Now Gretchen felt guilty. She got up and retrieved the TV remote from the coffee table to give herself a distraction.

News, sports, reality shows, more news. She tuned it to CNN and settled back in her chair.

"Amy, your fork, honey." Gretchen slid the fork toward her, and she picked it up reluctantly. Her sister followed suit.

"Mommy, what's a massacre?"

Gretchen darted a glance at the television. It was that school shooting down in Texas again.

"It's when someone kills a lot of people."

Both girls looked up.

"Why would someone kill a lot of people?" Angela asked.

Gretchen cast a wary look at the screen. Why, indeed? Why did men beat their wives, or drink too much, or do *anything*? "I don't know, honey. Amy, your *fork*."

"But hot dogs are *finger* food. You said so."

A knock sounded at the door, and Gretchen got up.

"Not without a bun," she said. "And don't argue with me."

She shifted the curtain on the window beside the door and peered out.

Her heart skittered.

A pair of men in army dress uniforms stood on her doorstep. During every one of Jim's deployments, she'd had nightmares about a scene like this. But Jim was out now, and anyway they were divorced. These men must have the wrong apartment.

She swung open the door and looked them over. Two crew cuts, two pairs of broad shoulders, two stony expressions.

"Gretchen Himmel?"

"No," she said, her heart pounding now. "That is, not anymore."

They stared at her.

"Are you the former wife of James K. Himmel?"

"I am."

Gretchen's chest tightened. Jim was *out*. What were these men doing here?

The TV droned behind her, talking about the sniper who'd climbed to the top of that library and shot all those people.

One of the soldiers glanced behind her at the television, and suddenly she *knew*. Her blood turned to ice.

"Ma'am, we need to talk to you about your ex-husband."

Oh, no. Oh, Jim, how could you?

She clamped a hand over her mouth and thought about the girls.

James Himmel had spent his final night on earth in the Happy Trails Motel cleaning his guns.

Jonah watched one of the crime-scene techs lift a pair of oily rags from the trash.

"CLP oil, by the smell of it," Jonah said.

The technician dropped the rags into a paper evidence bag and dipped his gloved hand back into the waste basket. In about the only stroke of luck they'd had in this case, Himmel's room hadn't been cleaned yet when Sean called the motel to check on a credit-card transaction.

Jonah had his secondary crime scene now, and it wasn't nearly as grisly as he'd feared.

"Just heard from Sean," Ric said. "They had the ex in there for more than two hours, and she swears she hasn't seen him in more than a year. No recent fights or harassment."

Jonah muttered a curse. Another dead end on the motive front.

But then again, Dr. Froehler's discovery this afternoon had given them plenty to build on. They were running tests on some tissue samples to confirm it, but it looked as though their shooter had been dealing with not only a recently finalized divorce, but terminal cancer. Either one would have constituted a triggering event that could drive someone to murder. The two taken together were pretty overwhelming.

Still, there were matters left to investigate, the most important being Himmel's connection to the university and whether he was acting alone at the time of the shooting. Even with the gunman dead and identified, even with Himmel's immediate family safe and accounted for, Jonah wouldn't rest easy until those questions were answered.

He stepped out of the way so several CSIs could wrap Himmel's green canvas duffel bag with butcher paper to be transported to the lab.

"Army or police?" Jonah asked.

Ric glanced up from a pile of bank statements that was sitting on the dresser. "What's that?"

"Who interviewed the ex?"

"Both. Couple of MPs picked her up, but I think they're pretty eager to turn this over to the locals. He was let go from the army about two years ago, and sounds like they've washed their hands of him."

Jonah didn't blame them. He hadn't seen the news since Noonan's press conference, but he could only imagine the field day the media was having with Himmel's military connection.

Jonah had spent five years in the army before becoming a cop, and he disliked anything that reflected badly on the uniform. At the same time, what he *really* disliked were people who thought they were above the law. The law was the law, and no one was exempt.

"Here, look at this." Ric held up one of the statements. "Looks like he printed these last week."

"What's his money situation?"

"Pretty bad. Nothing but withdrawals for the past three months."

Ric continued to shuffle papers as Jonah crossed the cramped little room and poked his head into the bathroom for an update. Minh was crouched beside the john, lifting prints from the handle.

"You can bet your ass I'm putting in for overtime on this." The CSI was ticked, and Jonah could see why. They'd probably turn up fifty different sets of prints in this crummy little motel suite, and it would take an ungodly number of man-hours to run them all.

"Got to cover all the bases," Jonah said.

"You mean cover Noonan's ass. I got that."

"Hey, Jonah," Ric called from the other room. "Get some gloves and come see this."

Jonah swiped some gloves from Minh's evidence kit and went to the bed, where one of the CSIs was on his knees photographing something.

Jonah crouched beside them. "What you got?"

"Looks like a teddy bear." Ric pulled it from under the bed. On closer inspection, they saw that it wasn't a teddy bear but a blanket with a bear head on top. The thing had dingy gray fur and one of its eyes was missing.

"What would a suicidal thirty-seven-year-old be doing with a kid's teddy bear?" Ric asked. "Manager said he was alone in here."

"Maybe it's not his. Could be someone else left it."

"Could be. Fleabag place like this, they probably don't clean the rooms too well."

Ric passed him the blanket, and Jonah frowned down at it. The thing was worn, even threadbare in places. It had obviously been well-loved—probably some kid's security blanket—but it looked creepy for some reason. Jonah ran his hands over the natty fabric.

"Hey, it's not a bear, it's a rabbit." Jonah glanced at Ric. "Looks like someone cut off its ears."

Sophie's date pulled into the parking lot and found an empty space right next to her Tahoe.

"Sorry to cut our evening short," she told him.

"It's no problem." Mark slid out of his shiny black Acura and came around to open her door, demonstrating more of the perfect manners that had impressed her all evening.

"Are you sure I can't get you anything?" he asked, offering her a hand out of the car. His voice was genuinely concerned, and she felt bad for doing this to him.

"I'm fine. Really. Usually just a few aspirin and a good night's sleep do the trick."

They walked up the stairs together and her nerves

began to jump. She hated this part. Was he going to try to kiss her, or was he perceptive enough to let it go?

They reached her door, and she made a production of fishing for her keys.

"Well," she said lamely. "Thanks for dinner."

"You barely ate anything." He smiled down at her, making sure she knew he wasn't criticizing. More manners again. This guy was perfect, really. He was smart, courteous, interesting to talk to. He had a warm smile, and—an added bonus—he was two inches taller than she was. With all those pluses, she could get past the overly large Adam's apple.

"It wasn't the food," she said. "I just don't feel myself tonight."

"You don't have to explain. You've had a trying week. To be honest, I was surprised you didn't cancel."

Now she realized that she should have. At least then she wouldn't have wasted his money on a piece of salmon she hardly touched.

He bent down and kissed her forehead. "Good night, Sophie. We can try this again when you're feeling better." And then he stepped back, ending the awkward good-night-kiss moment before it even began. This man was a prince.

Sophie gave him the first genuine smile of the night. "Thanks," she said, and slipped into her apartment. She leaned back against the door and listened as his footsteps faded away.

Alone at last. Another night with just her thoughts and her nervous energy for company. Despite what she'd told Mark, she knew a good night's sleep was not in her near future.

She tossed her purse on the chair and flipped on the TV to keep her company as she retrieved a Diet Coke from the fridge. She downed a few aspirin and stood there, waiting for the pills to slide down her throat.

Her head was throbbing. It had worsened after Jonah's visit. Was it the construction noise at the lab or the stress of talking to him? Probably a combination of both.

Sophie pulled off her high-heeled sandals and went to change from her date clothes into her most comfortable sleepwear—an old Austin City Limits tank top and a pair of boxers. Then she scrubbed the makeup off her face and looked at her reflection in the bathroom mirror.

What had Mark seen tonight? The cut on her face, obviously. It was a reminder that she'd been caught up in yesterday's shooting. Maybe it was also the reason he'd been so understanding when she'd bailed out early on him. She hoped she hadn't hurt his feelings. Nice guys were few and far between, and she didn't want to discourage them.

Still, she couldn't fake it. Despite her hopes when she'd agreed to go out with him, there had been no chemistry between them—no shiver when he touched her waist, no flutter in the pit of her stomach when he smiled at her. It was just . . . flat. It had been a long, long time since she'd felt anything but flat around a man. Yesterday had been an exception. She'd felt a flicker of that warm, tingly feeling she'd been missing. And so she'd acted on it, much too impulsively. But as usual, acting on impulse when it came to men was a bad idea—evidenced by the fact that Jonah now clearly thought she was up for some casual sex.

Which was not what she needed right now. Or ever.

Sophie looked at her reflection and sighed. Maybe Mark would have been good for her. He was different from the guys she usually dated. Not that she'd done much dating lately. Mark was bright, successful, a scientist. Her parents would fall in love with him on sight.

But they'd never get the chance, because there wasn't going to be a second date, much less a meet-the-parents. If the tingle wasn't there, what was the point?

Tom Rollins's perfectly modulated television voice drifted in from the living room. The Summer School Massacre continued to dominate the news, and Sophie listened to new developments as she moisturized her face. Investigators had made an ID, evidently, and now Rollins was busy recounting the details of the murderer's life: James Himmel had grown up in Mobile, Alabama. Star of his high-school track team. An Eagle Scout.

As if any of that mattered now.

She stared at her reflection, and it was back again. Ever since the winter, it had haunted her—all those imaginings of what *could* have happened, what *almost* had. The possibilities whispered around her like ghosts as she sat at the reception desk when the phones were quiet, or stood in the grocery aisle, or lay in bed at night thinking back over the day.

Sometimes she found herself stuck in a moment, and her life felt pointless. Insubstantial. As light as dust motes floating through a sunbeam. And all she could think of was, *Why me?* Why had *she* lived when those other women hadn't?

Survivor's guilt. She knew what it was. But that didn't help banish it, didn't make it go away.

Lately, when it had crept up on her like that, she'd

started to feel angry. Galvanized toward something—although she couldn't pinpoint exactly what it was. But it made her long for a purpose beyond answering phones at the Delphi Center. She wanted to be part of a mission, part of something that mattered. She wanted there to be a reason why she was here, beyond just dumb luck.

Sophie closed the door, shutting out the broadcast. She leaned closer to the mirror and examined the cut from yesterday. Maybe she *should* have had stitches. But after meeting Robert Kincaid and handing off Becca, she'd wanted nothing more than to get out of that hospital.

Sophie went back to her living room, searching for the ointment she'd picked up at the pharmacy.

"—a team of investigators combed a motel room where Himmel allegedly had spent the night recently," Rollins was saying. "Meanwhile, yet another team of investigators was on campus today, processing the scene where Himmel's car was said to have been abandoned."

Sophie found the cream and returned to the bathroom.

"His green Volkswagen Beetle was seized by police and hauled away for further testing."

Sophie froze. A green *what*?

She rushed back into the living room, but the broadcast was wrapping up. No footage of the car, the campus—just a bronze-skinned newscaster standing before the camera. Sophie snatched up the remote and turned up the volume.

"Come on, Tom," she murmured. "Come on, come on, come on. Say it again."

But Tom was done reporting, and his over-whitened smile beamed into her living room as he signed off for the night.

CHAPTER 7

Jonah emptied another beer in an effort to drown out the day.

"Three a record for you?"

"Yeah."

"I once did four."

"Shit." Jonah looked at his partner. "Drive-by?"

"Nah, this was a triple shooting down in Bexar County, back when I was a rookie," Ric said. "Drug deal gone bad. When we cornered the perp, he took a shot at one of our officers, too, so it ended up being four."

"You had to watch the cop's autopsy?" Jonah shook his head.

"I'd never met him, so they nominated me. Didn't seem right for one of his buddies to do it."

Jonah signaled the bartender for another beer, and Ric ordered one, too.

"This round's on me." A big hand clapped Jonah on the back. "I knew Walt Graham. He was a good man."

Jonah recognized the guy from SMFD. El Patio was a hangout for emergency workers of every stripe, probably because of its location between the cop shop and the firehouse.

"Thanks," Jonah told him, echoed by Ric.

"I mean it." Another hearty slap on the back. "You guys went above and beyond."

The man put some money on the bar and walked off, and Jonah watched him uneasily. He didn't like all this thank-you crap. People meant well, but it didn't seem right to get applauded just for doing his job.

He flicked a glance at the television behind the bar, where Headline News was running taped coverage of Noonan's press conference earlier.

Ric watched the chief and muttered something in Spanish. Jonah didn't catch the words, but he got the gist. Ric was pissed. As soon as those prints had come back, Noonan had stepped up to the podium and wrapped the case up with a big red bow, even though the police work was far from finished.

Another swig of beer, and Jonah started thinking about the mountain of paperwork on his desk and how early he had to get up tomorrow and how little sleep he was going to get with those autopsies playing through his head. He could still hear the Stryker saw.

"So, what's the deal with you and Sophie?"

He turned his tired gaze to Ric. "What do you mean?"

"She doesn't seem like your type."

"Since when are leggy, big-breasted women not my type?"

Ric tipped back his beer, then set it on the bar. "You want to watch yourself there. That girl's got issues."

Jonah stared at him. Even in his brain-fried state,

he realized he was getting relationship advice from Ric Santos, of all people.

"Are you serious, man?"

"Completely."

"Issues. You mean like boil-a-rabbit-on-the-stove issues? Guy issues? What?"

"You should know," Ric said, heavy on the disapproval.

"What the hell's that supposed to mean?"

"Just what I said. Watch your step with her."

Jonah gritted his teeth. He reminded himself that Ric had endured pretty much the same shitty forty-eight hours he had. For that reason alone, he refrained from telling him to mind his own fucking business.

Jonah pretended to watch TV as his temper festered. Ric thought he was taking advantage of a girl who'd been traumatized. Twice. The implication pissed him off—first, because it assumed Sophie was screwed up enough to be taken advantage of, and second, because it assumed Jonah would do that.

But then again, maybe he would.

He *had* gone over to her place last night hoping for some post–near-death-experience sex. He could admit that. But he'd come to his senses and backed the hell off. And anyway, *she* came on to *him*.

Proving Ric's point that she was traumatized.

Shit. Ric was right. Sophie was vulnerable, and he was taking advantage of her trust. He should leave her alone.

Jonah scrubbed a hand over his face. Goddamn, but he was too tired to even think about it right now. He just needed to get home.

"There you are! God, I've been looking everywhere!"

He turned around, and for a second he thought he

was hallucinating. But when he blinked his eyes, Sophie was still standing there, looking flushed and wild-eyed, both hands fisted on her hips. She wore jean shorts with a skimpy tank top and had a purse dangling from her shoulder that Jonah knew from personal experience concealed a LadySmith revolver.

And she was about the least vulnerable-looking woman he'd ever laid eyes on.

"*Where* have you been?" she demanded. "I've been all over town. Don't you answer your phone?"

Ric slid Jonah a look.

"And you." She pointed a finger at Ric. "Mia has no idea where you are. Nobody does."

Ric gave Jonah an I-rest-my-case look as he got off his bar stool. He pulled a billfold from his pocket and left a twenty on the counter.

"Think I'll be leaving." He nodded at Sophie and then carefully stepped around her, as if she might reach out and sock him. It seemed pretty crazy, but . . . she looked pretty crazy at the moment.

"What's wrong?" Jonah asked her when Ric was gone.

"I have *important* information for you! I called you twice."

He hadn't recognized her number or he would have picked up, even though she'd rejected him just a few short hours ago. Despite her brush-off—or maybe because of it—Jonah had had Sophie and her honey-sweet mouth on his mind all night.

"What are you staring at? Did you hear what I said?"

He pushed his beer away. "What kind of information?"

"It's about the case. The shooting. James *Himmel*."

That got his attention, along with about four other cops at the bar.

Jonah studied her more carefully now. She didn't *look* like she'd been out on a date tonight. She wasn't wearing makeup, and her hair was piled on top of her head in a messy knot. And then there was the little tank top, which had been through the wash so many times, Jonah could practically see through it. Not her usual fashion statement—not by a long stretch.

But it was the look in her eyes that worried him. She seemed a little unhinged.

"Let's get out of here." Jonah stood up, blocking his buddies' view of her. They were staring, and he didn't blame them.

A hot-tempered blonde walks into a bar . . .

It sounded like the start of a bad joke, and Jonah had a feeling he was at the butt of it. He tossed some money on the bar and took Sophie's arm to steer her to the door.

When they were outside, he turned to look at her.

"*Now* can I talk?" She shook off his hold.

"Please."

"It said on the news that James Himmel drove a green VW. You guys towed it from campus and took it into evidence."

"Okay."

"I *saw* that car on the street that day, just minutes before the shooting."

"Okay."

"He cut me off! He stole my parking space!"

Jonah crossed his arms and gazed down at her. "I'm not following."

"Don't you *get* it?" She shook his arm. "James Himmel

wasn't in the car. Somebody else was. He had an accomplice."

Sophie zipped through town, running every yellow light between El Patio and campus. She darted Jonah a look as he sat in her passenger seat, rubbing the bridge of his nose.

"How much have you had to drink tonight?"

He scoffed. "Not nearly enough."

"Well, I need you to get your head in the game. Here." She grabbed her travel mug of coffee from that morning and passed it to him.

Jonah took a gulp, then scowled. "How old is this?"

"Just a few hours. I need you alert so I can show you." She whipped into a faculty lot near the registrar's office and screeched to a halt.

Jonah shoved the mug back into the cup holder. "Let's go."

He climbed out, and Sophie followed, slamming the door with a little too much force. She was steamed. Very. She'd laid out her entire theory for him back at the bar and he'd simply stared at her.

"Come here. I'll show you." She led him across the parking lot to a street that was normally lined with cars. The university was oddly quiet now, even for summer session. Classes had been canceled until further notice, and many of the students had simply packed up and gone home.

At the intersection of University and Meadowlark, she stopped to glance around. The sidewalk was punctuated by gray parking meters.

"Here." She stopped in front of a space. "*This* was my spot. He pulled right into it."

Jonah sidled up beside her and sighed. He gazed at the space, completely nonplussed.

"Why aren't you on the phone, calling the chief of police or something?" Sophie stomped her foot. "There's an accomplice on the loose out there!"

Jonah rubbed his hands over his face. "Sophie. This proves nothing. So you saw a car park here. So what?"

"I told you, the timing doesn't make sense. When I drove by here it was, like, twelve-thirty. The shooting started at twelve-forty. How does someone park a car here and get all the way across campus and to the top of the library in that amount of time?"

"The first shot was at twelve forty-one. A security guard heard it, called it in immediately." He looked more alert now, as if he'd finally shaken the beer buzz. But he didn't seem to be getting it.

"The timing still doesn't make sense," she said.

"Assuming you've got your time line straight."

She stepped back. "What do you mean, 'assuming'? I'm telling you right now exactly what happened. Just because I don't have a badge doesn't mean I can't notice something when it's right in front of my face."

"And you were looking at your watch every minute?"

"No."

"So, isn't it possible you're off by a few minutes?"

She crossed her arms. "Why are you resisting this? Why can't you just believe me when I tell you there's a hole in this case?"

"I would believe you, if there really was a hole in this case. Our guy fingerprinted the car already."

"And?"

"And there were prints all over it. Belonging to James Himmel."

"You're saying I don't know what I saw?" She couldn't believe this. "That green Beetle cut me *off*! I yelled at the man inside. I remember it vividly."

"James Himmel cut you off."

"It wasn't him. There couldn't have been time. This was someone else—someone who must have dropped Himmel off at the library and then abandoned his car on campus."

"Okay, walk me through it." He gestured at the empty space. "The VW cut you off. Then what?"

She took a deep breath and made an effort to calm down. "Then I drove around the block."

"How many times?"

"Once. Still no spaces. So I pulled into a parking garage—that one near the basketball court. Then I walked up the sidewalk a ways toward the registrar's office. And then the shooting started."

"And you did all this in ten minutes. You're sure?"

"Why is that so impossible to believe?"

"It seems pretty unlikely you covered all that ground so fast."

"I was on my lunch break. I was in a hurry."

"It also seems pretty unlikely our suicidal gunman— who'd just gotten divorced and been diagnosed with cancer and was nearly broke, by the way—had some random guy valet his car for him while he hiked up to the top of that library to unleash his rage on everyone." Jonah looked up the hill and nodded. "I was there, Sophie. There was *one* shooter on that roof, and he murdered three people and wounded twenty-five others. All the bullets came from one rifle, except the bullet he fired through his own skull. The rifle has *one* person's prints all over it: James Himmel's. The shell casings collected from that rooftop have one person's prints on them: James Himmel's. The pistol he used to kill himself has one person's prints on it: James Himmel's. He did this on his own, Sophie. Why would he need an accomplice?"

Her arms dropped to her sides. Her chest ached. She couldn't be hearing this.

"You don't believe me."

Jonah sighed. "Sophie . . ." He looked off toward the library. "It doesn't add up. We've got one very angry and disturbed individual. One rifle. One source of deadly fire. Whatever messed-up goal he had when he went to the top of that building, he accomplished it alone. Where does the accomplice fit in?"

She looked toward the library. The lights were on, and the building glowed like a beacon at the top of the hill. She thought of the carnage that had happened there just a few short hours ago and shuddered.

"You should get home," he advised, "get some sleep. You're tired."

And crazy.

He didn't say it, but he didn't have to. It was in his voice, his body language, the pity she saw in his eyes.

She swallowed a lump of frustration. He could chalk it up to nerves, or fatigue, or whatever he wanted, but Sophie knew she was right.

Now she just had to prove it.

CHAPTER 8

"You mean to tell me this woman combed the campus looking for a parking space, pulled into a paid garage on Elm Street, then hauled her buns a quarter of a mile *uphill* to the registrar's office, all inside of eleven minutes?"

In high heels, Jonah could have added, but he didn't.

The lieutenant's look of disbelief was mirrored by the other guys at the table, including Chief Noonan, who'd shown up at this meeting specifically to hear Jonah's new theory of the case.

Which was sounding a hell of a lot shakier than it had at two in the morning.

"The timing's tight but doable," Jonah said. "I did it myself, twice." He didn't mention that he'd conducted the reenactment in the middle of the night, fueled by about sixteen ounces of gas station coffee. "I also clocked the walk from the parking space where we recovered the Beetle to the library. Including the six flights of stairs, that walk takes thirteen minutes, at least. And I've got a long stride. Which means if she saw that car being parked, Himmel wasn't the one behind the wheel."

Reynolds shot a dismayed look at Noonan, who was sitting back in his chair silently.

"What else we got on the car?" Ric asked, taking some of the heat off Jonah. "Minh? You done running the prints yet?"

Their fingerprint expert looked even worse than Jonah this morning. His eyes were bloodshot and he was swigging coffee like it was water. After staying up half the night processing prints from Himmel's motel room, he'd met Jonah at the police station at seven A.M. to go over the VW again.

"I've combed that thing top to bottom. Every print I have is consistent with Himmel." He sent Jonah an exasperated look. "There was some mystery guy driving his car, he had to have been wearing gloves. Not exactly inconspicuous in hundred-degree heat."

Impatient looks from around the table. No one wanted to listen to what, as Sophie had correctly pointed out, could be a hole in the case. The media spotlight was still on them, and now they had added pressure from a slew of attorneys representing injured students and—as of this morning—the family of the slain professor. The university and the police department were being sued left and right for failing to prevent Wednesday's events and failing to respond in a timely manner—whatever that meant. The pressure was intense, and no one was looking forward to some new setback in the case, such as an unidentified accomplice. The department had an opportunity here, and every one of them knew it. When James Himmel put that gun in his mouth and pulled the trigger, he provided all of them with an easy out. And

Noonan and Reynolds were tempted to take it—Jonah could see it in their eyes. Hell, he was tempted, too. But he couldn't, not until he knew the truth. People were dead, and he couldn't let that go by without getting all the answers.

"What's his motive?" This from Sean, who at least looked to be considering the idea.

"The driver?" Jonah asked.

"Yeah, you're talking about a team job now, right? Are you saying this driver's just some unsuspecting schmuck who maybe took a little money to give Himmel a ride to the library and then ditch his car for him? Or are you talking conspiracy to commit murder?"

"I don't know."

Reynolds looked aggravated. "A conspiracy? Come on, we're not talking about a couple of teens here. Himmel was thirty-seven. He didn't need a buddy on this."

Silence settled over the conference table.

"Anyway, his motive stands on its own," Reynolds continued. "He'd been cut loose from the army. His wife had dumped him. He had money problems *and* he'd been given a virtual death sentence by some cancer center." He ticked the reasons off on his fingers. "Throw in the fact that he's a gun nut, and he's the textbook candidate for one of these rampage shootings."

Jonah sat back and folded his arms over his chest. "What if it wasn't a rampage?"

Reynolds frowned. "What do you mean? He shot up twenty-eight people."

"Yes, but a rampage implies a random burst of violence," Jonah said. "I'm saying, what if it wasn't random?"

"You're suggesting this was a targeted hit." Noonan leaned forward on his elbows.

"Why not? I mean, we were pretty quick to jump to the conclusion that this was another senseless school shooting. Maybe it wasn't senseless at all."

"Who's the target?" Reynolds asked.

"I don't know," Jonah said. "We'll have to investigate the victims more thoroughly." And he was being diplomatic here. In truth, they hadn't investigated the victims at all. They'd been too busy racing around trying to come up with an ID so Noonan could announce that they'd solved the case. And the shooter, now safely identified as some outsider who wasn't even part of their community, was safely in hell, where he belonged.

This whole investigation had been a rush to judgment, and Jonah couldn't believe it had taken a receptionist to point it out to him.

"You're suggesting we blow up our own case theory and throw this town into an uproar on the basis of *one* witness account?" Reynolds leaned forward, scowling. "Who the hell is this girl, anyway?"

"Her name's Sophie Barrett."

"Who?" This from Noonan.

"Sophia Barrett."

Noonan turned to Reynolds. "Why do I know that name?"

"She works at the Delphi Center," Jonah said. "She—"

"She's the girl from January," Reynolds cut in. "That one who was kidnapped."

"Who?" Noonan continued to look flummoxed.

"She was kidnapped from a bar up in Austin," Ric

clarified. "Man who abducted her was responsible for several stabbing deaths—"

"The singer." Noonan slapped the table. "I remember her now. She was all over the news."

Reynolds turned to Jonah. "You don't think this is another one of her stunts, do you?"

"Stunts?" Anger welled up in Jonah's chest. "She was smashed in the head with a Maglite and thrown in the trunk of a car."

"Maybe she's doing this for media attention, hoping to get on TV again." Reynolds glanced around the table. "You said she's a singer, right? Maybe she's trying to get discovered."

Jonah's fist curled into a ball.

"I'd say that's unlikely." Ric shot Jonah a look that said, *Cool it.* "But if you're worried about her credibility, I'm happy to interview her, get a second take."

Jonah bit his tongue, intensely aware that the chief was sitting in on this meeting and could have him suspended in about two seconds for insubordination. He was also intensely aware that he'd never had such a powerful urge to pop someone's jaw.

Jonah glared at Reynolds. The man showed no leadership. In the army, there were colonels Jonah would have followed down the barrel of a cannon. He wouldn't follow Reynolds around the block.

"Get Doyle to talk to her," Noonan said. "She's more likely to get a straight read. Where is she, anyway?"

"On campus," Reynolds said, "flashing our suspect sketch and trying to figure out how Himmel got hold of those door codes."

"Have her interview this girl. And Minh, go over that car again, make sure nothing matches any of the prints we got from that motel room. We get a phone dump on this guy?"

"He didn't have one," Sean reported. "Or at least he didn't have a contract. He might have had a disposable phone, but if he did, we haven't found it yet."

"Keep looking. If he had a partner, they probably traded phone calls."

"Will do, sir."

"I'll call Doyle in," Reynolds said, clearly unhappy about the new direction the investigation had taken. "Sooner we check out this girl's story, sooner we can put this thing to bed."

"Let's get to it, people." Noonan stood up and pointed a finger at Jonah. "In the meantime, none of this leaves this room." He glanced around the table sternly. "I hear one word on the news about some mystery accomplice, I'm going to have someone's badge."

The Delphi Center was bigger than Allison had expected, and she'd expected big.

She steered her department-issue Buick up the winding drive and stared with wonder at the Parthenon-like structure at the top of the hill. It looked like something she'd expect to see on the Mall in Washington, not nestled in the hills of central Texas.

She parked in a visitor's space and worked on not looking like an awestruck kid as she hiked up the steps and passed through a pair of Greek columns. Corinthian? Ionic? Allison had a head for details, but her long-ago "Survey of Western Art" course eluded her now.

Pulling open the tinted glass door, she took a moment to feel the air-conditioning. Her eyes adjusted, and she noticed she was being sized up by a dark-skinned security guard and a smiling receptionist. Allison recognized the woman from the quadrangle, where she'd been pinned down behind a statue on the day of the shooting.

"You must be Detective Doyle. I'm Sophie."

The meet-and-greet was interrupted by some hammering down the hall. Allison peeled off her sunglasses and approached the desk.

"Sorry I'm late," Allison said. "I underestimated the drive out here. Very winding highway." She tucked the shades into the pocket of the lightweight blazer she wore to conceal her holster.

"No problem. I'll just need to see some ID."

Allison dug out her creds as a delivery guy walked up behind her and handed an electronic clipboard over the counter. Sophie signed for a package and then entered Allison's badge number into her computer. She handed over a visitor's pass.

"This goes on your lapel," Sophie said as she stood up to collect a stack of cardboard mailers from the edge of her desk. "Just these today, Leo." She handed them over with a smile that could have sold toothpaste. "You have a great weekend."

"You, too, Sophie."

She turned to Allison. "The Delphi Center. How may I help you?"

It took Allison a moment to realize she was speaking into a receiver clipped to her ear.

"One moment, please, while I see if he's in." She pressed a button on the phone and looked at Allison again. "Ready? I've reserved us a conference room." Then back to the caller: "I'm sorry, Dr. Snyder's in a meeting. Would you like to leave a message?" Pause. "Let me put you through to his voice mail. The Delphi Center. How may I help you?"

Allison watched her field a few more calls. She had one of those velvety phone voices that projected calm even amid a flurry of activity.

A dour woman appeared at the desk and looked Allison up and down. Sophie handed her the headset.

"Clovis is out sick today, and Lemberger and Snyder are still at lunch." Sophie looked at her watch. "A detective out of Harris County has been calling all morning to pester Mia about some lab work, but she's running behind. If he calls again, just tell him she's in a meeting and route him to voice mail. I'll be back at one."

The woman mumbled something that may or may not have been friendly, and Sophie nodded for Allison to follow her down a long corridor, away from the construction noise.

"You guys renovating?" Allison asked.

"Expanding our evidence room. You'd never believe how much stuff comes in."

Actually, Allison would. With some of the nation's top forensic scientists on staff, the Delphi Center had a reputation that rivaled Quantico's. If it weren't for the hefty price tag, every law enforcement agency in the country would be sending its stuff here.

Sophie opened a door, and Allison followed her into a conference room that was disappointingly ordinary.

"I'd offer you coffee, but honestly? We don't have time. Diane can only cover me until one o'clock."

Allison checked her watch. Fifteen minutes. "I'll get straight to it, Ms. Barrett."

"It's Sophie." She smiled and gestured her to the chair at the head of the table, putting Allison in the power position. Allison thought it was odd, but maybe the woman was being strategic.

Allison sat down and flipped open her notebook. "I'm just here to clear up a few details related to the information you relayed to Detective Macon."

A perfectly shaped eyebrow lifted. "Anything I can do to help."

"Okay, so I understand you went to the university on Wednesday. What were you doing there?"

She crossed her legs. "Enrolling in classes."

"So, you're a student?"

"Just taking a few hours. I'm trying to beef up my résumé before September."

"What happens in September?"

"The assistant director of public relations is leaving to have a baby," Sophie said. "They're going to need a replacement, and I want a chance to interview. Right now, my work experience doesn't exactly get me there."

"What's your work experience?" Allison put her pencil down. She didn't really need this info, but it didn't hurt to have a more complete picture of her interview subject. If this witness was credible, she stood to knock a hole the size of a barn door in this case.

"Well, let's see." Sophie leaned back and drummed her manicured fingernails on the table. She had pretty hands. Of course, given that she also had a body to die for, hands probably weren't the feature most detectives noticed about her. "There was a six-month stint at the mall," she said. "I graduated from peddling hair extensions to cell phones. Then I decided I might do better working for tips, so I waited tables at a nightclub in Dallas until I got my big break and started singing there. Only it wasn't such a big break when the manager told me I needed to get down on my knees to collect my paycheck."

Allison looked at her, startled.

"Don't worry, he got busted soon after that."

"For sexual harassment?" That was a tough charge to prove.

"Back child support," Sophie said. "*Then* I went to work for the woman who busted him. She was a PI with a specialty in computer crime and deadbeat dads. That was my first real office job. Then I followed Alex here—"

"I'm sorry, Alex is . . . ?"

"The private investigator. Alexandra Lovell. She's a genius with computers, so Delphi recruited her for the cyber crimes lab, and she was nice enough to get me my first gig here, which was working in the accounting office as a file clerk. *Extremely* boring, if you want to know the truth. But the pay was good, so I wasn't complaining. Plus, I didn't have to spend a lot of money on clothes then. The dress code gets stricter the closer you get to the front door, as you can see." She gestured to her black linen dress and patent-leather slingbacks. "And then the receptionist left. I'm much better with people than filing, so I interviewed and got *this* job, which I've had for the past year. That enough background?"

Allison looked down at her blank notebook page. She didn't have time to write it all, so she'd have to remember it. She glanced at the clock on the wall and realized Sophie Barrett had just seamlessly eaten up half of their interview time. Intentional or not? Allison wasn't sure, but she was annoyed with herself for letting it happen.

"Okay, so . . . you were on campus Wednesday. What time did you arrive?"

"About twelve twenty-five." She smiled. "I spotted the open parking space at twelve-thirty."

"You're sure about that?"

"Absolutely."

They walked through the next critical minutes, step by step, from the time the driver of a green VW allegedly took Sophie's spot until the first rifle shot rang out. Allison made careful notes—not just of the events as they were being told to her but of Sophie's mannerisms.

"And did you get a good look at the driver?"

"I didn't see much," she said. "It was only a glimpse."

"Okay, what about the car? Any other details you didn't mention?"

Sophie's gaze moved up and to the right, which according to body language experts meant the subject was recalling a fact, not constructing a lie—assuming Sophie was right-handed, which Allison knew from watching her sign for the delivery a few minutes ago. Of course, it also assumed the shrinks who wrote those textbooks weren't full of crap. Allison had her suspicions.

"Like I said, a dark green VW. An old-model Beetle."

"What about body damage?"

"No."

"Are you sure?" Allison asked.

"Yes."

"You didn't notice a crumpled bumper?" Allison

flipped to the front of her notepad. "Left side, if you're facing the front of the car?"

"No."

"And you're certain?"

She paused. "Yes."

Allison made a few notes. "And once again, you noticed the time when this happened and it was—"

"Twelve-thirty. I'm sure. I've even got my parking ticket for you, just to confirm what time I pulled into the garage. Would you like to see it?"

"I would."

"It's in my purse." She looked at her watch. "I'm sorry, but speaking of time, we're running over, which means my post is empty. Is there anything else you need to ask me?"

Allison pushed her chair back and stood up. "That about does it."

Sophie led her out of the room and back to the lobby, where her desk was indeed empty, as she'd predicted. She pulled her purse from the drawer and handed over a yellow parking ticket with the date and time stamped on it. It said 12:36.

"You know, eyewitness accounts are notoriously unreliable," Sophie said.

Allison watched her warily as she handed back her visitor's badge.

"I assume that's why you're here?" Sophie asked.

"You assumed right."

Something sparked in her eyes. "That and the fact that I could be just some hysterical woman who doesn't know what she saw?"

"Listen, Ms. Barrett—"

"If you really want to know what happened, why don't you send that Volkswagen up to our lab here? We're already running all the rest of your evidence, and we've got the world's top DNA experts. They can get a profile off a *single* hair follicle. It's really amazing. If someone besides James Himmel was in that car, our tracers will find evidence of it."

Allison couldn't help but smile. "Sounds like you're already trying out the PR job."

"I believe in the mission here."

"Mission?" She made it sound like a religious quest.

"The lab's main goal is to process the enormous backlog of evidence so that DNA can be used to *solve* cases, not just prosecute cases that have already been solved." She paused. "It's important work. It saves lives."

"I'm sure it does."

Some hammering started up down the hall, and Allison studied the woman's face. The pleasant hostess was gone, replaced by a razor-sharp woman with a glint in her eyes. Far from the ditzy blonde Allison had expected, Sophie Barrett was smart. And she knew exactly how much credibility the task force had given her story.

The banging ceased, and the phone sang out from the reception desk.

"Is there anything else?" Sophie asked pleasantly.

"Not for now."

She reached for her headset and gave another perfect smile. "Thanks for coming, Detective Doyle. Let me know if there's anything more I can do to help."

Gretchen's heart ached as she watched her daughters silently playing on the living-room floor.

"I appreciate the offer, Marianne. I really do. I just . . . I don't know."

"What don't you know?" her sister demanded over the phone. "How could it be any worse than what you're dealing with now?"

Her sister had a point. Between the reporters camped out in front of their apartment complex, the dirty looks from neighbors, and the incessant phone calls, she was on the verge of a meltdown.

"Gretch?"

"You don't have room for us," she said, navigating a minefield of toys so she could peek out the window. "And if anyone finds out we're there . . . Trust me, you don't want these vultures discovering where you live." Gretchen parted the curtains and surveyed the vultures in question. Some of them had given up since she'd come home from work and given another round of "No comment." But there were still a few stragglers, and she wouldn't be surprised if they came pounding on her door with one last request for an interview before the ten o'clock news.

"Gretch? Did you hear what I said?"

"Sorry, what?"

"Just *come*, okay? You need to get out of there. It isn't good for the girls."

Gretchen looked at Amy and Angela amid the sea of Legos—a ridiculously belated birthday gift from the father they hardly knew. When the package had come in the mail last week, Gretchen had been annoyed. Angry, even. But now she saw it for what it was—some sort of pathetic last effort by a desperate man.

God, Jim, how could you do this to us?

"Gretch?"

"I just . . . I can't afford to leave my job, Mar. What on earth could I do in Houston?"

"We'll figure that out when you get here."

"Marianne—"

"Just think about it, okay? Promise me."

"I'll think about it."

Gretchen got off the phone and sank onto the rug. Angela looked up from her Legos.

"Do you like my house, Mommy?"

"I do."

Angela's house had a bright red roof and yellow shutters and looked nothing like any of the low-rent apartments where she'd lived during her six years.

Gretchen studied her daughter's face, looking for signs of grief. She hadn't cried yet. Neither had Amy. She wondered if they ever would. Gretchen wasn't sure how much they remembered about the man who'd come in and out of their lives so sporadically. Did they remember him in uniform, when he'd looked so handsome? Did they remember him taking them to the zoo when they were three or playing airplane with them on the living-room floor?

Or did they remember him yelling and breaking things and reeking of gin?

"You want to play, Mommy?" Amy looked up at her somberly.

Gretchen realized she was crying. She wiped her tears away and forced a smile. "Sure, honey."

"You can be whites." Amy pushed a pile of plastic bricks across the carpet. "I'm yellows and Angie's blues."

"Sounds like a plan," Gretchen said, dragging the bin closer to cull through it.

A plan. For the twins' sake, she *needed* to pull herself together and come up with a plan. She couldn't take another day of clutching her daughters' little hands in hers as they dodged the mob of reporters.

Did you know your ex-husband was homicidal?

Had you seen any warning signs?

Did you know he was about to snap?

Gretchen poked through the Legos. Maybe Houston would be the best thing for all of them. Gretchen's job was nothing special, and she no longer had a reason to live near the base. Maybe it was time to start over.

Something white peeked out from beneath the sea of color. She cleared away the Legos. An envelope, taped to the bottom of the bin. Her stomach tightened with dread.

Scrawled across it, in Jim's familiar handwriting, was her name.

CHAPTER 9

Jonah spotted Sophie Saturday afternoon at the Squeaky Clean Car Wash on Riverview, and he almost kept driving. But a glimpse in his rearview mirror changed his mind. He had some questions for Sophie related to the investigation, and the sooner he got answers, the sooner he could move forward.

Yeah. *That* was the reason he was pulling an illegal U-turn and whipping into a steamy car wash while dressed in a suit and tie.

She was up on tiptoes spraying down her Tahoe, singing along to whatever music was playing on her iPod. Cutoff shorts again, a Cowboys T-shirt, and for once she was wearing flip-flops instead of heels.

He got out and shrugged off of his jacket, then tossed it over the passenger seat. As he rolled up his sleeves, Sophie stopped what she was doing and gazed at him over the tops of her trendy sunglasses.

"Well, look at you." She plucked out her earbuds as he approached. "You clean up nicely, Detective Macon."

He took the hose from her, annoyed to be reminded that he was the detective and she was the witness here, a fact that made the wet-T-shirt-and-soapsuds fantasies swirling through his head pretty inappropriate.

"Careful," she warned, "you'll ruin your good shoes."

He didn't comment as he doused the roof with water. She picked up another hose and started spraying the foam.

"Ric saw you at the funeral," he said.

"I saw him, too."

Jonah was surprised she'd been there. Walter Graham and Jodi Kincaid's funerals had overlapped, and he would have figured she'd go to the woman's, especially after bonding with her kid the way she had.

She stopped the soap spray and wiped her forehead with the back of her arm. Her skin was damp and locks of hair clung to her neck. "You were at the other one, I guess?"

"Yep."

She looked away, at the passing cars. "I wanted to be there, but—" She shook her head. "Anyway, it's probably for the best."

"It was nice of you to go to the professor's."

She scoffed at him. "It wasn't *nice*, it was selfish. I didn't even know the man."

"Still, you paid your respects."

"I was trapped next to his bloody corpse for thirty minutes. I needed a different image of him to replace the one in my mind." Her gray eyes gazed up at him tentatively. "I guess that sounds kind of sick, doesn't it?"

Jonah traded the water hose for the soap one she was holding. "Makes sense to me."

After witnessing Jodi Kincaid's autopsy, he could relate completely. He was still trying to make the portrait he'd seen at the front of the church replace his mental picture of her being dissected on that steel table. But it was probably forever lodged in his brain.

Jonah crouched down to do Sophie's wheel wells.

"So, was it civic duty or professional obligation?" she asked.

He glanced up at her. "A little of both, I guess."

Despite the developments in the case this morning, Jonah couldn't let it go. He felt compelled to investigate the victims, even though everyone but Ric seemed to think it was a waste of time. So he'd gone to one funeral, Ric to another. Eric Emrick was being buried in Oklahoma, so it wasn't going to be possible to attend that one, but Jonah still planned to do some basic investigating. These were murder victims in his jurisdiction, and he owed them that much.

He finished the front two tires and moved to the back. When he looked up, Sophie was watching him, the corner of her mouth lifted in a half-smile.

"What?"

"I've got a guy in a black suit washing my car. People are going to think you're my chauffeur."

She smiled fully now, and Jonah felt a warm pull. This one was the real deal. She smiled all the time, but mostly it was for show.

He stood up and moved to the back bumper. She retrieved a rag and some Windex from her backseat and started polishing the side mirror. She'd come prepared.

"So, how was your date?" he asked.

She glanced at him. "Fine."

"Anyone I know?"

She hesitated a moment, which answered his question.

"Mark Royers."

He frowned.

"What's wrong?"

"Nothing," he said. "I'm trying to place the name."

"He works at Delphi. He did some of the DNA work for your case last winter."

"Mark *Royers*? The DNA guy?"

"That's what I said." She stopped polishing. "What?"

"Nothing."

She fisted her hand on her hip. "What is it?"

"I just wouldn't think you two would have much in common."

"What's that supposed to mean?"

"Nothing. Forget it."

"You mean because he's a doctor? I don't have enough letters after my name to date someone who's smart?"

Jonah didn't much feel like getting beamed in the nuts with a high-power hose, so he took that as a rhetorical question.

She shook her head and stalked around to the other mirror.

When he finished her tires, she was still fuming.

"That's not what I meant, and you know it."

She muttered something he didn't catch.

He hung up the nozzles and snagged the towel out of her hand. "Thank you, Jonah, for helping me wash my car in this hundred-degree heat," he said.

"Thank you," she parroted. Then she reached into her backseat again and pulled a diet soft drink from a cooler. She popped it open, took a gulp, then passed it to him. He hated diet sodas, but it was a furnace out here, so he downed half of it.

"I meant he doesn't *look* like your type," he said. "Physically. He's kind of skinny, isn't he?"

She didn't like that, either. The genuine smile from a few minutes ago had been replaced by a genuine scowl. Time for a new subject.

"Listen, I stopped by to tell you something." He tossed the towel on the floor of her car and shut the door.

"Hmm, let me guess. I passed the test?"

"What test?"

"Detective Doyle. She was sent out to vet me, right?" Sophie drained the last of the soda and pitched the can in a trash bin. "That thing about the crumpled bumper was good. I almost fell for it. She had me doubting my own story."

Jonah pretended not to know what she was talking about.

"So, when we took Himmel's car into evidence," he said, "you know what we found in the trunk?"

"What?"

"A box containing an eight-inch hunting knife, a twenty-two-caliber pistol, and five grenades."

"*Grenades?*" She looked alarmed. "What was he planning to do with those?"

"Your guess is as good as mine. Here's what we didn't find in that car: prints belonging to anyone besides Himmel. We went over it three times."

She sighed and looked away. "I know what I saw."

"What you *think* you saw. We haven't found one witness who can corroborate seeing a green VW on campus that day."

Her eyes flashed with anger. "Are you saying—"

"Just hear me out. We ran every vehicle registered on

that campus, and there're four VW Beetles. One of them happens to be dark blue." He watched her face as she figured out what he was getting at. "Allison interviewed the vehicle owner this morning, and turns out he parked on University Avenue just a block north of Meadowlark sometime after twelve o'clock the day of the shooting."

She stared up at him. Her mouth dropped open. "But—"

"Is there *any* possibility that could be the car you saw?"

"The car I saw was green."

"You're sure?" He held his breath, waiting for her answer. The entire case hinged on this *one* witness account, and Jonah needed to be certain.

"It was green."

He blew out a sigh. She was convinced of what she saw. Or *thought* she saw. And meanwhile, news of the dark blue VW had all but annihilated any chance he'd had of convincing the rest of the task force to take him seriously with this.

Or take Sophie seriously, which was really the problem. They didn't.

"So, what does this mean?"

She knew exactly what it meant because she was looking up at him with disappointment in her eyes. She thought he didn't believe her.

And honestly, he wasn't sure he did. Every shred of physical evidence pointed to a lone perpetrator. And the one eyewitness account that might indicate otherwise could be explained now by a coincidence.

"It means we're back to the original case theory," he said.

"In other words, that's it? It's over? You guys have

your man, and we don't need to ask any more questions?"

Jonah didn't feel that way, but she'd described Reynolds and Noonan to a T.

"Sophie—"

"Forget it." She jerked open her door. "Believe what you want, Jonah. But I know what I saw."

Wyatt Macon lived in an area that had once been considered the boondocks but was quickly becoming the outskirts of town. Jonah passed yet another brand-new subdivision before turning up the narrow gravel drive to the one-story clapboard house where he'd grown up.

He parked his pickup under an oak tree and pushed open the door. A golden retriever instantly poked her head in and pawed his thigh.

"Hey, girl." He scratched Duchess between the ears, and she gleefully followed him across the lawn to where his dad was pushing his Toro mower. His face was red as a tomato, and he stopped as Jonah approached.

"You should do that in the morning," Jonah said.

In truth, he shouldn't do it at all anymore, but you couldn't tell his father a damn thing.

"I had company this morning." He pulled a bandanna out of his pocket and wiped the sweat off his face, and Jonah turned to look back toward the house, shaking his head. In one of life's bigger surprises, his parents had just last summer ended thirty-nine years of marriage. Apparently, they'd "grown apart." Now his dad had sleepovers on weekends and his mom had an account at eHarmony.

"Thought you'd be by today." His dad trudged across the lawn and hiked up the steps to the front porch, where a pitcher of lemonade was waiting with slices of lemon floating on top. Jonah's dad didn't make anything that couldn't be thrown on a Weber.

He poured a glass and downed half of it in one sip, then looked at Jonah. "Want some?"

"No." Jonah leaned back against the wooden porch railing.

"Macey makes good lemonade."

"I'm fine."

Jonah liked Macey well enough, but he couldn't drink another woman's lemonade in a house he still thought of as his mom's, and it didn't matter who had asked for the divorce.

"Supposed to be hot tomorrow." His dad slumped back in a chair and stared out at the yard. "Hundred and one, if you can believe that." Another gulp of lemonade and he looked at Jonah. "You been to the funeral, I take it."

"Jodi Kincaid."

Duchess settled at Jonah's feet and he bent down to scrub her ears.

"Hell of a thing. I read in the paper this Himmel had pancreatic cancer. Think it got to his brain?"

"The ME says no."

Jonah knew what his dad was thinking. When Charles Whitman was autopsied back in '66, doctors found a tumor in his brain, which confirmed a lot of people's feelings that his ninety-six-minute shooting spree was the work of someone sick in the head.

Jonah wasn't so sure. Some experts said that given the size and location of the tumor, it probably had no effect on the sniper's behavior that day. It made for a convenient explanation, though.

Jonah's dad had been a rookie cop in Austin the day of the Whitman shooting. It had to have been one of his toughest days on the job, but he rarely talked about it— which was probably why over the years Jonah had read everything he could find on the subject. His mom had once told him Charles Whitman was the reason they'd left Austin. The clock tower was the tallest building in the city, and she couldn't look at it every day and think about what had happened.

Jonah folded his arms over his chest and glanced at his dad. "We've got evidence that could indicate someone else might have played a role in the attack."

His gray eyebrows tipped up. "A second shooter?"

"Maybe a driver. A witness thinks she saw someone besides Himmel driving his car."

"Just one witness?"

"So far, yeah."

He rubbed his chin, as he always did when he was considering something. "Eyewitnesses are a tricky thing." He shook his head. "Sometimes they lie, or they forget, or sometimes they just see things funny. Pretty unreliable, you want to know the truth. You got DNA or prints or anything?"

"No."

"Hmm."

"There are some other things that bug me, too. This guy wasn't from around here. We still don't know what his connection was to the university. Why'd he do this here? And he took the trouble to file the serial numbers off his guns. Why bother? He had to know we'd run down his prints eventually. He was in the army."

His dad emptied his glass, then sighed. For a few minutes, they looked out over the lawn. No matter how many times Jonah offered, the man wouldn't accept help. One of these days, Jonah was just going to show up and do it.

Jonah checked his watch. He needed to get home and do his own yard. "Do me a favor, don't give yourself a heart attack out here."

His father heaved himself out of the chair. "You sound like Macey," he groused.

Jonah stepped off the porch. "About the investigation—"

"You don't have to say it."

It was understood that when they talked shop, it was confidential. But Jonah needed to emphasize the point. This case was the talk of the town, and he knew neighbors would be looking to Wyatt for details that weren't in the newspaper.

His dad put his cap back on and turned to look at him. "Don't beat yourself up over all these questions. You're trying to make sense of something crazy."

Jonah shook his head and looked away. He'd said almost the same thing to Sophie just the other day, but now he was having trouble following his own advice.

"It's just, where do I go from here?" Jonah felt foolish voicing the question, but if there was one person on earth he could talk to, it was his dad. "I'm not sure what I should do."

He slapped him on the back. "Do your job, Jonah. This town's hurting. They need you. Close this case and let these folks get on down the road."

• • •

Sophie lay in her bed, listening to her neighbor's television and trying not to think about Jodi Kincaid. She'd done everything she could to distract herself before bed tonight. She'd washed her car, she'd done her grocery shopping, she'd even gone to the gym for a double spin class. But although her muscles were sore and her energy was spent, the insomnia wouldn't leave her alone.

She closed her eyes and she was back behind that statue, watching a woman's life drain out of her.

Why hadn't she done something?

She could have sprinted over and pressed some clothes against her to stop the bleeding. Maybe she could have given CPR or even dragged her out of there.

And he would have shot you, too.

The answer came back, again and again. Every time someone had tried to move, or get up, or run for safety, they got hit with a bullet. She'd done the only thing she *could* have done, which was wait for Jonah's team to go up there.

So that *they* could be the ones to put their lives on the line for other people.

The irony didn't sit well with Sophie. Why was she still here, in her cheap, single-girl apartment where nobody needed her, while Becca Kincaid was sleeping in a house tonight without a mother?

Robert Kincaid had called this morning, just as Sophie had been turning her place upside down looking for the obituary she'd clipped from the newspaper.

Please don't take offense, but it might be better if you didn't come today. If Becca sees you, I'm worried it might upset her.

The logic seemed pretty backward to Sophie. What could be more upsetting to a child than attending her mom's funeral, no matter who was there? But Sophie had respected the request and instead gone to the professor's service, where she'd heard about his distinguished career and his academic achievements. The eulogies had been long, the ceremony somber and dignified.

At least you paid your respects. Jonah's words came back to her, along with the stark realization that she hadn't paid anyone anything. She shouldn't have gone. Sitting in that service, she'd felt a suffocating anger, and being there had done nothing to help her get past the utter pointlessness of it all.

At last the TV next door went silent, and Sophie could hear the music drifting from her stereo. It was the rain-forest track, and she took a deep breath and tried to relax. Insomnia sucked, and she'd tried everything these last few months, but music was the only thing that worked.

Snick.

Her eyes popped open. The noise came from her living room. She didn't move, didn't breathe.

Was someone in her apartment?

She listened through the soft patter of rain and tried to discern what she'd heard.

Snick.

Someone was at her door.

Sophie slid open the nightstand drawer and reached for her gun. With the revolver heavy in her hand, she kicked the covers off and crept to the hallway. Maybe she'd been hearing things. She'd been so rattled lately, even a little paranoid—although she'd never admit it to Jonah.

She peered down the hallway, but the apartment was dark and still.

Sophie crept into the living room, listening for the slightest sound out of place. She parted the blinds on the window facing the balcony. No one there. She peered through the peephole. Nothing. She double-checked the dead bolt and then secured the chain she'd forgotten to attach before going to bed.

Was that all it was? She'd forgotten the chain on the door and so she'd felt jumpy? Or had she really heard a noise?

Sophie despised this feeling. One of the worst aftereffects of her attack was the persistent self-doubt. Her trust in her own instincts had been shattered, and she went around all the time now second-guessing herself.

Sophie eyed the cell phone on the coffee table and had the urge to call Jonah. It was a stupid urge, and she hated herself for it, but still her fingers itched to pick up the phone. Jonah was a good cop. He had a protective streak a mile wide. If she called and told him she was scared, he'd be over in a heartbeat.

And he'd think she was more delusional than ever.

Sophie picked up the chenille throw from her armchair and sank onto her sofa. She rested her gun on the table and cast a longing look at the phone before reaching for the TV remote. She knew this feeling well, and there was no use fighting it. No matter what she did, tonight would be endless.

And so would tomorrow night. And the next night. And the next. And she knew that the restless, itchy feeling keeping her from sleep wasn't going to go away.

Not until she did what she had to do.

CHAPTER 10

Sophie wasn't home when Jonah dropped by the next morning, and when her phone went unanswered after two calls, he started to get uneasy. That shiny silver cell phone went everywhere with her.

But then he saw her rounding the corner and jogging up the path to her apartment complex. When she reached the parking lot, she halted and bent at the waist, panting.

He smiled as he sauntered over. Not exactly an ad for *Runner's World,* but those long legs got the job done.

"Didn't know you were a jogger."

She stood up straight and sucked down big gulps of air. "I practice many forms of torture."

She watched him curiously as she caught her breath, probably wondering what he was doing showing up at her place on a Sunday morning. She wore a blue spandex running top and black shorts. Her body was covered with a thin sheen of sweat, and he suddenly had a vision of her wrestling with him in his bed.

She started for the stairs to her apartment. He followed.

"Is this a social call or something about the case?"

"The case," he lied. "I had a few follow-up questions."

She pulled a key from a little pouch in her shorts and unlocked her door.

"Give me a minute to shower." She dropped her key on the coffee table and disappeared into the bathroom. He heard the shower go on, and then she poked her head out. "You had breakfast yet?"

"No." Another lie. But as he stood there in her living room, he realized it was imperative that they get out of her apartment. From his place near the door, he could see down the hallway to the corner of her unmade bed. And hearing that water running . . . But the most disconcerting feature was the laundry basket on her coffee table, brimming with a rainbow assortment of lingerie.

He wandered over to the breakfast bar to distract himself. On the counter was a newspaper article profiling Eric Emrick. Beside it was a steno pad with notes jotted in Sophie's loopy script.

> *SWM 19*
> *Norman, OK*
> *Comp sci / Math*
> *Microsoft*
> *D-Syst*
> *Shelley Harris??*

He unfolded the paper: *The San Marcos Bee*. The reporter was someone named Tyler P. Dorion. "Special to the Bee," it said under the name.

A college kid? Maybe someone on the school paper, with an eye toward a job after graduation? Jonah didn't know who else would use a byline like that in such a rinky-dink newspaper.

He skimmed the rest of the story as his subconscious brain registered the water shutting off. The door popping open. The rustle of air in the hallway as steam escaped and a damp, towel-clad, sexy-as-hell woman breezed down the hallway into the bedroom.

Jonah read the entire article, but what he was really thinking about was how much he needed to get laid. Soon. Before he lost the tenuous control he had over himself and did something extremely stupid with a woman who was now—for better or for worse—actively involved in his investigation.

"Ready?"

She stood there watching him. Denim shorts, black T-shirt with the word *PINK* emblazoned across the front. Her damp hair was twisted up in some kind of clip, but it was the little purple straps behind her neck that captured his attention. She had a swimsuit on under those clothes.

"Who's Shelley Harris?" he asked.

"Eric Emrick's girlfriend."

"You're researching the victims?"

"Sure, why not?"

He just looked at her.

"It's pretty obvious that if Himmel had an accomplice, there must be more going on here than a typical school shooting," she said. "Maybe he meant to kill one of those people."

"Didn't realize you were an investigator."

"I'm more of a concerned citizen. Are you ready? I'm starving."

"I've been ready." He took out his keys and followed her out of the apartment. As she locked the door, she shot him one of her looks.

"Are you actually *complaining* about how much time I spent getting dressed?"

"You put on makeup."

"So?"

"So, kind of high-maintenance for breakfast." He headed down the stairs, and he could feel her heated gaze boring into his back.

"High-maintenance? I took all of ten minutes!"

"Fifteen."

"Oh, please. I showered, shaved my legs, put on makeup, *and* returned two text messages in the time it took you to snoop around my kitchen. I'd say that's pretty good."

He led the way across the parking lot to his truck, her sandals making little snapping noises against the pavement. He opened the door for her and managed not to glance at her legs as she climbed in.

He went around to the driver's side, and she eyed him narrowly as he slid behind the wheel.

"When was the last time you had a girlfriend?"

He looked at her.

"It's been a while, hasn't it?"

"Pancakes or doughnuts?" He started up the truck.

"I can tell, it has been."

"How do you figure that?"

"Because you're completely out of touch with the typical woman's beauty regimen." She flipped down the vanity mirror and pulled a lipstick from her purse as if to emphasize her point. She put some on, then turned to look at him. "Well?"

"Well what?"

"I'm guessing two years, right? Since you've had anything besides a casual fling? I'm not saying you haven't had *sex,* because obviously you have."

"Obviously?"

"Oh, come on. Look at you. You've got the swagger, and it's not just because you're a cop. I've seen plenty of that, too, but some of those guys are losers. They're not fooling anyone. Come on, how long has it been?"

"None of your business."

"God, is it three years? Please tell me it hasn't been. Guys go too long without a woman in their life, they start to have weird views about personal hygiene. And I have two brothers—one who's divorced—so I've seen this phenomenon firsthand. Seriously, you can tell me. I won't make fun of you."

"How 'bout the Pancake Pantry? They've got the best omelets in town."

She rolled her eyes. "Coward."

Ten minutes later, they were seated across from each other in a brown vinyl booth. Jonah had his back to the wall, as was his habit. While Sophie chatted up the waitress, he kept an eye on the door and watched the parade of hungover young people filing in for morning-after eats.

When the waitress disappeared, Sophie guzzled half her ice water and plunked the plastic cup on the table.

"Okay, I'm ready."

"Ready for?"

"You said you had questions. There must be a new development in the case. I'm all ears."

Jonah watched her for a long moment. There *was* a new development, but he didn't plan to share it with her. She was a witness. There was a small—but growing—possibility that her account of events might become critical to the investigation, which meant that from here on out the information was going to flow one way.

"Tell me about the VW driver."

She sighed. "This again?"

"It's important."

"I told you, I barely saw him."

"But you saw something, right? I mean, he cut you off. According to your story."

That got a rise out of her. "Are we back to *this* now? Why even bring me here if—"

"Relax." He held up a hand. "I didn't mean I don't believe you. It's just that if he took your parking space, which probably ticked you off, I'd think you'd at least notice something about what he looked like."

She searched his face warily. Trust was a big thing with Sophie, he'd figured out. She didn't like her credibility questioned—or her intelligence, for that matter. Maybe she'd heard a few too many blonde jokes over the years. He didn't know why, but he knew she was sensitive.

She closed her eyes now and leaned back against the booth. "Let me think."

He took the opportunity to study those little purple straps again. Bikini or one-piece? What was she doing after this?

And was she doing it alone?

"He was tall."

"Tall?"

She opened her eyes. "Well, the way the light was, he was kind of in shadow. But I'm remembering now that his head almost touched the roof of the car. That would make him tall, wouldn't it?"

"A Volkswagen's pretty small. It might make him average."

"Well, that's all I got, Detective."

He looked at her for a long moment. She could probably provide more, under the right circumstances.

"You know, I'm pretty good at interviews," he said.

"Are you?" She feigned surprise.

"Yeah, actually, I am. But there are forensic artists out there who can get amazing things from witnesses—stuff they didn't even know they had. Would you be willing to talk to one?"

"What would I say? I told you, we're talking about a fleeting glimpse."

Jonah thought about the pushback he was going to get if and when he teed this up to Reynolds. It would help if he had some corroboration first. Anything at all that didn't come from Sophie.

She leaned forward conspiratorially. "What's this about, anyway? What did you guys find?"

It wasn't what they'd found, but what they *hadn't* found that had kept Jonah up most of last night. Not a single fingerprint on the box of items in the back of that VW. Not on the knife, or the pistol, or any of the five grenades. Not even on the box itself.

Where were Himmel's prints? If those were *his* possessions, wouldn't there be at least a partial print of his on something? Or had those items been planted there by someone to reinforce the lone-nutjob scenario?

It was a minor detail, but it nagged at him. He couldn't let it go. Jonah didn't just want the truth about this case, he wanted the *whole* truth. And he didn't think he was getting it. He knew this case wouldn't turn loose of him until he did.

"Well?" Sophie's eyebrows tipped up.

"I can't comment on an ongoing investigation."

"Oh, come on. We're friends, aren't we?"

He didn't answer that, and their breakfasts arrived before she had a chance to push the point.

"One Early Riser, side of links. One oatmeal." The server slid a platter in front of Jonah and a bowl in front of Sophie.

"I thought you said you were hungry." He eyed her breakfast as he doused his with Tabasco sauce.

"I am."

"You realize that's the most boring thing on the menu, right?"

She picked up her spoon. "It's low fat."

"You just went jogging."

"Yes, and you may have noticed I'm five-eleven."

"So?"

"So, people use words like *statuesque* to describe me. If they mean like Claudia Schiffer, I'm fine with it. Lady Liberty, not so much."

Jonah watched her dig into her cereal. It had never occurred to him that she thought of herself as anything but smokin' hot, which she was. Women baffled him sometimes—which was probably why he hadn't been in a relationship in close to three years. Not that he planned to tell her that.

"And anyway, do you realize what goes into those processed meats?" She nodded at his ham-and-cheese omelet, which was accompanied by three greasy sausages. "It's *so* bad for you. I shudder to think of it."

"Then don't. You don't want to know how your laws or your sausages are made." He stabbed a link with his fork. "That's what my granddad always said, anyway."

"What else about the case?" she asked. "You said 'questions' plural."

"Do you remember any other cars parked there along the sidewalk? We're trying to run down vehicle owners who may have seen something but haven't been interviewed."

"You mean to corroborate my story?"

Instead of confirming this, he focused on his food.

"I don't remember," she said. "I was in a hurry. Maybe you could talk to the shop owners."

"Been there, done that."

"And?"

He looked at her.

"I know what I witnessed, Jonah. A *green* VW. Why can't you just take me at my word?"

"Maybe it's not up to me."

She shook her head. "I know what this is about. I'm not an idiot."

"Why do you have this chip on your shoulder?"

"I don't have a chip."

"You definitely have a chip."

"Look, I come from a family of doctors. My dad, my two brothers. And then there's me."

"The beautiful daughter who works for a world-renowned forensic lab?"

She made a face. "Thanks for the compliment, but let's get real. I answer phones. It's not exactly open-heart surgery."

"It's an important job."

"It's an important *place*," she corrected. "Anyway, you're changing the subject. We were talking about what this is really about."

"What is what really about?"

"Your chief wants this case closed, am I right? Then we can all talk about how this was just some wacko who luckily is dead now. And we can all sleep fine at night, knowing our little town is safe again. Parents can send their kids back to campus, right along with their tuition dollars. Move along now, people, nothing to see here."

Close this case and let these folks get on down the road.

It was so similar to what his dad had said, Jonah could hardly believe he was hearing it.

"Am I right?"

He just looked at her.

"Here's the thing, Jonah. I *can't* sleep." She leaned forward and looked at him, and those gray eyes were vulnerable. That vulnerability got to him because she so rarely let it show. "I haven't had a good night's sleep in months, Jonah. Not since January."

Something twisted in his gut. He hated what had happened to her. He hated even more what *would* have happened if he'd been even an hour longer getting her away from that psychopath. She'd be dead right now. And the world would be a much dimmer place.

And suddenly he knew Ric was right. This woman

had some serious issues. She was probably dealing with posttraumatic stress syndrome, and the last thing he should do was take advantage of her trust.

"There's something more going on here than some crazed gunman who shot up a school. I can *feel* it." She held up a hand. "And before you say anything about psychic mumbo jumbo, let me just tell you this: I *know* you feel things, too. Call it cop instinct or gut instinct or whatever you want, but I know that's how you solved *my* case and put a very dangerous person behind bars. So don't talk to me about corroboration and lack of evidence and whatever else. There *is* something more, and I sure as hell hope I'm not the only one willing to see it."

Jonah didn't answer that.

She leaned back and looked at him expectantly.

"What?" he asked.

"Are you going to pursue this?"

"I told you, it's not up to me."

She looked disappointed in him. And he didn't blame her because it was a bullshit, cop-out answer, and they both knew it.

The fountain in front of the library had become a makeshift memorial to the victims of Wednesday's attack. Allison had passed by multiple times during the course of her interviews with faculty and maintenance workers who might be able to shed some light on the shooter's connection to the university. That had been during the daytime, though. Now it was Sunday night, and she found herself seeing the memorial in a whole new light.

Allison stood there for a moment, just looking. It was

late. She needed to get back to her desk and catch up on the weekend's paperwork. But the soft glow of candles captivated her, and she couldn't tear her eyes away. She approached the fountain.

Three simple wooden crosses displaying the victims' names had been erected by the Campus Christians. Flower bouquets were heaped at the base of each, and votives glimmered in the humid summer night. Allison stopped in front of Jodi Kincaid's cross, where someone had left a white teddy bear holding a light blue baby rattle.

A lump formed in Allison's throat. She thought about the baby who would never be born, or grow up, or go to high school and maybe college someday. Her gaze moved to the photograph of Eric Emrick with his Ultimate Frisbee team. A blue Frisbee sat next to it, covered with signatures—his teammates, she guessed. Sadness swelled in her chest as she surveyed the rest of the mementos. It was a sadness she'd been feeling for days, but the longer she looked, the more it gave way to anger.

Who had done this to her town? To this peaceful campus where people came to expand their minds? Who could do such a thing *here,* in the place she'd always thought was immune to the sort of heartless violence that plagued the big cities to the north and south of her? She'd become a cop here to get to know people, to be part of a community instead of just some anonymous person in uniform. She'd expected her job to be protecting neighborhoods, and keeping drugs out of children's hands, and pulling over drunken college kids before they had a chance to hurt someone.

She hadn't expected *this.*

A flicker of red appeared on the edge of the fountain. It danced over the water before disappearing into the darkness of the quadrangle. A laser pointer? Allison glanced behind her and saw the faint red line beaming down from the top of the library.

She turned to look at the south quadrangle, where a man was crouched on the ground, holding a heavy-duty flashlight. Jonah Macon. This would be the bullet trajectory test she'd heard about at this morning's task force meeting. The lieutenant had told Jonah to forget about it; they didn't have the time or the budget to run tests to prove what they already knew.

Jonah had nodded respectfully and dropped the subject, which should have been Allison's first clue that he—like so many cops she knew, including herself—didn't like to take no for an answer.

She tromped across the sidewalk to join him as he knelt beside a laptop computer.

"Hi," she said.

"Hi." He didn't look up, so she stepped closer and peered over his shoulder. On the screen was a digital simulation of the buildings surrounding the quadrangle. Jonah tapped away at some keys while Allison's gaze followed the red laser beam from the base of the statue to the top of the library.

"Who's up there?"

"No one."

"I'm guessing that buddy of yours from Delphi? Scott Black?"

Jonah glanced up at her. "Scott's not here." Then back down at his computer. "I'm not here. And *you* definitely shouldn't be here."

He picked up a walkie-talkie and stood up. "Okay, last one."

"Roger that."

The red beam vanished and Allison glanced up at the rooftop. Soon another beam shone down from the far corner. This one hit the bronze horse statue behind her, making a red dot on its chest.

"Little higher," Jonah said into his radio. "Higher. About another inch. Okay, got it."

The beam settled on a little dent in the metal.

"Hold it there," Jonah said. He pulled a laser pointer out of his pocket and aimed it at the indention made by the bullet, then directed it toward a concrete bench just a few feet away.

"You're thinking a ricochet?" she asked.

"Yep."

Allison picked up the flashlight and shone it on the bench but didn't see any chinks in the stone.

"You won't find it. The bullet ended up in Jodi Kincaid's neck. How tall are you?"

"Five-four, why?"

"She was five-two. Here, stand there." He walked over and positioned her on top of an X that was still visible on the grass. It had been made with spray paint by CSIs several days ago. Then he went back to the statue and aimed the laser. A red dot settled on Allison's collarbone.

"Bingo." Jonah crouched down and typed some more notes on the computer. "You can move now."

"We all set?" the guy on the other end of the radio asked.

"Yeah, that'll do it."

Allison rested her hands on her hips and watched him. "Not that I don't enjoy a covert laser light show as much as the next guy, but what exactly is the point of all this?"

He didn't look up from the computer.

Allison glanced around impatiently. "I mean, does anyone seriously think some mystery person was out here picking off victims from behind a tree or something while everyone was focused on the library?"

"No."

"So, how does this prove anything?"

"It doesn't."

She stared at him, and he kept tapping away. She could tell by the intent look on his face that tonight's little experiment had revealed something of interest. Frustration bubbled up. Yes, this was her first homicide case, but she'd been a cop for years and she was tired of being treated like a rookie.

"Listen, damn it, I'm on this task force, too, and I want to know what's going on."

Jonah finally stopped what he was doing and looked up. "I'm interested in his aim."

"What about it?"

"Two head shots. Instant kills. Then a shot that pings off a statue, ends up hitting a pregnant woman in the throat."

"You mean he didn't mean to kill her?"

"Maybe not."

Allison felt a twinge of relief, as if somehow his intention made the slightest bit of difference to Jodi Kincaid's husband or her little girl.

"But he meant to kill the student and the professor?"

"I don't know what he meant to do. If he was around, maybe I could ask him."

Allison rolled her eyes and turned back to look at the library. She noticed a shadowy figure moving toward them across the quadrangle. As he got close to the flashlight, she confirmed her guess that it was Scott Black, the Delphi firearms expert whom she'd met once before at the police station. They traded nods.

"You get what you need?"

"Yeah." Jonah shut down the laptop, zipped it into a backpack, and stood up. "All fifty-three shots accounted for."

"Fifty-three? I didn't realize he fired so many," Allison said.

"Lotta rounds," Scott stated. "I'm starting to see your point."

"Fifty-three shots and only three kills, and one of those was probably unintentional. What does that tell you?" Jonah turned to look at Allison.

"He has crappy aim?"

"This guy went to Army Sniper School at Fort Benning," Scott said. "Same place Jonah went."

"Maybe he didn't do so well there," Allison suggested.

Scott shook his head. "Just to get in the door, you have to have a hell of a lot better than a six percent success rate."

"One shot, one kill," Jonah said. "That's the sniper motto."

"Maybe his aim was off because of his cancer," Allison said. "Or maybe he'd been drinking or taking drugs."

"Maybe," Jonah said.

"We get his tox screen back yet?"

"Not yet."

"So it might come back and show that he was zoned out on pain meds or something."

"It might."

But she could tell he didn't believe it. He believed there was something more going on here and they'd barely scratched the surface.

Sophie pulled up to Jonah's address and stared. It wasn't at all like she'd pictured. For one thing, she hadn't pictured a house, but an apartment. And for another, she hadn't pictured anything so homey. It was a 1950s tract house—similar to all the others in this working-class neighborhood—with a wide front porch, a neatly trimmed lawn, and a hedge of monkey grass lining the sidewalk.

Sophie got out of the car and nervously approached the front door. It was a quiet Sunday night. No parties, no traffic noise. Just the bark of a dog in the distance as she walked up the sidewalk and inhaled the scent of freshly cut grass. The blue Chevy pickup in the driveway told her Jonah was home, but she had no idea if he was awake.

Or alone.

A television flickered behind the blinds, and she decided it was a good sign. He was home. And probably by himself, because if he'd had a woman in there, they'd likely be in the bedroom by this time of night. At least Sophie knew *she* would be if she were with Jonah. Not that she ever would be. In fact, after tomorrow it was doubtful he'd ever talk to her again, much less have her over to spend the night.

Sophie hiked up the porch steps, took a deep breath, and knocked on the door.

Seconds ticked by. Then minutes. She heard the dog again. Then a distant car.

She tried the bell.

A few seconds later, the door swung back and he was standing there in the gray-blue light of his TV. He wore jeans and a rumpled T-shirt. His hair was matted on one side, and from the dazed look on his face, she figured he'd been asleep.

"Hi," she said.

"Hey." His voice sounded gravelly. He ran a hand through his hair as he looked her up and down, lingering for a moment on her bare legs.

Maybe she should have worn jeans instead of shorts, but this was an impulsive visit. She'd grabbed the first clothes she'd spotted on the floor when she'd gotten out of bed to do this.

"Sorry to wake you."

"I'm just watching the game." He looked more alert now as his gaze dropped to her legs again, then lifted to her face.

"May I come in?"

He stepped back to let her inside, and she stood in his foyer with her hands clasped. She turned to look at things. With a pizza box on the floor and a mound of sneakers piled in the corner, the interior was more like what she'd expected. A beer bottle sat on the coffee table beside a closed laptop computer.

"Sorry it's late. I—"

She didn't finish because he kissed her. Gently, not hard, but it was shocking anyway, especially when he backed her up against the door and slid his fingers into her hair. He'd been drinking beer, and she wondered how much as his tongue swept into her mouth without the slightest hesitation. *This.* This was the tingle she'd been desperately missing and only seemed to feel anymore when she was with him. It felt natural, completely, as if he'd been waiting around all night for her to just show up here and interrupt his baseball watching. She slid her arms up around his neck and pulled him closer and savored the big, solid feel of him pressed against her. This, this, *this.* God, why had it taken her so long to figure it out?

And now it was too late. He was going to hate her tomorrow.

She braced her hands against his shoulders and gave a little push, but he didn't stop kissing her until she turned her face away.

"Stop."

He pulled back and gazed down at her with a look of disbelief.

"Sorry."

His eyebrows tipped up. *"Why?"*

"I didn't mean to come over here and do that."

The heat in his eyes told her he didn't mind at all. His hand slid out of her hair and dropped to his side. He made no effort to hide the fact that he was totally aroused as he stepped back from her. And he shouldn't have to, because this was her fault.

"Sorry," she said again. "I came by to talk about something. Could we sit down maybe?" Without waiting for an answer, she went to the sofa and perched on the edge of a cushion. He watched her with a mistrustful, heavy-lidded gaze as he sank down beside her.

She cleared her throat. "I just want to tell you that I think you're a really good cop. I may have made you think otherwise. At breakfast this morning, I mean."

He rested his forearms on his thighs and turned to stare at her, looking wary now.

"I have so much respect for what you do, you have no idea. And I want you to know that."

"You came here to tell me that." He said it as a statement, not a question.

"Yes, and also, thank you. For being . . . good at what you do. Not just now but before." She'd thought she'd be able to talk about last winter and how he'd helped her in the aftermath of her attack, but now the words were stuck in her throat, and she thought she'd choke if she tried to get them out. Tears stung her eyes, and the thought of unraveling in front of him made her panicky. That wasn't why she'd come here.

Or was it? Maybe her friends were right. Maybe she did need counseling.

He turned to look at her, and his expression grew concerned. "Come here." He draped an arm over her shoulders, and she started to pull away. "Relax, I'm not going to jump on you."

She rested her cheek against his chest and for a few moments she closed her eyes and let herself feel safe. The tight, strangled feeling went away and she relaxed. Just the smell of his T-shirt had a calming effect on her.

It felt so nice just to sit next to him. She realized this was the most unguarded moment they'd ever had together, probably because she'd interrupted his sleep.

"Are you okay?" he asked quietly.

"Yeah."

It wasn't a lie. She *was* okay now. But as the silence stretched out, she knew she needed to leave.

He took her hand and played with her fingers. "You're sure?"

"Yes."

"That's good." Pause. "Can I jump on you now?"

She laughed and felt the tension drain out of her. She ducked out of his arm and stood up. "I have to go."

He stood, too, and rested his hands on his hips and gazed down at her with a look that was both puzzled and worried.

"Go back to your game," she said.

"Actually, I was sleeping."

"I know."

She went to the door and was relieved when he reached over to open it for her. He wasn't going to twist her arm, which was good, because she wasn't sure she could resist even a little persuasion.

"Thanks for listening." She stepped onto the porch, into the warm summer night that smelled like lawn clippings, and she felt a pinch of regret.

It seemed like she was saying good-bye.

Sophia climbed the steps up to her apartment as he watched from the shadows. Out late again. With the cop this time? He wasn't sure. He also wasn't sure what she knew.

The man dug the key fob from his pocket and waited

for the light to go on in the bedroom. Then he crossed the parking lot and opened her locks with a chirp. He scanned the area for witnesses before inserting the spare key he'd stolen from her kitchen drawer and bringing the Tahoe to life. He reached for the navigation system. A few taps of his finger, and he discovered what she'd been up to the last few days—starting with Friday night, when video footage of Himmel's car being towed away had been plastered all over the news.

The man surveyed the screen in front of him. She'd seen the pictures. And then she'd gone exploring.

He stared at the map for a moment, then took out his phone. He punched in a ten-digit number he'd memorized years ago but never used.

Someone picked up, but there was no greeting. He hadn't expected one.

"It's Sharpe," he said.

A long silence, and then finally, "Go ahead."

He glanced up at the bedroom window, where the light was still on. "We've got a problem."

CHAPTER 11

Jonah made his way through the bullpen and dumped his keys on the desk he hadn't sat behind in more than five days. Neglected case files were stacked beside his phone. Messages and faxes were piled in his in-box. He tossed the ballistics report he'd just picked up on top of all of it and logged on to his computer.

His phone trilled at him, but he ignored it as he searched for a message from Minh, who'd promised him a fingerprint update this morning.

The trilling stopped, but then his cell started up. Cursing, he jerked it from his pocket.

"Macon."

"We're in the interview room. We need you in here."

Jonah fired off a reminder to the CSI before joining Reynolds in the cramped, windowless chamber that doubled as a conference room for private meetings. Four unhappy faces greeted him as he entered.

"Another lawsuit's been slapped on us," Reynolds said without preamble. "Got word this morning."

Jonah's gaze skimmed over his lieutenant, Chief Noonan, and Ric, before coming to rest on the county's district attorney. It had to be serious for them to be seeking a legal perspective so early in the game.

"Someone's suing the department or . . . ?"

Reynolds tossed his pencil down. "The department, the university, me, you, Ric."

"Suing us personally?" Jonah looked at the D.A.

"You're not listed as defendants, but your names are in the body of the petition," she said. "It's unlikely they'll go after you individually because of the sovereign immunity rule, which basically means you can't personally get sued for doing your job."

"Still this is a major pain in the ass, not to mention a publicity nightmare," Noonan said.

Jonah looked at his partner, who sat at the end of the table with his arms crossed. The grim look on his face was even worse news than the D.A.'s presence. Ric wasn't a worrier.

"Who's the plaintiff?" Jonah asked the D.A.

"Robert C. Kincaid."

"*Kincaid's* suing us?"

"For the wrongful death of his wife," Ric said. "Evidently if we'd stormed the roof sooner, she'd be alive today."

Jonah remembered the grieving widower with the kid on his lap during Saturday's service. He'd looked stricken. Helpless. Overwhelmed by sadness.

Apparently not too overwhelmed to be thinking about cashing in on his wife's death.

Jonah turned to the D.A. "Do we need to be worried?"

"What kind of question is that?" Reynolds demanded. "We sure as shit better be worried! He's going to try and squeeze us for millions of dollars in front of a sympathetic jury!"

"I'd like to say no, that it's just a frivolous money grab," she said. "However, you never know with these things. You all will have to consult a defense attorney who specializes in these sorts of cases. But I'll say this: It's definitely not good."

"The department's legal counsel is on his way up from San Antonio," Noonan said. "We've got a whole stack of these things to sort through. This is just the most recent."

"And the most personal," Ric said tightly. "Every one of us from the takedown team is mentioned in the lawsuit."

The door opened, and Sean poked his head in the room. "Yo, you guys need to see this. CNN's on campus again."

Noonan grumbled something and left the room. Reynolds followed.

Jonah stayed behind. He'd had it up to his eyeballs with the media coverage, and about the last thing he needed to see was yet another "inside story" about the Summer School Massacre. He felt a hard ball of bitterness forming in his gut. A lawsuit from Kincaid, of all people.

"We should have expected this," Ric said bitterly. "Can't have a tragedy in this country without people lining up to get rich off it."

Allison stepped into the room and looked at Jonah. "You get my message?"

"What?"

"Those door codes are a dead end," she said. "At least in terms of establishing some inside connection between the shooter and the university. I was in the central maintenance office this morning and they've got a master list posted there, right by the door, listing all the access codes. Anybody could have gotten a look at them with minimal effort."

Jonah shook his head. Another lead gone. Just what he needed today.

"Yo, Jonah." Sean looked in again. "You need to come out here, man."

Jonah stepped out of the room and fixed his attention on the department's only television, which was mounted on the wall in the waiting area beyond the reception counter. A couple of uniforms and plainclothes cops were gazing up at it now.

Jonah plunked his hands on his hips as he recognized the reporter, Tom Rollins. "That guy's local. I thought you said CNN."

"Just watch," Sean told him. "CNN picked this up from some station out of Austin."

"Turn it up!" Reynolds yelled across the room, and the woman at the reception desk scrambled for the remote.

"—another chilling firsthand account from a part-time student caught in the crossfire during Wednesday's deadly massacre. Is there anything else you want the victims' families or the viewers at home to know about your harrowing experience?"

The camera panned away from the reporter and came to rest on a woman.

Jonah's stomach dropped. Sophie wore a conservative navy blazer and had her hair pulled back in a neat bun. Far from the wild-eyed woman who'd shown up ranting at the bar the other night, this one was completely calm and composed.

"Christ, she looks like a Sunday-school teacher," Ric muttered. "What'd she do to her hair?"

"It was just so frightening," Sophie told the reporter. "As I said, I just kept thinking I was next. My heart breaks for the victims and their families, but it's a comfort knowing the police have been doing everything they can to identify the person or persons responsible for this."

"I'm sorry, did you say 'persons'?" The microphone inched closer. "Are you saying there could be more than one?"

"What the hell is she doing?" Reynolds flashed an accusing look at Jonah. "What is she talking about?"

"I can't comment on that," Sophie answered. "I've already been interviewed at length by investigators, and beyond that, I have nothing to say."

"But you think there's someone else responsible? Besides James Himmel?"

"I can't comment on what I saw that day. I will say this, though . . ." Jonah's stomach took another dive as Sophie looked straight at the camera. "The police have made it clear they are totally committed to this case. They've sent all the evidence to our nation's top private forensic lab—"

"How does she know that?" Noonan demanded.

"—and I think the public can rest assured that they will leave *no* stone unturned as they investigate these killings."

"Someone put a muzzle on that girl!" Reynolds exclaimed.

"But just to be clear, are you saying you believe there was someone *else* involved in the attack?"

A chorus of telephones started ringing across the station house. Jonah's throat tightened with fury as he gazed at the TV.

"I'm sorry, but I really can't comment." Sophie smiled apologetically at the reporter. "That's a question for the police."

The heavy thrum of bass pulsated through the darkened room, making Sophie's stomach vibrate as she pushed herself to the limit.

"Harder, everyone, harder! You're almost there! Don't stop now!"

Sophie squeezed her eyes shut and blocked out her spin teacher's voice as she focused on her burning muscles. Three more minutes of pain. And then two. And then one. She pushed and panted until she was dizzy, and just when it felt as if her heart would pound right out of her chest, she heard a collective sigh of exhaustion.

The lights came up on Sophie and a dozen other sweat-drenched people on stationary bikes. The music downshifted to melodic for the optional cooldown, and Sophie opted to get the hell off. She slid from her bike, grabbing the handle as she did because her legs were like noodles. She snatched the towel off the floor to mop her face.

"Great spin, Sophie! Woo-hoo!"

Her instructor's bright smile beamed at her from across the room. The woman was as soaked as everyone else, but there wasn't a hair out of place and her makeup remained perfect, despite the sixty minutes of torture she'd just meted out. Sophie somehow managed a friendly wave instead of an obscene gesture as she staggered from the room on trembling legs. In the hallway, she downed three cones of water at the cooler before going to the locker room for her gym bag, which was singing as she picked it up. She'd forgotten to turn off the ringtone.

Her brother's number flashed on the screen.

"Ted? What's wrong?"

Silence on the other end, and Sophie's stomach filled with dread. Ted was an intern at a hospital in Dallas, and he didn't have time to sleep, much less chat on the phone. She pictured her dad in ICU.

"Did you just run up some stairs?" His voice sounded oddly normal.

"I'm at a spin class. What's wrong?"

"You spin?"

"Is this an emergency?"

"Why do you say that?"

"Because you *never* call me. What's going on?"

"I was going to ask you that," he said as she plowed through the locker-room door. "How come you didn't give the parental units a little ET-phone-home about your brush with death last week? We have to hear about you on the news now?"

"Damn it." Sophie sighed and leaned back against the wall. "Mom and Dad saw that? I was going to call them."

"Yeah, well, dial a little faster next time. Mom's left three messages on my phone tonight, like I know anything about all this. Are you okay?"

The note of genuine concern in his voice made Sophie feel guilty. She hadn't told her family what had happened because every last one of them was a worrier. They'd been horrified by her ordeal last winter, and now every conversation with her mother ended with a recommendation for some therapist she should talk to. All in Dallas, of course.

"Sophie? Hey, you want me to come down there? I can probably take some time off—"

"Absolutely not," she said. That he would even offer showed just how concerned her family must be. "I'm totally fine."

"Then why are you on CNN talking about your 'harrowing experience'? You weren't injured, were you?"

"I'm fine. I just . . . The reporter asked me for an interview and I thought maybe it would be, you know, cathartic. So I decided, Why not?"

She waited to see if he was buying any of this. When he didn't comment, she knew it was time to get off the phone.

"Sophie . . . are you all right?"

"For the last time, *yes*! Listen, I've got to go. Call Mom for me. Tell her—"

"*You* tell her." Commotion in the background, and her brother exchanged ER jargon with someone. "Shit, I have to run. We just got an OD in here."

He clicked off, and Sophie took a minute to wrestle with some daughterly guilt. She gulped down one more cone of water and stepped into the muggy night. Her gaze scanned the parking lot for her Tahoe but got hung up on the pickup parked beside it.

Jonah was there, leaning against the grille with his arms crossed over his beefy chest and his fingers tucked under his armpits. Sophie's still-racing heart took off at a sprint.

His gaze was dark, ominous. He looked like a dam about to burst, and she felt a shiver of fear right down to the soles of her Reeboks.

Damn. She hadn't expected him to do this now. But then, he was a warrior by nature and she should have known he wouldn't shy away from a fight.

She tried not to look shaken as she rummaged for her keys and made her way to the row of cars. She paused in front of his pickup.

"Hi."

He didn't say anything, simply pushed off the grille and took a menacing step forward.

Sophie tossed her head and sauntered to her door, but he blocked her path.

"*Excuse* me."

"I need to talk to you."

"Why don't you go home and call me after I've had a chance to take a shower?"

"Now."

"If you don't mind, I'd prefer to de-slime myself first."

"I do mind." He reached behind her and opened the passenger's-side door to his truck. "Get in."

The hard set of his jaw told her arguing was only going to make things worse. If he was determined to talk about this, they might as well get it over with.

She sighed heavily and got into his truck.

Rather than looking triumphant or even pleased by her acquiescence, he continued to look supremely unhappy as he jerked his keys from his pocket and walked around to the driver's side. He fired up the engine as Sophie dug through her purse for a tissue to dab her still-sweating temples. Her yoga pants and T-shirt were wet, and she probably reeked. But as they exited the parking lot, Jonah seemed too preoccupied to notice.

The driver in front of them missed a chance to pull out, and Jonah laid on the horn.

Sophie slid a glance at him. "In a hurry?"

He looked straight ahead.

"Where are we going, anyway?"

"For a drive."

Sophie glanced out the window and waited for him to start. He needed to vent his temper, apparently, and she was up for the challenge. She'd expected a cold sulk from him, but she could deal with this, too. She just wanted to get on with it.

"So, I guess you saw the interview," she said as he pulled into traffic.

"Did you accomplish your objective?" he asked without looking at her.

"Well, I haven't seen the broadcast, but I'd say yes, I'm guessing I did."

"Was your objective to piss off every cop in town? Or just me in particular?"

She rolled her eyes. "This isn't about you."

"What was your objective, Sophie?"

"I think it's pretty obvious, isn't it?"

"Not to me. Maybe you could explain it. Because if your objective was to further this investigation, it's just taken a big step backward, thanks to you." He turned to look at her, and hostility flashed in his eyes.

"Oh, really? How's that?" She said it with the right amount of sarcasm, but underneath her confidence was a twinge of anxiety.

"You set the media on us, for one thing. How easy do you think it's going to be for us to pursue your theory with that pack of dogs nipping at our heels?"

"My 'theory,' huh?" He still didn't believe her.

"And even if there was something to it, you just tipped our hand. If there *is* some mystery accomplice out there, he's probably busy covering his tracks now. You want to go into PR? Here's the first rule of talking to reporters: Don't. They fuck everything up."

She folded her arms over her damp shirt. God, she hated this. Sex appeal was one of her go-to weapons, and she didn't like fighting with a man when she looked and smelled like dead fish.

"He was already covering his tracks," she said. "His prints weren't in the car, which means he wore gloves. Speaking of which, you need to get that car to the Delphi Center so our tracers can take a look at it."

Jonah shook his head.

"I mean it. There could be hair, dirt, carpet fiber, latent prints, skin cells, any number of things you could have tested—"

"Since when did you become a CSI?" he thundered. "You're a freaking *receptionist,* Sophie! Get that through your head! And your meddling is mucking up an already impossible investigation. Now thanks to you, besides an uncontrollable crime scene and angry parents and lawsuits to worry about, I've got the media wailing about conspiracy theories. And on top of everything, I have to leave town and worry about your safety the whole time I'm gone!"

She let a moment tick by to make sure he'd finished shouting before she responded. "Why would you have to worry about my safety?"

He turned to glare at her. "Because if by some chance you're right about this, then you just announced to the world that you're an eyewitness who can identify a coconspirator! What the hell were you thinking?"

Sophie turned to look out the window. "You can scratch my safety off your list of concerns. I barely saw the guy."

"And I'm sure he knows that, right?"

She felt a prick of unease. "I can take care of myself."

"Oh, yeah? Like you did last winter?"

She turned to look at him, stung by his vehemence. He must be seriously upset to take a cheap shot like that. But if he didn't think her story had merit, he wouldn't be worried about this. Was it possible he *did* believe her?

And where was he going, anyway? She hadn't figured on him leaving town in the middle of this, and it made her uneasy. And the fact that his whereabouts should even matter bugged her.

"When do you leave?" she asked.

"Tonight."

"Tonight?"

"I've got a meeting at oh-ten-hundred tomorrow. With gas stops, I'll probably just make it."

"You're *driving*?"

He didn't answer, just stared straight ahead. She studied his profile. His teeth were clenched, and she'd never seen him so angry.

"So, you're worried I'll give another interview while you're gone?"

"Among other things, yeah."

"Well, I'm not going to. And if it's my safety you're concerned about, Ric or someone else can keep an eye on me. Or tell one of your patrol cars to put me on his route or something. You don't need to worry about it."

Jonah shook his head. "You still don't get it."

"*What* don't I get?"

Whatever short fuse he'd had ran out. He jerked the wheel right and whipped into a parking lot, then slammed on the brakes, making them both pitch forward.

"Damn it, Sophie! There *is* no patrol car to keep an eye on you, or Ric to keep an eye on you. There's nobody but me. Don't you understand? *Nobody* believes you!" She shrunk away from the blast, but he kept going. "You pulled a publicity stunt, and guess what everyone in my department thinks this is about? Publicity. As in, here comes Sophie Barrett again, looking for a chance to get her face on the news. Congratulations. Your credibility is completely shot. Was that what you wanted?"

She felt as if he'd slapped her. "Nobody believes me?"

"That's right."

"Not even Ric?"

His silence answered her question. It dragged on, and she started to feel sick to her stomach. Ric was her friend. Mia was her friend. Did everyone she knew doubt her credibility? Did they really think she'd lie about something like this to get attention?

Jonah sat there, jaw twitching with suppressed emotion. A cold feeling settled over her.

"What about you?"

He didn't look at her.

"You know this case better than anybody. You think I'm lying?"

He sighed heavily and some of the anger seemed to go out of him. "Sophie . . ."

"Just tell me what you think. I'm a big girl. I can handle it."

"I think you gave an honest account of what you *thought* you saw."

She turned away, hoping he didn't see how much this conversation hurt her.

"The other VW is a pretty big coincidence for me," he said. "It brings reasonable doubt into it. I think it's reasonable to believe that's the car you saw, not James Himmel's. And not some mystery accomplice."

"So the case is closed, then," she said bitterly.

"Far from it. Especially not after today."

Sophie looked at him, and she knew it was all just for appearances. She'd been on the news, and now the department had to at least *look* as though they were following up, even if they weren't.

Sophie turned off her emotions. "Where are you going tonight?"

"Georgia," he said.

"This is related to the investigation?"

"I can't talk about it."

Which meant it was. She should take it as a good sign, although the fact that he was driving made her wonder if the department was paying for the trip or if he was off on his own. He could be kind of a maverick.

Sophie glanced around. "Take me back to the gym," she said. "You need to get on the road."

A tense silence filled the truck as he took a few turns and drove them back to the gym. He pulled up beside her Tahoe. The lot had nearly emptied, and she glanced around apprehensively. She hated parking lots at nighttime.

She unzipped her big purse and pulled out a sheaf of papers. "Here," she said, handing them to him. "I'd planned to give you these tomorrow, but sounds like you won't be here."

"What is this?"

"Victim profiles. Even though I'm just a *receptionist,* I managed to find some good info and I wanted you to have it. You might be interested to know Walter Graham took out a two-million-dollar life insurance policy just a few months ago."

Jonah thumbed through the papers, frowning. "How'd you get all this?"

"I'm resourceful."

He glared at her.

"Alex Lovell helped me."

"How did *she* get it?"

She gave him a baleful look. "You don't really want to know that, do you? It's like you said about the sausages."

She shoved the door open and started to climb out, but he caught her elbow. "Want me to follow you home?"

"Don't bother. You need to get going."

He watched her grimly. "Keep a low profile." He released her arm. "And try not to get in any trouble while I'm gone."

CHAPTER 12

Colonel William Fowler was rumored to be a hardass, and that was pretty much what Jonah found when he arrived on time for his meeting at Fort Benning and was left waiting without explanation for more than two hours. When the colonel finally showed up, his gaze zeroed in on the only person in his entire office wearing civilian clothes.

"Detective Macon, this way." He directed Jonah past his assistant's desk and into his private office. "Sorry to put you on hold."

"No problem, sir."

Fowler was tall, slim, and had the super-erect posture of an army lifer. Jonah waited for him to sit and took a plastic chair on the other side of a gray metal desk. The colonel's desktop, like his uniform, was immaculate.

"All the way up from Texas." Fowler leaned back in his chair and laced his fingers behind his head. "What do you think of Benning?"

"Same as I remember it." Jonah was playing the veteran card here, and both of them knew it.

"Long trip. Wish I had better news for you."

"How's that, sir?"

"You're here about James Himmel. I'm afraid I don't remember a damn thing about him, besides what I read in his file on Friday. Believe we sent you guys a copy of that."

They had. Jonah had found it to be amazingly lacking in any detail that would help his investigation. The file had been scrubbed clean of anything that might reflect negatively on the army.

"The file was pretty thin, sir. I'm here to get more. For example, the paperwork says Himmel's commanding officer refused to reenlist him, but it doesn't say why."

Jonah waited for an explanation, but it didn't come.

"I also need more on his shooting skills. I'd like to talk to someone who worked with him here at the base. I understand you were one of his instructors when he went through sniper school? That would have been nine years ago this summer."

Fowler smiled. "Not bad, Detective. You've obviously done your homework. Problem is, we get more than twenty-five thousand new soldiers a year through here, and I don't remember this one. 'Fraid you've wasted your trip."

Fowler stood.

Jonah stood, too, and set his jaw. He hadn't spent fourteen goddamn hours on the road and two hours sitting in a chair to be dismissed after five minutes.

"With all due respect, sir, I'm not finished yet."

Fowler's eyebrows tipped up. "Finished?"

"I'm investigating a triple homicide committed by one of *your* soldiers, and I have some questions I need answered."

Fowler gave him a long, hard look, and Jonah could tell he'd just gained some ground.

"You were here in '04, if I'm not mistaken," the colonel said.

"That's correct, sir."

"How about a tour of the base? For old times' sake." Fowler crossed the room and opened his office door. "Get me Wolchansky," he told his assistant. He turned and gave Jonah a crisp nod. "Master Sergeant David Wolchansky's your man. He'll get you what you need."

The speed with which the master sergeant responded to the summons told Jonah two things: first, that he'd passed some sort of litmus test, and second, that this hand-off had been planned all along.

Jonah rode alongside the man now in a doorless Jeep with the windshield flipped down. The base was just like he remembered it—from the sound of rounds popping off on the small-arms range complex to the stifling humidity. Jonah watched a line of new recruits with their faces in the dirt and remembered the hell of physical training—the push-ups, the flutter kicks, the mountain climbers, the cherry-pickers. He remembered thirty-second showers and meals wolfed down on the way to more PT. He remembered running and ruck-marching hundreds of miles and then collapsing into his bed at night and getting up to do it all over again. He remembered days spent in shoot houses, and the cuts and bruises on his body from the clay simulation rounds. And he recalled thinking at the time that it was hard, but then realizing months later that none of it even compared to the brutality of real combat.

Wolchansky pulled over at an empty firing range and

ground to a stop beside a wooden cabinet. Jonah climbed out of the Jeep and surveyed the area as the soldier unlocked the box and pulled out some gear.

Jonah had noticed the M24 in back and figured he was in for another test. He peeled off his jacket and tossed it over the passenger seat, then rolled up the cuffs of his white oxford shirt.

"You still shoot?" Wolchansky asked, handing him a pair of earplugs.

"Here and there."

He nodded at the range. "I was out here this morning with a team of Rangers. One guy hit the T-zone on a target from six hundred yards."

Well, shit. The T-zone was forehead and nose on a human silhouette.

Wolchansky handed him the rifle. "See what you can do with that five hundred."

Any doubt Jonah had that these guys were fucking with him was long gone. He took the rifle and looked it over. It was painted a flat desert camo and had a Leupold scope.

Wolchansky grabbed a pair of binoculars off the floor of the Jeep and started walking toward the range. "I'll be on glass."

Jonah followed Wolchansky across the turf and tried to get in the zone. The air smelled like spent ammo and CLP oil and dirt. Jonah breathed it in and let it sit in his lungs. He found a good, flat shooting position and crouched down to look around from the lower vantage point.

The range went to a thousand yards, with signs marking each hundred. The sole target at the moment was dead center in the field at the five-hundred-yard mark. It had a red flag on top, giving him wind direction as well as another hint that this was all part of the colonel's plan.

Jonah turned to Wolchansky. The man was typical army—thin, muscular, confident. He had the cool look in his eye of an experienced operator, versus the new Ranger recruits Jonah had seen on the way in. Those guys were hyper-aggressive and amped up on ego and adrenaline, but Wolchansky had a maturity about him that told Jonah he'd seen his share of combat. Jonah pegged him for Special Operations.

"You a Ranger?" Jonah asked him.

"I am."

"How long you been an instructor here?"

"Two years," he said. "I train spec ops, mostly."

Jonah had confidence in his shooting abilities, but he wasn't stupid. He wanted to get some info up front, just in case he failed this test.

"You ever meet Jim Himmel?"

The Ranger pulled a few rounds from his pocket and handed them to Jonah. "Worked with him in Ramadi, back in 2005." Jonah loaded the rifle as Wolchansky gazed downrange. "He was on one of the sniper teams. Back then, our guys were clearing a hundred IEDs a week. Our mission was to find the people placing them and take them out."

"How'd you do?"

"We got the job done, for the most part."

Jonah examined the weapon. It was slightly heavier than the Remington he had at home because of the more sophisticated optics.

He laid the rifle on the ground and settled on his stomach beside it. From there, it was a ritual. He zeroed the scope to five hundred yards, then pulled the gun in and adjusted the butt snugly against his shoulder. He lowered the bipod to the ground, shifted his hips and his legs, and dug his toes into the dirt. Then he tucked his cheek against the stock.

He peered through the scope and was sucked into a world five football fields away.

Wolchansky settled prone on the ground beside him and picked up the binoculars.

"It was a hot area," he continued. "We were busy round the clock. I remember in training they told us only stay on scope forty-five minutes at a time, but back then, we couldn't stop. It was an obsession. Those crosshairs get burned into your brain, even when you close your eyes. And you don't want to close your eyes because you think, What if I miss someone? How many of our guys are going to die because I wasn't paying attention?"

Jonah could relate to what he was saying. He felt that way about being a cop. He thought a lot about not just the rapists and murderers and gangbangers he took off the streets, but also the ones he missed, the ones who would go out someday and hurt someone.

"First cold-bore shot, just get the splash," Wolchansky said.

The man was giving him a warm-up shot. Jonah knew he needed it. He practiced all the time, but law enforcement snipers focused on shorter ranges—typically under a hundred yards.

Jonah settled in. He looked at the flag and got wind direction. He did some mental adjustments for drop and spin, and shifted the crosshairs up and to the left of the target.

Then he relaxed and got his heart rate down. Three deep breaths. He waited for the natural respiratory pause—the most relaxed point in the breathing cycle.

Then he stopped thinking about breathing. He stopped thinking at all. He squeezed the trigger.

The gun jerked against his shoulder.

"You're low, about four o'clock."

Jonah peered through the scope again. He adjusted the crosshairs. Three more breaths. Three more pauses. He squeezed the trigger.

Another kick in the shoulder.

Wolchansky whistled. "That's a hit."

Jonah took a moment to absorb what he'd done. He didn't know whether it was luck or skill, but he was glad he'd done it.

He let go of the rifle and kneeled beside it.

"Not bad." The Ranger picked up the gun and got to his feet.

Jonah stood and dusted his hands on his pants as Wolchansky gazed downrange. The sun blazed down on them, but Jonah stood there and waited because he knew he was about to get what he'd come for.

"I remember this one day with Himmel, back in Ramadi. We were in two teams, both of us on overwatch while some of our guys were out looking for IEDs. We get intel there's this group of insurgents approaching an alley. They're loaded down with RPGs." The Ranger looked at him, and Jonah pictured the band of insurgents toting rocket-propelled grenades. "Finally, one of them darts across. I watched Himmel thread the needle on a sprinting target from eight hundred fifty yards."

Jonah stood there in his dirty civilian clothes and knew he'd passed the test. And his prize was this Ranger's information. He absorbed the words, along with their implications.

The guy had made a head shot from almost half a mile away. A *moving* target, no taller than ten inches.

Himmel was a sniper. A force multiplier. A deadly weapon. He'd taken fifty-three shots last week and missed most of them. And Jonah knew now what he'd only suspected before.

James Himmel hadn't missed a thing.

Allison was finishing the remnants of her very late lunch when someone tall, dark, and handsome walked into the shop and peeled off his shades. He looked straight at Allison and approached her table as she swallowed the last bite of her soggy Italian sub.

"This seat taken?" He pulled out the chair across from her and flashed a smile.

Make that tall, dark, and arrogant. And young. Holy crap, he was young enough to be—well, not her son, but maybe a nephew.

Still sporting the smile, he sank into the chair and stuck his hand out. "I'm Tyler Dorion. And you're Detective Doyle, if I'm not mistaken."

She wiped her fingers on a napkin before shaking his hand. "How's it going, Tyler?"

Was he here to report an on-campus theft? Maybe a car break-in? She took in his pale blue oxford and clean-shaven face. Or maybe he was with the Young Republicans and looking to make a sales pitch.

"I saw you at the scene."

"Scene?"

"The crime scene. Last Wednesday." His smile dimmed a bit—but not enough for Allison's tastes—as he pulled a business card from his shirt pocket and slid it across the table. "I'm with the *Bee*."

"The who?"

He smiled. "You're familiar with our local paper?"

She glanced down at the business card. *Tyler P. Dorion*.

Beneath the name was a list of Web sites, none of which belonged to the *Bee*.

Allison crumpled her sandwich trash into a neat ball. "What can I do for you, Tyler?"

"It's Ty."

"What can I do for you, Ty?"

He leaned forward on his elbows, suddenly somber as he looked up at her. His eyes exactly matched his shirt, and she wondered if he practiced that earnest look in the mirror.

"Listen, Detective Doyle. Can I call you Allison?"

"No."

He nodded. "All right. Detective. It's come to my attention that your task force is investigating a conspiracy angle in connection with the Summer School Massacre."

He said it like it was a movie title. *High School Musical. Summer School Massacre.* Allison folded her arms over her chest. "I can't discuss an ongoing investigation."

"Understood. But allow me to tell *you* something I've uncovered about the case. Something you may not be aware of."

"How old are you, Ty?"

He frowned. "Why?"

"Standard question in a police interview."

He gave a serious nod. "Twenty-one."

"You're about to be a senior."

"That's right."

"And you're interning at the *Bee* this summer, I take it?"

"Not exactly."

"You just said you were with—"

"I'm more of a mojo. I work for various news outlets." His confidence was back as he tapped his card. "They're listed there, if you need to run a background check."

"What's a mojo?" Allison asked, letting her curiosity get the best of her.

"A mobile journalist." He smiled. "I cover stories from the road. Post them on the Net, do podcasts. You know."

Allison's phone vibrated at her side, and she looked down to check the number. It was her dentist's office. She let it go to voice mail, which seemed to increase Tyler's sense of importance.

"Trust me, Detective. You want to hear what I have to say."

"Okay, let's hear it."

He looked startled. "What, you mean here?"

She glanced around the empty sandwich shop and shrugged. "Sure, why not?"

"This is sensitive information." He cast a look over his shoulder at the hair-netted woman dumping out coffee grounds.

"Lay it on me."

"Okay." He took a deep breath. "Eric Emrick contacted me two weeks before his death. He said he wanted an interview."

Allison watched him for a long moment. The skin at the back of her neck prickled, and she wasn't sure why.

"An interview about what?"

"I don't know. But it was serious. And he was scared."

"Scared of what?"

"I don't know that, either."

Allison leaned forward on her elbows. The smarmy smile was gone, and he looked serious. His entire tone had changed.

"What do you *think* he was scared of?"

"He thought someone was trying to kill him."

Sophie hauled her third basket of laundry down the stairs and chided herself for being a clotheshorse. Granted, she did much of her shopping at outlet stores, but her savings account would be in a lot better shape if she managed to squirrel away a paycheck every once in a while.

A college-aged guy she'd never met before was seated cross-legged on one of the washers when she entered the room. Tuesday nights weren't usually a big laundry time, and she'd hoped to have the place to herself.

He glanced up from his Kierkegaard and gave her a once-over.

"Hot enough for you?" she quipped, dropping her basket on the floor by one of the open washers. The room felt like a sauna, probably because all three dryers were running.

"That one's out of order," he said as she started to dump her clothes in.

Sophie sighed. "Thanks."

The other two washers were in use. She was going to be here all night.

She glanced at her watch. Another twenty minutes until her first load would be dry. Just enough time to run to the corner store for more detergent. She could always ask to borrow some from the young philosopher, but she didn't see any. Maybe he was using the water-only method.

"Mind watching my stuff? I'll be right back."

He didn't look up. "Sure."

Sophie did the one-block dash to the corner store and grabbed the last bottle of soap. She plucked a diet root beer from the fridge, then caved in to temptation and picked up an Almond Joy before heading to the register.

Her phone sang out, and she pulled it from her pocket. Jonah calling with an update? But Kelsey's number came up on the screen.

"Have you been watching the news tonight?"

"No, why?" Sophie slid her twenty across the counter and smiled at the silver-haired store manager. She'd always liked him. He kept his shelves neat, his coffee fresh, and mopped the floors twice a day.

"Well, they're running you again," Kelsey said. "And you're going to love this. They've got a kook panel. Tom Rollins dug up a bunch of conspiracy theorists who are going gaga over your possible accomplice sighting. He's interviewing all of them at once, too, like he's Larry King or someone."

"Keep the change," Sophie whispered to the manager as he passed her a bag. Then to Kelsey: "What do you mean, 'kooks'?"

"Oh, you know. One of them's a Second Amendment nut, says the whole thing was staged by the gun-control lobby to draw attention to their cause. Another one is spouting something about Free Masons and secret societies. And I'm still trying to figure out the last one, but he seems to believe Himmel is not actually Himmel but someone disguised as human who may have been put here to . . . I'm not sure, really. His point is still *emerging*."

"God, what a sideshow." Sophie walked briskly down the sidewalk, checking up and down the street for creepy-looking shadows. "Guess I opened a can of worms. Are there any sane people on?"

"You be the judge. They had a police spokesman on a few minutes ago with the basic 'We can't comment on an ongoing investigation' comment. And then there was—"

Something rammed her from behind, and she flew forward onto the pavement. A weight crushed down on her and someone yanked her head back by the hair. She screamed and kicked. She groped for her purse, her phone, anything—

Smack! Her head hit concrete. Pain roared through her skull and she saw stars. Her hand curled around something hard. A bottle. She struggled to breathe, to yell, to kick. She flailed her arm back.

A curse boomed in her ear.

"Hey!" Footsteps, coming closer. *"Hey!"*

The weight disappeared. More footsteps. The unmistakable sound of a shell being chambered. On a burst of panic, she rolled sideways just as a shotgun blast ripped through the night.

She lay there, shocked, blinking up at the night sky and waiting for the pain. It was in her back, her head. But she hadn't been shot.

The store manager's face loomed over her. "Are you okay? I called 911!"

He reached for her head, and she jerked away. She tried to roll onto her side, but she still couldn't really move. She couldn't really breathe, either. She wheezed and choked and tried to get air into her lungs.

A gnarled hand reached for her arm and helped her sit up. "Are you okay? Did he get ya? He had a knife on him, looked like a big one."

Sophie's tongue felt numb. She registered the coppery taste of blood as she lifted her hand to her lip and glanced around. She heard a dog barking and the ever-increasing wail of a siren.

The manager planted the butt of the gun on the sidewalk and heaved himself to his feet. He offered her a hand. She looked at it and suddenly felt woozy.

The siren shrieked closer, and she sank back against the warm concrete. Her head pounded. Her ears rang. She blinked up at the sky and it seemed to be falling down on her.

CHAPTER 13

"Are you sure you didn't see *anything*?" Allison asked. "Not even his hair color?"

Sophie leaned against the back of the Buick and glanced over her shoulder for the hundredth time. "All I saw was an arm. I told you. He had one of those tribal tattoos—a full sleeve, I think."

Allison made another note on her pad. *Full sleeve?* It was a good detail, but those tats were so common now, it might not get her very far. She glanced down the sidewalk to where a patrol officer was interviewing the store manager, and hoped he was having better luck. Purse snatchings were a dime a dozen, but the knife bumped things up to a whole new level.

Allison eyed the blood spatter on the sidewalk. When she first arrived on the scene, she'd thought it was Sophie's, but turned out it belonged to the perp. She'd apparently nicked him with a broken root beer bottle before the manager chased him off with his twelve-gauge.

"Okay, anything else in that coin purse?"

Sophie looked at her. "Huh?"

"The coin purse he stole," Allison said. "Anything in it besides cash? Maybe an ID? Credit card? Social Security card?"

Sophie adjusted the ice pack against the side of her head. "Um, no. Just the money. My purse is upstairs. I was doing laundry, so . . ." The words trailed off and she swung her head the other way, toward the apartment building. "Oh crap, my clothes."

"Excuse me?"

"Nothing." Sophie glanced over to the patrol officer, who was still talking with the store clerk near the door. The red-white-and-blue police strobes were creating a scene, and Allison would bet the manager was hoping to finish up soon so he could get back to selling his beer and cigarettes.

"You know, there is one thing," Sophie said. "His voice."

"What about it?"

"He yelled something when I cut him. I don't know what it meant, but it sounded like Spanish."

Now, there was a useful detail. Allison jotted it down as Sophie glanced around nervously.

"Do you think the clerk saw enough to identify him? Like maybe in a lineup or something?"

"We'll have him come in to look at some photo books," Allison said. "Are you sure you don't want to do the same?"

"I told you, I didn't see his face. He was behind me." Another nervous look around. She rearranged the ice pack, and Allison noticed her hands were still trembling.

"You know, you should probably get to the ER, get that head checked out. I can run you over there."

"I'm okay."

"You should seek medical treatment," Allison pressed. "You could have a concussion."

"I know what a concussion feels like, and it hurts way more than this."

Sophie bent down to pick grit out of a scrape on her knee, and Allison watched with annoyance. This woman didn't take orders well.

"Actually, there is something you could do for me." She stood up. "I left my door unlocked when I went down to the laundry room. I'd appreciate it if you'd do a walk-through with me, just to be safe."

Allison signaled the patrol officer before following Sophie across the parking lot to an exterior stairwell. Instead of going up, Sophie darted through a door beside a vending machine alcove.

"Son of a bitch!"

Allison stepped into the room, which was a few degrees cooler than a pizza oven. Sophie stood beside an open dryer, hands planted on her hips, scowling down at a mound of wet clothes on the floor.

"He *stole* my dryer cycle, the little prick." She heaped the damp clothes onto an already-full laundry basket.

"Who?"

"Philosophy Boy." Sophie huffed out a breath and propped the basket against her hip, then strode out the door.

Allison followed her up the stairs, taking in the feel of the apartment complex. It wasn't the nicest place in town, but it wasn't the seediest, either. There was a tiny pool on-site. The tenants drove halfway decent cars, and many were students, judging from the parking stickers.

But from a security perspective, the place was abysmal. Only one light in the entire parking lot. Half the lights illuminating the balcony were burned out, and the ones that weren't gave off a pathetic amount of wattage.

Sophie stopped in front of one of the doors. Allison rested a hand on her weapon and then turned the doorknob. Unlocked, as Sophie had said.

A lamp was on in the living room. Allison recognized the soulful voice of Diana Krall coming from a pair of Bose speakers perched on a bookshelf. A laptop computer sat open on the breakfast bar beside a leather purse, which Allison took for a good sign. If some intruder had been up here tonight, he would have taken at least the purse.

Allison checked the bathroom, the bedroom, and the apartment's two tiny closets. She returned to the living room.

"All clear."

Sophie had deposited the basket of wet laundry on the kitchen table and was glancing around anxiously. Clearly, the woman was unnerved.

"You check your purse?"

"Everything's there."

A snippet of music rang out, and Sophie pulled her phone from her pocket. She'd dropped it during the attack. It was all scuffed up, but still working apparently.

"Hello?" She sighed. "Really, that's *not* necessary. I'm fine." Pause. "Just my coin purse. About twenty bucks . . . I know. I know. Listen, lemme call you later, Kels. I'm talking to the police."

Sophie hung up and set the phone on the counter. Her hands were still shaking and she actually looked worse in this light than she had outside. All her color was gone.

"You know, you probably won't get a wink of sleep here all by yourself. Way too much adrenaline."

Sophie looked at her.

"It's happened to me before."

"What, getting mugged?" She sounded surprised.

"Long time ago, but I remember the feeling."

Sophie glanced at Allison's sidearm. Her nervous gaze darted around the apartment.

"You have a friend you could call, or maybe a relative?" Allison pressed. "Someplace you could stay tonight?"

She looked away and seemed to decide something. "There is someone who probably wouldn't mind, actually." She looked at Allison and smiled weakly. "That's not a bad idea."

Sophie found Kelsey the next day in the subterranean suite of offices known to Delphi staffers as the Bones Unit.

"How's the head?" Kelsey asked, glancing up from the skull she had perched on some sort of tripod.

It was a human skull, and Sophie stifled a shudder. She'd never quite gotten used to the fact that some of her best friends spent their days studying dead people.

"I feel fine," Sophie reported. "All it really needed was an ice pack."

Kelsey watched her skeptically, probably trying to read whether she was lying. And she was. Sophie's head felt okay now, but the attack itself had shaken her much more than she wanted to admit.

Nevertheless, she'd come down to the bowels of the

lab to assure Kelsey that (a) she wasn't seriously injured and (b) Kelsey's ill-timed phone call wasn't to blame for the mugging.

"So." Sophie pulled up a stool near the worktable and mustered a smile. "What are you working on? Who's this?"

"As of now, her name's Jane Doe." Kelsey put down the laser pointer she was using to take digital measurements. "A couple of cavers found her near a nature trail out in Menard County. Sheriff there asked me to get him the Big Four: race, sex, age, stature."

"Will you be able to do it?"

"The skeleton's incomplete, but I've got the skull and the pelvis, so that shouldn't be a problem. The bigger challenge is getting an ID. I've got some ideas for him on that front, though." Kelsey crossed her arms. "Anyway, enough about me. How's your case coming?"

Which one? Sophie wanted to ask, but she wasn't sure how much Kelsey knew about her involvement with the university shooting.

"The store clerk looked at some photo books, may have identified someone," Sophie said. "It sounded pretty tentative, but at least it's a lead."

"Did Jonah bring him in?"

"Jonah?"

"You two looked pretty chummy at the picnic tables the other day. I figured he was probably involved. Are you guys dating now?"

"Ha. Dating hasn't been high on my list lately," Sophie said, dodging the issue. "Anyway, he's out of town. Allison Doyle's on the case."

"Never met her." Kelsey stripped off her latex gloves and tossed them in a bin. "Hey, while you're here, I should tell you the rumor I heard about you when I was up in the director's office this morning."

"About *me*?"

"Yep." Kelsey smiled. "The director's admin is kind of a gossip queen, and according to *her*, you're on the short list of candidates for the PR opening."

"You're kidding."

"The director caught your interview and believes we're wasting you on phones. He thinks someone with your, quote, 'poise in front of a camera' belongs in our public relations office."

"Wow." Sophie felt slightly stunned by the compliment. She hadn't thought the director even knew she existed. "He's probably just happy because I plugged the lab and it ended up on CNN."

"Shrewd move, by the way. You may have just gotten yourself promoted."

"I wasn't doing it to get *promoted*. I think the police are missing something."

"And you're probably right." Kelsey gave her a long look. "What did Jonah think? I'm guessing he wasn't too happy about you sharing your accomplice sighting with the media?"

Sophie remembered the look on his face when he'd met her at the gym. "You guessed right. I think I may have ticked off the whole department."

Kelsey waved her off. "I wouldn't worry about it. They're probably just embarrassed you caught something they missed. Jonah will probably be thanking you someday for having the guts to come forward."

Sophie snorted. "I don't know about *that*. Last time I saw him, he looked ready to wring my neck."

• • •

The 1976 Volkswagen Beetle arrived at the Delphi Center in a moving van, and Allison couldn't help thinking that if the lawsuits didn't bankrupt her department, the bill from this crime lab could certainly do the trick. She stood inside the large enclosed garage and watched as the driver of the van completed his delivery. The truck began to hiss and groan.

"What's that sound?"

"Hydraulics," said the tracer who was standing by to take the vehicle's interior apart in search of evidence.

Allison looked at him to elaborate, but then looked away. With his athletic build, sun-bronzed skin, and faded baseball cap, Roland Delgado was quickly dispelling her notion of a lab geek. If not for his Tyvek coveralls, she would have thought he was a kayaking instructor, not a scientist.

"We like gravity to do the work," he said as a ramp emerged from the cargo space, tilted down toward the floor. "The last thing we want is someone getting behind the wheel and contaminating the crime scene."

More groaning as the Beetle emerged, attached to a winch that was slowly being let out. The truck spit out the Bug, Roland stepped forward to unhook the winch from the front bumper, and the platform receded like a giant metal tongue.

Allison stood on the sidelines as the tracer snapped on some surgical gloves and got to work. Task one: photographing the car from every angle, which he did with a small digital camera.

"Hey, you mind aiming that light for me?" He

glanced up at Allison as he opened the passenger's-side door and crouched down.

This was the strangest garage Allison had ever seen. Besides having a floor that looked clean enough to double as an operating table, it had an abundance of lights—overhead lamps, portable lamps, handheld flashlights. Roland nodded at the standing spotlight closest to her, and she tilted it to shine inside the car.

"Not much of a neat freak," Roland told her, bending over something on the floor with his tweezers. "I like this guy already."

"You're aware he shot twenty-eight people, right?"

The tracer deposited something Allison couldn't see into a small paper bag.

"Yeah, but look at all the goodies he left behind. Soil, plant matter, synthetic fiber . . . The plant matter alone could keep us entertained for days."

Okay, maybe he was more of a geek than she'd given him credit for.

"Whoa."

Allison stepped closer and ducked her head. "What?"

He snapped a few pictures, then dug some extra-long tweezers from his pocket and reached under the passenger seat. He pulled out a small gray wad.

"Chewing gum," he announced with a smile. "Mia's going to love this. She's our DNA tracer. She can run an STR analysis and develop a profile."

"Not bad," Allison said. "And if our mystery man was smart enough to wear gloves but dumb enough to spit out his gum, I'll take you out for a beer to celebrate."

He lifted an eyebrow but didn't look up. "I'll hold you

to that beer. And you never know. Perps can do stupid things."

"Won't argue with that one." Allison stepped closer again. "I once worked an apartment burglary where the guy used a flexible plastic card to get past the lock on a door. You know those phony credit cards you get in the mail?"

"Yeah?"

"They're the best kind. Nice and thin. Anyway, this guy must not have had one handy because he used his driver's license instead. Didn't manage to get the door open, ended up dropping the thing in her apartment, and it was waiting right there when she came home from work."

Roland snapped another picture. "So, if he didn't get into the apartment, how do you know he was planning to burglarize it?"

"He hit the other apartments on her hall first." She leaned closer, trying to see what had his attention. "What are you photographing?"

"McDonald's wrapper. And a receipt."

"Tell me it's a credit-card purchase."

"Sorry."

He collected the bits of paper in separate bags, then moved around to the driver's side, which was Allison's primary area of interest. If Sophie Barrett's claims had any merit, here's where they'd be most likely to find evidence.

Roland arranged more lamps before crouching down and shaking his head. "Damn. Your fingerprint guy really went nuts in here. There's powder everywhere."

"He was trying to be thorough."

"Next time, send it straight to the best." He glanced up at her with warm brown eyes and a cocky smile that made her pulse pick up.

"I'll remember that." She shifted away from Roland and pretended to be examining the car instead of wondering what he looked like under those coveralls. She needed to get out more. She hadn't been on a date in ages, and she was starting to get itchy around all the men she worked with.

The door behind her squeaked open and a lab-coated woman stepped into the room. She had reddish-blond hair and a smattering of freckles covering her nose.

"Mia, baby, you're going to love me."

"What have you got?" She came over to stand next to Allison, and they traded greetings.

"Some ABC gum, for starters."

Allison looked at the woman. "ABC?"

"Already been chewed." She smiled. "We like our acronyms around here."

"Unfortunately, it's pretty petrified and it came from the passenger side. I doubt it's the guy you're looking for."

Mia donned a pair of surgical gloves and pulled a small glass vial from her pocket. Inside was a cotton swab.

"You finish the door yet?" she asked, walking over to Roland.

"Thought I'd save that for you."

"How thoughtful." She pulled out a small container of liquid, dampened the cotton swab, and began rubbing it in tiny circles along the top of the car door.

Allison eased closer, intrigued. "You're looking for skin cells?"

"Skin cells, maybe traces of sweat." She glanced up at Allison. "Anyone driving this little car probably rested an elbow on the door here. He may have worn gloves, but it was nearly a hundred degrees last Wednesday, and I'd be surprised if he was in long sleeves. If we're lucky, we'll get DNA."

"And it looks like this is our lucky day."

Allison and Mia both looked at Roland as he pulled the camera from his pocket and snapped a picture of the headrest.

"What is it?" Mia asked.

He traded the camera for tweezers. "A hair." He gently tugged it loose from a crease in the headrest, then lifted it up for them to see.

"About six centimeters, brown." He glanced at Allison. "Does your fingerprint tech have brown hair?"

"Black. He's Vietnamese." Allison's stomach tensed with excitement as she gazed at the strand.

Mia looked at Allison hopefully. "What about the shooter? What color was his hair?"

"He didn't have any," Allison said. "Head smooth as a cue ball."

"It wasn't random at all. I'd bet my badge on it," Jonah told Ric over the phone. He drove past yet another set of golden arches and felt a pang in his stomach. After fourteen hours of driving, he was tired, cranky, and running on fumes. "It was damn near surgical. Ankles, hands, wrists. He shot up windows and statues. He wasn't trying to kill students, he was trying to terrorize. I think the whole thing was staged."

"Who was the target, then? Or was he aiming for all three?"

Jonah stared ahead and concentrated on keeping to his lane. Only a few more miles to go, but he could hardly hold his head up. He'd driven almost eighteen hundred miles over the past two days and had a shitty night's sleep in a cheap motel in Columbus after wasting the remainder of yesterday looking for Himmel's ex-wife. She was MIA.

The phone was silent, and he remembered Ric had asked him a question. Shit. The target.

"I don't think it was Jodi Kincaid," Jonah said. "He didn't mean to kill her. It was a ricochet bullet. Confirmed it with Scott Black just the other day."

"So he didn't mean to kill the pregnant lady, but he had no problem killing a student and a professor. Good to know. The question is, why?"

"I'm still working on that." Jonah sailed past another exit, ignoring the fast-food signs. He planned to raid whatever was in his pantry before falling into bed. "Allison's helping me, too. She's pulling together victimology reports on all three. If we can get to motive, we can get to who else might be involved, if anyone."

"That's sounding more and more likely. By the way, Noonan finally broke down and sent the car up to Delphi."

"The VW?" Jonah couldn't believe the chief had sprung for the cost. But considering the media uproar, he probably thought covering his ass was a good use of funds.

"They found a hair in the headrest of the driver's seat," Ric informed him. "Mia's working on the DNA."

It took Jonah's fried brain an extra second to process the words. "Shit."

"That's what I was thinking."

Himmel's head had been shaved. Because he liked it that way? Because of chemotherapy? Jonah didn't know yet. But a hair recovered from the headrest of Himmel's car, assuming it wasn't his, would be the first physical evidence of a possible accomplice.

A pause on the other end. Even in Jonah's wiped-out state, he could tell there was something more on Ric's mind.

"Whatever it is, fucking spit it out. I'm too tired to play guessing games."

"This new info . . ." Ric paused, clearly uncomfortable with whatever it was he had to say. "It goes a long way toward proving this was a targeted murder. That conspiracy theory is looking more and more believable. You understand where this puts Sophie, don't you?"

"Right in the fucking middle of our fucking investigation."

"She's a critical witness," Ric said.

"She's our only witness."

"You hear what I'm saying, man?"

"Yeah."

"Whatever you got going with her——"

"I got it. Jesus."

"I'm pointing out the obvious, I know, but you sound pretty beat."

"I am."

"Get some sleep," Ric advised. "I'll catch up with you tomorrow."

Jonah tossed the phone onto the passenger seat as the

burning in his gut intensified. It wasn't just hunger. It was disappointment, too—the stinging kind. Because suddenly he knew he'd been counting on Sophie's story falling apart. Not just counting on it, hoping for it, desperately, because somehow in his sleep-deprived, food-deprived, sex-deprived state, he'd decided she was fair game. He wanted her. Issues or not, head case or not, he wanted her and he'd decided to go after her. He'd decided to quit thinking about right and wrong and finally give in to the lust that had been gnawing away at him for months now.

That plan had been obliterated.

Now Sophie wasn't just involved in this thing, she was a witness. And now she wasn't just *a* witness, she was *the* witness—the only one who mattered. If he cared anything about his job, she was off-limits.

The badge can get you tail, but tail can get your badge. The advice he'd heard during his first year on the job came back to him. He hadn't fully understood it then, but he understood it now. When it came to witnesses and confidential informants and especially crime victims, the badge inspired trust, sometimes even lust. And while that sounded good, it could mean a shitload of problems if a man wasn't careful.

His whole career, Jonah had never been anything *but* careful. Until he'd met Sophie.

Jonah finally reached his neighborhood and turned onto his street. He slowed as he neared his house, where a subcompact car was just pulling up from the opposite direction. The car had a glowing delivery sign on top.

Jonah pulled into his driveway, grabbed his duffel, and climbed out. The aroma of fresh pizza nearly knocked him over. He glanced at his house, where a TV was on in the living room. He glanced at his closed garage door and got a sneaking suspicion about what was behind it.

"This for you?" A skinny kid with about ten rings in his eyebrow came up to him.

"What is it?"

"Veggie Supreme."

Sighing, Jonah reached for his wallet. He handed the kid a couple twenties and waited for some change, all the while staring at his front door. Finally, it swung open, and Sophie stood there, perfectly silhouetted in the light from his living room. She wore a tank top and cutoffs, but it might as well have been a G-string, because backlit like that, she looked like every X-rated fantasy he'd ever had—in the flesh. Standing in his doorway, waiting to welcome him home from a business trip. It was a dream come true and a goddamn nightmare, all at the same time.

The kid made a strangled sound in his throat, and Jonah looked at him. His jaw had practically hit the sidewalk. Jonah jerked the change from his hand and scowled at him.

"Well, *hello*." Sophie tipped her head to the side and smiled as Jonah collected the pizza box from the dazed delivery boy. "I didn't expect you home so early."

He hiked up the steps to his door and glared down at her. She didn't even flinch.

"What are you doing here?"

She took the warm box from him and gave him a sultry smile. "It's a *really* long story. Come in and I'll tell you."

CHAPTER 14

Jonah seemed tense. Not just tense, he seemed . . . bitter about something. Sophie had hoped two days would have been enough time for him to work through his anger over her television appearance, but evidently not. Maybe he was one of those macho guys who didn't "work through" their emotions, but instead let them stew.

He looked good, though. Instead of his typical detective garb, he wore faded jeans, a gray T-shirt, and a two-day beard.

She carried the pizza into the kitchen and put it on the counter, then remembered the bread sticks and let out a gasp. She spun around and raced back out the door.

But the hatchback's taillights were already fading down the street.

She returned to the kitchen, where Jonah was leaning back against the counter, watching her coldly.

"Well, no bread sticks," she chirped. "But that's probably for the best, right? Who needs garlic breath?"

He folded his arms over his chest, clearly not amused by her attempt to lighten the mood.

"What's going on, Sophie?"

"Well." She walked over to the cabinet and got down several plates as she stalled for time. She'd had her speech all planned out, but she hadn't counted on quite this level of hostility. "Before you left, you told me to keep a low profile. And to stay out of trouble." She picked up a slice of pizza and tore a few strands of cheese before setting it on his plate. Then she smiled up at him. "I was having a hard time doing that at my apartment, so I decided to crash here."

She handed him a plate, and he put it on the counter without looking at it.

"How'd you get in?"

"Your Hide-a-Key."

He frowned.

"Magnetic box behind the gutter near the back door." She smiled. "I've always been a champ at finding them, but I would have expected a better hiding place from a cop."

Jonah shook his head and looked away.

She served herself a slice. "Don't you like pizza?"

"That's not pizza, that's salad."

"Extra veggies. Yum." She chomped into her slice and chewed, watching him. He practically radiated stress. Must have been a long drive.

Sophie put her food aside and fetched a Vitamin Water from the fridge. She offered him one, but he refused. Obviously, her beverage choices were lacking, too.

"Is the media camped out at your apartment?" he asked. "Is that what this is?"

She tipped her head to the side. "I'm not sure. Not last time I looked."

"And when was that?"

"Yesterday."

"You've been here since yesterday?"

He seemed angry, and she felt a tug of doubt. Maybe she'd picked the wrong tactic. She could have just called him up and asked his permission to stay here, but she'd been afraid he'd say no.

"I figured you wouldn't mind." She smiled up at him. "You *did* tell me to keep a low profile."

He looked away, shook his head again. On an impulse, she eased closer, but that seemed to ratchet up his tension another notch. The muscles in his jaw hardened.

"Why are you so upset?" she asked.

"Why are you lying to me?"

"I'm not."

"Okay, have it your way. But you can't stay here."

"How come?"

"Because you can't. End of story."

"But—"

"Call Mia if you need a place to crash."

She crossed her arms. "Ric's living there. And you're the one who told me he thinks I'm full of crap, so I don't exactly feel comfortable hanging out with them."

"Then go to a motel."

"Our motels are full of news people."

"Then call Mark."

"Who?"

"Mark Royers." He glared at her. "Your date from the other night. I'm sure he'd be glad to put you up."

"I hardly know Mark. We don't have that kind of relationship."

"Sophie, *we* don't have that kind of relationship."

"I'll be out by tomorrow. It's only for a night. What's the big deal?"

"It's my career, Sophie. *That's* the big deal. I'm a homicide detective. You're a witness. I can't just have you shacked up at my house."

"Why are you being so uptight? All I'm asking for is a place to stay. For one *night*!" She felt her cheeks flush as his rejection sank in. "God, just . . . forget it. I'll stay somewhere else." She stalked out of the kitchen, and he grabbed her arm. "Let *go* of me!"

"No."

"*No?*" She tried to shake off his grip, but it was like an iron cuff.

"Not until you give me an honest answer."

"What is that supposed to mean?"

"You think I'm buying this little act?" he demanded. "'Oh, hey, Jonah, didn't expect you home so early'? You're wearing a red lace bra, Sophie. And you didn't expect me?"

Fury bubbled up. "Screw you."

"Yeah, that's what I thought."

She hauled back to hit him, but he caught her hand. She tried with the other one, and he caught that, too. He scowled down at her, both of her hands clamped in his huge mitts, and frustration burned in her throat.

"Cut the bullshit, Sophie, and tell me what happened."

"Let *go* of me!" She jerked away from him, and this time he released her. She retreated to the corner between the stove and the sink, and tried to incinerate him with a look.

He just watched her.

"I got mugged, okay? And I'm terrified of my

apartment. And I'm terrified of everything. And so I came *here*. Are you happy now?" Her shrill words hung in the air, and she felt like a child.

Jonah stepped closer, his brow furrowed. "When did this happen?"

She looked down at her feet and tried to compose herself. "Yesterday."

"Are you hurt?"

He reached a hand to her face, but she backed away. She didn't want to be touched, and he seemed to get the message.

She took a deep breath. "I was doing laundry. I went down the street to get detergent—"

"At *night*?"

Her gaze snapped up. "Do you want to hear this or not?"

He tucked his hands in his pockets. "I want to hear it. All of it. Don't leave anything out."

And so she told him, glossing over the part where she was still talking on her cell phone when she walked out of the store. But he caught it, anyway—she could tell from the way his jaw tightened. When she reached the end, he was watching her, his face hard and unhappy.

He stayed like that for a long moment, and then he stepped forward. "Can I touch you now?"

She shrugged.

Gently, he took her face in his hands and seemed to be examining her for bruises. She stared at his chest as he checked her head. Her pulse picked up. She wanted to lean into him and wrap her arms around his waist and feel safe.

His thumb grazed over the goose egg just behind her hairline.

"Ouch." She pulled away.

"You could have a concussion. You should have let Allison take you to the ER."

"I'm fine." She cleared her throat. "But it freaked me out. Combined with everything else, I just—" She turned away. She looked at his clean, spare kitchen. At the fridge he kept stocked with beer and salsa. At the back door where he left his muddy work boots. Then she faced him again and looked at his hazel eyes, which were gazing down at her now with so much intensity, so much intelligence. "It seems connected somehow. Don't ask me why I think that, but I do. I can't explain it—it's just a hunch. And I feel safer here than I do anywhere else. Even when you're not here, I feel safer. Last night I got a better night's sleep than I have in months."

"Why the ambush, Sophie? You should have just called me."

"And you would have said, 'Sure thing, babe, come on over'?"

He didn't answer.

"I figured there might be some rules," she said, "or, I don't know, at least guidelines about us having a personal relationship because I'm involved in your case." She paused, trying to read his face. "I'm not reading this wrong, am I? I'm guessing there was some kind of break while you were in Georgia because you've been gone two full days. And you just said I'm a witness, so—"

"I can't discuss the investigation."

Which answered her question.

"Anyway, I figure your letting me stay here is kind of a favor," she continued, "and I've always had better luck asking for favors in person than over the phone."

He just looked at her. She noticed the bra strap peeking out and tugged at the neck of her T-shirt.

He didn't miss that, either. And then she felt ashamed of herself for assuming he was like every other man she'd ever known, for assuming if he helped her, he'd want something in return.

But then again, maybe he did. There was no mistaking the heat in his eyes, underneath all that genuine concern. She'd seen it before, and she knew exactly what it meant.

She crossed her arms and gazed up at him defiantly. "So that's it. That's why I'm here. Are you going to let me stay or not?"

Jonah looked at Sophie standing just inches away from him in his kitchen and knew that he was well and truly fucked. There was no way he could turn her out after what she'd told him. It simply wasn't happening. He didn't like her getting mugged, period, and he sure as hell didn't like it occurring at the same time as all this other stuff. Jonah didn't know what exactly was going on, but until he figured it out, he wanted her here with him, even though there was no way he could let himself touch her—especially not after calling bullshit on her little seduction scheme.

Did she think he was like that? Did she really think he'd expect sex just for giving her a place to stay for a few nights?

Evidently, she did. And while part of him knew he had way more self-discipline, way more *decency* than that, a whole other part of him was at this very moment picturing her on her back on his kitchen table, wearing nothing but that damn red bra.

Maybe *he* was the head case.

"You can stay here tonight," he said. "Then we'll figure something out."

"Thank you." She smiled, clearly relieved. "You won't even know I'm here."

That blatant falsehood was still hovering over them as Jonah's phone buzzed. He took it out and checked the number.

"This is work," he told her. "I probably have to go in."

"No biggie. I'll lock up after you."

The phone buzzed again.

"Macon." He listened for a few moments, while Sophie stood there, pretending not to eavesdrop. She'd painted her toenails, he noticed—cherry red.

"All right. I'm on my way." He hung up and looked at her. "Does anyone know you're here?"

"Beside you? Not a soul."

"Will you be okay here alone? I might be late, depending."

She nodded at the gun on the counter beside the cookie jar. "I've got LadySmith here to keep me company."

"Yeah, I saw that." He looked at the revolver, which usually resided in her purse. She didn't have a permit for it, but far be it from him to try to enforce the law with this girl. Anyway, lately he was glad she had it.

He scooped his keys off the bar and grabbed his leather jacket off the chair. "Lock up behind me," he said sternly. "And do me a favor when I get home and try not to shoot me."

Sean noticed the tail the second he pulled out of the police station parking lot. It was interesting for two reasons: One, it was so easy to spot, and two, the person behind the wheel of the blue Ford Focus was a woman.

Sean kept an eye on his rearview mirror as he culled through the list of women he'd met recently for anyone slightly stalker-ish. He came up empty. Whoever she was, he didn't particularly want to lead her home, though, so he reshuffled his plans for the night and pulled into the parking lot of El Patio.

Ten minutes later he was seated on a stool nursing a Budweiser when he spotted her in another mirror—this one behind the bar. She stepped through the door and glanced around apprehensively. Short dark hair, average height. She wore jeans, a black T-shirt, and sneakers. She definitely wasn't an ex. She wasn't even his type, but that didn't keep him from watching as she made her way across the room and tentatively approached the empty stool to his right.

He shifted his gaze to the baseball game and waited to see if she'd have a clever opening line.

"Is this seat taken?"

He turned to look at her. Pale skin, full lips, and a very nice rack that for some reason she'd decided not to show off. She looked at him expectantly.

"It's all yours. Do I know you from someplace?"

This seemed to catch her off guard, and she froze for a second before sliding onto the stool.

"Um, I don't think so. Why?"

"Could have sworn I saw you in my rearview mirror a few minutes back."

Her mouth dropped open, and the bartender picked that moment to wander over and ask for her drink order.

She glanced at Sean's bottle and ordered the same. He took a sip and waited.

"Sorry about that. I thought about calling you at work, but . . ." She let that puzzling admission trail off as she glanced around the bar. "Is it okay to talk here? I mean, you know, about something important?"

Sean turned to face her now, getting impatient with the games. "Who are you, exactly?"

"Marianne Parker." She held out her hand, and Sean waited a beat before shaking it. It felt cool and small, and his grip enveloped hers. She pulled away and tucked the hand in her lap just as her beer arrived.

"Sean Byrne," he said. "But I guess you already know that."

She didn't answer, and he watched her sip her beer.

"You from around here, Marianne?"

"Not really."

"And you're in town because . . . ?"

She shifted on her stool and seemed to decide something. She looked straight at him for the first time. "You're one of the homicide detectives working the Himmel case."

He raised an eyebrow.

"I saw your picture in the paper," she explained. "You were there at the crime scene?"

She was talking about a photo of him and a CSI crouched beside a pool of blood where the pregnant woman had gone down. He hadn't given the reporter his name that day, but the guy was local and he'd known it, anyway.

"What is it you wanted to tell me?" Sean watched her with interest. Obviously, she was nervous about something, and she sat there, turning her bottle on the bar as she decided how to answer his question.

"My sister is Gretchen Parker." She waited a beat. "Jim Himmel's ex-wife."

"Okay." He wasn't going to make this easy for her. Maybe it was mean, but he was enjoying watching her squirm. Payback for pulling this cloak-and-dagger crap when what she should have done was walk into the station and simply ask for a detective.

She cleared her throat. "I have some information— from my sister—that I think is important to the investigation."

"Why isn't your sister here, then?"

Last he'd heard, Gretchen Himmel was missing. She'd disappeared after the last round of interviews with Columbus PD.

"My sister has two young daughters." She fidgeted with her bottle. "She thought it would be better if she and the twins lay low for a while."

"All right." Sean watched her skeptically. Something about her story didn't ring true, but he wasn't sure what it was yet. "Tell me about your sister's information."

She cleared her throat. "Gretchen came into a large amount of money recently."

"How large?"

"A lot. It was given to her children. Put in two separate bank accounts under their names."

Sean watched her pick at the label on her bottle. He didn't like her evasiveness, and he *really* didn't like where this conversation was heading.

"Where'd the money come from?"

"Jim." She glanced up. "I'm almost sure of it."

"Last we checked, Jim was broke."

"He was." She paused. Bit her lip. "But I think he might have taken a job recently. As a hired assassin."

The alley behind Mario's Bar smelled like piss and vomit, and it didn't take Jonah long to identify the source.

"That the kid?" he asked the patrol officer who'd been called to the scene by the bar owner.

"Yep. Said he just stopped off to take a leak when he saw the leg sticking out."

Jonah glanced back at the green-faced kid sitting on the curb near the patrol unit, then sidestepped a puddle of fresh puke and made his way down the alley. Behind a pile of cardboard beer boxes, he saw a sneaker peeking out of a doorway.

He looked at the kid again. "He underage?"

"Nineteen. Fake ID. Probably accounts for at least some of why he's scared shitless right now."

Jonah glanced up and down the narrow passageway, which had already been roped off with yellow tape. The side of the alley belonging to the bar was red brick that had been tagged with layers of graffiti. The other side belonged to a music store that had been out of business for months.

"Barkeep know the victim?"

"Says he wasn't in tonight," the patrol officer reported. "Least he doesn't recognize him."

Jonah stepped closer to the victim, who was facedown on the pavement. He wore a cheap leather jacket and jeans, and his pockets had been turned inside out, indicating a possible robbery. No wallet in sight, no bulge in the back pocket. He'd been shot in the back, near the right kidney, and the pool of blood beneath the body had already coagulated.

Jonah looked at the jacket again. Only one reason to wear one in this heat. Whatever he'd been packing tonight was probably gone now, along with his wallet.

"What time did the kid call it in?" Jonah asked.

"Ten fifty-two. Called 911 first, then went inside and told the bartender."

Jonah checked his watch. It was 11:25. He kneeled beside the body and pulled a mini-Maglite from his back pocket so he could look at the face. Young Hispanic male. Gang tats. The kid looked familiar for some reason, but it was hard to tell for sure because of all the flies buzzing around the eyes, mouth, and nose. Maybe he'd been through the system before. Jonah aimed his flashlight at the second bullet wound—this one on the side of the neck. An army of ants, marching single file, had already gone to work.

Two or more gunshot wounds, at least one that was up close and personal, judging by the stippling. He probably knew his attacker if he let him get this close without pulling his gun.

Jonah glanced up at patrol officer. "No one heard the shots?"

"If they did, we haven't found 'em yet."

"We need to interview everyone in the bar, also the gas station on the corner. Everything else around here looks closed."

The cop sighed. He'd been about to come off a shift when the call came in, and he obviously wasn't looking forward to spending the better part of his night interviewing a bunch of barflies.

"Where's the manager?" Jonah looked at the ever-increasing crowd of spectators on the bright end of the alley, where it opened out to the street.

"Inside. None too happy about having a DOA behind his bar, believe me."

"Yeah, this guy doesn't look too happy about it, either."

"Hey, I'm just sayin'."

Jonah gazed down the alley. It led to a parking lot, but he doubted they'd find the victim's vehicle there, which would speed up an ID. That would be too easy, and nothing about tonight had been easy.

He rubbed his eyes tiredly. His argument with Sophie had woken him up some, but now he felt the weight of the past few days bearing down on him again.

"Shit, I recognize this guy."

Jonah glanced over. The patrol officer was crouched beside the body now, frowning.

"Who?"

"Roberto Consuelo. Saw his mug just today at roll call. We been looking to bring him in for questioning. Store clerk picked him out of a photo lineup."

Jonah got a bad feeling in his stomach. "What photo lineup?"

"Mugging yesterday night, other side of town. He pulled a knife on some girl, took off with her purse."

CHAPTER 15

Sophie opened her eyes and saw Jonah staring down at her.

"Morning," he said brusquely.

She sat up and glanced around the living room. Sunlight slanted through the blinds, making a pattern on the blanket she'd dragged from his closet. She stretched her arms over her head and looked at him. "Your hair's wet."

"Comes from showering." He rested a cup of coffee on the end table. "You could have had the bed, you know. I would have taken the couch."

He sounded peevish—as though maybe she'd offended his Southern manners—but she ignored him and reached for the coffee. It smelled like the super-robust blend she'd made yesterday. Jonah took his coffee seriously. Not a vegetable in the house, but he kept about a year's supply of java in the freezer.

"So." She brushed her hair out of her face. "Homicide case last night, I take it?"

"Yep."

"I didn't hear you come in."

"You were too busy snoring."

"I do not *snore*."

"How would you know?"

She sipped some more coffee as she noted his clean-shaven face, the sidearm and badge snug against his hip. He looked so *cop,* and her heart gave a little squeeze.

"How much sleep did you get?" she asked.

"Enough. You going to be around later? I might drop by." He went into the kitchen and snagged his keys off the counter.

"You mean at work?"

"Yeah. I may need to talk to you."

She kicked the quilt away and swung her legs off the sofa. "Talk to me now. What's up?"

"Nothing yet. I'll let you know. Stay alert today."

And with that, he walked out the door. She heard the key in the lock and then the grumble of his truck backing down the drive.

Sophie took her coffee into the house's only bathroom, which was still steamy from his shower. She turned on the water and tried to ignore the shaving cream scent lingering in the air. She conjured up a vision of him bare-chested, leaning over the sink shaving, and tried to ignore that, too.

A short while later, she was ready for work in a turquoise linen tank dress and peekaboo pumps. As she folded up the blanket she'd used, she heard another truck on the driveway, only this one was louder than Jonah's—maybe even diesel.

Sophie took her gun from her purse and stepped toward the kitchen just as a man stomped up the back steps. Confident gait, wide shoulders, strong jaw. He was the spitting image of Jonah, except for the white hair.

She tucked the revolver behind the cookie jar as the screen squeaked open. He tried the knob, then rapped on the glass.

"Jonah?"

She flipped the latch. "Hello," she said, swinging the door back.

He looked her up and down. He held a brown paper bag in his hands, and she glimpsed tomatoes inside.

"Jonah around?"

"He's at work." She stepped back to let him in. "Would you like some coffee?"

He hesitated a moment, then removed his John Deere cap and wiped his boots on the mat before stepping inside.

"You got a pot going, I could use a cup." He deposited his hat on the counter and rested the bag by the sink. "I'm Wyatt Macon, Jonah's dad."

"I'm Sophie Barrett. You like sugar?" She opened up a cabinet and took down a mug.

"Black, thanks."

She poured his coffee as he leaned back against the counter and watched her. He wore a blue chambray work shirt and jeans. His scarred leather boots reminded her of Jonah's, as did his build—except for the slight paunch hanging over his belt. She wondered if Jonah would have one someday.

She set the coffee on the table, and he took the invitation to sit down.

"You're from the panhandle?" she asked, joining him.

"Lubbock." He paused. "Been down here fifty years, though. Thought my accent wore off."

She smiled. "I've got an ear for voices."

They sipped coffee and regarded each other over their mugs. His hands were big, brown, and callused, and she noticed he didn't wear any rings. Was he widowed or divorced? She watched him sip his coffee and realized how little she knew about Jonah's personal life.

"So." She glanced at the paper bag on the counter. "You grow your own tomatoes?"

"Brandywines, mostly. Along with some Italian plums, a few cherries."

She got up and went to the sink, mainly because she wanted something to do with her hands. She'd never particularly liked being scrutinized by people's parents. She grabbed a dish towel from the counter and spread it out by the sink. Then she unpacked the tomatoes and started rinsing them.

"How long you two been livin' together?"

Sophie looked at him over her shoulder. "Well, let's see." She glanced at her watch. "I guess about nine hours. Would you like one of these?"

"No, thanks."

She got a plate down and took a steak knife from the block near the stove. She picked a fat gold tomato and cut it into thick slices. Then she sprinkled salt and pepper and returned to the table.

"It's not what it looks like," she said.

He made a *humph* noise.

"What?"

"If it's not what it looks like, my son's either blind or stupid, and I know he's not blind."

Sophie smiled as she cut a bite of tomato. It was sweet

and juicy and she closed her eyes to savor it. "These are amazing."

"Homegrown. Only way to eat 'em."

"Best tomato I ever had."

He smiled. "I'll tell Jonah's mama you said that. Those plants are her pride and joy."

She glanced at his hand again. "I hope you kept some for yourself," she said.

"More than I need."

The kitchen got quiet except for the rotating fan and the sound of mockingbirds through the screen door. He got up from his chair and took his cap from the counter. "I 'preciate the coffee, but I better get back. Macey'll be thinking I ran off."

He settled his cap on his head and nodded at her.

"Nice meeting you, Mr. Macon."

"Wyatt," he said. "And it was nice meeting *you*." The screen squeaked as he pushed it open. "Take care now, Sophie. And don't be leaving that LadySmith on the counter when strangers come calling. You're liable to get in some trouble."

Roland entered the conference room and sank into the seat Allison had occupied when she'd been in here interviewing Sophie.

"Looks like you won't be buying me that beer," he said.

"No DNA on the gum?"

"No, there was. But according to Mia, it belonged to the gunman."

"What about the hair?"

"I analyzed the hell out of it, but I can't tell you whose it is." He held out a one-page report and Allison took it, sighing.

"What *can* you tell me?" she asked. "Is it animal or human? Can we get a race or gender?"

"Human *is* animal." He smiled slightly. "But I know what you mean, and yeah, it's human. I can also tell you the hair is not dyed, it's light brown, and it belongs to someone of European descent. It's impossible to determine the age or sex."

Allison scanned the report, which contained a lot of specialized vocabulary and acronyms.

"Your main problem is you've got no comparison sample. If you had one, I could say with near certainty that the contributor of the sample did or didn't leave that hair in the car. You guys have any suspects yet?"

"No," she said, deflated. She'd thought the hair was a good lead.

The door opened, and Mia stepped into the room. "Sorry I'm late." She didn't take a chair, and Allison could tell she was in a hurry. She could also tell she wasn't going to like Mia's news.

"No DNA?" Allison asked.

"Not nuclear DNA, no. This hair appears to have been shed naturally, so we didn't get any follicular cells." She passed her a slip of paper from the clipboard she was carrying, and Allison added it to her ever-growing stack of unhelpful reports. "Mitochondrial DNA can be useful *if* we have a known sample to compare it to."

"Mitochondrial?"

"It's more plentiful than nuclear DNA," Mia explained. "It can be found in nonliving tissue like hair and bone, which are extremely durable. So it's good for identifying remains. But to run a profile through the database of known offenders and get a cold hit—which is what you were hoping to do—I'm afraid it doesn't work that way. You need nuclear DNA."

"Tell her about the door," Roland said.

"What about it?" Allison pinned a hopeful gaze on Mia.

"I *did* recover some skin cells from the door, where someone rested his arm."

"You're kidding."

"Locard's Principle," Roland said. "Every contact leaves a trace. That's why Mia and I have a job."

Allison looked at Mia. " 'His' arm?"

"Got that Y chromosome." Mia smiled. "Very handy, isn't it? We're still running the profile, though. I'll let you know if we get lucky. I *can* tell you the profile doesn't match that of the gunman, James Himmel. We have his DNA sample from the autopsy." She looked at her watch. "Speaking of, have you seen Jonah? I thought he was riding out with you."

"Haven't seen him today. Why?"

"He's supposed to bring me another sample—some murder victim who was autopsied this afternoon."

"The gangbanger behind the bar?" Allison was surprised. "They're sending his DNA *here*?"

"Jonah wanted me to run it."

Allison stared at her, baffled. What did the guy in the alley have to do with this? And why was she being kept in the dark?

She tried not to let her annoyance show as she got to her feet and collected the paperwork.

"Thanks for the help," she said crisply. "Let me know if you get any hits."

"You'll be my first call. I don't like being cut out of the loop, either." Mia gave her a pointed look, and Allison remembered the woman lived with a cop. "Hey, and if you see Jonah, tell him I'm looking for him."

Jonah shot down the narrow highway, juggling his phone and the stack of Polaroids he'd snapped with the ME's camera.

"A phone call would have been nice," Allison said, continuing her rant. "I don't know how you expect me to contribute here if I'm constantly playing catch-up with the facts. Why is Roberto Consuelo getting the VIP treatment today?"

"I think he might have a link to the university shooting."

"He's a junior-grade gangbanger. I'm not seeing the connection."

"Sophie Barrett's the connection," Jonah said. "I think the guy who attacked her the other night could have been the one driving Himmel's car."

"Interesting theory. I would have liked a heads-up, though. I could have pitched in here."

"Fine. Next autopsy's all you." He found several photos of the forearms and tucked them in his jacket pocket, along with a face shot. Sophie said she hadn't seen him from the front, but maybe a picture would jog her memory. Or maybe she'd seen him around earlier. The guy could have been stalking her.

"You know, this isn't just a pissing contest." Allison was still at it.

"No?"

"It's about communication. And let me catch *you* up on a few facts. According to Delphi, the *light* brown hair recovered from Himmel's Volkswagen is of European descent. Consuelo is Mexican."

Jonah thought about that as he wended his way through the rolling hills. The late-afternoon sun cast long shadows on the hillsides, reminding him that it was closing in on five and he hadn't put anything in his system today besides coffee.

"Well?"

"Well what?"

"Mia's wasting her time. The guy in the VW isn't Consuelo."

"She's not wasting her time. Whether this links back to the Volkswagen or not, he's got tribal tattoos and a fresh gash on his arm, and I want to confirm whether he's responsible for Sophie's attack."

"And just how do you propose to do that? I was on the scene that night, Jonah. She didn't see his face. All you've got is a seventy-two-year-old eyewitness who was busy firing his shotgun into the air as this kid took off with a coin purse."

"We've also got blood on the sidewalk."

A pause. "You read my report."

"Of course I did."

Another pause, and Jonah could almost hear her mental wheels turning on the other end of the phone. Allison was smart, but it didn't take a brain surgeon to figure out that his interest in Sophie went beyond the normal cop interest in a case. If he wasn't careful, she'd also figure out he'd asked Mia to run the latest DNA test as a personal favor. Reynolds never would have approved ordering up a DNA test for something as minor as a mugging.

"You really think Consuelo is connected to Himmel?"

"I don't like the timing," Jonah said. "Maybe Sophie was targeted by Consuelo because she witnessed an accomplice."

"But why would he do that?"

"Why do people do most things? Probably someone paid him."

"And now he's dead. At the hands of that same someone?"

Jonah didn't say anything. He took another bend in the road and glanced at his watch.

"Jonah?"

"I'll let you know what I find out," he said. "I'm on my way out to Delphi to drop off this sample and run these autopsy pictures by Sophie."

"Well, you're going to be disappointed. I just left the lab. Mia's expecting you, but Sophie's already gone."

"Where the hell are you?"

She paused, absorbing the hostility.

"I'm in my car. Why?"

"Why aren't you at Delphi?" Jonah demanded. "I told you I'd come by today."

"And I told *you* I had an appointment to meet with a leasing agent after work."

"You didn't tell me that."

"I left you a message at your office."

He grumbled something, and Sophie figured he fell

into that annoying subset of people who never checked their voice mail, except on their cell phone.

"So, what's up?" she asked now. "Where are you and why are you ticked off?"

"I'm on my way to the lab. I need to show you something."

She heard the urgency in his voice, and her stomach tightened. "What is it?"

"That homicide I caught last night—I just attended the autopsy. Victim's Roberto Consuelo. I'm ninety percent sure he's the guy who attacked you in front of your building. I've got some photos to show you."

"All right." She tried to sound calm, but her pulse was racing. "You might be better off talking to the store manager. He's the one who—"

"Ric already talked to him. Got a tentative ID."

Sophie eased her foot off the gas as she rounded a bend. This was a curvy road, and she needed to concentrate, not let her imagination run wild with hypotheticals.

"Sophie?"

"I'm here. I just . . . Do you know who killed him?"

"We don't know who, but what. Two rounds, point-blank range. We haven't run the ballistics yet, but we could get lucky and get a match. I've got a couple of slugs here for Scott Black to look at."

"How long will that be? Don't ballistics tests usually take a while?"

"Depends. Where are you, exactly? We need to connect—the sooner, the better."

"Well, I could cancel my appointment." A truck appeared in her rearview mirror. It was moving fast, and she drifted over so it could pass. "I'm supposed to see an apartment at five-thirty and—"

"Cancel it. This is important."

"Yeah, and here I thought finding a safe place to live was important." She glanced in the mirror as the pickup loomed closer. "Jerk," she muttered.

"What?"

"Not you." She put on her turn indicator and eased toward the shoulder. The truck sped up. Her stomach tightened as she watched it close the gap.

"Sophie?"

He was right up on her bumper now, close enough for her to see the Dodge emblem and the mud spatter on the black hood. Her foot hovered over the brake. She didn't want to get rear-ended, but as he inched even closer, she realized that that was exactly his intention.

"Oh my God."

"What is it? *Sophie?*"

Her phone clattered to the floor as she gripped the wheel with both hands. He lurched closer. She instinctively hit the gas, even as her brain screamed for her to *slow down*.

She tore her gaze from the mirror and looked ahead, saw the black S on the yellow sign. Fear snaked down her spine. She was going much too fast.

The bend was upon her. She swerved, taking it wide. The tires skidded, and for an instant she had a bird's-eye view of her Tahoe as it careened across the yellow line. She hung on through the turn, praying that she wouldn't hit the oncoming car that was sure to be just around the corner.

"Please, please, please . . ."

To her right, an empty lane and a tree-dotted hillside. To the left, a steep drop-off. She clenched the wheel. She prayed. The curve finally eased, and she fought her way back into the right-hand lane.

Another glance in the mirror. Her heart seized. He was there again, black as death, as she hurtled into the next turn.

He's going to hit me.

She accepted the fact calmly as she pressed the brake in a last-ditch effort to keep control. But it was too late. She had too much speed. The tires squealed. The guardrail seemed to suck at her as she crossed the yellow line once more. She gripped the wheel, struggling for her lane, fighting for the hillside instead of the cliff.

Another sickening skid. A metallic crunch. She held her breath as the tires left the road.

Everything slowed, like a film in slow motion. She sailed through air and it felt like water, thick and blue around her. Her stomach dropped and her gaze fell on her hands, tight on the steering wheel. She registered the veins protruding beneath the white skin as she hung on for her life, for that fleeting, fragile life that was about to get ripped away from her. And she saw a thousand separate details leaping up at her, vying for her attention in the last endless moment: the flash of sun in the mirror, the green trees rushing past, Jonah's voice, calling her name from some unreachable place.

She knew he would find her. He'd be first on the scene, like he'd been once before, and he'd see her mangled, lifeless body, and she knew that it would cut him to the bone—the kind of cut that never really healed—because he saw himself as her protector. She realized that now in this tumbling, too-slow moment when her life stood stark and insignificant before her and she was flying headlong into death after too many wasted hours and days doing nothing much that mattered. She'd cheated death before, and now it was her turn.

She felt the relentless pull of gravity, yanking the front of her car down, dragging her straight back to earth and into the wall of trees. And she suddenly *rejected* death, with every fiber of her being, because even if it *was* her turn, she was a survivor, and she was going to fight until her very last heartbeat.

The wall of trees rushed up. The windshield *popped*. The entire world reached out and smacked her in the face.

Jonah raced through the curves and switchbacks, searching for the Tahoe. His heart thundered. His hands were slick on the steering wheel as he replayed the last few seconds over and over.

There had been a scream and then a high, excruciating shriek of metal just before a silence that froze him to the core.

And then he saw them, there on the highway. Two black parallel skid marks crossing over the yellow line.

"Fuck!"

He stomped on the brake and slammed to a jaw-rattling stop on the narrow shoulder. He jammed the gearshift into park and leaped from the truck, his heart pounding in his chest like a herd of cattle.

He followed the marks and spotted the twisted guardrail he'd missed just seconds earlier. It had been shorn from all but one of its posts and flung over the hillside like a piece of trash.

Jonah sprinted for the gaping hole in the foliage and caught himself on a tree branch as his feet slid out from under him. He landed hard and rode the next twenty feet on his ass before connecting with a boulder jutting out from the steep hillside. He glanced around frantically.

About forty feet below him, the roof of the Tahoe.

"Sophie!"

He jumped to his feet and crashed through the brush, catching himself on limbs and branches to keep from taking a header into the bowl of plants and trees where she'd landed. He felt sick. His stomach churned with dread as he half-slid, half-ran down the hillside. Was she conscious? Had she crawled out somehow? The one door he could see from this angle—the passenger's side—was shut. But the window was broken.

"Sophie!" The hoarse call echoed through the hills as he neared the wreckage. The cop part of his brain cataloged the scene while the rest of his brain shut down. The Tahoe had landed on top of an oak tree, splitting it in two. He noted the splintered limbs, the shards of glass, like ice crystals, blanketing the ground. The SUV perched on the splayed tree, its silver hubcaps still spinning like pinwheels in the open air.

And then it exploded.

CHAPTER 16

The blast knocked her off her feet. A bolt of pain zinged up her tailbone. She watched, awestruck, as a ball of fire billowed up from the wreck and reached high into the sky before sinking down again and dissipating into a cloud of smoke. Heat licked her cheeks. She flipped onto her stomach and cupped her hands over her head as chunks of debris rained down.

Seconds ticked by. She tasted dirt. She smelled smoke and dust, felt it tickling in her throat as she waited for the next wave of terror. Her pulse raced at some impossible speed, but it told her she was alive, and for now that was enough. Her ears rang. She pushed herself up. The earth seemed to shake under her hands and knees, but then she understood it was *her* shaking, from the top of her head to the soles of her very bare feet.

My shoes are gone. And that inane thought was followed by a more practical one: *Someone's trying to kill me.*

Sophie's heart skittered. That panicked inner voice she'd heard just moments ago—the one that had ordered her to break free from the tentacles of her seat belt and her air bag, the one that had ordered her to shimmy through that shattered window and brave the eight-foot drop from the tree like it was nothing—that voice was back again, louder than ever. And this time it was telling her to spit out the dirt and get to her feet and get a *move on*. Now. Before someone realized she'd made it out of that wreck alive.

Her ears continued to buzz as she grabbed for the nearest object—a sapling—and hauled herself to her feet. She wiped her dusty palms on her even dustier dress. She took a wobbly step for the cover of the bushes. Her legs felt stiff and rubbery all at the same time. Smoke stung her eyes. She couldn't hear. Her mind was jumbled, crowded. She had room for only one thought at a time, and at that instant, it was that her arm burned. She clutched it against her chest and used her other arm to push through the branches. And then a new thought took hold.

She needed to hide.

Jonah reached the fiery wreckage and glanced around, desperate.

"*Sophie!*"

She'd gotten out. He had to believe that. He clutched her shoe in his hand—her clean, intact shoe—and tried to believe it meant something good. It meant there was hope.

Beyond the crackle and hiss of flames, he heard the sirens of the coming cavalry. He hadn't called them. His phone was in his truck, sixty feet above him at the top of the ridge. Someone must have seen the smoke and called for help.

A rustle in the bushes. He dropped the shoe and plunged in after it.

"*Sophie?*" He swept aside vines and branches and searched for any sign of her. Movement. A flash of blue just beyond the green. He plowed through another layer, and she was there, right in front of him, staring up at him with wide gray eyes.

His heart flipped over in his chest.

She was bleeding. Filthy. Disoriented. But she was alive. She was on her feet, too, but that didn't last long as her legs crumpled, and he caught her just before she hit the ground. She reached out to touch him, as if he were an apparition.

"Jonah. I don't . . ." She didn't complete the sentence, just clutched the front of his shirt.

"It's okay. I got you. You're okay now."

She looked up at him, glassy-eyed. He touched her face, her shoulders, her neck, looking for any sign of injury. The most obvious—she was in shock. He'd seen it in Afghanistan. She had the look of a soldier whose bunker had just been hammered with a few too many mortar shells.

She held her arm against her chest, and he touched it gently.

"Are you hurt? Show me."

Tremors shook her, head to toe, but she held her arm out to him. It was streaked with blood, and he saw the chunk of glass embedded in her wrist.

"From the window." She stared down at her arm as if it belonged to someone else.

"You climbed out the window?"

She nodded.

"And then what, you jumped?"

She nodded again.

He laughed—a mix of relief and *you've got to be fucking kidding me*—as he looked into her face. He brushed the hair from her eyes. "That was a good call." He nodded. "Damn thing fireballed, but I guess you saw that."

Her gaze drifted over his shoulder. She was still in shock. *He* was in shock. He couldn't believe he was crouched here in front of her when just minutes ago he'd thought she was dead.

He'd thought she was dead.

He glanced over his shoulder at the plume of smoke above the trees. The sirens were louder now, and stationary. At any moment a crew would start combing the bushes, searching for survivors.

"Jonah."

He turned back to give her his full attention.

"We'll get your arm fixed, I promise." He kissed her forehead.

She sagged against him, and he shifted on his haunches to keep them both from tipping over. *He'd thought she was dead.* He held her tightly and watched the smoke drift up into the blue.

It smelled like a hospital, which made sense because it *was* a hospital. But for the past two hours, the thought kept popping into her brain each time a gurney rolled by or she got a fresh whiff of that antiseptic-scented air.

It wasn't crowded—not like last time—but Sophie was stuck in hospital purgatory as people in scrubs and lab coats bustled back and forth, ignoring her.

At last, a wispy-thin nurse in pink scrubs stepped up to her table.

"Here we are." She handed Sophie a small white tube, then picked up the nearby clipboard and jotted something down. "That's for your cuts. The script for the codeine is on its way, soon as Dr. Broomfield can get over here."

Sophie hadn't seen Dr. Broomfield since the first fifteen minutes, when he shone a light in her eyes and asked her what day it was. His bedside manner had been pretty abrupt, but he'd promised her something to help the pain in her tailbone, so she hadn't totally written him off.

"And after that I can go?"

The woman smiled. "Fine with me, if you can clear it with the authorities."

Sophie cast an impatient look at the patrol officer leaning against the reception desk, shooting the breeze with the nurses. He'd been there ever since Jonah and Ric had gone to "check on something" at the police station.

The two double doors swung open and—as if conjured up by her thoughts—Ric Santos strode in. To her disappointment, he was alone. He stopped to say something to the patrol officer before making a beeline for her exam room, which consisted of a padded table and a flimsy curtain that had been pulled back.

"Sophie," he said.

"Ric," she replied. Small talk was not Ric's strong suit.

"DPS is still on scene," he stated.

"Okay." She wasn't sure what that meant. The highway patrol was still investigating? Clearing the wreckage away? And then she realized she didn't give a flip.

"Where's Jonah?"

"At the station. Said he'd be here soon as he could get free."

Sophie glanced at the reception desk, where the cop was hanging out. He was still on babysitting detail, or Ric would have dismissed him.

Which meant Jonah was going to be awhile.

The doors opened again, and this time it was Allison. She was wearing another version of the jeans-shirt-blazer ensemble Sophie had seen twice before. She carried a large brown sack with the top folded over, and Sophie wondered what was in it. Detectives were constantly showing up at the lab with bags like that, and some of them contained some pretty nasty stuff.

Allison deposited the bag on the counter and joined their little powwow. "You hanging in?" she asked, looking concerned.

"I'm okay."

She reached into the blazer and pulled out an envelope. "Went by your apartment, got the manager to let me in. Your spare credit card was in the desk like you said."

"Thank you." Sophie took the envelope and stared down at it. Her purse, her phone, her gun—all of her most important possessions had been lost, and now she was down to one spare credit card with a thousand-dollar limit.

Enough to cover her ER co-pay, at least.

She turned back to Ric. "You were saying? What happened to my car?"

"They're still working the accident scene," Ric said.

"*Accident?* My Tahoe exploded, in case you didn't notice. How can that be called an accident?"

Allison shot Ric a look.

"It probably wasn't," he said.

"Probably." Sophie crossed her arms. "Where's Jonah? I want some straight answers."

"We have some questions first," Allison said. "Did you notice anyone lurking near your car in the last twenty-four hours? Maybe when you stopped at the store, say, or parked at the gym?"

"I didn't do either of those things in the last twenty-four hours."

"We ran the surveillance tapes for the parking lot at Delphi," Allison said. "If someone tampered with your vehicle during the past three days, they didn't do it there."

Sophie looked from Allison to Ric. "You think someone put a bomb in my car?"

Allison flicked a wary glance over her shoulder, probably worried about potential eavesdroppers. She looked at Sophie. "At this point, we can't confirm—"

"Jonah thinks it was a bomb," Ric said, cutting her off.

Sophie's blood chilled. Ric gave her a long, steady look, as if gauging her reaction.

"You have any threats recently?" he asked. "Phone calls or letters we should know about?"

"I haven't had any threats, no. I mean, I was *mugged*." She looked at Allison. "You could probably count that."

"We're looking into that," Allison said, and Sophie's blood turned colder.

It hadn't been a mugging, then. The man with the knife had meant to kill her and probably would have if someone hadn't chased him off with a shotgun.

"So, you're saying someone wanted to . . . to hurt me?" *To kill me,* she was thinking, but she couldn't seem to say the words.

Their two carefully blank expressions answered her question.

"*O-kay,*" she said. "Good to know. And now someone runs me off the road and tries to blow me up. Terrific."

"The explosive is just a theory at this point," Allison said. "We're still investigating."

Sophie looked at her. "Give me a little credit here. I work at a forensic lab, all right? I'm perfectly aware that cars don't just crash into trees and fireball, except in the movies."

"Investigators are working on it," Ric said. "But until we know more, it's being classified as a traffic accident."

She gaped at him. "Are you freaking kidding me? The son of a bitch *ran* me off the road! He was in a black Dodge pickup. It's all in the statement I gave to no fewer than *three* people at the scene. How is that an accident?" A few heads had turned, and Sophie lowered her voice. "I'm not making this up," she snapped. "I don't want media attention, or police attention, or whatever the hell you're thinking."

"No one's thinking that," Ric said. "At least not anymore. It's pretty clear you're being targeted by someone, maybe because you've come forward as a witness in the sniper attack. There's more going on there than we first thought, and someone wants to cover it up."

She stared at him, feeling a wave of relief. He'd just admitted he believed her. Right in front of Allison, too. It was almost like an apology for his earlier skepticism, and he probably had no idea how much it meant to her.

It had really bothered her that someone she considered a friend had doubted her credibility.

"So." She cleared her throat. "That's good, then. That you all believe me. Does that mean I can get some sort of witness protection now? Until you find the accomplice?"

Allison sent Ric a look.

"What?"

"It's not that simple," she said.

"The Federal Witness Protection Program is for federal witnesses," Ric said. "This isn't a federal case."

"Okay. What about local protection?"

"We're not equipped for that," Ric said.

"It sucks, but it's true," Allison added. "Our department is stretched to the last penny. A twenty-four-hour security detail just isn't in the cards—not with everything else we're juggling."

Sophie sat there, trying to digest that. She'd been shot at, mugged, and car-bombed, and they were telling her there was nothing they could do about it because of *budgets*? The sheer mundanity of the reason was almost funny. Almost. If she hadn't been so utterly panicked.

Ric turned to Allison and made a motion with his head.

"Think I'll go hit the vending machine," she said, taking the dismissal in stride.

When she was gone, Ric looked Sophie squarely in the eye.

"Jonah's sure it was a bomb, but right now there's no proof. He thinks the device—whatever it was—was planted last night while you were asleep."

Sophie's stomach clenched. They both knew where she'd spent the night.

"He's beating himself up over this."

She swallowed.

"He's working on your situation, but it's complicated. There's no budget, anywhere, and it's not just a matter of money. It's a matter of manpower. This thing has all of us slammed with work."

"Okay. So, what are you getting at?"

"Jonah's looking at alternatives. His dad has a deer lease about two hours from here. It would get you out of the thick of things."

"You mean out of the way."

He didn't say anything.

"If Jonah's slammed, how is he supposed to look after me at some deer lease?"

"He wouldn't be doing it."

"Who would?"

"I don't know yet. Maybe his dad."

Sophie's mind reeled. This was getting too, too weird. Someone had planted a bomb in her car, probably while it was parked *in Jonah's garage*. He hadn't even wanted her at his house to begin with—she'd practically had to beg him. And now he was having to turn his life upside down to find someone to look after her 24/7 while he had his hands full trying to solve a multiple murder case.

Someone had been to his *house*.

Sophie pictured his white-haired father coming by with his tomatoes, and she felt sick.

Allison reappeared with a soft drink in hand. She caught Ric's eye and tapped her watch.

"We need to get going," Ric told Sophie. "Jonah will be by as soon as he can. He'll give you a ride to wherever you're headed next."

If Allison noticed his evasiveness, she didn't let on. "That bag's for you," she said. "A couple things from your place."

Sophie muttered a thanks and watched the two of them disappear back through the beige double doors.

"Here we are!" The nurse breezed up with a brown prescription bottle and a slip of paper. "I got you started with a few doses. And a script for the rest, *if* you decide you need it."

Sophie took the bottle gratefully. She'd definitely be needing it. Her tailbone felt like it had been smacked with a baseball bat.

When the nurse was gone, she opened the paper bag and peered inside. Jeans and a T-shirt. Allison had also included a pair of sandals and some toiletries from Sophie's bathroom cabinet. Tucked in with everything was a king-size Almond Joy, which she must have picked up somewhere else. Tears sprang into her eyes at the tiny gesture of friendship.

Sophie dropped the meds into the bag. She slid off the examining table and took a few wobbly steps. There was a telephone on the wall, and she made two important phone calls, both to people she knew from work. Then she went looking for the nearest bath-room. Her spine was on fire. Her dress was in tat-ters. Her limbs were scraped and bandaged, and she smelled like Betadine. She changed into the fresh clothes and stuffed her formerly stylish Calvin Klein dress into the trash can.

A few minutes later, she walked as briskly as she could manage past the nurses' station.

"Um . . . ma'am?"

She halted with her hand on the door and turned. "Yes?"

The patrol officer stepped over. "You're not leaving, are you?"

Ah, uncertainty. This guy was toast. "Actually, yes." She flashed a smile. "It's been a rough day, and a nice hot bubble bath is calling my name."

He seemed at a loss for words. "I just . . . I thought you were supposed to wait for Detective Macon."

Another smile. "He knows where to find me." She pushed the door.

"I'm sorry, ma'am?" He caught the door, showing an irritating bit of gumption. "I was told you needed to wait for Detective Macon." An apologetic smile. "He's going to escort you home."

"Thanks, but I've got a ride."

"You do?"

"Yes, and Detective Macon has my number." She pushed through the door, and he followed her into the waiting room.

"Ma'am, *wait*."

Sophie stopped and sighed heavily. "Is there a problem"—she glanced at his name tag—"Officer Woods?"

"No. Yes." Woods was flustered. "I can't let you leave."

Her eyes widened. "*Let* me leave? Am I under arrest?"

"No, just—Detective Macon said—"

"Have Detective Macon call me."

"But—"

"Good night." She gave him a wave over her shoulder as she walked out the door.

• • •

Jonah spotted the canine unit just as he was leaving the police station to go get Sophie. The SUV's door popped open, and the handler climbed out while the German shepherd remained seated obediently in the front passenger seat.

"What'd you get out there?" Jonah asked.

"Still nothing."

"How is that possible?"

"Wish I could tell you. Hawkeye didn't alert on anything."

Jonah glanced at the dog. "He usually pretty good?"

"The best. All I can tell you is we'll try again tomorrow. I'm trying to get my hands on one of those electronic sniffers, see if we can come up with something he missed." He glanced at the building. "Hey, is Allison still there?"

"Don't know. Why?"

"She was asking all about the dogs. Thought I'd see if she wanted to grab a coffee or something."

Allison didn't date cops. Jonah wasn't sure she even dated men, but this guy could find out for himself.

"Try the break room. Someone just brought in a pizza."

Jonah's phone buzzed, and he pulled it out. He didn't recognize the number.

"And keep me posted," Jonah said.

"I'll call you when I get out there tomorrow. Should be pretty early."

Jonah's phone buzzed again, and he answered it as he headed for his truck.

"Macon."

"Glad I caught you." It was Sophie.

"Sit tight. I'm on my way over."

"There's been a slight change of plan."

He stopped beside his truck. "What's that?"

"I'm going out of town."

What?

"You know, it's been a *really* crappy week for me, considering everything. I could use a vacation."

Jonah stood there, stunned. And then his blood turned icy.

"Are you alone?"

For a second, she didn't answer.

"Sophie? Cough if someone's with you."

"You're wondering if I'm being held at gunpoint or something? The answer is no, I'm fine."

Fine?

"A little sore, but I've got some pills for that. And some R and R should help, too. Just what the doctor ordered."

"Sophie—" He tried to tamp down his frustration because the last time he'd seen her, she'd been pretty shell-shocked. "Someone's trying to hurt you. You need protection. You cannot just go on *vacation*—"

"Wanna bet?"

"Where the hell are you going?"

"That's the beauty of it. I don't know yet. Which means nobody else knows, either."

Jonah clenched his hand in a fist and worked on not pounding his truck. He reminded himself that she was terrified. The bravado was her response to being scared.

"Sophie." He took a deep breath. "Honey, where are you?"

"Why?"

"I'm coming to get you. I've got something lined up."

"What, you mean the deer lease?" The hint of revulsion in her voice ticked him off. "I appreciate the thought, but I'm going to have to veto that. No offense, but it sounds kind of like a pain in the ass. For you, your father, pretty much everyone. This way works better."

"Sophie . . ." He was practically choking on his anger now. "Don't be stupid! You can't just take off!"

"I'll check in tomorrow. Keep your phone on, okay? Gotta go."

"Goddamn it, Sophie, listen to me!"

But she'd already hung up.

CHAPTER 17

Sophie awoke with a sunbeam in her eyes. She turned her head away and was immediately zapped by a bolt of pain. It shot up her spine and pinged around before settling at the base of her skull, which was already throbbing from the noise outside.

Seagulls.

Slowly, carefully, Sophie turned onto her back and lay there, squinting at the window.

She'd forgotten to draw the curtains. She'd arrived late and exhausted and hadn't thought of anything except popping a blue pill and collapsing into bed. She lay there now on the lumpy mattress, listening to the gulls and making a mental list of all her aches and pains. Tailbone was at the top. Next was her wrist, which felt strangely hot underneath the bandage. She'd had four stitches in the ER last night, and she hoped they hadn't become infected. She also had a scraped elbow and two skinned knees, as well as that full-body soreness that came from doing an intense physical activity you hadn't done in a long time—such as moving boxes or waterskiing.

Or being smacked by an air bag and taking an eight-foot jump from a wrecked car.

Sophie sat up slowly and looked around the room. Daylight didn't help the decor. The blue bedspread was faded to almost gray, and the once-white walls were streaked with water marks. In a nod to the resort's sand-and-surf theme, someone had put a sea-shell border up around the ceiling, but it was peeling off at the corners.

Sophie didn't care. They'd had a vacancy and they'd taken her cash without questions. She'd used her credit card in San Marcos last night to get a cash advance that would buy her a few days of quiet anonymity. She just hoped the investigation made progress before her funds ran out.

Sophie rolled her sore shoulders and winced at the pain. She needed a long, hot shower. She walked gingerly into the cramped bathroom and stood briefly under a lukewarm trickle. At the rate she was paying, she couldn't really complain.

Wrapped in a micro-towel, she rummaged through her Walmart shopping bag and lined her purchases up on the dresser. She'd bought some clothes, toiletry items, and most important, a disposable phone. Her sleek little flip phone was probably a charred cinder somewhere. But she wouldn't have kept it anyway because someone could use the GPS on it to pinpoint her whereabouts.

One of the many tidbits she'd learned while working at a PI's office.

Sophie's new phone didn't have a clock, and neither did her room, but judging from the brilliant shade of blue outside her window, it was late morning. Perfect time for a swim, if she hadn't been nearly faint with hunger. First stop would have to be a restaurant.

She donned the bikini she'd purchased without even trying it on. It was turquoise with white polka dots, and it fit fine. What wasn't so fine was the line of purple bruises across her abdomen in the shape of a seat belt. So much for the beach babe look. She slipped into some jean shorts and grabbed her only piece of luggage—a faux leather tote bag. She dropped her keys and phone inside it, alongside her cash, and headed out the door.

It was almost like a hangover—the achy, woozy sensation she felt as she stepped into the sunshine. No cotton mouth, but a definite throbbing behind her eyes. She had a sharp craving for food and an even sharper one for coffee, and she set out on a quest for both.

Mustang Island was a lazy beach retreat populated by retirees, surf bums, and fishermen. It was the perfect refuge for people wanting to get away for a few days or drop out of sight for a while. Sophie had visited once before and knew it was ideally suited to her current purposes. The coastal island was small and rustic, and the village had enough transient young people to keep her from standing out.

She glanced up and down the street. The Island Breeze Motel was located four blocks off the shore, and Sophie thought she remembered a taco stand nearby. She decided to go on foot, leaving her borrowed transportation in the motel lot.

Sophie looked at the pickup. It belonged to Scott Black, who had responded to her SOS call last night and collected her at the hospital. Scott had been more than happy to lend her his truck, because, first, she needed it, and second, he also owned a Harley, which he sometimes took to work at the Delphi Center. The third reason was a bit more complicated. Scott was pretty attached to his truck, so Sophie knew this particular favor came with some as-yet-unspecified strings attached. But she'd deal with that later. She'd promised to return it in a few days with a full tank of gas, and *that* promise was definitely one she could keep.

She headed for the beach, keeping her eyes peeled for a thatched-roof hut with a picnic table out front. She found it without trouble and treated herself to a veggie breakfast taco and a grande coffee. Then she bought a refill. The woman who gave it to her kept eyeing her bruises, so Sophie took the refill to go and strolled down the street until she found a surf shop. She bought a blue-and-green sarong and tied it around herself so she could wander the streets without attracting stares. After thoroughly exploring the village, she decided to hit the beach. She slathered on sunblock, spread out her wearable beach blanket, and sat down facing the waves.

The surf was up today. Teenagers trudged up and down the shore with boards tucked under their arms. Children frolicked in the water. A snow-cone truck rolled by playing a reggae tune that told her not to worry, be happy. The lyrics mingled with the sound of the waves long after the truck had gone, and Sophie tried to heed the advice. But of course, that wasn't possible.

A child squealed. She turned to look at the rainbow umbrella nearby where a family had set up camp for the day. The mother lay on a beach towel reading a magazine while the father and daughter worked together on a sand castle.

Sophie watched the girl. She had long blond pigtails and reminded her of Becca Kincaid. Only Becca would never spend a day at the beach with her mother, ever again.

Sophie's chest hurt, and it wasn't from the bruises. She dialed a number she knew by heart and waited through five rings.

"Good afternoon. The Delphi Center. How can I direct your call?"

Young. East Texas. Sophie refrained from correcting her grammar.

"Extension five-thirty-nine, please."

"One moment," the temp said pleasantly.

Silence. Sophie counted sandpipers until finally the call went through.

"Botany."

Sophie hung up. She dialed again.

"Good afternoon. The Delphi Center. How can I direct your call?"

"Hi again. I'd like extension five-three-nine, please. I think that was five-three-six."

"Oh, sorry! Just . . . hang on a minute, please. There's another call coming in."

More silence. A few clicks. Another series of rings.

"Osteology."

"Hi, Kels."

"Sophie? Oh my God, where are you?"

"I'm out of town, actually. How's it going there?"

"Well . . . *I'm* fine. But what about you? I heard you were in a major wreck!"

"I'm okay, more or less. Thought I'd take a few days' vacation, though."

The other end went quiet, probably as Kelsey's bullshit meter clicked on.

"Hey, I need a favor," Sophie said. "Could you get a message to someone for me?"

"Let me guess. An SMPD homicide detective?"

Sophie's heart skipped. "How did you know?"

"Hmm, maybe because he was banging on my door at ten o'clock last night?"

"He went to your *house*?"

"He most certainly did."

"What did he want?"

"You mean besides you?"

"I mean, did he ask you a lot of questions or was he just, like, checking in to see if I was there?"

"He wasn't in detective mode, if that's what you mean. More like angry boyfriend." She paused. "And when did *that* happen, by the way? I thought you were in a dry spell."

Sophie examined her toes, which were covered in sand. She was definitely in a dry spell. Sahara-dry. She could hardly remember the last time she'd had real sex, and yet she'd never felt so abuzz with sexual energy. She blamed the red bra. All that buildup and no payoff. Come to think of it, the entire six months since she'd met Jonah had been that way.

"Sophie?"

She sighed. "Still dry as a bone. But I'm involved in Jonah's investigation, so he's just being thorough."

"Uh-huh. So, what's this message?"

Sophie cleared her throat. "If you could just tell him that I'm doing fine. I'm recouping from my injuries and getting plenty of rest, and I'll check in again over the weekend."

"I shouldn't tell him you're at the beach, I take it?"

"How'd you know that?"

"I can hear the waves. Don't worry, I'll relay your little message verbatim."

"Verbatim. Don't tell him anything else."

Jonah was a good detective. All he'd need was one little detail, and her plans would be screwed.

"Don't worry," Kelsey said. "I can pull that need-to-know crap with the best of them. Take care, all right?"

Sophie said good-bye and stared down at the phone. She would have liked to call Mia, too. And maybe even her brother. It seemed ridiculous when she'd been on vacation less than one day, but she was feeling lonely.

She distracted herself by people watching and taking a dip in the Gulf of Mexico. The salt water stung her cuts, but she knew it was good for them, too. And the surf churning against her skin made her feel rejuvenated. The beach was therapeutic for her—always had been. She'd come here after her attack last winter. She'd arrived feeling numb and robotic and stayed until she felt human again.

Sophie stared out at the distant horizon where blue met blue. Being near the vast expanse of water made her feel small and made her problems feel diminished, too. That was part of why she'd come—not just to get away from the dangers surrounding her, but to get some perspective on everything. The water did that for her.

After swimming, she stretched out on the beach and

thought about taking a nap, but her skin was getting pink. It was late afternoon. She wrapped her sarong around herself and wended her way back to the motel, making note of any suspicious-looking cars cruising through town.

She took a long route but didn't see anything worrisome. No black Dodge pickups, no one following her on foot. She spotted the same gray sedan twice in two blocks, but then it turned left at a stoplight and headed for the ferry docks. Sophie spent some time window shopping, and the red-white-and-blue bunting in some of the windows reminded her that it was a holiday weekend.

Sophie's stomach growled, and she checked her watch. Maybe instead of napping, she'd shower and grab a sandwich. She passed a hand-painted sign advertising dolphin-watching cruises. Or she could sign up for one of those. She loved boats, and she couldn't recall the last time she'd seen a sunset over the water. Sophie reached her motel and noted the glowing o VACANCY sign. She'd probably lucked out getting a room here, even a shabby one.

She dug her key card from her purse and slid it into the door. The light flashed green. She glanced in the window to her room and noticed the reflection.

A gray sedan pulling into the parking lot.

Sophie's heart jumped. She turned around and watched, paralyzed, as the sedan slid into a nearby space. An enormous man climbed out. He looked at her over the roof of the car before slamming the door and stalking straight toward her.

Sophie's throat went dry. She couldn't breathe. Jonah stopped in front of her and nodded at the key card in her now-quivering hand.

"You going to let me in, or you want to do this outside?"

CHAPTER 18

Do what?

The question stuck in her throat as she stared up at him. The set jaw, the tight mouth, the angry gleam in his eyes—all told her exactly what he wanted to do. He was spoiling for a fight.

He pulled the card from her hand and shoved it in the slot, then pushed open the door.

Sophie's gaze darted to Scott's pickup, just footsteps away. The keys were tucked inside the tote slung over her shoulder.

"Not an option."

She glanced up at him, and he shifted his massive body to block her view of the truck.

Sophie tossed her head and sauntered into the room, as if it were her choice instead of his.

"What are you doing here?" She dropped her bag on the dresser. "I told you I needed a vacation."

The door whisked shut behind her, and she turned to face him. He stood there, arms crossed, looking a lot like he had the other night at the gym, when he'd been waiting for her in the parking lot. Those hazel eyes were hot on her again, but it wasn't just anger this time, it was something else, too. Something that made her stomach flutter and her heart start to pound.

The room felt stuffy, too small. She went over to the window unit and flipped on the air conditioner, and it coughed and rattled before working its way to a steady hum.

When she turned around, Jonah was still watching her with that gleam in his eyes. He hadn't moved to touch her, and she felt a prickle of doubt. Was she reading him wrong? Had pure anger brought him here? With possibly some wounded pride mixed in? Maybe his cop buddies were ribbing him because he'd misplaced a witness.

"I'm not going back with you," she said calmly.

He didn't respond.

"You can't force me."

He lifted an eyebrow but still didn't move.

Her gaze went to the Glock tucked at his side. No badge or handcuffs that she could see, but still he commanded plenty of authority. She crossed her arms, mirroring his stance, except she didn't have quite the alpha effect in a sarong and flip-flops.

He took a few steps deeper into the room and glanced around. "Nice place you got here."

"I'm not going back with you," she repeated.

He surveyed the room some more, and his gaze came to rest on the top of her sarong. His attention lingered there for a moment, and then he looked at her face again.

"You know what pisses me off?"

She just looked at him.

"Being knee-deep in a murder investigation and having to drop everything to play your little game."

"This isn't a game."

"You wanted me to chase after you? Fine. I'm here, Sophie. But I'm not going back alone."

"You can't *make* me go with you."

He looked at her for a long moment. Then he stepped closer and gazed down at her with that intensity that made her heart thrum. Her insides tightened. There were just a few inches between them, and the space seemed charged with electricity.

He bent his head down, and his breath was warm against her temple. "Take it off."

She pulled back and looked up at him. *"What?"*

"That scarf thing." His voice was low and rough. "Take it off."

Her blood heated at the words. "You want me to—"

"Yes."

Her arms dropped to her sides. She felt ridiculously self-conscious. She had on a bathing suit, for heaven's sake, but this seemed like a striptease.

Which was the point. He wanted *her* to do it. It was a power thing.

She could have told him to go to hell. She could have walked out. She could have pretended she didn't want him here and his showing up hadn't sent her stupid, hopeful heart into a tizzy.

He watched her steadily, waiting for her to decide.

She reached up and tugged the knot. The fabric came loose and puddled on the floor at her feet. She held the last fringed corner in her hand, then let it go.

Jonah's gaze traveled over her, taking in the scrapes

and the bandage, before settling on her string of bruises. They were darker today, almost black. He didn't move, didn't flinch, but she saw his eyes go flat.

His gaze met hers, still cool. Then it moved back to her body and she felt even more self-conscious. She worked hard to stay in shape, and she liked the way she looked. But standing before him in only a few wisps of fabric, with his face so cold and emotionless, she wanted the sarong back.

He eased closer and rested his finger just above her hipbone. He traced a path along her bruise, and she held her breath as his finger trailed over her breast and stopped at her collarbone.

"Does it hurt?"

She shrugged. Her throat was too dry for words. Her pulse was racing, and she wondered if her nerves showed on her face.

His hand dropped away and his gaze moved over her again, but with none of the warm approval she'd expected when she'd imagined being alone in a bedroom with him for the first time. She *knew* he was attracted to her. She'd seen it, felt it. Where had that gone?

She mustered her courage and reached behind her back. She untied the string. A smolder came into his eyes as she reached for her neck and untied the string there, too. With a quiet *swish,* her top landed on the toes of his boots.

Her skin burned under his gaze. She went on tiptoes and kissed him, and for a moment, he didn't move. But then she pressed into him. She licked her tongue along the seam of his mouth, and when he pulled her against him and kissed her deeply, she felt the thrill of it down to her core. He tasted so good, so *male,* and his powerful arms came around her and made her feel protected, like she always felt with him. His big hands closed firmly over her butt, and she started to feel intoxicated.

She wanted to touch him, desperately. She tugged at his T-shirt, and he stopped what he was doing long enough to yank it over his head and fling it away. She clamped her hands over his pecs and slid them down, dragging her thumbs over that trail of hair that led beneath his jeans. She stopped at the belt buckle, but he brushed her hands aside so he could loosen his holster and get rid of the gun. He laid it beside her purse.

"Come here," he said, reaching for her again and leaning back against the dresser. He braced his legs apart and fit her snugly against him, so the ridge in his jeans was lined up with the one scrap of clothing she had left. Delight zinged through her as he cupped her breasts in his hands and dipped his head down to kiss them.

"You smell like coconuts," he murmured.

"I've been at the beach."

His mouth closed over her nipple and she bit back a yelp and tipped her head back. He licked her and kissed her and teased her while she combed her fingers through his hair. The stubble on his face scratched her skin, but his hands were careful—she could tell he was worried about her bruises. She pressed against him and tried to let him know she was up for whatever he could dish out. She wanted a real match up, no holds barred. She loved the strength of him, the feel of him, the intent way he was kissing and touching her. When his arms tightened around her, she let out a whimper.

He started to pull away, but she caught him. "No,

it's good." She nipped his earlobe. "You don't have to be gentle."

His eyes sparked and he took her mouth again in a fierce, hot kiss that went on and on until every cell in her body was *alive* and dying to be touched by him. She couldn't get enough of him as she ran her hands up and down his back, loving the muscles there and the deep indention along his spine, the smooth hardness of his skin. She rolled her hips against his, and got a low moan in response.

Suddenly she was up off her feet. He carried her the few steps to the bed and deposited her in the center of the low mattress. The springs creaked loudly and he glanced around.

"This place is a dump, Sophie." He slid his knee between hers and leaned over her, bracing his weight on his arms.

"It's affordable."

He smiled down at her. Then his gaze slid to her bruises, and the smile faded.

"I don't want to hurt you," he said, and the serious look on his face made tears spring into her eyes.

"I won't break, I promise." She smiled and tried to lighten the moment. This was supposed to be *fun*. And even though she did feel a little fragile, it wasn't because of her bruises—it was the emotions he'd stirred up by showing up here out of the blue. She reached out and cupped his cheek. "Really, I'm good. More than good."

He seemed to take her at her word, and the next kiss was a long, relentless assault on all her senses. He kissed her until the only thing she felt, the only thing she could think of, was the all-consuming *need* to have him. She wrapped her legs around him, and as his jeans rasped against her skin, she realized he was still wearing most of his clothes.

As if reading her mind, he stood up to pull his boots off and tug the wallet from his pocket. He tossed it on the nightstand and climbed back on the bed with her. She hooked a leg around him and pulled him to her, and the bed creaked even louder this time.

The look of exasperation on his face made her giggle.

"I swear, if this collapses under us . . ." He didn't finish the thought, but instead pinned her wrists beside her head and dipped his head down to nuzzle her breasts.

She squirmed under him, but he wouldn't let her wrists go, and she decided she liked that. She rolled her hips against him, over and over, showing him the rhythm she wanted, and then he finally released her and watched her hotly as he slid the rest of her bikini off and tossed it on the floor. Her eyes drifted shut as he touched her and she let herself get lost in the warm magic of his hands.

He found her mouth again, and she wound her legs around him and kissed him with all the pent-up heat and need that had been building inside her for months. God, she'd wanted this. *This* man. *This* feeling. This burning, insatiable hunger that made her dizzy and giddy and weepy all at the same time.

He braced himself on one arm and gazed down at her as he opened his jeans. He reached over her, for his wallet.

"You don't need that," she said.

For a split second, he hesitated. But then he shifted

over her. She closed her eyes and arched her hips up to meet him as he pushed in.

She gasped at the force of it. Her body clenched, and her nerves exploded with the white-hot, searing pleasure of being joined. For a moment, he didn't move. And then he pulled back and did it again, harder, and she clung to his shoulders as he set a powerful rhythm that made her nerves sing. She couldn't think. She couldn't talk. All she could do was wrap herself around him and hang on. The springs moaned. The air heated. Their bodies grew slick with sweat as they went on and on and on until she thought she would combust.

"Sophie . . ." His voice was raw, tight.

"Yes."

His shoulders tensed under her hands. She arched against him, and in a flashing, glorious moment, she flew over the edge. As she was gliding back to earth, he made a last, violent thrust and shuddered against her.

With a mighty groan, he rolled onto his back, leaving her cold and very naked beside him. The springs were still echoing as she opened her eyes and blinked up at the ceiling.

She lay there a few moments, dazed and winded. Then she rolled onto her side and propped up on an elbow.

His eyes were shut. Sweat beaded at his temples. His chest rose and fell as if he'd just run a marathon.

"What was that?" she asked.

He opened one eye and looked at her. "You coming, I hope."

She smiled. "I meant afterward. The roll-over thing."

He closed his eyes. "I didn't want to crush you."

She'd wanted him to crush her. There was something about him that made her crave the solid, heavy weight of him. She'd been yearning for it for months.

They'd just have to do it again. She liked the idea, even though it had taken a few too many near-death experiences to get them here.

His eyes were still closed, and she took advantage of the chance to look over his naked body. He scored a very big ten. She liked everything about him, from his size-fourteen feet to his work-roughened hands, which could be so gentle. And then there was all the other good stuff in between.

He opened his eyes and frowned at her. "Are you checking me out?"

"Yep."

He sighed.

"What?" She slapped his arm. "You check me out all the time."

"Come here." He slid his arm under her shoulders and scooped her into him. She nestled her cheek against his chest and heard his heart still thrumming from exertion.

"I'm still pissed at you," he muttered.

She slid her thigh over his. "And I'm still not going back."

Sean watched her walk up the sidewalk with her arms full of groceries. He should help her with those. He would, too, but for the moment he wanted to observe her unguarded. He wanted to see who she really was.

The short hair was recent, he confirmed. Probably

the color, too. The back of her neck was paler than her face, and he wondered why he hadn't noticed it last time. Instead of the unisex clothes from the other night, she had on a tank top and a long, flowing skirt. It was more the Earth Mother look, but it suited her.

He pushed off from the tree he'd been leaning on and stepped into her path.

"Hello, Gretchen."

She froze. Her eyes widened. She darted her gaze around, and he could see her deciding whether to bolt.

He stepped forward and took her grocery bags. "Run, if you want. It'll just take longer."

"Longer for what?"

"For me to talk to you. You've got some explaining to do."

She flicked a glance over his shoulder, to the door of her sister's patio home. Sean waited patiently, holding her bags.

"Is it only you?" she asked.

"Who else would it be?"

"I don't know. Another detective?"

"It's just me." He never would have asked one of his busy coworkers to join him on this little road trip. Not based on a hunch.

She squared her shoulders and seemed to decide something. "This way."

He followed her up the sidewalk, watching her skirt swish around her ankles. She took a set of keys from her oversized leather bag and opened the condo.

Two cats darted out to greet her. They rubbed up against Sean's legs, and he tried not to trip as he ferried the groceries inside and set them on the counter. The air smelled like cat and old marijuana. The living room was dark, except for a lamp glowing on an end table.

Another light went on in the kitchen, and Gretchen busied herself putting away groceries.

"Do you want anything?" she asked.

"No."

He wandered over to a bookcase and surveyed a row of framed photographs. Gretchen and her kids. Gretchen and her sister and her kids. Gretchen's kids with her sister. Apparently, these women were close.

"I'm not going to tell you where they are," she said, joining him in the living room.

He looked at her across the dimly lit space. She rested her arm on the counter casually, but he could tell she was nervous.

"I'm not going to ask you."

Relief flashed in her eyes.

"Are you worried about them?" he asked.

The look on her face answered the question. He turned back to the photographs.

"They're five?"

"Six." She cleared her throat. "They just had a birthday. Jim sent a gift and that's how I knew. About the money. He'd included a letter with the account numbers."

"I'm going to need to see that letter."

"I burned it."

Sean gritted his teeth. He wanted to lecture her, but then he looked at her face more closely. The color had gone out of her cheeks and her eyes were wide. She was terrified.

Of his being here? Or of something else?

"Are you worried someone will go after your children?"

She stood there for a moment, just looking at him. Then she rounded the sofa and sank down on it. "Fifty thousand dollars is a lot of money. Whoever paid it might decide they want it back."

"Maybe. On the other hand, they agreed to pay it, and he sure as hell earned it."

Her gaze snapped up.

"He killed three people, and at least one was probably his target. And then he offered himself up as a scapegoat for someone else's plot."

She clasped her hands in her lap. "He was dying, anyway. I didn't know until after, but—" She shook her head. "It's all so crazy. The whole thing. How could he do it? I keep thinking, I don't know, maybe he felt like he was doing something good for the girls. Maybe making amends."

Sean stared at her. Had she even read about the victims?

She glanced up. "Don't look at me like that. *I* don't think it was good. I don't care how much money he left them. But you didn't know Jim." She twisted her hands in her lap. "He had this weird . . . disconnect. It was like regular thinking didn't apply to him. He had a cold streak."

Sean knew all about Himmel's cold streak.

He stepped over to the sofa but didn't sit down. "Our task force has been investigating him. I've seen the police reports."

"You're probably wondering why I married him in the first place. But he wasn't always like that. It wasn't till later. After his first tour. He came home different than when he left."

Sean watched her but didn't say anything. He needed her to open up.

"What is it you came to ask me?" she asked. "San Marcos to Houston's a pretty long hike. It must be important."

He sat down in a nearby armchair as she watched him uneasily.

"Who recruited him for this job?"

"I told you last time, I don't know." She looked away. "All I know about is the money."

Sean waited for her gaze to return to his.

"What?" she asked.

"I don't believe you."

She leaned back, defensive now. "I hadn't spoken to Jim in more than a year. I told you this! I told the army this. And Columbus PD."

Sean kept staring at her.

"What?"

"You're a smart woman, Gretchen. You're intuitive, too."

She scoffed. "How would you know? You don't know anything about me."

"You're wrong about that. I know you have a degree in fine art. I know you'd rather be working for that gallery still, instead of cleaning bedpans at that nursing home. I know you care about your daughters and you knew your husband had a drinking problem and you knew to get your kids away from him before he dislocated *their* shoulders."

Her gaze flashed to his. That part hadn't been in the

police report, but Sean knew it anyway because he was thorough.

The defensiveness seemed to seep out of her. She rested her elbows on her knees and cradled her head in her hands.

"I don't know why he did this to us. The girls will have to live with this always." She looked up, tormented now. "It's one thing to have a father who's a mean drunk. It's another to have one who's a murderer. They're never going to get past this."

He waited for her to calm down. She looked at her hands and took a deep breath.

"You were his wife. You knew things. You still know things."

She didn't look up.

"Who was it, Gretchen? You're not the only one who might be in danger here. Anyone who knows there was a conspiracy is at risk."

She squinted her eyes shut and rubbed her forehead. "I don't have a name for you."

"What do you have?" His pulse quickened, because he could tell she had something.

"There was this guy." She heaved a sigh. "A couple years back. I don't know his name. Jim never said."

"An army guy? Who?"

"I'm not sure. Maybe." She glanced up guiltily. She should have told him this last time. "I'm fairly sure he and Jim went back pretty far, but that's just a guess. I got the feeling this man had done more, though, career-wise. Based on the way Jim talked about him, I figured he was Special Operations. 'Shadow Warriors,' Jim called them."

Jonah had researched Jim's career. He'd wanted to be a Ranger but hadn't made the cut. Not because of his shooting ability, but because he wasn't a team player.

Gretchen shook her head. "Anyway, after Jim got discharged, the guy showed up one weekend."

Sean leaned forward. "You met him?"

"I didn't, no. But Jim went out for beers with him." She rolled her eyes. "Or at least that's what he said. For all I know, they were picking up hookers or something. Anyway, I think this man wanted to recruit him into some kind of private security company."

"What was it called?"

"I don't know. I don't know anything about it. But I know my husband, all right? He was an adrenaline junkie. He worshipped all that covert operations stuff. When this guy contacted him, I could tell he was thinking about a change. He started talking about 'contracting out,' whatever that meant."

"What happened?"

"Well, that was about the same time he got drunk and yanked my arm out of the socket." Her tone was brittle now. "I moved out with the girls the next weekend, while he was off on one of his binges. Stopped asking about his career plans at that point."

The rest was pretty well documented. She'd filed for a restraining order, then filed for a divorce. And as she'd said, over and over, she hadn't seen him since then.

She was looking down now, at her hands. Her shoulders were slumped forward.

"I'm scared of these people," she said quietly. "If I had a name, I'd give it to you."

Sean believed her. He wasn't sure why, but he did. He'd gotten everything he was going to get tonight, and now it was time to go. He stood up, and she looked at him with somber brown eyes as he took a business card out of his pocket.

"My number's on the back. Home, cell, everything."

She stood up and turned the card over.

"If you think of anything else, call me."

She nodded.

"I also want you to call me if you feel threatened. If something feels off. If you feel like someone's following you, or watching you, or if you're worried about your kids." He paused to let it sink in. He didn't discount her fear. These people *were* dangerous. And they'd already killed a student, not to mention a pregnant woman and a grandfather. Why not a mom and kids?

"Are they somewhere safe?"

She nodded again.

"Good. I'll call you when we get this resolved. Until then, be careful."

"But . . . when will that be?"

"I don't know." He moved for the door. "I hope soon."

"Jonah?"

"Hmm?"

A naked breast pressed against his side. "Are you hungry?"

He opened his eyes and gazed at the woman lying next to him in the dark. The neon light from the parking lot seeped through the shade, giving her skin and everything else in the room a pale red hue.

"Like, for food?"

"Yes." She popped up onto her knees and sat back, looking at him.

Jonah's brain and his body kicked into gear. He slid his hand up her thigh. "I could eat."

"I'm serious."

He tugged her down on top of him and nibbled her neck. "Me, too."

She sat back again, scooting out of reach. "Jonah, I'm famished. When was the last time you ate?"

He sighed and took an inventory of his body. He felt worn out. He chalked it up to a combination of too much driving, not near enough sleep, and some of the most athletic sex he'd had in his life.

Come to think of it, he was starving.

Sophie hopped off the bed, and he watched her stumble around in the dark, picking up stuff off the floor.

"Let's go get dinner. It's probably not too late yet."

Jonah grabbed his jeans off the floor and dug his cell phone out. It was 9:25. And he'd missed two calls.

"Fuck," he muttered. He was pretty much AWOL right now. He'd left Reynolds a vague "following up on a lead" message today, which had bothered him some on the way down here. He usually showed more professionalism than that.

He glanced over at Sophie, who was shimmying her body into a pair of jeans. She grabbed a bra off the dresser and he watched, transfixed, as she scooped her breasts into it.

Jonah decided he didn't give a rat's ass about Reynolds right now because this was where he needed to be. And— despite Sophie's earlier protests—he fully intended to be back on the job tomorrow morning, with Sophie tucked safely away nearby.

He heaved himself out of the sorry excuse for a bed and got dressed.

"There's this *great* shrimp place," Sophie said. "I think they're open until ten. Let's hurry."

He grabbed his gun off the dresser and slid it into the back of his jeans, then left his shirt untucked over it.

He picked up his keys. "My car or Scott's?"

She froze.

"How did you . . . ? Forget it. We can walk."

Damn right they'd walk. He wasn't taking her out to dinner in some other man's truck. He'd said that just to needle her.

Jonah tugged her aside and stepped out of the room first, to check things out. He was reasonably sure they were safe down here. He doubted she'd been followed, and he knew for a fact that he hadn't.

"One block off the beach and three blocks that way," she said.

He fell into step beside her, taking in their surroundings. It was hot and humid. The air smelled briny, with a hint of car exhaust from the traffic cruising up and down the main drag. It was early still for a Friday night. Tourists filled the sidewalks, licking ice-cream cones and stopping to window-shop, just like Sophie had been doing when he'd spotted her earlier that afternoon.

His gut tightened with anger. He'd worked some of it off in bed with her, but a lot of it was still there. He couldn't believe she'd taken off like that. He couldn't believe she'd run away from him. He'd known she was scared, but he'd also thought she trusted him.

She shot him a sideways glance. "You realize what this is, don't you?"

"What's that?"

"It's a coping mechanism."

"What is?"

"Your coming all the way down here to have sex with me. It's your response to trauma." She caught his hand in hers and squeezed it. "You're hardwired for it: Near-death experience, must nail someone."

He scowled. "Are you trying to piss me off?"

"I'm just making an observation."

"It ever occur to you that I hauled my ass all the way down here to protect you?"

"Hmm." She seemed to consider it. "So, the jumping in bed part was just, what? A diversion?"

It was way more than a diversion. It was a release of more than six months' worth of stockpiled lust, and frustration, and—

He realized what she was doing. She was downplaying everything so no one would have to admit it mattered—including her.

She looked at him. "Well?"

"Well, I just figured out *your* coping mechanism."

Her gaze narrowed and he could see her replaying the conversation, looking for what she'd revealed. It was like a game with her, this male-female banter she was so good at. And she always wanted the upper hand.

"Whatever." She shrugged, a little too casually. "And I appreciate the thought, but I didn't actually *need* you to come here to take care of me."

He snorted.

"Did you forget I used to work for a private investigator?" she asked. "This is a woman who basically ran her own witness protection program. She made a living helping people in trouble disappear."

The smell of fried seafood told Jonah they were nearing their destination, and he glanced around. He spotted it on the next corner.

Sophie was looking at him as if expecting him to say something.

"So, that's what this is?" he asked. "You're trying to disappear? I thought you were here for some R and R."

"I am, but you underestimate the planning that went into this."

"Is that right?"

"That's right."

She squeezed around a trio of teenage girls who were giggling and looked like they'd had too much to drink. She halted in front of a weathered wooden building: Tony's Shrimp Shack. It was a walk-up place, with a cluster of umbrella tables out front where people were eating food out of cardboard baskets.

"Let's eat on the beach," Sophie said.

He slid his arm around her waist. "I watched you get dressed," he murmured in her ear.

"Yeah?"

"And I happen to know what you're not wearing under these jeans." He tucked a finger in the waistband. "Let's eat back in the room."

"Tempting." She smiled. "But I'd hate to spill crumbs and create an attraction for the local rodent population."

A few minutes later, they were sitting on a sand dune, facing the moonlit surf. Sophie had kicked off her sandals and arranged their food baskets side by side.

She chomped into her po'boy and made a moan of pleasure. She was right about the food, and it didn't take him long to make a pretty good dent.

"You were saying?" He finished off his fries. "About all the planning you put into this trip during your two-hour ER visit?"

Sophie took a sip of the beer she'd smuggled out here in Styrofoam cups. He'd told her she was wasting her time—any cop on this beach could spot a disguised beverage a mile away—but the woman had a stubborn streak.

"What I was *saying*," she told him now, "is that I know how to cover my tracks. I know how to stay off the radar. And I know I'm much safer here than I would be at my apartment, or your house, or some deer lease, because I'm next to invisible." She popped a fry into her mouth.

"If you're so invisible, how'd I find you?"

"You knew something about me that I never told anyone else."

Now, that surprised him.

"You never told anyone you like to come down here?"

"I don't." She looked down and fidgeted with her cup. "I only came here that one time, last winter."

He frowned at her, not sure he believed her. "You didn't tell anyone besides me?"

"I needed to be alone." She glanced up, and there was that sadness again. It was only a flicker, but he hated seeing it. "I kind of went to pieces, I guess you'd say. And then I pulled it together and got back to my life."

"Just like that, huh?"

She looked at him.

Maybe he shouldn't press the point, but he happened to know that was bullshit. It hadn't been "just like that."

"So, why'd you tell me?" he asked.

"You were worried about me. I could tell." She shrugged. "I wanted you to know I was taking care of myself. And I also knew you'd leave me alone and not crowd me. You're good at leaving me alone."

She was dead wrong. He wasn't good at leaving her alone. He was amazingly *not* good at it. He'd tried to do it for months, and he'd blown it, and now he doubted he'd be able to leave her alone for a very long time.

She glanced up at him. "How'd you know about Scott's truck?"

"I've seen it before, in the lot at Delphi. When I saw it here, I ran the plate."

"And what's with the sedan?"

"It's a rental," he said. "Didn't want you spotting me before I got a chance to spot you."

Sophie didn't look at him, and Jonah knew that if she *had* spotted him first, she would have made a run for it.

"He lend you a pistol, too?"

She looked up, startled.

"He's a weapons guy. I know he at least offered."

She glanced at her tote bag, and Jonah dragged it across the sand. He poked through it and saw the Beretta.

"Is it loaded?"

"Yes."

Jonah looked out at the waves and tried to lose the jealousy. Was she involved with the guy? First Mark, now Scott. She seemed to be pretty friendly with the men at her job, and the knowledge didn't sit well with him. He wasn't sure why he cared. It wasn't as if he was looking for a big relationship or anything. At least he hadn't been. He wasn't sure what he wanted now, but he knew the thought of her with someone else made him crazy.

Sophie dusted the sand off her knees, and he looked at her bare arms. He could still taste her skin. He could still feel the squeeze of her thighs. He wanted her all over again, right here on this beach.

And she knew what she did to him, because she leaned against him and rested her hand on his knee. She looked at him with that slow burn in her eyes.

"We done eating?" he asked.

She nodded.

They walked back to the motel, not touching or even talking. She seemed moody now. He wasn't the greatest at reading women, but he could tell she had something on her mind.

Maybe it was the promise he'd made her—that he didn't intend to go back without her. Or maybe she was having second thoughts about sleeping with him.

When they got back to the room it was cool and dark, the A/C still rattling away in the corner. Jonah tossed the key card on the dresser and pulled her against him. He tucked his hands inside the back of her jeans and felt the warm skin he'd been craving for an hour.

"You're not a diversion," he said.

"I'm not?" Her hands slid up, over his chest, to link behind his neck. "And here I thought I was pretty diverting." She settled her breasts against him, and he knew she was doing it again—making it all about sex— but at the moment he didn't care, because all he could think about was taking her to bed.

"I'm still hungry," she whispered.

Jonah laid his Glock on the dresser. And then he pulled her down with him onto the squeaky bed.

"It's Sharpe."

Silence. "Is this a secure line?"

"What do you think?"

"You said yesterday. I wanted a status report yesterday."

The man dropped the cigarette on the asphalt and let it smolder. He glanced at the fireworks stand across the street. Twenty Thunder Snaps for a dollar. It was a business model he hadn't figured out. They operated only a few days a year and practically gave the shit away.

"What the hell's going on? You said you'd be finished."

"I will be." He ground the cigarette with the heel of his boot. "Everything's on schedule."

More silence. He could picture this guy at his fancy, glass-topped desk, getting red in the face.

"There was an article today in the newspaper. A car crash out near the lab, then an explosion. Was that you?"

The man clenched his teeth.

"*No* fatalities. That's what it said in the paper. So if it *was* you, you may want to rethink your battle plan."

Rethink your battle plan. When had this fucker ever seen a battle plan? He didn't know the meaning of *battle* or *combat* or *country,* for that matter.

"Fear and intimidation," he answered calmly. "That's what this is. I've got her attention now. She'll think before she opens her mouth again."

Two kids left the stand with an armload of Roman candles. He and his dad used to make their own and set them off down by the river. He'd learned to shoot down on that river. Learned to build bombs. Thirty years later, he was doing the same shit, only now he'd elevated it to an art form.

"So, if she's intimidated . . . maybe we don't need to kill her after all?"

Squeamish bastard.

"We need to."

"Are you sure? We're already at three. Maybe it's better to scare her enough to guarantee her silence. I mean, she might not even know anything. Maybe she was just running her mouth off to that reporter."

The man pictured her behind the wheel of that black Tahoe. He could still see the blond hair, the stylish black sunglasses. If he'd gotten that good a look at her, she'd definitely seen something.

"She dies," he said. "That's your guarantee."

Pop.

Sophie bolted upright, looking around frantically.

Her heart leaped into her throat, and she nudged Jonah, a giant dark lump in the bed beside her.

"Did you hear that?" she hissed.

Pop! Pop! Pop!

She started to lunge for her purse, but he caught her arm.

"Firecrackers."

She stopped to listen. It was silent now, but she replayed the sound in her head. She shook off Jonah's grip and went to the window. She parted the curtains and peered out at the parking lot.

A long whistle. *Pop!*

"See?" Jonah sat up in bed. "Bottle rockets."

Sophie took a deep breath. She couldn't see them, but she recognized the sound. She checked the lock on the door. Then she took her bag off the dresser and dropped it beside the bed.

"Come here." His voice was rough from sleep. She slid into bed beside him, and he wrapped his arm around her and pulled her against him.

She tugged the sheet up and rested her head on his chest. She listened to his heart. It was a steady *thump-bump*. Pause. *Thump-bump*. Hers was racing. Her breath felt shallow. She could feel her chest tightening, like it did sometimes. She closed her eyes and hoped she wouldn't have a panic attack.

"You okay?" His breath was warm against the top of her head.

"I'm fine."

His hand stroked slowly up her arm, then down again, and she took a deep breath. She nestled against him and breathed in his scent. She felt her chest loosen. And her pulse slow. Seconds ticked by. Minutes.

He reached under the covers and found her knee, then pulled it up so her thigh rested across his stomach.

"Better?"

She laughed. "No."

He stroked his hand lazily over her leg, her hip, then back to her knee. She heard the low hum of the air conditioner across the room. She heard the fireworks, too, but they didn't bother her now.

Her head felt good against his chest. Too good. His arms were strong and warm around her. The solidity of him put an ache inside her.

"Better now?"

"Yeah." She cleared her throat, felt her stomach flutter. "Sometimes I have trouble sleeping."

"You told me."

"I did?" She looked up at him.

"At breakfast that time."

"Oh." She laid her head back down and closed her eyes.

"You ever seen a doctor or anyone?"

"You mean a shrink?"

He didn't answer, but she knew that's what he meant.

"My mom tried to get me to see a therapist, but I don't know. I don't know what good it would do."

Nothing would erase it. No matter what she did, she'd always remember coming to in that cold, dark space and realizing she was trapped in the trunk. She remembered the metal vibrating under her body. She remembered her aching wrists, which had been bound so tightly she couldn't feel her fingertips. She remembered the icy grip of panic as understanding dawned and she realized she couldn't scream and she couldn't move and she couldn't do anything but listen to the tires spinning over miles and miles of highway.

Jonah stroked her leg some more, and she absorbed the heat of him.

"It's just . . . You never think it can happen to you. And then when it does, you know anything can happen to you."

She lay her hand on his sternum and felt his heart thud under her palm. He was listening to her, and for once she didn't mind talking about this.

"I'm different now. Some expensive doctor's not going to change that."

"Different how?"

She sighed. "I don't know. Less carefree, I guess." Less happy. Moodier. Bitchier. But she didn't want to run down the list of all her flaws, so she tried to focus on something good. "I don't take things for granted now. Not a day. Not a breath."

He didn't say anything as the moment stretched out. She turned and pressed a kiss to his chest. She wanted him to know she didn't take him for granted, either, but she couldn't bring herself to tell him outright. Maybe he knew. Part of her hoped he did and another part of her panicked at the thought. He stirred up such strong emotions in her, and she wasn't sure what she stirred up in him beyond simple lust. But even if that was all it was, she'd take it—for now, at least. He made her feel more alive than she had in ages, and she liked it.

He pulled his arm out from under her shoulders and shifted himself over her, pinning her to the bed with his hips. It was a nice, heavy feeling, even though he propped most of his weight on his elbows. The intense look in his eyes made her pulse quicken.

"So, this insomnia thing." He kissed her neck. "I think I can help with that."

"You do?"

"I do."

His voice was serious, and she smiled.

"I bet you can."

CHAPTER 19

Allison trailed the bulky security guard down the windowed corridor.

"That dock belong to D-Systems?" Sean asked beside her.

The guard glanced out the window, and Allison followed his gaze. At the base of a green lawn that sloped down toward the water was a dock with several pontoon boats.

"The property covers all twenty acres from the bridge to the greenbelt area to the west."

"Guess that means the boat dock, too, then," Sean said. "You all use those boats for parties? Corporate picnics? Must be nice working for a place that has money to burn like that."

The guard didn't respond, and Allison could tell he didn't appreciate being grilled all the way up here from the lobby. He swiped his way into a reception room using a security badge, then crossed the empty seating area to a pair of wood-paneled doors.

"Wait here," he said, before rapping lightly on the door and entering.

Allison looked at Sean. "What gives?"

He gave her a "Who, me?" look.

"You've had a burr up your butt all morning. What is it?"

The wooden door opened. "Mr. Maxwell will see you now."

Allison stepped into the inner sanctum of D-System's CEO and nodded her thanks to the guard. Sean followed, without the nod. He was in a pissy mood, and she hadn't figured out why yet.

She turned her attention to the room. Or, more accurately, to the man seated behind the glass-topped desk. Ryan Maxwell leaned back in a black leather chair and gave them a cool once-over.

"Have it to me by Monday," he said into the phone clipped to his ear. He had a lean, tan face and short brown hair with a touch of gray at the temples. Allison put him at forty, which struck her as young to be in command of one of the biggest tech companies in the state.

After ending the call, he unhooked the ear clip, tossed it on the desk, and stood up.

"Detectives, good to see you this morning." He stepped out from behind the desk and thrust out a hand. Like so many young Austinites, this guy sported the cyclist look, complete with biker shorts, a spandex shirt, and a yellow bracelet.

Allison shook his hand. "I'm Detective Doyle, and this is Detective Byrne."

Sean shook hands and nodded but didn't say anything.

"Thanks for seeing us on a weekend," she added.

He shrugged. "Weekend. Weekday." He gestured to the pile of papers on his desk beside the computer. "The work doesn't stop. I'm sure it's the same for you guys. What can I do for you?"

Allison cut a glance at Sean, but he remained mute.

"We just have a few questions this morning about Eric Emrick."

A grave expression came over Maxwell's face, and he shook his head. "Terrible news. We're still in shock around here."

"Yes, I saw the flag at half-staff on our way in."

"Eric will be missed. He was well liked by everyone on our staff."

"I didn't see you at the funeral," Allison said.

Maxwell's mouth tightened. "Yes, well. I didn't know him personally. He was an intern. A contingent of his coworkers attended, though." He glanced at Sean. "Can I offer you some refreshment?"

"We're good, thanks," Allison said.

"How about a seat?" Maxwell gestured them to a black leather sofa and chairs in front of a huge floor-to-ceiling window that offered a panoramic view of the lake. Allison took a chair. Sean stepped over to the window and looked out at the scenery. Maxwell gave him a mildly curious look before taking a seat himself.

"So, what did Eric do for you here?" Allison pulled the notebook out of her jacket and flipped to a clean page.

"He was in our R and D group. Research and development for some of our software applications."

"Maybe we should back up a sec and you can tell me what exactly your company does." She smiled sheepishly. "I'm not much on computers. You make software or something? Is that what I read?"

Maxwell smiled. "We create an array of leading-edge software solutions for a wide range of customers."

"And your customers are?"

"Blue chips, mostly—computer manufacturers, cellular phone companies."

"The Defense Department?"

Allison glanced up at Sean, startled by both the question and the sharp tone.

"We have, in the past, worked with the Department of Defense." Maxwell looked at Allison. "Most of our software utilizes GPS technology," he explained. "It has some useful military applications."

"Okay. And did Eric work on any of those?"

Another smile. "I'm afraid Eric didn't have the security clearance for anything that sensitive. Anyway, we're no longer working for the DoD."

"Is that right?" This from Sean.

"That's right." The smiled flickered but stayed in place. "We've currently got our hands full with projects for our private-sector clients."

"And Eric was working on which project?" Allison held her pencil poised above her notepad.

"Some of our cell phone applications. We create programs that essentially serve up various services to the user, and we like to test-drive them, so to speak, before we take them to market." He nodded. "That's where our interns come in. We recruit people who are smart, tech-savvy. In Eric's case, he's also got the engineering background."

"Had," Sean said.

"Excuse me?"

"He *had* the engineering background. Before he was killed."

"Yes, well . . ." Maxwell floundered. "These college kids have a feel for what people want. A finger on the pulse of the market, you could say. That's why we hire them, and sometimes offer them jobs after graduation."

"How about an example?" Allison asked. "For someone who *doesn't* have her finger on the pulse of all that."

"Well, for instance, say you're driving past a movie theater on the evening the new Matt Damon movie comes out." Maxwell leaned his elbows on his knees, warming to the topic. "You've used your phone in the past to look up movie times for some of the Jason Bourne films, so we know you're a fan of the actor."

"You do?"

"Our software stores the information digitally. Anyway, so now you're driving by this theater, and the GPS on your phone sends a message to our software, which in turn checks the movie listings and overlaps *that* with your past movie preferences, and *ping*."

"Ping?"

"You get an e-mail letting you know it's opening night for a movie you might want to see. You can even buy your tickets with a few keystrokes."

It sounded invasive to Allison. "And what if you don't want to be 'pinged' with this advertising?"

"Some people don't, which is why it's optional. If you don't want it, simply set the preferences on your phone to block the capability."

Allison jotted some notes. "So Eric was working on this?"

"Well, this particular feature isn't really new. He was working on some added functionality. Along with the rest of his team."

"And was any of this sensitive?" Allison asked. "The stuff Eric was working on?"

"He was a college junior, Detective."

She looked at him expectantly.

"In other words, no. We don't let our interns have access to sensitive projects."

An electronic bell chimed. Allison glanced around for the source of the noise as a baritone voice came over an intercom.

"Your nine o'clock appointment is here, sir," the security guard announced.

Maxwell smiled and stood up. "That takes care of your questions, I hope?"

Allison traded looks with Sean. They were being dismissed. And she'd bet a thousand dollars this appointment was as phony as Maxwell's persona.

The guard was waiting in the reception room to escort them back to the exit. He took a route that bypassed the lobby, depriving Allison of the chance to get a look at Maxwell's nine o'clock.

They exited the glass-and-steel building and walked silently to the parking lot, where Sean had parked his battered Buick within dinging distance of the silver Land Rover that probably belonged to Maxwell.

"What did you think?" Allison asked as Sean started the car. It was a hundred thousand degrees, and she reached over to crank up the A/C.

"Interesting."

She sighed. "You want to be more specific?"

"He didn't like us there."

"I got that part. The question is, why?"

"I don't know."

Sean pulled out of the lot while Allison looked out her window, admiring the landscaped office park with its hike-and-bike trails. Twenty acres on a hill overlooking the lake. D-Systems had to be doing well.

She looked at Sean. "That software they make—sounds very Big Brother."

"Yep." He glanced at her. "You know what D-Systems stands for, don't you?"

She waited.

"Defense Systems. Their original name, back in the eighties. They were founded to do top-secret projects for the Pentagon, but funding dried up after the Cold War. They changed their name and started developing software and technology for the American consumer. Much more lucrative."

She looked at him, impressed. "You've checked into this."

"I'm an investigator." He slanted a look at her. "That's what I do."

"So, you think Eric was on to some top-secret project? Seems unlikely. I mean, he was an intern making four hundred bucks a week. He probably would have been a nobody over there if his death hadn't made headlines."

"Just think it's interesting."

Allison drummed her fingers on the door beside her. "You know, it isn't what he said that bothers me, so much as what he didn't."

"How do you mean?"

"Maxwell didn't make a single comment about our case," she said. "To most people, our investigation ended when Himmel put that gun in his mouth. So, why are we still going around asking questions about the victims?"

She gazed out at the lake. "Just strikes me as weird, that's all. He didn't seem all that surprised to see us."

Maxwell watched the Buick wind its way up the drive. He took out his phone and dialed the number he'd been given for emergencies.

"The police were just here," Maxwell said.

Silence.

"Well?"

"What did you tell them?" Sharpe asked.

"Nothing."

"Are you sure?"

"Don't insult me," Maxwell said. "But they were here, and I didn't like their questions."

"I'll take care of it."

"Goddamn it, this is getting out of control!"

"I'll take care of it," he repeated, and the line went dead.

Sophie woke in an empty room. It was eerily quiet, but darker than it had been the day before. The curtains were drawn. Her clothes were strewn across the floor. Jonah's gun was gone from its place on the nightstand, and she felt a spurt of panic.

She heard the door click, and he stepped in carrying a cardboard coffee cup in each hand and a small sack between his teeth. Sophie sat up. He deposited the cups on the dresser and tossed her the bag.

"Breakfast," he said.

She put the bag on the nightstand without looking inside, then tucked the sheet under her arms as she eyed him critically. He was in the clothes he'd worn yesterday, including the holster. He didn't look at all like someone who planned to hit the beach today.

He checked his cell phone, muttered something, and stuffed it back in his pocket. Then he looked at her. "We need to get going."

"Where are you going?"

"*We* are going back to San Marcos."

Calmly, she slipped out of bed and picked up her sarong. She wrapped it around herself like a towel before striding toward the bathroom.

"*I'm* going to the beach today." She smiled at him over her shoulder. "Have a safe trip." She started to close the door on him, but he stuck his boot in the opening.

She snatched her toothbrush off the counter, turned on the faucet, and started brushing her teeth. Jonah squeezed his way into the minuscule bathroom and stood behind her.

"Do you mind?" She bumped him back so she could bend down to spit into the sink.

A swift snap, and the sarong disappeared.

"Hey!" She glared at him over her shoulder, but he was too busy looking at her in the mirror. He lifted her arms up and examined her body. The bruises had taken on a sickly green hue, and Sophie pulled her arms down.

"How are you feeling?"

The concern in his voice made her stomach flutter. "I'm fine."

"Did you take one of your pills?"

"Not yet."

He disappeared into the bedroom and came back with a cup of coffee. He held a blue pill in his big palm.

"Thank you."

She downed it with a sip of coffee, reconsidering her strategy. He was acting all sensitive now, and it was going to be tougher to argue with him—which was probably why he was doing it.

His hands settled on her hips, and his gaze met hers in the mirror.

"I understand why you came down here," he said.

She didn't reply.

"You're freaked out, and you needed to pull it together. I was mad at first, but I get it now." He looked at her steadily. "You *should* be freaked out, Sophie. Someone planted a bomb in your car."

Her stomach clenched. "Is that confirmed?"

"As of this morning, yes. They found traces of residue at the crash scene. The explosion was intentional."

"I could have told you that. I *did* tell you. I told everyone there—that person *ran* me off the road."

Jonah nodded. "Probably the same person who drove Jim Himmel's car to campus. This person left it there, along with a box full of extra equipment—a knife, a gun, grenades—that Himmel never intended to use. This is the person you saw, Sophie. He wants to emphasize the whole idea of the crazed gunman up there shooting people at random before killing himself. But there was nothing random about it. It was a targeted hit."

Sophie watched him in the mirror. A lump formed in her throat. He was talking to her candidly, like a real person, not some outsider who couldn't be let in on any information.

And he believed her.

"Who was the target?" she asked.

"We've got some ideas on that. You can help us."

"*I* can?" She turned to look at him over her shoulder.

"I've got you an appointment with a forensic artist today at one o'clock. She's the one who did the postmortem drawing of Himmel."

"But—"

"She's the best there is, and Reynolds offered to spring for the expense. The task force needs your input, Sophie. If you saw anything, even briefly, this artist can probably get a sketch." He waited a beat. "It would really help the investigation."

"It would also help you get me up to your *deer* lease." She turned to face him, grabbing a towel off the rack as she did so because it felt strange having this conversation while she was naked and he was fully dressed. She leaned back against the sink and held the towel over herself.

He looked annoyed by her sudden modesty. "What have you got against a deer lease, anyway? I can come out there at night when I get off work. And compared to this rat hole, it's practically a resort."

"I don't care about that," she said, although she did. Her father and brothers had a deer lease, and *primitive* was an understatement. "It's your dad."

Jonah's brow furrowed. "What about him?"

"I met him the other day at your house. Didn't he tell you? He came by with his *tomatoes,* Jonah."

"So?" He looked baffled.

"He's retired. He's *old*. And he's so sweet and— Why are you laughing?"

Jonah leaned back against the wall, silently cracking up.

"What?" she demanded.

He squeezed his eyes shut and laughed so hard, she thought he was going to cry. "You're worried about my *father*?"

"Yes! What is wrong with you? He's *elderly*, Jonah! How can you ask him to go out to some deer lease in the hundred-degree heat and sit around guarding me from a hit man? It's a terrible plan! I can't believe you thought of it!"

"Sophie." He pulled her against him. "Let me tell you about my dad, okay? First off, he's a cop. He's retired now, but he'll always be a cop. Second, he's a lifelong gun collector and a crack shot to boot." He grinned down at her. "I can't believe you called him 'sweet,' though. Don't say that to his face."

"Jonah—"

"Anyway, I trust him." The smile faded, and he looked serious now. "There's no better person to keep an eye on you while I work on this case—with the help of the suspect sketch that you're going to provide for us"—he jerked his phone out of his pocket and checked the clock—"in about four hours." He slapped her butt. "Better get a move on if you want a shower. We're leaving in ten minutes."

She stared up at him, frustrated beyond words. They were leaving. She was going with him. She was going to do the exact thing she'd told him she *wouldn't* do at least half a dozen times.

The task force wanted her help. They needed it. Instead of treating her like a crazy woman, they actually believed her and wanted her input.

And Jonah had known all along this was his ace in the

hole. She cared about those victims. She'd been a victim herself, and he knew she'd do anything to find the man who'd helped take three innocent lives.

He swatted her butt again, and she caught the glint of triumph in his eyes. "Hop to it, Sophie. We don't want to be late for your appointment."

"Fine." She shrugged. "I'll meet with the artist. You mind getting out of here? I'd like to shower, please."

"So you'll come?" He looked wary as he stepped out of the bathroom.

"I said I would." She shut the door almost all the way but then poked her head out. "Oh, but I should tell you up front. You'll be pulling up to the self-serve from now on, because there is *no* way I'm having sex with you at some deer lease while your father's just a stone's throw away."

She slammed the door on his startled expression and stepped into the shower.

CHAPTER 20

The forensic artist lived in Austin, and Sophie wasn't sure why she'd agreed to waste her Saturday afternoon driving down to San Marcos to do a sketch with someone who'd barely seen anything.

But when she walked into the interview room and introduced herself, Sophie got a big hint about her motives.

"Sorry I'm late. Didn't expect traffic on a Saturday." Fiona Glass smiled and plopped a bottle of V8 Juice on the table, then began unfolding a portable metal easel.

Sophie rushed forward to help. "You need a hand?"

"I got it." She waved Sophie off, setting the easel up with fluid efficiency and then clipping a sheet of gray paper to the front of it. She pulled up a chair and settled her hugely pregnant body into it.

"Hope you don't mind if I sit today," she said. "My feet are killing me. Everyone tells you about the baby showers and the first kicks. No one mentions the cankles."

She glanced down at the woman's feet. Her ankles looked painfully swollen, and Sophie felt a wave of guilt.

"You know, I'm not sure how much they told you," Sophie said, "but I'm really not certain I can do this."

Fiona smiled pleasantly as she took out an array of pencils and erasers.

"I only got a glimpse," Sophie continued. "Very fleeting. I can't imagine how I'm going to be able to do a picture."

"Well, here's the thing, Sophie. You don't have to. That's my job." She adjusted her paper and tossed a lock of wavy, strawberry-blond hair over her shoulder. "All you have to do is relax and tell me what you saw."

"But that's just it. I only saw him for a second. I mostly saw the car."

Fiona opened her juice and took a swig. Then she set the bottle on the floor beside her puffy feet.

"I've interviewed all sorts of witnesses—children who have been sexually assaulted, elderly people who have been robbed at gunpoint, cops who have been shot in the chest. The one thing they all have in common is that they never think they can do this."

Sophie watched her skeptically. This woman was being overly optimistic here, and Sophie had a feeling she knew why. She surveyed her glowing complexion and her loose, hippie-style maternity dress, and she couldn't help but be reminded of Jodi Kincaid.

"I really want to help this investigation, but—"

"Listen, Sophie." Fiona leaned forward, suddenly serious. "I'm going to cut to the chase with you because my husband's at home right now, trying to assemble a crib with instructions that are entirely in Swedish, and he could really use my help."

Sophie sat back in her chair.

"Let me tell you what I hear all the time, all right? I hear 'It happened too quick.' Or 'All I saw was the gun.' Or 'It was too dark.' I understand your reservations, but we can *still* do this. We don't have to get a perfect sketch. We just have to get *a* sketch. I've seen it over and over again—even an imperfect likeness can spark recognition and lead to an ID."

Sophie bit her lip.

"And you know what? I'm eight months pregnant, just like Jodi Kincaid, and I'd really, *really* like to help these cops nail the bastards who killed her. You want to help me do that?"

Sophie took a deep breath. "I'll try. What do I need to do?"

Fiona shifted the easel so that it was across from Sophie but not facing her directly. Strangely, the minor adjustment put her at ease. She didn't feel as though she was being stared at.

"Just relax and close your eyes," Fiona said. "We want to activate your visual memory."

Sophie closed her eyes.

"Now, take a deep breath."

She did.

"And describe what happened."

"Well . . . his face was in shadow at first."

"Why don't we get to the face in a minute? Just tell me everything you saw."

Sophie took a few moments to collect her thoughts. Then she started with the car. She remembered it well. She remembered thinking about how rare those old VWs were and getting sputtering mad when it stole her space.

"And he was tall," Sophie said. "I remember that. He seemed too big for that little car. Like somehow it didn't fit."

"That's good."

Sophie heard the pencil moving over the paper, but she didn't open her eyes.

"What about hair color? Most people notice that first."

"Brown," Sophie said, surprised by her level of certainty.

"And skin?"

"Light. He was definitely Caucasian. I'm remembering his arm on the door now. I guess the window was open? I hadn't even thought of that until just now."

"Keep going."

Sophie did. She just sat back and talked. And in about an hour, Fiona was putting the finishing touches on an amazingly detailed drawing.

Sophie stood behind the easel and stared at it, astonished. "How did you *do* that? It's . . . God, it's so *real*."

"Practice," Fiona said. "Men between the ages of eighteen and forty are my specialty. They commit the most crimes."

Sophie glanced at her. Something in Fiona's tone struck a chord with her. Had she been the victim of a crime herself? She had a certain empathy that Sophie had just begun to recognize in other women. It was like a club, only there was no secret handshake—just a silent understanding.

She looked at the drawing again. "There's something off with his eyes."

"Okay."

"They need to be . . . I don't know. Meaner? Does that make sense?"

"Maybe a furrowed brow?" Fiona was open to suggestions. "Or maybe narrower?"

"That's it—*narrower*. More predatory, I guess. He had this look. I mean, I only saw it for a moment, but it was like he was on a *mission*."

Fiona took a charcoal pencil and added some shadows. "I hear that a lot, actually. Sometimes that's exactly what you're seeing. They've got a laser-sharp focus on what they're about to do. Sometimes it makes them slip up, forget the little things—like the woman walking her dog who might witness something, or the security camera mounted in the corner of the room."

Sophie studied the drawing. "Wow, that's him. That's the guy. Whatever was missing, you fixed it."

"Glad you're happy with it."

"I'd be even happier if we could get an ID. Do the police need help circulating this? Because I know a reporter who would be *very* eager to put this on the news."

Sean entered the conference room and immediately picked up on the grim mood.

"This smells more and more like a conspiracy," Reynolds was saying, as if this were a new insight.

Sean glanced at Jonah as he took an empty seat. The man had his arms folded over his chest and looked like he was grinding his teeth to nubs. No doubt he was pissed. He'd floated the conspiracy theory over a week ago, and the lieutenant had blown him off.

"Question is, who was the target?" Reynolds asked

the room at large. His gaze scanned the people convened around the table and came to rest on Sean. "You checked up on that life insurance lead, didn't you? Is it the professor?"

Sean suddenly felt like he was in a game of Clue. "I think we can scratch off Graham," he said. "Allison and I talked to the widow, and it doesn't gel."

"Two million dollars is a lot of insurance money," Ric observed.

"Have you met the woman?" Sean asked him.

"Just briefly at the funeral."

"Well, Allison and I interviewed her. She heads a Bible study at her church. She organizes fund-raisers for cancer kids. I don't see her taking a hit out on her husband of forty-two years. Not to mention, we checked out her financials and she's independently wealthy. Her family owns a string of car dealerships."

"I don't think Graham's our real target," Jonah said. "I'm pretty convinced the professor was collateral damage, that he was shot just to make it seem more like a rampage than a hit, same as all those wounded students."

"What about the Kincaid woman?" Reynolds asked.

"Jodi," Ric said.

"She was hit by accident," Jonah put in. "Ricochet bullet. I confirmed it with ballistics just the other day." His gaze swung to Sean. "Which leaves Eric Emrick. Where's Allison? I thought you two had a lead on him."

"We do," Sean said. "And she's following up. She's meeting with the reporter who first gave her the tip about it. Thinks he's holding out on her."

"Holding out on her how?" Reynolds asked.

Sean wasn't sure how much Reynolds was in the loop,

so he decided just to dive in. "This reporter's convinced there's something going on over at D-Systems."

"D-Systems?" Reynolds looked blank.

"Tech company where Eric interned," Jonah said. "What'd you get on it?"

"Nothing solid, just an off feeling during the interview. They used to do projects for the Defense Department. Their CEO claims Eric Emrick was never working on anything that sensitive, and anyway, the government contracts have dried up. But still, this military connection keeps cropping up." Sean looked at Reynolds. "Himmel's ex says before their divorce, he was contacted by an old army buddy, possibly to do some contract work."

"You know the name of the outfit?" Jonah had gone from Code Yellow to Code Orange.

"No."

He muttered a curse.

"What?" Sean asked.

"A second K-9 team just went over the crash scene," Jonah said, and Sean knew he was talking about the site where Sophie Barrett had nearly been killed. Probably that explained his extra-unhappy mood today. "The original dog was trained to pick up a group of commonly used explosives. He didn't alert on anything."

The door swung open, and Allison blew into the room, looking frazzled. She took the empty chair beside Jonah.

"Today we got another dog over there—a newer one trained to detect a broader range of chemicals—and he picked up PETN."

"PETN?" Sean asked.

"Military-grade plastic explosive," Jonah said.

"You're saying someone ran this woman off the road and then blew up her car?" Sean asked.

"Probably used a remote detonator," Jonah said. "A cell phone, something like that. Given her rate of speed and the skid marks, it would have looked like an accident except that she walked away and was able to tell us what happened."

The room got quiet as the weight of Jonah's information seemed to press down on everyone. Whoever this man was, he wasn't playing around.

"Where is she now?" Reynolds asked. "The Barrett girl."

"In an interview room talking to Fiona Glass," Jonah said.

"Fiona Glass?" Allison asked.

"A forensic artist. We've used her before."

"What did you get from the reporter?" Sean asked Allison now. He doubted it was good, based on her frustrated look when she'd walked in here.

"I got zip," she said. "He didn't show for the interview. He's not answering his phone, either. I think he's dodging me."

"Is this CNN or one of the locals?" Reynolds asked, obviously worried about controlling the spin.

"Neither," Allison said. "Dorion is a blogger who's written a few articles for the *Bee*. But I can tell he has more of the story than he's letting on. I think he's holding out so he can get a big headline somewhere."

"You said Dorion?" Ric leaned forward on his elbows.

"The reporter who first handed me this tip."

"We just got a call from the Blanco County Sheriff about a Dorion."

Allison stiffened. "What happened?"

"There was a fire early this morning at the Rolling Hills Motel out Highway Twelve."

"Did anyone—"

"One fatality. No positive ID yet," Ric said, "but the room was registered to a Tyler P. Dorion."

Jonah crossed paths with Fiona in the bullpen.

"You finished already?" he asked.

She held out a thick piece of paper about the size of a legal pad. It had a protective flap over it, and Jonah flipped it open.

"This is him?"

"It's the man she described."

"Damn, it's so detailed." He glanced at Fiona. "I was worried you might not get much. It's been ten days."

"My average lag time is three weeks," Fiona said. "Unfortunately, many investigators think of forensic artists as a last resort. Ten days is nothing."

Jonah studied the face of the mystery accomplice no one but Sophie had even believed existed. The man looked to be mid-thirties, medium build. He had slightly shaggy hair, but no distinctive scars or tattoos. It was his eyes that stood out. They looked cold. Focused. And Jonah would bet money this was the shadow warrior who'd recruited Jim Himmel for his suicide mission.

He glanced up. "You think this is an accurate sketch? I mean, was she pretty confident?"

"Actually, witness confidence has very little bearing on accuracy," Fiona said. "Some of the most reluctant, insecure witnesses can provide loads of details. And the timing's not an issue here, either. Studies have shown that whatever details are still with you seventy-two hours after an incident will stay with you for a long, long time. So, yes, I'd say it's good." She hitched her bag up on her shoulder. "Anyway, it's yours now. I hope it leads to an ID for you."

"You ready?"

Jonah turned to see Allison standing at his elbow, looking anxious. They were heading out to the Delphi Center to learn more about the victim of last night's motel fire. Even the medical examiner's office didn't keep a forensic anthropologist on staff.

"I'm coming," he told her. "Just need to talk to Sophie." He glanced at Fiona. "She still in the interview room, I take it?"

"Not anymore. She left about ten minutes ago. Said she had to run an errand."

Sophie combed the aisles looking for anything that could remotely qualify as health food. Or at least healthy. She settled for a box of shredded wheat and a bunch of bananas. She fully expected the deer lease to have either an empty pantry or one stocked with beef jerky and Beanie Weenies.

She plunked her groceries on the counter, along with a six-pack of diet soda.

"And pump number two, please," she told the clerk.

The man rattled off her total, and Sophie sighed as she handed over her twenties. At this rate, she was going to be out of cash in no time. But she'd promised Scott a full tank of gas, and she intended to deliver.

After leaving the store, Sophie tossed her grocery bags in the cab of the pickup, then cleared out the cup holders.

They'd dropped off Jonah's rental car in Corpus on the way back, and he'd insisted on driving the remainder of the three-hour journey. Sophie suspected he'd been worried she'd make a dash for it if he didn't personally escort her back here.

She replaced the fuel pump and slid behind the wheel, then pulled out of the parking lot. She checked her watch. Jonah had been stuck in a meeting when she'd left. If she could get Scott to take her to the police station right away, she could probably make it back before Jonah even noticed she was gone. But she'd have to hurry. She pulled into traffic and calculated the shortest route to Scott's house.

A siren sounded behind her.

She checked the mirror and felt a jolt of alarm at the flashing lights. She glanced around and confirmed that, yes, the cruiser was after her.

"Damn hell," she said, pulling into a parking lot. This was *not* good. She didn't even have a license with her. It had burned up in the explosion.

She glanced in the side mirror as the officer made a call on his radio. Then he climbed out and approached.

Woods, thank God. Her shoulders sagged with relief, and she rolled down her window.

"Fancy seeing you again!" she said brightly.

But Woods wasn't looking bright. He looked decidedly grumpy, in fact, and she wondered if he'd caught any flak for letting her slip out of the hospital the other night.

"License and registration," he said gruffly.

Sophie smiled. "You won't believe what happened. Actually, you probably *will* believe it—"

"License. And. Registration."

All righty, then. Woods was pissed. Sophie leaned over and popped the glove compartment. Maps, flashlight, condoms. She smiled at Woods over her shoulder, but he didn't look amused. She kept poking around and tugged an envelope loose from the pile. She peeked inside. Bingo.

"Here's the registration," she said, and her heart was pounding only a little now. Traffic stops always did it to her. She handed up the insurance slip and dug into the tote bag on the seat beside her. "I don't have my license *on* me, but I do have a credit card with a photo on it—you know, for security purposes? Maybe you could just—"

"Hands on the wheel."

She glanced up, startled.

"Hands on the wheel."

She slapped her hands on the wheel. Woods was clutching his holster now. She glanced up at his stern expression and followed his gaze to her tote bag.

Where a black Beretta was visible amid all the junk in her purse.

Oh, shit.

"You have a permit to carry a concealed firearm?"

"Actually, I don't." She smiled. "I was about to get one and—"

"Out of the car, ma'am."

Sophie's jaw dropped.

"Step *out* of the car." Woods kept a hand on his weapon and used the other to yank the door open.

"If you'll let me explain, I—"

"Ma'am, I'm ordering you to get—"

"I'm getting, I'm getting!" She thrust her hands in the

air, then slid out of the pickup. She stood on the asphalt, hands up, feeling ridiculous as cars whisked by on the road beside her.

"Hands on the car, ma'am."

"What?"

"Palms against the vehicle, feet apart."

Sophie stared at him.

"Now."

Sophie turned and rested her hands on the dusty truck cab. This couldn't be happening. Woods stepped up behind her.

"Feet apart."

Numbly, she spread her feet apart. Her stomach knotted as Woods crouched down and patted her legs through her jeans.

"You carrying any other weapons, ma'am?"

"No."

Traffic rushed back and forth behind her as Woods patted down her legs, her pockets, her sides. He ran his hand briefly between her breasts, and she cringed.

"Any other weapons in your bag or your vehicle?"

"No. I mean, I don't think so. It's not my vehicle, so—"

"You're under arrest for unlawful possession of a firearm."

Sophie's stomach plummeted.

"You have the right to remain silent."

Her vision dimmed at the edges and all she could see was the dusty window of Scott's truck. He was reading her her rights. She was being *arrested*. Her cheeks burned as she pictured what she looked like from the perspective of one of the passing cars.

This can't be happening.

Metal clinked behind her. Woods clasped her right wrist and pulled it behind her back. Then her left. She turned her head and saw a flash of silver.

Panic shot through her. She yanked her arms free and jabbed him in the face.

Jonah pulled into the apartment parking lot, and Allison glanced around. She saw no sign of the black Tacoma pickup Sophie Barrett was supposedly driving today.

Jonah cursed vividly.

"What about her gym?" Allison asked.

"You think she went to work out?"

"I don't know what the hell she's doing." Allison checked her watch impatiently. "But I know we've got an autopsy in thirty minutes, and it takes forty minutes to get there. Did you try Mia Voss?"

"Not answering."

Jonah's cell buzzed, and he jerked the phone to his ear. "Macon."

Allison watched as his face flooded with relief.

"Good . . . all right. So, you're bringing her in?" His brow furrowed. *"What?"* He leaned his head back against the seat. "Aw, shit. You've got to be kidding me."

CHAPTER 21

Kelsey Quinn didn't look happy when Jonah and Allison walked into the osteology section, and he figured she was still miffed about his pounding on her door the other night.

"Detectives," she said curtly.

Jonah introduced Allison, who had hardly said three words the entire drive out. She was still reeling from the fact that this college kid she'd interviewed might have been murdered.

Jonah was reeling, too. From the new fatality, yes, but also from the knowledge that at this very moment Sophie was being booked and tossed in jail. And there wasn't a damn thing he could do about it right now, even if he'd wanted to.

Which—truth be told—he didn't. This recent death was another screaming wake-up call about how dangerous the case had become, and Jonah would rather have Sophie cooling her heels in lockup than running around providing another target for some assassin.

"I've got a full load today," Kelsey said. "I couldn't

wait to begin the prelim, so come in and I'll catch you up.
Is the sheriff planning to make it?"

"One of his deputies is on the way," Jonah said.

Kelsey glanced at a clock on the wall as they headed
for the room behind her. "Well, he'll have to read the
report." She opened the door and ushered them into an
autopsy suite, then pulled a pair of latex gloves from the
pocket of her lab coat.

Jonah stepped into the room and was immediately hit
with the odor of burned flesh.

"It's bad, I know." Kelsey handed out blue surgical
masks. She applied a few drops of something to hers and
then passed the bottle around.

"What is it?" Allison asked.

"Orange oil. Works better than Vicks, at least for me."

Kelsey donned her mask and stepped over to a
stainless steel table where a blue sheet was stretched over
a large round lump. Jonah was still trying to understand
the underlying shape when Kelsey pulled back the cloth.

Behind him, Allison sucked in a breath. The charred
remains were curled up in a fetal position.

"Jesus," he muttered. He put on his mask and stepped
closer to the table. The childlike position underscored
how young this latest victim was.

And what a ruthless son of a bitch they were dealing
with.

"Can you confirm it's a homicide?" Jonah looked at
Kelsey.

"In my opinion, yes."

Allison stepped up beside him. Her face had gone pale,
and her eyes were wide and round above the surgical
mask. This was probably her first postmortem, Jonah

realized, and unfortunately it was someone she knew.

"I know this looks shocking," Kelsey said. "The victim is positioned this way because the heat causes the tendons and connective tissue to shrink, which makes the arms and legs draw up like this and the hands clench into fists."

It was impossible to look at the blackened remains without imagining intense suffering.

"So . . . did he die from the burns, or maybe smoke inhalation?" Jonah asked, hoping for the second one.

"Neither."

He looked up.

"Fire is an overrated means to conceal a crime," Kelsey said. "I haven't seen a single cremation that consumed all the remains of a human body. What usually happens is that instead of disguising a murder, the fire gives investigators a big red flag that a crime has been committed."

"You're telling us he was shot or something, and the killer tried to burn the evidence?" Jonah asked.

She moved across the room to a light board and switched it on. Several X-rays were mounted on it. "The films don't show any slugs or bullet wipe."

"Bullet wipe?" Allison asked.

"Embedded metal fragments that would indicate a gunshot wound, even if the bullet passed through the body. Nothing like that turned up."

Jonah was running through scenarios in his head. As a detective, he tended to like bullets. They revealed all kinds of useful information about both the perpetrator and the crime itself.

"So you're thinking . . . ?"

"I don't know for certain," Kelsey said. "But the sheriff tells me the remains were recovered from the bed in this motel room. I think he might have been killed as he slept, or maybe killed and then moved to the bed to make it look like he died of smoke inhalation, when in fact he was murdered."

"Fire chief out there said something about faulty wiring at the motel. You're saying arson?"

"That's not my area," Kelsey said, "but I wouldn't be surprised if he comes back later with a different take. What I *can* tell you about is this victim. Everything is burned, but pretty much intact, which gives us a lot to work with from an investigative perspective." Kelsey pointed to something on the screen. "For example, I looked at the hyoid—a tiny bone in the neck. It's broken."

"Manual strangulation," Jonah said.

"That's what it looks like to me." Kelsey glanced at Allison. "It's different for children, but in most cases in which an adult is strangled manually, the hyoid is broken."

Jonah studied the film, then looked at Kelsey. "Any clues about how it went down?"

"There's no other sign of struggle, if that's what you're asking. No blunt-force trauma to the skull or bones that appear to have been broken around the time of death."

"What about an ID?" This from Allison, who was gazing at the body again. Jonah should probably get her out of here. She didn't really need to see this, but she'd insisted on being involved.

"I'll need dental records for that," Kelsey said. "The sheriff's working on it. We usually do a tooth pulp analysis for confirmation, using DNA. If speed is an issue—"

"It is," Allison said firmly.

"Then I can get the sample to Mia right away."

"We'd appreciate it," Jonah said.

Kelsey's gaze met his, and she suddenly looked like a worried friend instead of a detached scientist. "This is related to the school shooting, isn't it?"

"It's looking that way."

"I'm concerned about Sophie. I haven't heard from her since yesterday."

"I have," Jonah said. "And don't worry—she's somewhere safe."

The inside of the jail was a lot like a public restroom, only bigger and with worse smells coming up from the centralized drain. Sophie stared at it now, trying not to think about the odor as she shifted uncomfortably on the metal bench.

"God, what I wouldn't give for a cigarette." The woman beside Sophie turned and looked her up and down. "You got anything?"

"Sorry, don't smoke."

The woman squinted at her. "What're you in for, anyway?"

Sophie's throat tightened at the question. She looked away, but her gaze came to rest on the stainless steel toilet at the far end of the room—currently in use. She turned back to her neighbor.

"Assaulting a police officer."

"No shit?" The woman looked impressed. "Damn, girl, you're gonna be in awhile."

Sophie clenched her teeth and focused on the drain. Bodies shifted on the floor around it as people vied for space. Only midway through the holiday weekend and they were already full up on drunks and derelicts.

"I'm in for public intox," the woman said.

Sophie had deduced this herself when the woman stumbled in here, spewing obscenities. She promptly collapsed in the corner, where she spent the next four hours snoring.

Public Intox shifted beside her, and Sophie got a whiff of previously used alcohol. As revolting as it smelled, she would have traded her right arm right now for a stiff margarita.

Or a chance to kick Jonah Macon in the nuts.

"God*damn,* I want a smoke."

God*damn,* she wanted to kick him. Sophie sighed.

"You got *any*thing? Maybe some Nicorette gum?"

"Sorry." She glanced at the woman, curious now. Hadn't they been through the same booking procedure? How would she have smuggled gum in here? They hadn't even let her keep her shoes.

But then, maybe Woods had given the guards special instructions about how to handle her.

"Sophia Barrett."

Sophie glanced up, both mortified and insanely relieved to hear her name called. It was the guard from earlier, standing on the other side of the bars. Her brother must have come, *finally.*

Sophie jumped to her feet. Dozens of bleary eyes turned to look at her as she picked her way through the sea of bodies. They were holiday revelers, mostly— women who'd either had too much to drink on the river or gotten into trouble at one of the local pubs. Sophie stood beside the bars and watched the dour guard open the cell. She wore latex gloves again, and Sophie shuddered to think where her hands had been recently as the door slid open with a heavy *clink*.

Sophie followed the woman down a dim hallway, and her jail-issued rubber-soled shoes made squishing noises against the concrete. More foul smells. More drains. Sophie's legs felt stiff and sore, and she didn't know whether it was from hours of sitting or aftereffects of the car crash. She didn't even want to think of what she looked like. Ted was going to be appalled. He'd grill her endlessly. But she was so desperate to get out of here, she didn't care.

"This way."

The next room was lit by a painfully bright fluorescent fixture. Sophie blinked up at it. Her eyes adjusted, and she noticed the man standing across the room, leaning against the wall.

Not her brother, but Jonah.

Tears stung her eyes, and she quickly blinked them away.

She followed the guard to a counter, where a man was making notes on a clipboard.

"Sign these." He didn't look up, and Sophie thumbed through the papers, signing beside the X marks. A large brown envelope appeared on the counter in front of her, and the man emptied it out.

Her personal effects.

"One pair silver earrings," he droned. "One belt, leather. One tote bag. One pair sandals. One Visa credit card. One prescription bottle, codeine. One tube antibacterial ointment. One cellular telephone. One package contraceptive pills. One bottle Unisom—" She felt Jonah ease up beside her, but she didn't look at him. "—one bottle sunblock. And one envelope containing . . . five hundred eighty-six dollars and sixty-two cents."

Sophie's cheeks burned as she snatched up the tote bag and dropped the items inside.

"Sign here, ma'am." He slid a receipt of some sort in front of her, and once again she scrawled her name.

Then she bent down and slipped off the shower shoes. She handed them across the counter and dropped her sandals onto the floor.

"And my car keys?" she asked.

"Scott has them."

She turned to look at Jonah, making eye contact with him for the first time. He looked calm, cool.

"He picked up his truck earlier." Jonah glanced at the man behind the counter. "We good here?"

"That'll do it."

"Hey, what's the score on that game?" Jonah nodded at the small TV on the desk behind him.

Sophie's vision blurred with fury as she bent down to buckle her sandals. They were talking sports.

"Eleven-ten, Rangers," the man said. "Top of the ninth."

"Good to hear it. Thanks again, Phil."

Sophie cast one last glance around the room. The guard had disappeared, and Sophie hoped she never saw her again. She headed for the door marked with an Exit sign. Pretending to know exactly where she was going, she walked briskly down a corridor and took the first stairwell she spotted.

Jonah's footsteps echoed behind her. When they got to the bottom, he reached around her to push open the door. Another institutional-looking hallway, this one with linoleum flooring instead of concrete. Sophie made a beeline for a set of double glass doors.

"Would you wait up?"

She plowed through the doors and found herself outside the police station. It was hot and humid and smelled much less like a urinal than the room where she'd spent the past eight hours.

She was at a side exit. Jonah's pickup was parked beside the curb, and she took a deep breath. She was going to have to ride in it. With him. And she was so angry right now, she couldn't see straight.

She jerked the cell phone from her bag.

"Who are you calling?"

"My brother's on his way down here from Dallas."

"Not anymore. I called him."

She snapped the phone shut and glared at him.

He'd contacted her brother. He'd contacted Scott. He'd taken care of everything, and now he planned to drive her to some plot of dirt in the middle of nowhere where he probably expected to talk her down from the tower of rage she was standing on so he could get her naked tonight.

She dropped the phone back into her purse and walked to his truck. The locks chirped, and she jerked her door open before he could help her. She tried to pull it closed, but he caught it.

"Are you hungry?" he asked.

"No."

"It's pretty late."

"I'm not hungry."

Shaking his head, he went around and hitched himself behind the wheel. He started up the truck and steered out of the lot.

"You know, a little thanks would be nice."

She turned to look at him. He glanced at her and had the nerve to look irritated.

"You want *me* to thank *you*." She could practically feel the steam coming out of her ears.

"Yes, as a matter of fact. I called in a crapload of favors to get you out tonight."

Her eyes widened with outrage. "You *told* Woods to bring me in! I *heard* you on the phone with him! He was out looking for me!"

He glowered at her. "Yeah, and it never occurred to me you'd assault a police officer. What the hell were you thinking? The man has a shiner, Sophie. You know how hard it was for me to get him to drop the charges and forget about this?"

She clenched her teeth and looked away.

"Not to mention the D.A. I had to call her up at a freaking baseball game. Let me tell you how happy she was to hear from me."

Sophie bit her tongue and focused on looking out the window. If she opened the floodgates on her emotions, she doubted she could stem the tide. No way in hell did she plan to add crying in front of this man to her list of humiliations today.

She dragged her tote bag into her lap and found her sunglasses. She shoved them onto her face and leaned her head against the door.

"That's it?" he asked. "That's all you have to say?"

"What do you want me to say?"

"How 'bout explaining why you hauled off and hit a police officer?"

Her throat tightened. She remembered his hands clamping around her wrists. It had triggered something, some inner terror she didn't know she still had, and she'd panicked. Jonah knew about her kidnapping. She would have thought he, of all people, would understand. For him to be so dense made her feel physically sick. She'd been so wrong about him.

She closed her eyes and rested her cheek against the cool glass.

"Well?" he demanded.

"Wake me up when we get there."

She drifted off. For a long while she floated in and out of consciousness, only vaguely aware of the vibration of the truck and the changes in speed. It wasn't all that restful, but it kept her from having to keep up a conversation.

She thought of the waves crashing against her skin. She thought of the stench of that cell. She thought of Jonah, leaning against the wall and watching her shuffle out in those hideous shoes.

Her head jerked up and she turned to look at him.

"What baseball game?"

He glanced at her, obviously surprised by her sudden question after hours of silence. "Huh?"

"You said you called the D.A. at a baseball game. What game was it?"

"Rangers–White Sox. Why?"

She stared at him through her sunglasses, and the fury was back. She was fully awake now. She looked out the windshield as the truck bumped over a gravel road. It was pitch dark, and the headlights illuminated only a narrow swath.

"You waited *six hours* to call." She could hardly say the words, but she knew they were true. "You told my brother not to come get me and then you made me sit in that jail."

His silence confirmed it.

Sophie took off her shades and slid them into her tote bag. She hadn't thought it was possible to be angrier than she was leaving that police station, but she was learning all sorts of things about herself today.

Like she couldn't bear to have her hands bound.

Like the most shameful moment of her life was having her mug shot taken.

Like she was incapable of peeing in front of strangers.

She wished she'd never met Jonah Macon.

"We're here."

He drove past a grove of trees and pulled up to a camper. It was white. Old. Big, too, and Sophie was surprised to see it. She'd pictured a tiny silver Airstream, like her dad kept at his deer lease.

Sophie got out. She ignored Jonah as she stretched her legs and tried to get her bearings.

He came around the truck and stood in front of her, hands on hips. "You're still mad."

"You're perceptive."

"You want me to be honest with you?"

"No, lie to me."

He looked annoyed. The headlights on his truck switched off, and they stood there, staring at each other in the dark.

"I thought about getting you out right off the bat, but you were in the safest place you could be. And with your track record—"

"My *track record*?"

"Yeah, your track record. I tell you to stay at work, you go apartment hunting. I tell you to stay at the ER, you head for the beach. You're a flight risk, and there's a very dangerous person looking for you, and I've got too much fucking work to do to go chasing after you again if you take off. So, *yes,* I left you in jail for a few hours before moving heaven and earth to get you out. And this is the thanks I get!"

He stomped up the steps to the camper and opened it with a key. She followed him inside, fuming.

"*Thank you,* Jonah, for telling one of your buddies to arrest me! For having my gun confiscated! For having me strip-searched, and fingerprinted, and humiliated in front of a department full of police officers who *know* me, not to mention my entire family, who's going to hear about this. Thank you for treating me like some common criminal, like some *hostage,* after I agreed to come out here *voluntarily*!" Her hands were fisted at her sides as she glared up at him in the dim light of the camper. "I wasn't fleeing anywhere! I was returning Scott's truck to him, with a full tank of gas, like I said I would. Because when I tell someone I'll do something, I do it. I'm trustworthy, Jonah. If you ever took the slightest interest in getting to know me instead of just screwing me, you would *know* that, and none of this would have happened!"

She stood there, chest heaving, as he gazed down at her with a steely expression. The side of his jaw twitched. He was extremely pissed.

Well, so was she.

She turned away from him.

And suddenly she felt exhausted—more tired than she'd ever been in her life. She slumped into the nearest chair. It was a worn armchair, avocado green, and she didn't think she'd ever be able to move from it.

Jonah closed the door and locked it. For a few minutes, he moved around the camper, slinging groceries, opening and slamming cabinets, showing her just what he thought of her little speech.

Sophie glanced around. The place was spacious, for a camper. At one end was a living room with a built-in table and a U-shaped bench. There was a cramped kitchen and what looked to be a tiny bathroom. On the far end was a queen-size bed with an army-green blanket on it.

Sophie closed herself in the bathroom. She turned on the water and stripped naked for the third time that day. Then she stood under the spray and tried to wash away the stress. It didn't work. She got out just as tense and furious as she'd been when she stepped in. Of course, there was no towel, so she stood in the little room drip-drying and squeezing water from her hair into the sink. Finally, she wrestled herself back into her T-shirt and panties and stalked out of the bathroom.

The camper was dark, and Jonah was a massive lump on the left side of the bed. She stared at him and tried to tell whether he was asleep.

He sat up and looked at her. The light from the bathroom fell across his face, and she saw his eyes linger on her damp T-shirt.

She walked over to the empty side of the mattress, and he watched her warily.

"You coming to bed?"

She snatched the pillow up and took it across the room, where she tossed it down on an empty patch of carpet.

"I'd rather sleep in hell."

CHAPTER 22

Sophie awoke with a crick in her neck and a large man scowling down at her.

"My dad's here."

She sat up and brushed hair from her eyes. She tried to move her neck and winced at the pain.

"How'd you sleep?" His tone was smug, and she narrowed her gaze at him.

"Fine. You?"

"Fine."

She glanced around. The bed had been straightened, and she looked longingly at the mattress. Then she glanced back at Jonah. He was still scowling.

"What's wrong?"

"Damn coffeepot's not working."

Sophie looked over her shoulder at the kitchen. A lousy night's sleep she could handle. Lack of coffee was another matter. She got to her feet. He handed her a blue pill and rested a cup of water on the table beside her. She took the pill without comment but couldn't bring herself to thank him.

"I'll be gone all day. Stay out of trouble." He grabbed

his keys off the table and left, leaving her staring out the window after him as he trekked across the grass to meet the approaching pickup. She recognized Wyatt Macon behind the wheel.

Sophie watched them talk to each other through the open window. Jonah was in his full detective outfit—slacks, button-down, holster, badge. He had a big day ahead of him, apparently, despite the fact that it was Sunday.

He was a dedicated cop. And she admired him. And as angry as she felt, she knew that she was half in love with him, too, and that scared her. Because as good a cop as he was, as good a *man* as he was, he could be infuriating. And controlling. And arrogant. She wasn't sure she could handle a man like that for any length of time. She wasn't sure she even wanted to try.

She went into the kitchen and discovered a dismantled coffeepot in the sink beside a mug. All of it was covered in a layer of wet coffee grounds.

Jonah had gone to war with the French press and lost.

Sophie rinsed the pot. She found a saucepan and set some water to boil on the propane stove. As she waited, her gaze landed on a familiar gym bag sitting in the corner.

He'd been to her apartment.

Her chest tightened with remorse. She went over to the bag and crouched down to look through it. He'd packed T-shirts. Gym socks. Sneakers. A dizzying amount of racy underwear. Sophie sighed. What was she going to do with this man?

She picked the most practical items she could find and got dressed. She compiled a mental to-do list and resolved to have a better day. Then she made two cups of strong black coffee and went out to greet Wyatt.

Allison watched the sun come through the trees lining the winding highway. She passed an S-curve sign and tapped the brakes as a plastic orange fence came into view.

Allison slowed as she neared the spot where Sophie Barrett's Tahoe had sailed off the road. She cut a glance to the side and noticed the singed patch of brush that marked the site of the explosion. More than three days had gone by, and now Allison had even more questions than answers.

Focus.

She trained her gaze on the road in front of her. She worked on mapping out the day ahead. She worked on ignoring her emotions. She worked on analyzing her case objectively, instead of letting this gut-churning anger get the best of her.

Five victims, and those were just the ones they knew about. There could be more. And it wasn't even the body count that shocked her, it was the way in which they'd all been killed. So coldly. As if a human life was worth nothing more than the squeeze of a trigger or the toss of a match.

She rounded a bend, and the sun flashed in her eyes. She pulled her shades from her pocket, and her fingers brushed over the business card she'd tucked there days ago at the sandwich shop.

Allison slid on her sunglasses. She pictured Tyler Dorion, with his hearty handshake and ambitious smile.

In his quest for headlines, he'd gotten in over his head. He wasn't the first journalist to do it, but he had to be one of the youngest, and Allison couldn't seem to get a handle on the rage that had been consuming her since she'd seen his charred remains.

When she finally reached the Delphi Center, she was feeling calm and determined. She badged her way past the security gate and parked in the nearly empty lot. Not too many people working this holiday weekend, but she'd managed to pull in the expert she needed. She collected the brown paper evidence bag from the passenger seat and made her way up the wide marble stairs for the third time this week.

A few minutes later, she stood inside a sterile laboratory, with a visitor's badge clipped to her lapel and a lab-coated scientist at her elbow.

"This is the subject's backpack?" he asked.

"The victim's, yes."

Allison watched as Dr. David Lemberger unzipped the bag and lined up the contents neatly on a worktable, atop a piece of fresh butcher paper. As head of Delphi's QD section, Lemberger specialized in questioned documents, and his talents included everything from tracing printer toner to authenticating ransom notes. Mia had described him as a word wizard. With his round spectacles and trimmed gray beard, he seemed to fit the image.

She watched him gaze down at the tattered spirals of a budding reporter. "Three notebooks, eighty pages each," he muttered, stroking his beard. "And what is it you need exactly? I assume you've read through these."

"I have, yes. They were recovered from the victim's apartment. I'm interested in the story he was working on at the time of his death."

He reached for a box of gloves, but to Allison's surprise, they were made of cloth. He must have seen her curious look.

"Cotton," he said. "Latex can smear pencil and ink."

After donning the gloves, he lifted the corner of one of the reporter's pads. "There are some pages torn out."

"Exactly." Allison looked at the torn paper caught in the spiral. "I think those pages might have been important, because of what came immediately before. In one case, he writes the name and cell phone number of another murder victim—Eric Emrick—and then starts taking notes, like from a phone interview. Next page, it cuts off."

Lemberger made a *tsking* sound as he counted the pages. "Seventy-four here, so six missing. Not necessarily consecutive, although we can find out. He used a ballpoint pen, which is good."

"It is?"

"Requires more pressure. I can most likely recover the words for you."

Allison sighed with relief. "I was hoping you'd be able to do that. Can you rub over it with graphite or something?"

He smiled up at her. "You've been watching too much television, Detective Doyle."

"Allison." She'd dragged him in on a Sunday morning—the least she could do was keep this informal. "And, what? That's not how it works?"

"The rubbing method typically fails to visualize the

indented writing and also destroys it for other, workable methods. As a general rule around here, we prefer to use nondestructive techniques when dealing with evidence."

"Other methods being?"

"Oblique lighting should do the trick."

He walked over to the wall and switched off the lights, then took a handheld spotlight and positioned it beside the first page beneath the missing interview notes.

"Let's just hope all the important stuff was on the last page," Allison said. "Deeper indentions, right?"

"It's easier that way, but I can go several layers deep."

"You can?" Allison looked at the page he was examining. The task was made more difficult by the fact that several pages' worth of writing were overlaid. "Doesn't the writing get all jumbled together?"

"It does, but we can pull it apart. Determine which words go with which page based on the depth of the indentions, the angle of the writing, the meaning of the words."

"You can sort through all that?"

"Absolutely." He smiled slightly. "That's why we're called tracers."

Allison stared at the page, trying to decipher the shadows.

"I'm seeing numbers," she ventured.

"Dates, it looks like. And the word 'D-Syst'?"

"D-Systems." Allison's heart skipped. "The company where the victim interned this summer and last. How are you getting that? It looks like chicken scratch to me."

"Years of practice," he said. "Hold the light, please?"

Allison tried to hold it at the same angle he had as he

pulled a magnifying glass from his pocket and studied the page.

"Something about 'Project Shadow Tracker.' That's underlined three times, heavy pressure. Possibly something important."

Allison had never heard of it. "Are you seeing any names?" she asked hopefully. "Dates?"

"Says here '07 AFG' and a few more acronyms: SO, AR, USNS, RM." He glanced up. "That mean anything to you?"

"Nope." Allison pulled a notebook from her pocket and jotted it all down.

"I'll prepare a report," he told her. "But you said this is a high-priority investigation, so maybe you can at least get started." He flipped to the next page, but the indentions there were so faint, they were practically invisible.

"We can try one more method. Ever heard of an Electrostatic Detection Apparatus?"

She shook her head.

"It's an instrument that uses a toner that collects within the indentions so they can be visualized. It'll take me some time to complete an ESDA analysis, though. It's a bit more complicated." He checked his watch. "I'll have to get back to you later today."

Allison gazed down at her cryptic notes. What did these letters mean? She wished she had an audio recording to work with instead of all this jumble. But she remembered what Sean had said after their meeting at D-Systems. He was an investigator, and so he investigated. Allison should adopt that attitude. This was a homicide, not a bike theft, and no one had promised it would be easy.

She tucked her hand in her pocket and fingered the

business card. She planned to keep it there as a reminder, until whoever killed Ty Dorion was in jail or hell, whichever came first.

Jonah spotted four familiar cars when he pulled into the station and found the better part of the task force gathered around a box of doughnuts. Looked like the hub of the investigation had moved from the bullpen to the break room. Noonan's constant hovering and spin-doctoring had the effect of quashing creativity, which was what they needed right now to crack this case open.

"I knew Maxwell was holding out on us," Sean said. "I should go right back there and kick his scrawny ass."

Allison rolled her eyes. "Perfect. Just what we need. How about a police brutality lawsuit on top of everything else?"

Jonah stepped into the room and traded looks with Ric. "I miss something?"

"Project Shadow Tracker mean anything to you?"

"No. Should it?"

"I took Dorion's reporter notebooks to Delphi to be looked at by their questioned documents expert," Allison said. "He uncovered a bunch of writing from an interview with Eric Emrick. Acronyms, mostly, but there are a few full words."

"Lemme see." Jonah took the notebook from her.

"Those are just my notes," she told him. "Dr. Lemberger has the originals. He's trying to get more for us with some high-tech method."

" '2007 Afghanistan,' " Jonah read. "Looks like abbreviations for different spec-ops groups: Army Rangers, U.S. Navy SEALs, Recon Marines."

He glanced up, and everyone was staring at him.

"How the hell'd you get that?" Sean demanded.

"Years in the military." He handed back the notebook. "Place is a fucking alphabet soup." He glanced at Allison. "Sorry."

Another eye roll. "Yeah, apologize for swearing as you *break open our goddamn case*. Jesus, Macon. We should have had you in the interview with Maxwell. This whole thing has to do with some military project—I'd bet my life on it."

"I knew that guy was dirty," Sean said. "Everything out of his mouth was a fucking lie."

"Back up a sec." Jonah leaned against the door frame. "Someone wanna explain why any of this is a break in the case? So Eric worked for D-Systems. And they were working on some Defense Department project. You think that's what got him killed?"

"We think it's possible," Allison said. "What I'd really like to know is what this Project Shadow Tracker thing is about. Any chance one of your army contacts might know?"

"I wasn't exactly on the Joint Chiefs, but I can poke around." Jonah looked at Sean. "I don't much like all these leads pointing to some off-the-grid spec-ops stuff. Shadow Tracker. Shadow Warriors. We have any actual names?"

"Mia's still working on that DNA from the Beetle," Ric said, tossing a half-eaten doughnut in the trash. "No hits yet. Our best hope right now is that suspect sketch."

"What about Himmel's ex?" Jonah looked at Sean.

"I left a message to call me so I can fax her the suspect sketch. No answer."

"Convert it to digital, then e-mail it," Jonah suggested. "She might get it faster. Where is she, anyway?"

"Laying low with her sister and her children."

Ric's eyebrows tipped up. "She's worried about her children?"

"Wouldn't you be?" Sean asked. "So far, whoever's doing this has killed a grandfather, two college kids, and a pregnant woman, and tried to blow up a receptionist. Looks to me like the gloves are off."

"You tell him about the teddy bear blanket?" Ric looked at Jonah.

"What teddy bear blanket?" Sean asked.

"It was a rabbit," Jonah said. "Looked like a kid's security blanket. We found it in Himmel's motel room. Someone cut the ears off it."

"A veiled threat against Himmel's kids if he didn't complete the mission?" Allison suggested.

"*Veiled*?" Sean looked at her like she was crazy. "Ears cut off is veiled? Fuck, these witnesses need to be in lockdown!"

Jonah understood Sean's frustration, but it wasn't getting them anywhere. He looked at Allison. "Speaking of motel rooms, what's the sheriff's update on that surveillance cam at the fire scene?"

"No go," she said. "They had one pointed at the parking lot but—you're going to love this—the motel manager said it's a 'decoy.' Thing conked out years ago, they never bothered to get it fixed."

"There goes our chance of getting a look at whoever Dorion was out there meeting," Jonah said.

"How do we know he was meeting someone?" Ric asked.

"He told a friend he had a meeting Friday evening with a 'source' for some big story he was working on." Allison gave Jonah a somber look. "And Kelsey just called, by the way. Tyler Dorion's identity has been confirmed."

Silence settled over the room.

"We need motive," Jonah said. "That's what will tell us who's doing this. I'll see what I can find out about Shadow Tracker. Allison, see if you can get an update on those interview notes."

"I'll work the motel fire angle," Ric said. "Got a buddy over there who's a sheriff's deputy. Maybe there's some stuff they haven't tried or some employees over there who could use another interview."

"Sean?" Jonah gave him a hard look. "You want to come with me?"

Understanding passed between them. Maxwell needed leaning on, and Sean looked more than game.

"I'm in," he answered. "Let's go."

"Whoa, whoa, whoa, hold up." Allison stood. "You two are going to what, show up at Maxwell's house and play Good Cop Bad Cop? Which one of you's Good Cop? You look like a pair of raging bulls."

Sean sneered. "What are you planning to do, have a tea party with him?"

She shot him a glare, and Jonah knew she didn't like being discounted because she was a woman. Allison Doyle was tougher than she looked, he was discovering.

"Jonah, you focus on the military angle," she said firmly. "I'll go with Sean."

"Why?" Sean asked.

"Because he likes me," she said. "I'll disarm him with my charming smile."

Allison rode shotgun and navigated as Sean wove through the posh neighborhood just west of Austin.

"Hang a right here."

Sean cut her a glance as he pulled into a driveway lined with cars. It looked like a luxury auto show.

Allison whistled. "Nice party. Too bad I forgot my engraved invitation."

They pulled past a pair of young guys in matching golf shirts—the valets, presumably—and slid into a space beside a red Porsche Carrera. Allison smiled. If waterboarding was out as a means of getting information, they could at least use plain old embarrassment. They walked, badges visible, straight up to the front door.

"Mr. Maxwell around?" Sean asked, flashing his ID at the maid who answered the door.

"One moment, please." She gave his sidearm a nervous look, then directed them into a small sitting room off the foyer. They remained in the hallway as she hurried away, and Allison's gaze came to rest on the giant canvas that dominated the far wall. It was a Warhol-like silkscreen print of a pretty brunette. Allison stepped closer and examined the green and orange dots.

"Think it's real?" she asked.

Sean gave the picture a dismissive look. "Real what?"

Allison shook her head and turned away. More modern paintings, several abstract sculptures. Every piece of furniture she could see was made of leather, glass, or steel.

A very tense-looking Maxwell strode into the hallway. He wore taupe slacks and a trendy sports shirt that would have looked at home on the clay at the French Open.

"What are you doing here?"

Allison stepped forward. "Mr. Maxwell, good to see you again."

A young couple walked in, and he pasted a smile on his face as he greeted them. They cast curious glances at Allison and Sean, and Maxwell shuttled them to the back of the house. He reappeared, clearly rattled.

"*This* way." With a jerk of his head, he led them down a long tile hallway to an office. More modern furniture and abstract art. A large window looked out over the pool and patio, where the Fourth of July bash was in full swing.

The door clicked shut behind them.

"What is the meaning of this?"

Allison smiled. "Sorry to interrupt the party, Mr. Maxwell. We just had a few follow-up questions."

"Can't it wait? This is a private function."

Sean's eyebrows tipped up. "You want, we can take it down to the station. Nice and public there." He turned to Allison. "Think we got room in the back of the car, you don't mind moving all those case files."

Maxwell's face hardened. "What are your questions?"

Allison pulled out a notebook and made a production of leafing through the pages. She glanced up to see Sean taking a spot beside the window, much like he'd done last time. She knew he hadn't missed the security cam mounted in the corner. There had been one in the hallway, too, making her wonder again about that painting.

"You may recall, we were asking about Eric Emrick's internship over at D-Systems?"

"What about it?" Maxwell cut a glance at the window, probably worried about whether Sean's badge was visible to the guests milling around the negative-edge pool.

"We wondered if he might have been working on something called Project Shadow Tracker."

Maxwell stiffened. His gaze went from Allison to Sean, then back to Allison.

"I don't know of any such project."

Allison tipped her head to the side. "Are you sure?"

"Eric was an intern," Maxwell said. "He worked on applications for our cellular phone clients. I already told you this."

"You didn't answer her question," Sean said mildly.

"What was it?"

"Are you *sure* you've never heard of Project Shadow Tracker?"

Maxwell tucked his hands into his pockets and looked defiant. "No, I haven't."

Allison didn't like his glib tone. And his attitude was getting on her nerves. "We have a source that says otherwise."

"Who?" Disdainful now.

"Fella by the name of Tyler Dorion?" Sean folded his arms over his chest. "Newspaper reporter? Turned up dead yesterday morning in his motel room, by the way. Homicide."

"We're going through all his files right now," Allison added. "Lots of detailed information about you, your company, Eric Emrick."

"Yeah, we told the D.A. about it," Sean lied. "She

thinks it's going to make some interesting reading for the grand jury."

Maxwell blanched.

"Sure you want to stick with that story you've been shoveling?" Sean asked. "We might be able to help you out if you can explain what your name was doing all over this reporter's files."

"I never heard of him." He jabbed a finger at Sean. "And if you tell the media I had something to do with some pissant reporter getting killed, I'll sue both of you into next week."

Sean drew back in mock surprise. "Is that right?"

"Don't push me, Detective. You have no idea who you're dealing with. I've put up with enough of these slanderous allegations."

"It's not slander if it's true."

"I've had enough of this." Maxwell moved for a door on the other side of the room.

"Going to call your lawyer?"

He shot him a venomous look and disappeared behind the door.

"Fucking prick," Sean muttered.

"You think he's lying?"

He looked at her as if she were slow. "Are you kidding?"

Allison strode across the room and pulled open the door. It was a bathroom. Maxwell was backed up against the black granite counter, dialing a number on his cell phone. She closed the door behind her, then pulled the phone from his hand and ended the call.

"Ex*cuse* me!"

"Listen, Ryan." She grabbed his crotch and twisted,

hard. His mouth dropped open, and he let out a gasp. "You seem to be missing something. Tyler Dorion is dead." She twisted harder. "Four other people are dead, too, and I think you know something about it." His eyes rolled back and he made a choking sound. "Now, I need you to answer some very simple questions, or I'm going to get very pissed off very soon, all right?" He made another noise, and she squeezed again. "All right?"

A slight nod.

"All right, then." She let go and opened the door. She resumed her place in the other room and avoided Sean's gaze.

A few moments later, Maxwell shuffled from the bathroom and collapsed into his desk chair. Sean shot her a what-the-fuck look.

"Ask your questions," she said.

Maxwell was slumped forward, clutching his groin. His face was colorless and his haughty attitude had disappeared.

"Ask him."

Sean stepped up to the desk. "Have you ever heard of a Project Shadow Tracker?"

He nodded.

"Did Eric Emrick know about it?"

"Yes," he wheezed.

"Is that why he's dead?"

Maxwell glanced up at Sean. He looked at Allison. He squeezed his eyes shut and rubbed his forehead. "Yes."

CHAPTER 23

"I never told him to hurt anybody," Maxwell said. "He did that on his own."

"Who did?" Sean stepped closer and towered over him.

Maxwell glanced up. He looked pale and clammy, and Sean could smell the fear on him. He was screwed, and he knew it. Now it was just a matter of degree.

"Our security guy. I don't know his name."

Allison shook her head. "You're going to have to do better than that."

He shot her a hateful look. "I don't know, all right? He uses an alias."

Sean stepped closer, crowding him back in his chair. "You expect me to believe some security guy your company uses—whose name you don't even know— went off and arranged for these murders, all on his own?"

"I don't know what he arranged to do."

Sean planted a palm on the desk and got right in his grille. "I'm not buying it."

Maxwell scooted back in his chair and glanced

miserably around the room. "I didn't do this, all right? I swear. All I did was call someone in to deal with a security issue, and things started *happening*."

Sean straightened and looked him over. He could tell Maxwell was lying. But he also got the impression that there was some truth mixed in.

"You need to explain that," Allison said.

Maxwell rubbed his forehead. "Eric was a security problem. He'd hacked into our secure storage area and started downloading files about some of our top-secret projects."

"Like Shadow Tracker," Sean said.

"Like that, yeah. But that one was shut down." Maxwell shifted uncomfortably in his chair. "The government pulled the plug on it two years ago, but all the specs are still sitting there, in encrypted files, and Eric hacked into them. Threatened to sell them on the black market."

"Shadow Tracker," Allison said. "Explain what that is."

"I can't." He looked at her guiltily. "I signed a contract with the Defense Department. There could be sanctions."

Sean sneered. "You expect us to believe a college kid's going to know where to market top-secret military plans?"

"He was threatening to. It was probably a bluff, but he wanted money." Maxwell looked at Allison. "He was out of control! Everything was a game to him! I called our security guy in to go talk him out of whatever he was planning."

"You mean torture him." Allison said.

"No, *talk* to him. That's all. We needed him to be reminded of the gravity of what he was doing."

"Why didn't you report this to the police or the FBI?" Sean asked.

"I should have. I realize that now. But we do a lot of sensitive work here, and I didn't want it leaking out that some student hacker had compromised our security."

"I want a name," Sean said.

"I told you, I don't know. Just an alias."

"What is it?"

"Sharpe. That's all I have. That and a phone number."

Allison flipped open her notepad and tossed it on the desk in front of him. "Let's see it."

Maxwell hesitated. She tossed him a pen, and he started writing. When he was done, she picked up the pad.

"I'm going to call this in," she told Sean. "See what we get."

She slipped out of the room, leaving Sean alone with Maxwell and a very inconvenient security camera.

"Who's this guy work for?" Sean demanded.

"I don't know."

"Where'd you get his name?"

He sighed. "My predecessor gave it to me. Said if I ever had anything really sensitive come up, I should call this consultant."

"A *consultant*." Sean edged closer. "He's orchestrated the deaths of at least five people. Who paid him?"

This seemed to catch Maxwell off guard.

Follow the money. It was one of the first things he'd learned as a homicide cop.

"Well?" Sean pressed. "Five hits? Six, if you include having Himmel off himself to cover the tracks? Sounds like an expensive job."

"I didn't tell him to kill anyone! He was just supposed to handle a difficult employee."

"Sounds like he handled it. How much did you pay him?"

Maxwell hesitated, and Sean waited for the lie. "He wanted up-front payment. In full. That's how he did business, he said."

"How much?"

"Five thousand dollars to talk to Eric and find out how much hacking he'd done, how much damage control we needed to implement."

The room grew quiet except for the sounds of music and conversation coming up from the patio.

Much of this was bullshit. Sean knew it. But it gave him a direction.

It also gave him a renewed sense of urgency.

He stepped forward and leaned a palm on the desk again. He got up in Maxwell's face and felt a fresh wave of fear rolling off him. The man smelled like vinegar and cowardice.

"Let me tell you something, Maxwell. A lot of innocent people have been sucked into this thing that *you* created. You know what that means?"

Maxwell leaned back.

"Means I don't like you." Sean eased forward and lowered his voice. "If anyone else gets hurt in this, I will personally track you down, to a place where there aren't any cameras. And I will rip your goddamn head off."

The Rolling Hills Motel sat twelve miles outside of town on a state highway. The one-story building was old, run-down, and concealed from the road by a grove of oak trees. Jonah could see why someone might choose it as a place for a covert meeting and a deadly "electrical" fire.

Ric stood outside the smoke-blackened door of Room 119, which had been sealed shut by investigators. He was interviewing a Spanish-speaking maid whose statement sheriff's deputies had somehow failed to include in their report. Ric had been talking to her for a while now, and Jonah hoped he was having some luck.

Jonah sure wasn't having any. He'd been trying for over an hour to reach Wolchansky at Fort Benning, but the man was in the midst of a training exercise, and the woman who'd answered the phone at the base had been unable to track him down.

Jonah scrolled through his mental list of military contacts. There were plenty of people he'd have an easier time reaching, but none were special ops, with the exception of a SEAL he knew who was currently overseas. He could try his former CO and see if—

"Wolchansky."

Jonah snapped to attention. "Hey, she found you."

"Just got in. What's up? She said it was urgent."

"New lead in the case. Another military connection."

"Shit."

"Yeah, I know. You ever heard of Project Shadow Tracker?"

A pause on the other end, and Jonah's pulse picked up. He'd expected a flat, "Nah, man, never heard of it."

"It's been a while."

"So, you've heard of it?"

"Not recently," Wolchansky said. "Although I'm not even sure it's the same thing you're talking about. You said *Project* Shadow Tracker? I don't remember it being called 'Project.'"

"What do you remember?"

"Nothing concrete, really. This was just a rumor circulating awhile back in spec-ops circles. I didn't even think it was true."

Jonah pulled out his notepad. He could tell he'd hit pay dirt. "What was the rumor?"

"Some new technology being developed by, like, the Pentagon or someone. You know, black-ops kind of stuff."

"What was the big secret?"

"Well, supposedly they were piloting some project where Special Operations guys—Rangers, SEALs, think it was across the board—were having these chips implanted."

"Chips?"

"You know, computer things. At the time I heard about it, I remember thinking it was like my dog. He had one of those, where if he ever got lost, the pound could just scan his chip and find out where he lived. It was like that, but with GPS capability. I remember it supposedly worked off a battery, like a pacemaker or something."

"Soldiers were being implanted with these?"

"That's the thing—it was a rumor," Wolchansky said. "I never heard of anyone actually doing it. Most guys I talked to were kind of paranoid about it."

"How come? I can think of some benefits. Lot of those teams operate behind enemy lines. Mission goes south, they risk getting taken prisoner or killed before we can find them and pull them out."

"Exactly," Wolchansky said. "And yeah, some people thought it sounded good. But me? No way. I mean, it's too much like the Matrix or something."

"So, was it temporary? Permanent?"

He paused. "I haven't heard about this in a couple years. I'm thinking it was removable. Yeah, that's right, because I remember a guy—one of those paranoid types, but he had a point—he was saying how they put you under to implant the chip. So then how do you know, say, that they didn't put in more than one? You've got Uncle Sam tracking your every move for life."

"When did you hear about this?"

"Let's see . . ." Heavy sigh. "I was just back from Iraq at the time. Had to have been '07? Like I said, it's an old rumor. Far as I know, the program never got off the ground."

Maxwell had told Sean that the government had pulled the plug on the funding. But if the thing was shut down, why all this interest?

And it sounded expensive. If the program *had* been shut down, wouldn't the technology be worth something, at least on the black market, where Eric Emrick supposedly would have tried to sell it?

But how would some college kid—a very bright college kid, but still—realistically believe he could find a buyer for that sort of technology? It would have to be a government buyer, some intelligence agency or spy operation. Jonah's brain clicked with possibilities. Project Shadow Tracker—sounded like a LoJack for the government's most highly trained operatives, every one of whom represented a significant investment. It was the kind of thing that could be good if used by the right people for the right purposes—such as retrieving a wounded soldier from behind enemy lines. But that same technology in the hands of the enemy could be disastrous.

"You there?"

"I'm here," Jonah said.

"I need to go. Was there anything else?"

"Nah, that's it. Unless you think of something relevant, and in that case call me."

"Will do."

"And don't mention this—"

"Goes without saying."

Jonah ended the call and stared out the windshield. All sorts of scenarios were running through his brain now, and none of them was good. They all involved big dollar amounts, and highly sensitive information, and the sort of nasty people Jonah didn't like to think about even operating within American borders, much less right in his own backyard. He had the impulse to call his dad and check on Sophie.

He felt a strong surge of protectiveness. He wanted to lock her up somewhere and lose the key until Sharpe was six feet underground. The fact that someone like that had her on his hit list was bringing out some visceral, violent urges . . . along with some softer ones that made him just as uneasy, for different reasons.

This was why he shouldn't have let it get personal. His feelings for Sophie were messing with his brain, and he couldn't afford any distractions.

Because much of what Maxwell had told Sean had sounded like bullshit. He'd paid some guy five K to *talk* to Emrick? That kind of sum didn't ring true—not by a long shot. What *did* ring true was the other part: that Sharpe had wanted up-front payment and been paid in full before the job even got done. If that's what happened, it meant there was a price on Sophie's head, and even with Maxwell neutralized, she was still in danger. She was an unfinished job, or worse, a *botched* job. And a guy like Sharpe wouldn't want it getting out that he couldn't get the job done. He'd be seen as impotent, in every sense of the word.

Ric jerked open the door and slid inside. "I got a vehicle."

Jonah looked at him as he started the car. "I take it it's not a black Dodge pickup."

Ric cut a glance at him. "Think we've determined our guy's too smart for that."

"And too well-funded," Jonah added. There was some big money involved here, which made him worried about how this was going to go down. The stakes were higher than he'd ever imagined.

"White Ford Explorer, tinted windows, missing hubcaps," Ric stated.

"Maid see the driver?"

Ric slid his copy of the suspect sketch into the file as Jonah pulled out of the lot. "No luck there. But the vehicle's a pretty good lead. Especially since Sharpe might not know we know about it." Ric glanced at Jonah and frowned. "What happened?"

"I got ahold of my contact. He's heard of Shadow Tracker."

"And?"

"It's worse than we thought."

CHAPTER 24

Jonah heard his dad before he saw him. He stood near the fire pit just south of the camper, taking potshots at a line of cans on a distant fence. Sophie stood beside him. She turned to look as Jonah pulled up the road, and the sight of her very intact, very healthy body reduced at least some of his stress.

Jonah parked under an oak tree and went inside to change his work clothes for jeans and boots. Grabbing a beer from the fridge, he popped the top and brought it to his mouth, but stopped mid-sip as his gaze landed on the sleeping bag sitting in the corner.

It was his goddamn Cub Scout sleeping bag, and she'd dug it out from some cabinet and left it there, no doubt to piss him off with a hint about where she planned to sleep tonight.

Not happening.

He'd spent the better part of last night listening to her tossing and turning on that floor until his head was about to explode, and he was damned if he'd listen to it again.

He strapped on his holster and went outside.

Now Sophie was shooting. He studied her form as he

approached from behind. She had a wide stance, a two-handed grip, and a steady aim. She fired off a round, and the aluminum can flipped off the fence post thirty feet in front of her.

"Not bad."

Jonah glanced at his dad. Sophie didn't know it, but she'd just received Wyatt Macon's highest compliment when it came to target shooting.

He nodded at Jonah. "I lent her the nine-mil."

Again, Jonah was surprised. It was the pistol his mom had always used.

Sophie fired another round, and another can went sailing. Now that the sun was lower, she'd taken off her sunglasses and hooked them in the V-neck of her T-shirt. A little crease formed between her brows as she squinted at the fence again.

"Relax your shoulders," Jonah told her.

She ignored him, and his dad gave him a stern look.

She squeezed the trigger, missed, and mumbled a curse.

His dad smiled. "Ah, let's call it a day, Sophie. You been at it two hours now."

She turned around and huffed out a breath. "Yeah, I guess you're right." She glanced at Jonah, but only for a second. "I'm going to get a drink. You want a beer or anything?"

The question was obviously not directed at Jonah, as he was holding one already and she had yet to acknowledge him.

"I better be getting back," his dad said.

Sophie looked concerned. "You're not staying?"

"Can't do it." He pulled off his John Deere cap and

wiped his brow with his forearm. "Got to get home, take the dog out. I'll be back tomorrow, though. We can get out the long gun, if you want."

She gave him one of her rare genuine smiles. "I'd like that, Wyatt. Thanks."

"You hang on to that pistol now." He nodded at it. "It's yours until you get your other one replaced."

"Well, thanks. That's really sweet. See you tomorrow, then."

She turned to Jonah with a dim imitation of the bright smile she'd had for his father. "Hi."

"Hi."

She walked off toward the camper, and Jonah watched her go.

His dad slapped him on the back. "You got your work cut out for you, son. I'll be back at eight." He pulled his keys from his pocket and headed for his truck. The beer he'd refused, along with the spring in his step, told him his dad had a date tonight.

Jonah sighed. "Thanks for coming."

He waved without turning around and climbed into his truck. As his taillights faded down the road, Jonah heard the camper door open and shut again.

Sophie walked up beside him. She swigged her beer and then rested it on the ground at her feet.

"Want to shoot?" she asked.

"You go ahead."

"Suit yourself." She lifted the gun and aimed it. "So. How was your day?"

How was your day, dear? The question was so June Cleaver, and it sounded strange coming from a woman in tight jeans and strappy heels, who was holding a pistol.

She turned to look at him and lifted an eyebrow. "Well?"

"Busy."

She sighed and shook her head, probably miffed not to be let in on all the details. She returned her attention to the target.

Squeezed the trigger. Can was history.

"Who taught you to shoot?" he asked, impressed.

"My father."

"He give you the LadySmith?"

She took aim again. "I bought it for myself."

"Here." Jonah moved behind her and rested his hands on her hips. "Wider stance."

She moved her legs apart without complaint, and Jonah let his hands drop away.

She fired. Hit.

He whistled.

She glanced at him over her shoulder, and for a moment, they just looked at each other. She was still really pissed, and he felt guilty.

"It was the cuffs that set you off, wasn't it?"

She turned away and pretended not to know what he was talking about.

"Sophie?" He took her arm and turned her to face him, then carefully slipped the pistol from her hand.

"Hey, I'm not finished."

"Never argue with a woman holding a loaded gun." He smiled down at her. "Personal rule."

She plunked a hand on her hip. "I didn't realize we were arguing."

"Next time you want to hit a cop, hit me."

She rolled her eyes. "I don't want to hit you."

"Yeah, you do." He flipped the safety and tucked the pistol into the back of his jeans. "Come on. I deserve it."

"Don't be ridiculous."

"Gimme your best shot."

She looked him up and down and pursed her lips. Then she reached out and smacked his chest.

"Aw, come on. You hit like a girl."

"I am a girl." This time she made her hand into a fist and gave him a solid thunk on the chest.

He shook his head. "Didn't your brothers teach you anything?" He lifted her hand in his and adjusted her fist. "Thumb out. Now pop me one."

She hesitated. Then took a lightning-fast swing at his jaw and caught it with the palm of her hand.

He grinned down at her, and she eyed him suspiciously. "You're getting turned on by this."

"Honey, everything you do turns me on."

"I'm still mad at you."

He decided to quit while he was ahead. He reached down and laced his fingers through hers. "Come on. I want you to see something." He tugged her toward his truck, but she kept her feet planted. "Come on."

She followed. "Where are we going?"

"You'll see." He opened the passenger's-side door and resisted the urge to cop a feel as she slid inside. This woman had his number. He wasn't sure if it was the jeans or the shoes or the attitude, but he couldn't be around her and not think about sex.

He got behind the wheel and made a bumpy circle around the camper to loop back to the road. The sun was getting low now, and even the small rocks cast long shadows on the gravel road. He hooked a right onto an overgrown path and then loosened his grip on the wheel and let the tires find the ruts in the dirt.

"Where are we going?"

"I'll show you."

They drove in silence for a few minutes past scrub brush and boulders and clumps of prickly pear. The grade started to get steep as he maneuvered north.

It felt good to be out here in familiar country with Sophie riding beside him. He hadn't realized how much of his stress was about her being out of his sight, and now that she was right here—even though she was still in a snit—he was finally able to ratchet down his tension level from an eleven to maybe a nine-point-five.

He spotted a familiar tree stump and skirted around it before rolling to a stop.

Sophie stared through the windshield. "Wow."

They looked out over a meadow. From their vantage point on the edge of a ridge, they could see straight over a line of trees to a thick carpet of grass.

"The row of trees there, that marks the creek. It's the lowest part of the property, so it stays pretty wet."

An orange longhorn stood in the shade of an oak on the far end of the meadow.

"This is a cattle ranch?"

"About a hundred head. He's got about five thousand acres, manages it remotely from San Antonio. Caretaker lives on a few acres across the highway. That bull there, he's a troublemaker. He gets his own separate pasture."

They looked out over the field. The high grass was golden in the fading sunlight. It was the nicest spot on the property. Jonah had been coming out here all his life, and this was his favorite place.

He turned off the engine, and everything got quiet and still. The only sound was the low hum of cicadas.

"I'm sorry I told Woods to bring you in."

Sophie looked at him. She looked down at her lap. "I shouldn't have hit him. He was just doing his job."

She was right. And she'd deserved to get arrested. But Jonah wasn't about to point that out right now.

"I need to apologize to him at some point." She gazed out the window.

Jonah reached over and rested his hand on the back of her seat. He stroked his thumb over her neck. Her cheeks were pink, as was the tip of her nose. Looked like she'd spent most of the day outside.

She turned and gave him a curious look. "Did you bring me here to make out?"

"Yep." He brushed her hair off her shoulder.

"Isn't that a little high school?"

He let his hand trail down to her waist and tugged at her jeans to reveal a strip of skin and a narrow band of lace.

"Purple." He looked at her.

"Yes. And thanks, by the way. Your clothing selections were very interesting."

"Just trying to help." He slid his arm around her waist and pulled her closer. "You're not really still mad at me, are you?"

"Very."

He brushed the hair out of her eyes. "Really?"

She nodded, and the hurt on her face made his chest tighten.

"Sophie." He kissed her forehead. "I need you to forgive me."

She looked at him for a long moment and he waited, anxious. He could hardly breathe for wanting this girl, and he realized he'd never had so much riding on one apology.

"I'll think about it," she finally said, and leaned forward to kiss him.

CHAPTER 25

His arms tightened around her, and he lifted her right out of her seat and into his lap. She fell against his chest, and he shifted her legs so she was straddling him.

"Wow, you really put the moves on." She settled onto his thighs, and he was already tugging up her T-shirt.

"Hey." She slapped his hand. "We aren't even to first base yet."

Heat sparked in his eyes, and he jerked her against him. His mouth was hard and hungry. His tongue swept against hers, and she melted into the familiar taste of him, the familiar feel of his arms around her as he kissed her. She'd thought about this last night from her spot on the floor, and it was all she could do not to swallow her pride and crawl into bed with him. But she'd wanted an apology first, and now he'd given it to her, and she knew him well enough to know it hadn't been easy, because he was every bit as stubborn as she was.

As evidenced by the fact that his hands were still sneaking under her shirt. He cupped her breasts and moved the lace aside with his thumbs, and she decided she didn't care if he was rushing this. They could take it slow later, when they'd gotten this blinding lust out of the way. He squeezed her gently with his big hands.

She loved the way he touched her. Tipping back her head, she pulled the shirt off, and he helped her free it from her arms. He flung it on the floor and locked his mouth on her breast.

She closed her eyes and combed her fingers into his hair. It was thick and surprisingly soft, and she liked that he had so much of it. She hoped he wouldn't be one of those men who lost it all early. And then she pushed the thought away because it was way, way too long range, and she couldn't let herself think like that. She just wanted to think about the here and now, and how amazing his mouth felt against her skin, and how everything he did to her made her blood rush.

She shifted on his lap, and he groaned, deep in his chest. She did it again and watched his eyes drift open. He glanced down at her breasts and froze.

"Damn, Sophie."

She followed his gaze to her line of bruises, green today. He traced his finger over her abdomen, and she saw his jaw harden.

"It doesn't hurt," she whispered, reaching back to unhook her bra. She tossed it away and distracted him by kissing him.

Her fingers trailed over the bristles along his jaw as she licked into his mouth and he played with her breasts. She rolled her hips against the hard bulge in his jeans.

He pulled back and gave her a desperate look. "Are you trying to kill me?"

She smiled and reached for his shirt. He pulled it over his head and dropped it on the floor. Man. Jeans. Gun.

She sat back and sighed contentedly as he unbuckled his belt and loosened it from his holster. She watched his muscles ripple as he pulled the belt loose and stretched his arm back to stow the holster in the space behind the seat. Then he reached his arms around her to adjust the steering wheel, and she felt a shiver of lust as their bare skin touched. He racked the seat back, giving them more room.

"Seems like you've done this before."

He pulled her hips, and she tipped forward and fell against him.

"True," he said. "But I think I was about sixteen."

She braced her hand against his shoulder, and he glanced down at her breasts.

"Sixteen, huh? I'm impressed."

"Don't be. It lasted maybe two minutes."

His lips moved down her neck, and he shifted lower in the seat until she was leaning over him. He kissed her and licked her until she squirmed away from him and scooted back. She undid the snap of his jeans, then slid her hand inside and smiled at the very male groan he made as she touched him. The next thing she knew, he'd rolled her onto her back, swapping their places, and he was working on her zipper. There was an urgency now, and she could tell he was done playing around. She kicked off her sandals. Together, they wrestled with her jeans, and he ended up in the seat beside her so she could stretch her legs out while he tugged the cuffs free. Now she was down to a skimpy bit of purple lace, and he moved it aside impatiently so he could touch her.

She closed her eyes and gasped, gripping his shoulders as he hovered over her. It was too good, too much, and she started to see stars behind her eyelids. She felt the last bit of fabric being slipped down her legs, and then he moved under her, rolling her on top again, only this time she was naked. She glanced around and couldn't believe she was doing this out in the open this way.

"Jonah, do you think—"

"No one can see us." He hurriedly unzipped his jeans, and then grabbed her hips and—

She gasped. He moved beneath her, and she gasped again. And then he clutched her hips and pulled her against him, hard, and she yelped. As she gripped his shoulders and ground herself against him, she felt the heat building and building between them. His eyes were closed, his face taut. He looked almost in pain, and she felt the exact same way because that full, perfect feeling she wanted stayed just out of reach.

"Jonah. Oh my God."

"Tell me when, honey."

She grasped his shoulders and closed her eyes and strained to get closer and closer and . . . he shifted beneath her. "*Yes*. Oh, yes. I love that. I love you. *Jonah!*"

He plunged deeper, and suddenly everything was too hard, and too bright, and too intense. A wave of pleasure crashed over her, and she shuddered in his arms and went to pieces. She slumped against him as he squeezed her tight and finished riding the same wave.

The truck went silent. The only sound was the buzz of insects outside. Her cheek was pressed against his shoulder. Their chests were glued together with sweat. She felt his arms, draped heavily over her back, anchoring her against him.

Her words came back to her, and she felt a flush all

the way to her scalp. Maybe he hadn't heard. Maybe he'd been too caught up in the moment to notice. Or maybe he'd think it was one of those things she said in the throes of passion.

Only she'd never said it to anyone. Not like this. She didn't know whether to be embarrassed or panicked.

His arms slid off of her and he groaned.

She was crushing him. She pushed back from his chest and brushed her hair out of her face. His eyes were still shut, and he looked totally blissed out. She took advantage of the chance to compose herself. Her bra was draped over the gearshift, and she pulled it on.

"How did we manage to steam up the windows? It's ninety degrees out."

He opened his eyes slightly. "It's hotter in here." He reached out and pulled her against his chest, and she tentatively settled her head there.

"You're sweaty," he said.

"Um, hello? So are you."

"Just an observation."

"This was your idea."

He wrapped his arms around her and sighed heavily. "Best sunset I ever saw."

They lay there for a while and she listened to his heart slow. She traced her finger over his chest and hoped this wasn't going to be awkward now. She could handle him ignoring what she'd said, but she didn't know if she could handle his rejection. She imagined him giving her some line about how he liked her, he just didn't want a commitment, and her stomach twisted into a knot.

"You hungry?" he asked.

"Starving. How'd you know?"

"You were starving last time, too. I figured maybe it's a thing."

She sat up, and this time he sat with her. She slid into the passenger seat and tried—with as much grace as she could—to locate and reassemble her clothes. She glanced up and caught him watching her as she leaned back against the seat and zipped up her jeans.

"What?" she asked.

"Nothing."

She tossed his shirt at him, and he pulled it on. Another sideways look.

"What?" she demanded.

He shook his head and started the truck. He blasted the A/C and pointed a vent in her direction. "How about steaks and potatoes?"

"Sounds good."

"I'll fire up the grill." He looked at her. "And then we need to talk."

Gretchen opened the door to her sister's condo and wasn't surprised to see Sean.

"Long way from San Marcos, aren't you?"

"I've left you three messages. Why haven't you called me?" He stepped inside without an invitation.

"I was about to. I've been busy all afternoon."

"With what?"

"I met with an attorney. He's a friend of my sister's. I wanted to get his advice, make sure I'm not breaking any laws here."

"And what'd he tell you?"

"That I should be careful what I say to you." She looked him over and sighed. He'd driven a long way just to talk to her, so it must be important. So much for the legal advice.

"Come on in." She led him into the kitchen, and he watched her impatiently as she took a few glasses down from a cabinet and filled them with water.

"Did you read my e-mail, at least?" he asked.

"What e-mail?"

"I sent you a drawing. We have a witness who may have seen Sharpe."

"Sharpe?" She handed him a glass and he set it down on the bar.

"That's his alias. He's the man who hired your husband. We need an ID on him ASAP, and we finally got a suspect sketch from this witness who saw him on campus, parking Jim's car."

Gretchen stared at him, her pulse racing now. Thank God her children were in hiding with Marianne. They were at an out-of-the-way place no one could possibly know about.

"I didn't get the picture. Maybe it went into my spam folder." Gretchen walked into her sister's bedroom, which doubled as an office. The bed was unmade, but she ignored it as she sat down in the chair and turned on the system.

"Something happened, didn't it?" She turned to look at Sean and felt a wave of alarm.

"Why aren't you with your kids?" he asked.

She didn't answer.

"You shouldn't be here, Gretchen. This location's too obvious."

"I figure, if someone wants to come looking for me or the money, they'll find me but not the girls."

"They may not want *money*," Sean said. "We think Sharpe's responsible for a hit on a reporter and the attempted murder of the witness who gave us the sketch."

Gretchen looked at the computer and bit her lip. The screen came to life, and she entered Marianne's password.

"Maybe I'll join them," she said. "I don't know. I just thought it would be safer this way."

"Gretchen, did either of your girls ever have a security blanket with a rabbit on it?"

She turned to look at him and felt the blood drain from her face. "Mr. Bunny?"

"Was it beige? A stuffed animal with a blanket attached?"

"What happened?" She jumped to her feet and darted across the room to snatch up the phone. She dialed Marianne's cell number.

"Calm down. Nothing happened."

"That's Angela's blanket! It's been missing for weeks. How did you know about it?"

"Hello?" Marianne said on the other end.

"It's me. Where's Angie?" Gretchen held her breath.

"She's right here, why?"

"What about Amy? Are you all okay?"

"We're fine." Pause. "Gretch, what's wrong?"

She looked across the room at Sean.

"Gretchen?"

"Nothing. I was just checking in." She didn't want to terrify her. "Sorry. I'll call you later, okay? Give the girls a hug for me."

She hung up the phone and stared down at her hands. She was shaking now. She felt sick. She glanced up.

"Tell me what happened," she said. "I need to know."

He hesitated.

"Sean—"

"The blanket was recovered from Jim's motel room—the place he stayed the night before the shooting."

"I don't understand. How would Jim have Angie's blanket? He hadn't seen her in a year."

"Someone else might have taken it. To threaten him. To make sure he didn't back out at the last minute." Sean paused. "The rabbit's ears were cut off."

Gretchen felt the world falling out from under her.

"Whoa." Sean lunged over and caught her as she slid to the floor. He helped her up onto the bed. "Head between your knees." He pushed her head down, and Gretchen stared at her bare feet.

He was threatening the girls. Whoever this was knew about the twins and was threatening them.

"You okay?"

She sat up, slowly. She felt dizzy. Terrified.

"Who *is* this?" She jumped up. "I want to know who this is! I'll kill him myself!"

"Calm down."

"Don't you *dare* tell me to calm down! These are my *children*! What do you know about children? You don't even have any!" Tears streamed down her cheeks and she looked helplessly at the phone. God, if anything happened to her daughters, she'd die. She'd just curl up and die.

She looked at the detective, who was eyeing her warily.

"Sorry." She covered her face with her hands. "That wasn't fair. I didn't mean to attack you like that. I'm just—" She swiped the tears away. "I'm just terrified."

She looked over at him. "What can I do? I need to do something."

"You need to go be with your kids. Are they somewhere safe?"

She took a deep breath and tried to pull it together. "They're in a state park in Georgia. My sister rented a cabin. They're hours from anywhere. No one knows about them. I'm going to go there," she said, making the decision right there on the spot. "I need to be with them."

"That's probably best."

She returned to the computer. "Now, show me this picture you sent. I doubt I can help, though. I didn't know that many of Jim's army friends. Most of them were single. When did you send the photo?"

"This morning, around eleven."

She sat down and opened her account. Sure enough, there was an e-mail from him in the spam folder. She opened the message and then the attachment.

A picture came up on the screen, and Gretchen's blood ran cold. She brought her hand to her throat. "Oh my God. *This* is him? This is the man calling himself Sharpe?"

"What? Who is it?"

"Joe Shugart. He's not some army buddy—they grew up together." She looked at Sean. "This man was in our wedding."

Sophie was a conversational pro, and she managed to keep the small talk going all the way through dinner. And afterward, just when Jonah was ready to bring up something serious, she distracted him again by taking off her clothes.

She lay beside him now, pretending to be asleep as Jonah stared at the ceiling and tried to map out a plan. She couldn't stay here, not after tonight, anyway. Things were escalating, and he no longer felt safe with this ad hoc arrangement. He'd talked to Ric earlier about bringing in the FBI, and they'd hatched a plan to do it, even at the risk of going over Chief Noonan's head. Some of what Maxwell had told Allison and Sean involved federal defense contracts, which meant federal charges—possibly even treason. No one on the task force would be thrilled to bring in the feds, but their involvement would mean help on the witness protection front. The possible sale of military secrets qualified as a Big Fucking Deal and made the whole investigation—literally—a federal case.

Jonah's cell buzzed from the floor. He gently rolled Sophie onto her side and grabbed his jeans off the carpet. He fished the phone out.

"Yeah?"

"We got an ID," Sean said.

"Hang on." Jonah tossed the phone down and pulled his jeans on. He tucked his Glock in the back of his pants as he watched Sophie still pretending to be asleep while she eavesdropped. He knew she was pretending because she wasn't making that faint sniffling noise she did when she was actually out. Jonah stepped outside of the camper and put the phone to his ear again.

"DNA came back?"

"No, based on the picture," Sean said. "Himmel's ex recognized him. Joe Shugart, aka John Sharpe. Guy was a Ranger, special-ops regiment, before he got dishonorably discharged back in '05."

"Why'd he get discharged?"

"Still working on the details there. Anyway, after that he went rogue, joined some private mercenary outfit where he worked under an alias."

"Name doesn't ring a bell," Jonah said. "They go through any training together? I thought I checked everyone out."

"Connection's deeper than that. Turns out they went to high school together. This guy was in their wedding."

"Damn."

"And listen to this. I've spent the last three hours running down his background. He hasn't filed a tax return in five years. No current address. No bank account. He's living totally off the grid."

Jonah paused. That wasn't the sort of background check they had access to down at the station. "You brought in Ric's brother, who was with the FBI."

"We need some help on this thing," Sean said. "These witnesses—"

"Hey, I'm with you. What did he say?"

"He's working on it. Might have something by tomorrow. Then it's going to be a matter of getting Sophie Barrett and Gretchen Parker on board. Neither one strikes me as the type to go quietly into hiding while a bunch of feds track down their man and prepare a trial. And what about afterwards? Not sure they're going to want to just start their lives over somewhere."

"There's not going to be a trial for Sharpe," Jonah said.

Silence as Sean absorbed his meaning.

"It may not be up to us."

Jonah didn't dispute that, but he knew what he knew.

If someone managed to track down Sharpe, only one person was walking away.

Jonah intended to be that person.

"I've been thinking about this technology," Sean said now.

"So have I."

"Some college student isn't likely to find a buyer for information like that, no matter how smart he is."

"No shit," Jonah said. "I buy that Emrick was a hacker and stumbled into something important. I don't believe he was trying to sell it, though. Maybe he figured out someone else was."

"Maxwell," Sean said.

"Exactly. He was probably looking for a buyer after the government pulled the plug on the project. He was using Sharpe to do the legwork for him because of his network. Sharpe probably cut himself into the deal, too."

"So, your military connection—he know whether they actually started implementing this thing before the funding got yanked?"

"You mean do some of our operators actually have those chips implanted?" Jonah asked.

"Yeah."

"I don't know, but just the possibility makes this stuff all the more attractive on the black market. Every hostile government and radical terrorist org in the world will be chomping at the bit to get ahold of this technology. Maxwell could probably get a fortune for it."

"This guy Sharpe wore a uniform once," Sean said. "Hard to believe he'd do that to his own country."

"His country fired him. Probably with good reason, but still. Could be he's lashing back at the army here.

Or maybe this is about greed, plain and simple, and he uses his beef with the government to justify taking the money."

"Either way," Sean said, "sounds to me like Eric discovered what Maxwell was up to through his hacking and *that's* why he was a 'security problem.' Maxwell's a fucking liar."

Jonah didn't say anything. It was the only kind of suspect he'd ever interviewed. Why was Sean so surprised?

"Where is he, anyway?" Jonah asked. Last he'd heard, the man had clammed up and called an attorney.

"We got him in custody on some obstruction charges," Sean said. "We're going to try and make them stick until the feds pull together something better, but there's a chance he'll get out on bond. He's got connections."

"There probably *is* one thing he was telling the truth about," Jonah said. "Sharpe getting paid up front. That sounds like his MO. Get paid, get the job done, get out."

Silence on the other end of the phone.

"Is Himmel's ex someplace safe? Until the feds come through?"

"I'm working on it," Sean said. "How about Sophie?"

"I got it covered." Jonah opened the door and stepped back inside the camper. She lay on her stomach now in the center of the bed, so he'd have to move her when he got back in. Which would lead to other stuff he'd have to do.

All before he could get around to the really fun conversation of how she needed to take an extended—and possibly permanent—vacation from her job while investigators tracked down a highly trained operator who'd been paid to kill her.

"Anyway, tell her thanks for me," Sean said.

"What's that?"

Sophie stirred in the bed.

"Her suspect sketch. It was the break we needed. We wouldn't have an ID if it hadn't been for her."

"I'll tell her," Jonah said, and ended the call.

Sophie blinked her eyes open and looked up at him. A slow smile spread across her face, and Jonah's pulse picked up. He recognized the look. That tough conversation was going to have to wait.

Half moon. Clear sky. Moderate breeze out of the southwest. He would have preferred a little more cloud cover, but overall, not bad conditions for a hunt.

Sharpe dragged out his pack. A quick check of his equipment and he was good to go. He crouched in the grass beside the SUV and used the nearby brush to conceal himself as he applied camo paint by the light of his flashlight. He checked the side mirror a couple of times until he was satisfied with the result, then tossed the paint back in his pack and moved on to more important matters.

He took out his Leupold spotting scope, which he kept in a camo zipper case, and looped the strap around his neck. Next decision, ammo. The mission called for .308 bullets, and he considered taking only two—one for each target. *One shot, one kill.* But although he could do this job with his eyes closed, he made a habit of being prepared for contingencies. He stuffed ten rounds in the zippered pocket of his tactical pants and grabbed an extra magazine for his sidearm.

Finally, his rifle. It was an M40A1, fitted with a Schmitt

& Bender telescopic sight. It was a nice gun, nicely tricked out, but still similar to the Remington 700 he'd used in the beginning. From the time he'd first touched it, he'd been in love with that gun. He'd wanted to be a sniper. He'd wanted to hunt something that could hunt him back.

And he had.

Now his missions were more mundane, and he missed the rush of a good challenge, the thrill of the hunt and not just the kill. But thrill or no, he had a job to do. He lived off his reputation, and he had a reputation for reliable execution.

Sharpe looked out into the darkness and let his eyes adjust. He slung the gun across his back and slipped into the woods.

CHAPTER 26

Sophie put the finishing touches on her makeup and stepped out of the bathroom to find Jonah leaning impatiently against the wall.

"It's about time." He glanced at his watch. "How long does it take to get dressed for a day in the sticks?"

She squeezed past him and reached for the coffeepot. "Aren't we in a cheery mood this morning?"

He caught her arm and turned her around. "No more distractions, Sophie. We need to talk."

She huffed out a breath and cocked her head. "You're not going to get all male on me, are you?"

"What's that supposed to mean?"

"Never listen to what a woman says in the throes of ecstasy." She reached around him and took a mug from the cabinet. She poured some coffee and turned around.

The side of his mouth was curved up in a cocky smile.

"What?"

"Ecstasy, huh?"

She rolled her eyes. "Oh, please. We both know we've got a certain . . . chemistry going here. Doesn't mean I'm planning to rush out and get your name tattooed on my arm. You don't have to get all skittish on me."

He looked annoyed now. "That's not what I wanted to talk about."

"It's not?"

"No." He folded his arms over his chest. "We need to talk about your security situation."

Sophie took a sip of coffee and tried to settle her nerves. "What about it?"

"I don't like it."

"Why not?"

"Because there are some new developments in the case."

Sophie set the mug down. "Such as?"

"Such as stuff I can't talk about. You're going to have to take my word for it that it's serious."

It was her turn to get annoyed. "Yeah, I kind of figured that out when someone *blew up my car.* Why won't you just be straight with me?"

Jonah looked at her long and hard, as if debating whether to trust her. "How do you feel about taking a leave of absence?"

"From my job?" The minute she said it, she felt stupid. Of course that's what he meant. "For . . . for how long?"

"I'm not sure. A week or two. Maybe a month."

She gaped at him. "Are you kidding? I'll get fired!"

His blank expression pissed her off.

"*Why* would I want to do that?"

"Does it really matter? You said you were looking for a new job, anyway."

"Yeah, I'm looking for a *promotion.* At the Delphi

Center. I have a good shot at getting it, too. There's no way I'd just up and leave right now. What's this about, anyway? Tell me what happened."

He hesitated.

"Don't you dare give me some crap about how it's confidential. This is my life we're talking about. My livelihood. How would you like it if I suggested you just walk in and turn in your badge?"

He paused, but she still wasn't sure he was getting how she felt about this.

"The FBI is involved now, and I think I can get you federal protection."

Her hands dropped to her sides. "What? Why?"

"Because we've IDed the person we're looking for, and I'm no longer comfortable with this security setup. You need something more sustainable until we can close the net and bring this guy in."

Sophie's blood chilled. "Does someone know I'm here?"

"Just my dad and Ric. That's not the issue."

"But—"

"I think I can get the details hammered out today, hopefully have something together by tonight." His serious expression told her she wasn't going to like what he was planning.

"What does that mean, exactly?"

"I'm not sure yet. Probably one or two agents, a rotating watch." He paused. "The San Antonio field office is working with a couple of others, seeing who can spare the manpower."

"You mean, like, another state?"

"Possibly."

"For how long?" Sophie's stomach tightened. The thought of being shuttled off somewhere, away from her work and her friends and Jonah, made her queasy.

"It depends on the investigation. We're doing everything we can to bring this guy in, not just for your sake but other people's, too."

Sophie looked at him and felt a stab of hurt. He made it sound so impersonal, as if she was just some random member of the public he was sworn to protect. As if he hadn't spent most of the last twelve hours with his hands all over her.

Jonah turned abruptly and peered out the window. She heard the sound of an approaching truck.

"My dad." He turned back to look at her. "I need to get going."

She stared at him, and suddenly she felt helpless and powerless and *furious* all at the same time. She was flooded with resentment toward all the forces beyond her control that were turning her life upside down.

He stepped closer and gazed down at her. From outside came the sound of Wyatt's pickup grinding to a halt. The door screeching open, slamming shut.

Jonah put his hand on her shoulder. "You okay?"

"Fine."

His mouth tightened, as if he knew she was lying. "Keep your phone on. I'll call you when I have a plan."

He dropped a kiss on her forehead and walked out the door.

"Baltimore, Maryland," Ric said. "They just wrapped up some big investigation there, have a couple rookie agents with not a lot to do, so . . ."

"Shit," Jonah muttered.

"There's a flight at six-fifty out of San Antonio. Reservation's all set. If you can get her on the plane, my brother's got someone lined up to meet her on the other end."

Jonah didn't say anything as he pulled off the gravel road and onto the highway. Baltimore sounded very far away. And he didn't like handing this job over to someone else.

"She'll be at a safe house," Ric continued. "Round-the-clock surveillance, a two-agent team."

"How'd your brother swing that?"

"Evidently, we're not the first agency to take an interest in this guy. Soon as Sharpe's name came up, the Bureau was all over it."

Jonah slammed on the brakes and screeched to a halt. He threw the truck in reverse and rocketed backward to the patch of grass he'd just passed going sixty miles an hour.

Parallel tire tracks, heading off-road into the brush.

"Jonah?"

"Lemme call you back." He hung up on Ric and tossed his phone on the seat beside him as he glanced around at the landmarks. This property was part of the ranch.

Jonah's gut tightened as he jumped out of the truck and followed the line of tracks into some cedar trees. Maybe the caretaker was out repairing fences. Jonah swiped at the brush, and his gut tightened some more because he didn't really believe that.

Beyond the foliage, a barbed-wire fence . . . with wire missing between two posts. Beyond the fence, another thick line of brush. Jonah unholstered his gun and approached it, darting his gaze around as he drew near. He grabbed hold of a giant branch and moved it aside.

And discovered a white Ford Explorer, tinted windows, no hubcaps.

Sophie was too angry to talk, so she distracted herself by focusing on breakfast. She opened a cabinet and rooted around. Chicken soup, beef jerky, Spam. The pickings were slim, but she found a box of cinnamon Pop-Tarts.

"You hungry?" she asked Wyatt.

"I'm fine. Wouldn't mind a cup of that coffee, though."

"I should probably make some more." She poured the remains of the first pot down the drain, then cleaned out the carafe.

"Ah, that French coffeepot," Wyatt grumbled. "Macey swears by it. Seems to me like a pain in the neck."

"You just can't let it sit, or it gets bitter." She filled a saucepan with water and reached down to switch on the stove.

The window exploded.

She dropped to the floor, shrieking, a barrage of stings on her face and neck. Glass blanketed the carpet under her hands and knees. She glanced around frantically.

"Wyatt!"

He blinked at her, his eyes wide with surprise. A spot of red bloomed on his shoulder as he slid down the wall.

CHAPTER 27

Jonah floored it all the way to the camper, praying he'd get there before someone else did. His truck jerked and lurched over the tire ruts. He was all over the road, doing everything he could to keep his head down and not provide an easy target.

The camper door stood open, and Jonah's heart skittered. His dad's truck was missing. Jonah pulled right up to the camper, shoved the door open, and lunged directly into the RV, gun in hand.

"Sophie!"

Glass on the floor. No one there. He did a quick search.

Blood on the wall beside the door. A trail on the carpet. Jonah's stomach plummeted. He glanced at the shattered window, the hole in the faux wood paneling. The shot had come out of the northeast, which put the shooter on the ridge.

At least one of them was hit.

But Jonah hadn't heard any shots. The gunman was using a suppressor.

He jerked open the cabinet where they stored the guns

and ammo. The twelve-gauge was missing. So were the pistols. Sophie would have known where they were, so that didn't necessarily tell him who was injured and who wasn't. Either one or both of them could have grabbed the guns and taken off.

He rushed back outside, remembering at the last second to keep his head low as he dove back into his truck. He yanked the door shut and took a second to make a plan.

Think.

If Sophie was driving, he would have passed her on his way in, since she only knew that one road. But his dad knew the back ways on and off the property.

Sophie was hit.

Jonah pushed the thought away and tried to focus. Northeast ridge. Shooting out of the sun, directly into the kitchen window. It was a good position. A tougher shot than the door, but no one wanted to shoot into the sun, and there were far fewer places to set up to the west with a view of the camper. Plus, the ridge wasn't far from the Explorer, so easy insertion and extraction.

Jonah thrust the truck in gear and kept his head low. His dad would cut east, then south toward one of the back roads, assuming his dad was behind the wheel.

He pictured Sophie in the front seat, bleeding.

Sophie bumped along the dirt path, barely peeking over the steering wheel.

"Is this right? Wyatt?"

God, he was drifting in and out now. He was losing too much blood. The homemade bandage she'd fashioned from a few T-shirts was soaked through.

His eyes fluttered open. "Sun. East," he mumbled. "Then go . . . south."

Sophie looked at the sun. It was in her eyes, blinding her as she peeked over the wheel. She couldn't drive like this. She was sure she'd run into a tree or a boulder, or steer them off a cliff. But she was terrified to sit up straight for fear—

The truck lurched right. Then pitched left. At first she didn't understand, and then it hit her. *The tires!*

"Gun!" she screamed as the windshield shattered.

She slid to the floor, under the steering column. Wyatt was already slumped low in the reclined seat, but she reached over and covered his head with her hands and pressed it down against the console. The gearshift dug into her armpit, and she thrust it into park, even though they'd stopped moving.

He'd shot out the tires! They were sitting ducks!

She hadn't even heard the shot.

Again, it had come out of nowhere. No warning. No noise. Her entire body quivered as she waited for the next explosion of glass.

Beside her, Wyatt groaned.

She heard an engine approaching, coming fast. Terror gripped her and she grabbed the pistol on the floor at Wyatt's feet.

Two quick horn blasts. Oh God, was it—

Jonah's pickup roared up beside them. His passenger door pushed open, and she fumbled for the handle of her own door.

"Jonah!"

The door swung back, and he was there, reaching for her. "Are you hurt? Oh, shit! *Dad!*"

"Get down! He's still shooting!"

Jonah reached over her and checked his father's pulse.

"It's his shoulder. I tried to bandage it, but—"

"We have to get you out of here. Get low. Get into my truck. Stay on the floor, behind the engine block."

"But—"

"Are you hurt?" His hands were on her arms now, which were streaked with Wyatt's blood as well as her own, from the flying glass. His gaze met hers, and his eyes burned with some emotion she'd never seen.

"I'm fine. It's your father I'm worried about."

"I'll get him, you get in the truck," he commanded. "Stay low."

Sophie scrambled from the seat and used the two open doors for cover as she climbed into Jonah's truck. Behind her, she heard him exchanging words with his dad. Wyatt was conscious. That was good. But the voices were low, and Sophie knew he was weak.

"Sophie, give me a hand getting him in. Recline the seat back. And stay down!"

She quickly found the lever and adjusted the seat. Then she glanced at the surrounding prairie, visible through the gap between the trucks. All the shots had come from the direction of that ridge—the same ridge where she and Jonah had parked last night and made love. Someone was up there shooting at them, and the fact that they couldn't even *hear* the shots was unnerving.

"Sophie!"

She reached forward and helped Jonah guide Wyatt's shoulders into the truck. But now what? Were they going to just drive out of here?

"Get low! At his feet!"

Sophie crouched on the floor beside Wyatt's dusty cowboy boots. Her heart missed a beat as Jonah climbed over both of them, making himself a target for a brief moment as he slid behind the wheel. Then he ducked low and thrust the gearshift into drive.

"How can you see?" she squeaked.

He wasn't even looking over the wheel, just driving by feel.

"Try your cell phone," he ordered as they bounded over the uneven terrain.

"I tried already. It's not working. It's like it's dead or something, but the battery was fully charged."

"*Shit*. Try mine." He dug a phone from his pocket and tossed it to her, and she saw his gaze dart to his dad. He was white as chalk now, and his bandage was soaked through. He needed a hospital, fast.

Sophie snatched up Jonah's phone and jabbed at the buttons with trembling fingers. Nothing.

"It's dead. I don't understand."

"He jammed the signal. *Fuck*." Jonah's face was slick with sweat. He cast another worried look at his father.

Suddenly the truck jerked right. Then tipped left.

"The tires!" Sophie screamed. "Get down!"

She braced herself for the inevitable explosion of glass, but it didn't come. Jonah pressed the gas. The truck struggled forward. Metal crunched as they slammed into something hard. A rock?

"*Shit!*" Jonah pounded a fist against the dash. He shoved the gear into park.

For a moment, all was quiet. Just the idling engine and the sound of Sophie's rapid, terrified breaths.

"Okay, new plan." Jonah's gaze met hers. "I'm going to draw his fire."

"*What?*"

"I'm going to put some distance between us and distract him. You two stay here. Low, behind the engine block."

"But—"

"Once I take him out, I'll come back to get you in another vehicle."

Sophie's head was spinning. He was serious.

He unbuttoned his white shirt and stripped it off. He reached into the back of the cab and pulled out a rifle, then a box of ammo.

"Jonah . . . you can't do this! Don't leave us here."

"We're all clustered together. Better to spread out the targets."

"But his target is *me*! Let *me* draw his fire." She clutched his arm as he reached for the door handle.

"This guy's a sniper, Sophie. He's lethal and he's patient. He's cut our communications, and he can wait us out all day if he has to." Jonah nodded at his dad, who was now deathly pale. "He doesn't have time."

"But what's to stop him from just walking out here and gunning us all down?"

"He could try. Shit, we left the shotgun in the other truck!" Jonah glanced around and grabbed the handgun off the floor. "Keep the pistol in your hand, and listen for anyone approaching, okay?"

"We should stay together."

"Then we're all dead." He looked at her, and he was so *certain,* so confident, she didn't understand. How could he want to do this? "Sophie, listen to me, all right? I know this guy. I know his type. He's got an ego and he thinks he's invincible. If all he wanted was to kill you, he could have planted a bomb last night, end of story. He wants the challenge, Sophie."

"But—"

"I'm going to give him one."

The grass was high and thick, and Jonah belly-crawled through it, keeping his gun ahead of him. About ten more yards to a stand of cedar trees, and from there he would issue his first shot.

He just had to get there before the gunman closed in on the pickup and finished off his prey.

He kept his head low and tried to think. He had to do this right, and he had to do it fast. His dad was bleeding. He needed a doctor. Jonah pulled himself through the dirt and grass and thought about his strategy.

The ridge to the camper was a four-hundred-yard shot. The gunman had a high-powered scope and probably a good pair of binoculars. He might be watching Jonah through them right now, but Jonah was counting on a different scenario.

Never fire more than two shots from a single position. It was the sniper's cardinal rule, and Jonah was counting on him following it, which meant he was on the move right now, looking for his next hide.

Sweat dripped from Jonah's chin as he heaved himself forward. He smelled the dew on the grass and the loamy scent of dirt under his belly. Two more yards. One. His world darkened as he pulled himself into a dense clump of brush. Now he had cover, but he couldn't get sloppy.

He had to get that shot off.

He crouched at the base of a mesquite tree and did some quick recon. Sun in the east. Wind out of the southwest, about ten miles per hour. To the northeast, the ridge. Jonah faced it now and imagined the property like a clock, with Sophie and his dad in the center. The ridge ran diagonally, from about two to three o'clock. The escape vehicle was at ten. The gunman's next logical firing position would be anywhere between ten and two, where he would have a quick route back to the Explorer with the benefit of tree cover all the way.

Jonah kneeled in the grass and rested the barrel of his rifle on a notch in the branches. He checked his scope, scanning the area from two o'clock to ten for potential positions. He doubted he'd be lucky enough to spot him, but if he judged this shot right, he could definitely give him a scare.

And issue a challenge, which was the whole point.

An outcropping of limestone at about eleven, topped by a few boulders. It was a good position, putting the gunman directly in line with the windshield of the pickup. He could set up there and wait patiently for someone to peek over the dash. Jonah adjusted his scope.

He rested his cheek against the stock and peered through the lens, and the world opened up for him six football fields away. Had he guessed right? Was the sniper there, watching the pickup through the crosshairs and preparing for his next shot?

He scanned the area, looking for anything that didn't belong—any movement, any color, the slightest branch that looked out of place. Jonah had hunted this property his whole life. He knew it like the back of his hand, and that was his only advantage. But everything looked natural. Wherever the shooter was, he was well-concealed.

And then he spotted it. A too-fast flutter near the rock. He squeezed the trigger.

The rifle kicked back as he heard the bullet report. A splash of dirt at the base of the rock. He'd missed the shooter, but he'd achieved his objective.

The shooter wasn't focused on the truck now. He was too busy thinking about where that shot had originated.

Jonah fired another, for good measure.

That's right, game on. Fuckin' come and get me.

Sophie cringed at the second shot. It was both reassuring and terrifying. It told her Jonah was alive, he'd made it, but it was also as if he'd stood up from those bushes to the east of them and shouted from a megaphone: *Here I am!*

Sophie busied herself tearing Jonah's shirt apart. She carefully removed the top layer of Wyatt's bandage and stuffed the new fabric on top. She didn't want to remove the layer closest to the skin and disrupt any clotting, even though not much seemed to be happening. God, he was bleeding a lot. She looked at his pale, clammy face as she wrapped a strip of fabric around the bandage.

Wyatt mumbled something, and her heart lurched.

"Wyatt? Can you hear me? You're going to be okay now. Jonah went to get help."

He winced as she tied the cloth.

"Sorry. I know this hurts. My whole family's doctors, but I'm afraid you're stuck with me."

"Florence . . . Nightingale."

A hysterical bubble of laughter rose up in her throat. Her eyes burned with tears. "I wish. Wyatt, I'm so sorry this happened. We're going to get you out of here, okay?"

His lids fluttered open, and he was staring at her with hazel eyes that looked so much like Jonah's.

"Jonah . . . will get him."

Sophie bit her lip. Had he heard Jonah's plan? They'd thought he was unconscious. If he'd heard, he knew how risky it was. How possible it was that all three of them could end up dead at the hands of this sniper.

Wyatt's hand moved on the console, and Sophie glanced around. He was reaching for something. A water bottle? The keys?

The pistol on the driver's seat. Sophie had put it down so she could re-dress his wound.

"You want the gun?" God, he was too weak to even hold it.

"You," he rasped.

Sophie took the pistol in her hand and crouched on the floorboard. She already had a cramp in her leg from squeezing herself between the steering column and the gearshift, but she knew they had to stay low.

Wyatt reached over and patted her arm, just once, with his limp hand.

"Good girl. Good . . . shot." Then he closed his eyes and drifted off.

Hide, blend, deceive.

Jonah sorted through concepts he hadn't thought about in years. He didn't have a ghillie suit, but he'd been taught to improvise. He dug his hand in the dirt until he got to a layer that was cooler and wetter than the topsoil. He rubbed it over his face, his neck, his chest and shoulders. His skin was tan from doing yard work all summer with his shirt off, which would keep him from standing out like a beacon. Also lucky was his choice of pants today—khaki. But in the not-so-lucky category was his gun. Black metal with a walnut stock. His opponent's would be painted with flat earth tones to blend in with the trees. He'd be wearing camo head to toe, maybe even a ghillie suit covered in foliage. Jonah was going to have to stay concealed. He smeared some more mud on his face and scanned the area. He'd already worked out his next position. He needed some elevation, which meant he had to get from the brush to the spot where the limestone rose up from the prairie. The route was covered, but not completely, and he'd have to be careful. No sudden movements that would draw the eye. No casting shadows. He glanced at the sun rising up over the eastern tree line and calculated his route.

Then he made his move.

Wyatt didn't look good.

His skin was ashen now, and the air rasped in and out of his lungs. He'd bled through Jonah's shirt, and she'd added her T-shirt to the bandage, which seemed to be holding now—the bleeding had stopped, at least. But something else was going on—although she didn't know what—and for the hundredth time today she wished she'd followed in her father's footsteps.

God, where was Jonah? It seemed like an eternity since that last gunshot.

The sniper had some kind of silencer. She couldn't

hear him; she could only see the horrifying results of his actions. She or Jonah could be in his crosshairs right now.

Or Jonah could be dead already, and she wouldn't even know it.

Jonah peered through the scope, looking for anything that didn't belong. A patch of color that didn't match. A sudden shift in the vegetation. A circular black hole in the bushes that would indicate a scope.

His gaze settled on a clump of trees about ten o'clock. He focused slightly to the right of it, hoping to catch any movement in his peripheral vision.

He caught it. There was something there.

His enemy was at ten o'clock, facing southwest if he was aiming at the pickup, facing due south if he was aiming at Jonah.

Jonah eased himself into a comfortable crouch. He pulled the butt of the gun snug against his shoulder and settled the barrel on his hand, which rested atop his knee.

Three deep breaths.

He waited for the pause.

He squeezed the trigger.

Two seconds later, a burst of bark, just above his head. *Holy shit.*

Jonah dove low, nose to the dirt, his gun out in front of him now. His heart galloped. The shot had missed him by less than three inches, and he hadn't even heard it.

He'd almost had his head taken off.

But he'd accomplished his goal. He'd engaged the enemy on *his* terms. He was one step closer to gaining the upper hand.

• • •

Sophie kneeled on the floor of the truck, holding the pistol in her hand as she watched the door. At any moment, she expected a man to appear in the window, and she'd be staring down the barrel of his rifle.

Or would he approach from Wyatt's side and ambush her from behind?

Something glistened on her leg. A chunk of glass. It was dripping from her hair. She had little cuts along her arm and cheek, but she hadn't had time to pick the shards out. She'd have time later, if they survived this.

If.

She glanced over her shoulder to the east, where she knew Jonah was hiding. She glanced west, where the sky was turning a bright, hard blue.

Jonah belly-crawled to the edge of the ridge and peered between the ears of a prickly pear cactus. He was on the southeast slope of the ledge, just elevated enough to see over the grass. He was eye-level with the truck, where Sophie and his dad waited and where he hadn't seen the slightest movement in more than fifteen minutes.

Which could be good or bad.

Were they hunkered down, waiting silently, as he'd instructed?

Or were they dead?

Jonah gazed through the scope and settled his attention on an outcropping of rock at exactly nine o'clock.

It was a bad position, facing directly into the sun.

But it was tempting because it provided solid cover and allowed an unobstructed view of both the pickup and Jonah's current firing position, which the gunman had probably figured out by now.

Jonah wanted the shooter at nine o'clock, but would he take the bait? Or would he make the prudent maneuver and drop down to eight? Or maybe he'd make the really smart move and abort the mission altogether.

Jonah knew he wouldn't. He knew it in his bones. This guy was swept up in the challenge, the thrill. And his need for that battle high was going to be his downfall. Jonah was counting on it.

He peered through the scope and waited. The familiar weight and shape of his rifle calmed him, made his heart slow. His scope was zeroed for eight hundred yards, and he wasn't sure he could make it even if the shot presented itself.

But failure was not an option.

A brief flash, and Jonah's breath caught. The sun, glinting off a scope. It was a serious mistake, and now it was up to Jonah to make it fatal.

Three deep breaths. He paused. He pulled the trigger and took the shot of his life.

A jolt of movement in the bushes behind the rock.

The shooter falling? Was he dead?

Jonah's ears were still ringing as he stared through the scope and tried to determine.

The shot had been clean. Steady. He thought he'd made it, but there was only one way to know for sure.

He had to go see.

Sophie squeezed her eyes shut and murmured a prayer. Jonah was alive. She'd just heard his gun.

But the shooter could have returned fire, and she wouldn't even know it.

She looked at Wyatt again, passed out and slumped over the console. He was breathing. He had a pulse. It wasn't strong, but it was there, and Sophie was praying it would be there when Jonah came back.

And if he didn't . . . She couldn't think that way. It was like a betrayal.

Sophie needed to be ready for anything. She needed to be alert. She adjusted her grip on the pistol and stared at the door.

The sniper wasn't there.

Jonah crept up on the hide and saw that it had, indeed, been recently used. He noted the flattened plants, the scuff marks in the dirt.

The trail of blood leading away.

Jonah gripped his Glock in his hand now as he glanced around. He followed the trail into the plants and saw the olive green object protruding from the base of a bush.

Another wary glance around. Jonah crouched down and slid the rifle out from where it had been discarded.

The scope was destroyed. The front layer of glass was shattered. The bullet had penetrated a good twelve inches through multiple layers of thick glass but hadn't come out the other end.

Son of a bitch. What were the odds? A perfect shot, and the fucker was saved by his own scope.

Maybe.

The impact would have been tremendous. Even at eight hundred yards, the force of a rifle absorbing that round would be a major blow to the head.

Hopefully, a mortal blow.

Jonah unslung his rifle from his back and slid it under some brush. This was up close and personal now, and he needed to be ready to move quickly.

His heart hammered as he tracked the blood through some bushes. It moved in the direction of the Explorer, but the path was erratic—either purposely so or because of a severe injury.

Then suddenly, nothing. No more trail.

Jonah stopped and listened.

A whisper of wind through the scrub brush. The buzz of insects. The distant croak of a bullfrog down near the creek.

Snap.

He dropped to a knee and whirled around, gun raised. A deafening *boom* an instant before he pulled the trigger. Jonah dove to the ground, rolled, and scrambled to his feet.

A flash of movement, so close he didn't even have time to aim, he just threw his weight into him. They crashed against a tree and a pistol went flying just as Jonah pointed his Glock. A burning twist of his wrist and it fell to the ground. Jonah brought his arm up and shoved it against the man's throat. He got his first good look at his attacker as the man's head snapped back against the tree trunk. Green and brown greasepaint, blood-matted hair. Sharpe's right eye was swollen shut, maybe even missing, from when the rifle had pummeled him.

Jonah felt a hot pain in his side and leaped back. Bad move. The sniper landed a knee in his kidney. Jonah sensed the knife swinging in again and dodged right, then spun around again, slamming his weight into him.

He hit him squarely in the solar plexus with 230 pounds of angry muscle, and in the instant of paralysis that followed, he seized the knife hand and crushed the wrist. The weapon dropped to the ground alongside Jonah's Glock. He lunged for the gun and Sharpe was on him. Jonah reached back and grabbed him by the shoulders, and with a giant heave, flipped him over his head to land on his back. Jonah rolled sideways to grab his Glock and brought it up just as the attacker got to his feet and charged him with the blade.

Pop.

Sharpe jolted back as if he'd hit an invisible wall. He fell against a cactus bush and rolled to the ground.

Jonah was on his knees in the dirt, staring at the dead gunman. Jonah's gun was still raised and aimed, as if the man might suddenly spring back to life.

Jonah stood up on unsteady legs and took a step forward. His heart thundered. Adrenaline coursed through his veins, and he could have taken on an entire enemy platoon with his bare hands.

This enemy was dead.

He stared down at the man with disgust. The streaks of blood on his face contrasted with the greasepaint and the greens and browns of his woodland camo. One eye was swollen shut while the other stared sightlessly up at the sky.

Jonah thought of his dad. And Sophie. He dropped to a knee and did a quick pulse check before rooting through the sniper's pockets. He came up with not one set of car keys but two.

Jonah's mind reeled. Was there another getaway car? Another accomplice?

He shoved both keys into his pocket and took off running.

Sophie couldn't wait any longer. Wyatt needed help *now*. She shoved the truck in gear and slowly pressed the gas.

The truck inched forward, then stopped. She heard the painful sound of something hard grinding against rock. She shifted into reverse and tried that way, with no better result.

Sophie cast a frantic look at Wyatt. His skin looked gray now and his pulse was thready. She didn't know what was going on with Jonah—couldn't even bear to think what those pistol shots meant—but she knew she had to do whatever she could to get them out of here. She engaged the four-wheel drive and tried backing up again.

Movement.

The truck lurched backward, bumping over something in the road. Or was it the tire tread? She had no idea, but they were rolling. She peered between the gap in the two front seats at the rectangle of blue behind her. Nothing tall, at least. She was still afraid to peek her head over the dash, but she did her best to navigate as she steered backward toward what felt like the direction of the woods. How far could she manage to go on one good tire? The air smelled like burning rubber, and an excruciating scraping noise was coming up from the front wheels. Was there any chance she could find the road and make it out to the highway?

They hit a bump, and Wyatt slid forward in the seat. Sophie stopped the truck and leaned over to catch him.

Noise outside. A vehicle approaching. Loud, bigger than a car. She grabbed the pistol off her lap and held her breath. Oh, Lord. Would she have the courage to shoot someone? Or would she be paralyzed with fear?

Sophie leaned back against Wyatt's body and pointed the gun.

CHAPTER 28

"Sophie!"

Jonah dashed for the truck and stopped short as he found himself staring down the barrel of a pistol. She was sprawled across the front seat, shielding his father's body with her own as she leveled that gun at him.

She went limp with relief, and Jonah yanked open the door.

"Is he alive?"

"Barely. He needs help."

Jonah was already rounding the hood to go to the other side. He jerked open the door.

"Is it safe now? The sniper's dead?"

He met her gaze over his father's motionless body. "He's dead." The words sent a chill down Jonah's spine as he scooped his dad up and heaved him over his shoulder in a fireman's carry. Jonah rounded the truck.

"Get in the back. Help me get him in."

She hurried to the Explorer and yanked open the door. Jonah tried to muscle his dad inside and onto the backseat without jarring his wound.

Sophie went around to the other side and helped pull him through using his uninjured arm. Then she climbed in the back and settled his head on her lap as she jerked shut the door.

"Go!"

Jonah grabbed a barn jacket from the pickup, rushed back to the Explorer, and jumped behind the wheel. He took off for the nearest road—a back route that skirted the south of the property before spitting out on the main highway.

"We need a phone. A landline," Sophie said. "We need to call an ambulance."

"No time." Jonah floored the pedal, going as fast as he dared over the rugged terrain. This SUV wasn't designed for these conditions and they had no time for a flat tire.

Jonah's heart pounded. He glanced at Sophie in the rearview mirror. She was adjusting the bandage, which seemed to consist of both of their shirts now. She had a determined fire in her eyes, and he thought about how she'd looked aiming that gun at him. She'd been shielding his father with her own body, and Jonah had no doubt that if he hadn't called her name out the second he did, she would have blown him away.

Jonah took the barn jacket off the seat beside him and shoved it back at her. "Put this on."

She grabbed it and pulled it into her lap, making it a pillow for his dad's head.

The SUV bounced as they hit a rut. Jonah eased his foot off the gas, but not much. They didn't have time.

Sophie glanced around impatiently. "Why aren't we taking the main road?"

"Get your head down," he told her. "There could be another shooter."

The frantic race to the hospital turned into an unbearable wait.

Sophie fetched a third soft drink from the vending machine and trudged back down the hallway to the waiting room, where Jonah sat with a pair of FBI agents. They'd been interviewing him for an hour now, and she could tell he'd had enough. Every few seconds his gaze darted to the double doors, where he was hoping a doctor would appear to deliver the outcome of Wyatt's surgery.

Sophie didn't think it was good. She wasn't normally a pessimist, but she couldn't keep the feeling of dread from closing in on her. She remembered way too many times when her father would come home after a marathon surgery, and the defeated look on his face would tell the story without him even having to utter a word.

Sophie glanced at the clock. Four and a half hours.

She strode into the waiting room, and all three men looked up.

"Hi." She offered Jonah the soft drink. It was a caffeine-and-sugar-packed Dr Pepper, and she'd hoped it would perk him up, but he shook his head.

"Everything all right?"

The two agents, whose names she'd been given and promptly forgotten several hours ago, looked up at her silently.

"It's okay," Jonah said. "You can tell her."

"Tell me what?"

The younger of the two men cleared his throat. "We just got word from our evidence response team. They're processing the crime scene now, which as you can imagine is quite extensive."

Sophie pictured a team of black-suited FBI agents swarming the deer lease like ants.

"And you found the sniper?"

"We did."

"Has he been IDed?"

The agents exchanged looks, and seemed to decide she merited this bit of information.

"Joe Shugart," the designated spokesman said. "Also known as John Sharpe. We intend to confirm that through fingerprints."

"Assuming they're on file," Sophie said.

"They are. He's ex-military."

Sophie looked at Jonah, whose gaze was trained once again on those double doors. He wore a gray T-shirt with the sheriff's department logo on it that some deputy had given him. He'd managed to clean some of the mud off in the restroom, but he still had streaks on his neck and arms—not to mention a slash on his left side that he'd refused to talk about as a nurse had bandaged him. Sophie would ask later.

She made eye contact with the agent who wasn't mute. "How did he find us at the deer lease? I was told no one knew we were there."

"I led him right to you."

Her startled gaze met Jonah's. "What?"

"We found a GPS tracking device," the agent informed her. "On Detective Macon's truck." He looked at Jonah. "It was well-hidden, underneath the back axle."

Jonah raked his hand through his hair and looked away. She could tell he was torturing himself about this.

"And he was acting alone?" Sophie asked, trying to change the subject. "What about the second set of keys?"

"All the evidence we have tells us he was a lone operator. Those keys belong to a Dodge, possibly the one that ran you off the road the other day. We've got some agents looking for the vehicle right now."

Sophie looked at the two men, who'd been summoned out to this rural hospital on a holiday weekend. She imagined dozens more trekking around the deer lease.

"A lot of agents on this thing," she observed.

"Sharpe has been on an FBI watch list for years." This was the first she'd heard from the silent agent.

"A watch list?"

"Suspected ties to governments hostile to the United States," he elaborated. "If he weren't dead right now, he'd probably be looking at treason charges."

The doors *whooshed* open behind her, and Jonah jumped to his feet. He was in front of the doctor in two strides. The man wore blue scrubs and had a surgical mask hanging around his neck. He was much shorter than Jonah, but he put a hand on Jonah's shoulder and guided him to a nearby row of chairs.

Sophie's heart squeezed.

Jonah watched the doctor, nodding. His face froze. He sank like a stone into the chair behind him.

Sophie clamped a hand over her mouth as the doctor walked away and disappeared back through the doors. Jonah rested his elbows on his knees and bowed his head.

Sophie crossed the waiting room and stood beside him. He didn't move. She kneeled down.

"Jonah?"

He glanced up, and the stricken look on his face tore her heart out.

"Is he . . . ?"

He nodded. He pressed the heels of his hands against his eyes. "He made it." His shoulders sagged forward and he heaved a sob. "He's going to be okay."

Jonah didn't talk the whole way home. He didn't think he could. Every time he started to say something, his throat closed up and it felt like a sandbag was pressing down on his chest.

He'd almost lost his dad today.

He'd almost had his head blown off.

He'd almost lost Sophie.

For the first time since he'd become a police officer, he'd fired his weapon in the line of duty, and he'd killed a man.

And although the last thing was the most permanent, it was the least disturbing thing that had happened, and Jonah knew he wouldn't lose a wink of sleep over it.

The rest was another story.

"Do you mind if I stay with you?"

He looked at Sophie, beside him in the rental car.

"I still don't have a key to my apartment," she said. "And even if I did, I don't have transportation, so . . ."

He stared at her.

"But if you'd rather be alone, I understand."

"No." Jonah trained his gaze on the highway. Shit, he was so distracted, he'd nearly missed his exit. He flipped on the blinker and skated across three lanes of traffic.

"No, you don't want to be alone? Or no, you don't want me to stay?"

Jonah pulled off the interstate and rolled to a stop at the light.

"Yes, I want you to stay."

They drove in silence the rest of the way to his house. Jonah reached for the automatic garage-door opener, only to discover it wasn't clipped to the visor. It was back in his pickup, where it belonged, but that truck was still out at the lease or maybe at some FBI lab by now being examined for evidence.

Jonah didn't know.

He didn't particularly care.

He only cared about one thing at the moment, and she was sitting beside him.

He parked in the driveway, got out, and waited for Sophie to come around. She wore his dusty barn jacket over the thin scrub top the hospital had given her to replace her T-shirt. She had blood and dirt under her nails. Glass in her hair. A pistol grip poking out of her jacket pocket. He remembered the steely look in her eye when she'd pointed that gun at him. She was brave and strong, a one-woman SWAT team, and his heart turned over just looking at her.

He took her hand and led her inside.

Jonah's house was cold, and she stood in the dimness, shivering as he locked the door behind them and turned on the porch light. He must have left the air-conditioning on, and they'd been gone for days. How many days? She counted backward and couldn't believe it when she came up with five.

Time was a blur. Her brain felt muddled. She

didn't even know how late it was, just that it was dark and she was beyond tired. She knew Jonah was, too.

He took her hand and led her down the hallway, straight into the bathroom. She stood beside the sink while he flipped on the light and turned on the shower.

He closed the door and the room started to fill with steam. She stood there, facing the sink and her reflection as Jonah eased up behind her. He reached around her and plugged the sink drain, not saying a word as he gently tipped her head forward and started picking through her hair. He dropped little chunks of glass in the basin and she stared down at them. A few of the chunks had blood on them, and she realized they were responsible for the tiny cuts along her cheek and jaw. When there was a little mound of glass in the sink, Jonah's arms came around her and unzipped the jacket, sliding it off her shoulders. She undressed, noticing how her neck and arms were covered with brown dabs of disinfectant from where they'd cleaned her up at the hospital.

Jonah swiped back the shower curtain. He took her arm and helped her over the side of the tub. The curtain closed again and she tilted her head back and let the hot water sluice over her hair. The curtain scraped back again and she felt Jonah climb in with her, completely disregarding the bandage on his side. He turned her around and reached for the shampoo. Then his hands were in her hair, lathering it and combing through.

"Careful," she said.

He turned her around again, and she leaned back and rinsed. She stood for a few minutes, eyes closed, under the scalding spray, as Jonah moved around, soaping himself. Then he took her shoulders and eased around her.

She stared down at her feet. The water was brown and sudsy as it swirled down the drain. He'd really coated on the mud out there, and she remembered how wild he'd looked when he'd come up on her in the pickup. She'd hardly recognized him, and she'd almost pulled the trigger. Just thinking about it made her want to throw up.

He turned off the water. The curtain scraped back again, and he held her arm as she stepped out. He pulled a towel off the rack and used it to squeeze water from the ends of her hair. Then he wiped her down, head to toe. As he crouched at her feet, she rested her hand on his head.

He stood up. He gazed down at her, and she couldn't read his face. She couldn't read anything about him now, hadn't been able to all day. Was he sad? Was he worried about his father, still recovering in that hospital? Was he angry at her for getting them both involved in this?

Did he feel numb, like she did?

She leaned her forehead against his sternum, right above his heart. She brought her hand up and traced the damp bandage on his right side.

A *nick*, he'd called it.

"Are you going to tell me about the knife?" She gazed up at him.

"Later."

He opened the door and let the steam escape. Then he scooped her into his arms and carried her to bed.

• • •

Allison sank into the chair and blew on her coffee. It had been a bitch of a day, and it wasn't even over yet.

Ric Santos collected his change from the airport coffee vendor and joined her at the table.

"Trade places with me," he said.

"Why?"

"Because if he gets a look at you, he'll bolt."

Allison got to her feet and surrendered the chair facing the terminal. Ric plunked his coffee on the table and sat down.

"I heard about your Good Cop bit."

Allison sat back, defensive. "I got the information, didn't I?"

"Won't hear me complaining." The side of Ric's mouth twitched up. "Just remind me never to piss you off."

Allison turned to the side and watched the security checkpoint in her peripheral vision. Any moment now, they were expecting Maxwell to pass by on his way to Gate 11, where the last plane to Seattle was departing in fifty minutes. The judge who'd released him on bond on the obstruction-of-justice charges had made him surrender his passport, but Allison had believed he was still a flight risk, so when the FBI got involved, she took advantage of their enviable computer access to look up outbound flight reservations for any Ryan Maxwells.

They'd come up with a hit.

"The feds have been doing some digging," Ric said. "Turns out our boy's got money problems."

She snorted. "Who doesn't?"

"These are the big kind. D-Systems lost its largest

client six months ago, and they're scrambling for cash. Company's way in the red. Maxwell personally has a two-million-dollar mortgage that's about to balloon on him and he's close to broke."

Allison thought about the artwork and the infinity pool. "Just goes to show," she said.

"What's that?"

"Looks can be deceiving."

Ric sipped his coffee and looked at her. Then his gaze veered behind her. "How 'bout this guy?"

Allison glanced subtly at the mouth of the security line, where passengers stopped to put on shoes after going through X-ray. A guy slipping into a pair of Nikes had Maxwell's build, but he was traveling with a woman and two kids. Allison studied him carefully.

"Not him."

"Kids could be a decoy."

"Nope."

Allison sipped her latte. It was going to keep her up all night, which was what she needed. She had a crapload of reports to do for this case, and it wasn't as if she had a personal life to get back to on this holiday weekend. So, hey, why not work?

A man stepped through the X-ray machine and stopped to collect a backpack and slip on a pair of Teva sandals. Five-foot-eight. Baseball cap. Goatee.

"This could be him," she said.

He was wearing a flannel shirt in July.

"It's him." Allison turned to Ric.

"You're sure?"

"Positive."

Ric dialed his brother. "Rey? Yeah we're here at the

coffee shop. He just cleared security." Pause. "Positive."

He clicked off and Allison sat there, waiting. "You okay?"

She shrugged. "A little nervous."

"Worried you're wrong?"

"I'm not."

Ric's gaze flicked over her shoulder. "Okay, here we go."

Allison glanced to her side as a pair of FBI agents in dark suits approached the backpacker. They flashed their badges. Allison caught the look of horror on the man's face.

"Got him," she said.

She and Ric stood up. They sauntered over to the man, who was now being turned around and frisked. That goatee hadn't been started yesterday, and it was going a long way toward confirming Allison's theory about his plan to slip into Canada on a fake passport.

Ric's brother turned the man around and cuffed his hands. "You're under arrest for soliciting the murder of Tyler P. Dorion."

"What? That's absurd."

Maxwell saw Allison and flinched.

"Hey, Ryan. How's it hanging?"

His cheeks flushed. "This is outrageous! I want to talk to my lawyer. I'll sue every one of you people!"

"You'll have to get in line," Ric said.

"You have the right to remain silent," Special Agent Rey Santos intoned. "Anything you say can and will be used against you in a court of law."

The other agent picked up his backpack while Rey led Maxwell away, still reciting his rights. His face went crimson as they passed the crowd of other travelers at the security gate, and Allison shook her head. Public humiliation was the least of his worries now. He was looking at treason and murder charges.

"Not bad, Doyle."

She looked at Ric.

"Don't be surprised if there's some reshuffling," Ric told her. "You'll probably be moving from property crimes to CAP."

Allison watched Maxwell getting smaller and smaller as he was escorted down the terminal. She was going to get a promotion out of this. Joining the Crimes Against Persons squad had been her goal for years.

"So, how's it feel? Your first big arrest?"

"Not like I thought," she said. "I expected to be happy, but I just feel . . . I don't know. Slimed."

"That's homicide. Even when it turns out for the best, it still sucks."

She looked up at him. "Why do you do it?"

Ric gazed off into the crowd. "Started out, I was doing it for the kick. The ego boost." He looked at Allison. "Homicide dicks, we think we're pretty hot shit."

"You guys? I hadn't noticed."

He looked away again. "Now I've got a teenage daughter. It's more complicated. When I take trash off the street, I'm doing it for her. And people like Becca Kincaid."

Way down the concourse, the agents and Maxwell reached a secure exit and disappeared through a door.

Allison slipped her hand into her pocket and felt Ty's business card.

"I figure it's not a bad reason to get up in the morning," Ric said.

Allison nodded. "Good enough for me."

• • •

Sean hung up with Allison and dialed Gretchen. She answered on the third ring.

"Any word?"

She must have seen his number on caller ID.

"Joe Shugart, aka John Sharpe, is dead," he told her.

She didn't say anything, but Sean watched through the window as her shoulders slumped with relief. She sank down on the arm of the couch.

"I never thought I'd be happy to hear news like that, but . . . thanks."

"Ryan Maxwell has been arrested," Sean added. "I thought you'd want to know."

"Ryan who?"

"The man who hired the hit on the witness. And probably, indirectly, the man who hired your husband."

"Ex-husband." She stood up and took the phone across the room, away from where her kids were seated at the kitchen table kneading Play-Doh with their aunt.

Gretchen stepped toward the window of the cabin and gazed out at the trees. She'd had the blinds open all night, which had been driving Sean crazy, even though he'd been running surveillance on the place for twelve hours and had detected nothing amiss.

"You okay?"

"Yeah. Just kind of . . . numb. I don't know. This all seems surreal. Do you think—" She sighed.

"Do I think what?"

"This may sound paranoid, but do you think that's it? Just those two? Is there anyone else I need to worry about, you know, coming to bother us?"

"I don't think so. Everything we've dug up so far points to one money person who hired Sharpe, and Sharpe hired Jim. We have no evidence of anyone else, but I'll let you know if that changes."

"Thank you."

He paused. "You're going to have to give the money back."

"I know."

"It's evidence."

"I understand. I don't want it, anyway, now that I know where it came from."

Sean hesitated. He didn't want to insult her, but he'd seen her bank accounts as part of the investigation. "Are you going to be okay?"

"Yeah." She looked to the side, at her children. "We were fine before. We'll be fine again. We've got each other, and that's really all I care about." She pressed her palm against the glass and looked out, wistful. "Where are you, anyway?"

Sean sat in the front seat of the rental car and felt a pang of regret for something he couldn't really name.

"On my way home from work," he said, and it wasn't really a lie.

She walked back into the living room and stood beside the sofa, looking at her kids. For the first time since he'd known her, she looked relaxed instead of tense.

"Good. You should get some rest. You've had a long week."

He laughed. "You've had a long life."

She smiled. Then she sighed. "I guess that's true." She cleared her throat. "Thank you for telling me. You don't know what a weight this is off my shoulders."

He did know.

Sean started the car. He pulled back onto the gravel road and pointed the sedan toward the entrance to the park. He had a long drive ahead of him and then a flight out of Atlanta. Gretchen had hidden herself well.

"You take care," he said. "And take care of those girls."

"Thanks, Sean, I'll do my best."

And he knew that she would.

CHAPTER 29

Sophie was home.

Jonah pulled up behind her new SUV, blocking her
in so she'd be less likely to tell him she didn't have time
to eat lunch with him. He trudged up the back steps and
toed off his dirty Nikes, then kicked them to the side of
the porch.

"Sounds interesting," she was saying into the phone
as he walked into the kitchen. He planted a kiss on her
forehead, and she cowered back against the sink and
made a face at him.

He didn't blame her. He was covered in sweat and
dirt and lawn clippings, and she looked all put together
in crisp white jeans and a silky green top.

"Okay, two o'clock. Right. See you there." She hung
up the phone and dropped it into her purse on the table.

"How's your dad?" she asked.

"Good."

"You get the yard all done?"

"Yep." He took a glass down and filled it with water.
"Where you heading?"

"That was a leasing agent. I found a place on the west

side of town that's running a two-months-free special. It's *slightly* out of my price range, but I'm going to take a look."

Jonah guzzled the water. He refilled the glass and guzzled some more, then plunked it down on the counter.

"You want to come?" she asked.

"No."

He watched her across the kitchen, and he could feel the tension in the air between them. This was the conversational land mine they'd been avoiding for the past two weeks.

He'd told her she could stay here as long as she needed, and she'd basically said thanks but no thanks. Jonah was still irked about it.

"I could change the appointment time." She glanced at her watch. "You could jump in the shower? Come along and give me your opinion?"

"Why would you want my opinion?"

She gave him a baleful look. "Well, you *are* a cop, so I was thinking you might have something to say about the safety aspects. I mean, that's the entire point of this move. My apartment isn't exactly the safest place on earth—"

"Your apartment's a dump."

"Right. And this is a gated community. It's supposed to be nice. It's even got a view." She crossed her arms. "And I was kind of hoping you might be spending some time there with me, so maybe you'd have an opinion."

Jonah didn't say anything. He just looked at her.

"You don't?"

"I've got plenty of opinions. You don't want to hear them."

"Like what?"

"Like you're signed up for two classes, right? Starting Monday?"

"Yeah."

"And you just got a new car, but the insurance check didn't cover all of it."

"Yeah. So?"

"So, you're wasting your hard-earned money," he said. "I think it's stupid."

"You think I'm stupid?"

He sighed. "I think this plan is stupid. What do you need a gated community for when you've got me?"

She rolled her eyes. "Don't be ridiculous."

"What's ridiculous?"

"I can't depend on a *man* to keep me safe and secure."

"Why not?"

She opened her mouth.

"Why can't you depend on me? I can do those things, Sophie. I'm good at that stuff."

She floundered for words. "Jonah . . . this isn't the Middle Ages. I don't need some knight to ride up and rescue me—"

"I'm talking about real life. I'm talking about you being with me. Staying at my house. In my bed. I'm talking about hanging out together, going to movies, washing your car. I'm talking about you waking me up to distract you when you can't sleep at night."

She stared at him. "You want me to move in here?"

He wanted way more than that. But it was a start. And she looked a little stunned by what he was saying.

"Screw the apartment search," he said simply.

• • •

She stood there looking at him, all dirty and sweaty on the other side of the kitchen. This wasn't exactly how she'd pictured this conversation. It was a step up from "Stay here as long as you need," but not by much.

Sophie's stomach cramped. There was a serious imbalance in this relationship, and it was only getting worse. She desperately wanted to move in with him, but she wanted him to love her first, even if he didn't say it all the time. She could do without the words as long as she knew the feeling was mutual.

But maybe it wasn't.

She looked at her feet. Her throat tightened. She glanced at her watch.

Across the room, Jonah muttered a curse. "Just hang on a minute, okay?"

She looked up, and he walked straight out the back door.

"Where are you going?" she called through the screen.

He didn't answer, but disappeared into the garage. She heard him rooting around. And then he came back inside carrying a red metal toolbox. He set it down beside the sink and turned on the faucet. He dampened a dish towel and scrubbed it over his face and neck. He took a deep breath and stared down at the sink while she watched him curiously.

He opened the toolbox and lifted the top tray. It was filled with screws and nails and plenty of other little metal things she couldn't identify.

He took out a black velvet box, and Sophie's heart skittered. She looked at him.

His eyes were dark and serious, and the tender expression on his face made her legs weak.

"I wasn't planning to do this yet, but . . ." He opened the little box and took out a diamond ring.

"Oh my God, *Jonah*." She sucked in a breath as he picked up her hand. His fingers were big and brown compared to hers, and he had dirt under his nails. He slid the ring onto her finger.

"My granddad gave it to me."

She glanced up at him, and he looked nervous. She could hear it in his voice, too.

"This was years ago, after my grandma died. He said she'd want me to have it for later, when I met someone." He cleared his throat. "I took it in the other day. Had it sized for you."

She blinked down, shocked. "And then you stored it in your *garage*?"

He smiled slightly. "Yeah, well, you're kind of nosy. And I was planning something nicer than this, but . . ."

She looked up, and his face was serious again.

"I love you, Sophie."

She couldn't move, couldn't talk. She could hardly breathe. He gazed down at her, patient as always, waiting for it to sink in. This was for real. *He* was for real.

He squeezed her hand. "Will you marry me?"

She looked into his eyes and knew that he meant what he said. She could trust him. Not just to protect her and keep her safe, but to keep her laughing and fighting and losing her temper and losing her mind with passion for many years to come. He could do all those things, and she could do them for him, too. He was giving her his heart right now, in the middle of his kitchen, in his sweaty T-shirt and bare feet. It was the most precious gift anyone had ever offered her.

"Yes." She wrapped her arms around him and squeezed him tightly. "I would love to marry you."

She felt his sigh of relief, and she pulled back, laughing. "I love you, too, you know. Just in case you were wondering."

The corner of his mouth lifted in a smile. He leaned down to kiss her.

"I know," he said. "I heard you the first time."

Turn the page for a sneak peek of

TWISTED

the next heart-stopping Tracers novel from

Laura Griffin

Coming in Spring 2012 from Pocket Star Books

Detective Allison Doyle knew better than to expect the whole night off. But she was an optimist at heart—and she was hungry—so she pulled into the parking lot of Sal's Quick Stop, savoring the idea of a hot Meat Lover's Supreme.

Everyone in the department had been working round the clock. Allison's reward was going to be a junk-food dinner and a mindless night in front of the tube. She pulled open the freezer and selected a sausage-and-double-pepperoni pizza with extra-thick crust. She made a quick detour through the dry goods section and approached the register.

The store owner's gaze darted to her. His tense expression morphed into relief.

Allison's skin prickled. Her attention snapped to the customer at the counter with his back to her. Greasy brown hair, oversize leather jacket, shoulders hunched up around his ears. His body moved back and forth with the agitated tic of a tweeker.

Holdup.

The flash of awareness was accompanied by a kick of dread, as she realized both her hands were full.

Always keep your gun hand free. Allison knew that. She'd had it drilled into her by every firearms instructor she'd ever met, and yet here she stood with an armed assailant, encumbered by a frozen pizza and a bag of kitten chow, her service weapon tucked neatly beneath her jacket. Panic threatened, but she tamped it down as she scrambled for a plan. If she dropped her groceries, she'd startle him—

The man whirled around, and she cursed her hesitation. She looked at his black pistol and widened her eyes in fake surprise.

"Step back!" He jabbed the gun at her with a shaking hand, then spun to Sal.

Allison scanned her surroundings. No other customers, thank God. Two cars in front, including hers. No getaway driver in the other vehicle, but the headlights glowed, hinting at a running engine. Why hadn't she noticed it? She was 0-for-3 here, and she blamed a marathon workweek that had now culminated in a string of potentially deadly mistakes.

The situation worsened as another car turned into the lot. It pulled up to a gas pump, and she hoped they were going to pay outside.

The perp spun toward her again with another panicked look. White male, five-ten, one-forty. Dilated pupils. The tremor in his gun hand extended to his whole body, and he was clearly jacked up. Bad news for everyone. So was the fact that he'd made no effort to disguise himself and seemed oblivious to the security camera mounted behind the cash register. Even from ten feet away, Allison could smell the desperation on him.

"I said *back*, bitch!"

She stepped back obediently and tried to look meek.

He turned to the register. "The *money*!"

Sal reached for the cash drawer. It slid open with a *ping,* and Allison watched the store owner, noting all the details she'd missed at first glance. He didn't just look tense, he looked frightened. But it was a fierce frightened, like a cornered animal. Sweat beaded at his temples as his angry gaze flashed to the man aiming the gun at him.

Allison eased forward. Sal glanced at her, and his defiant look had her pulse racing. She knew exactly what he thought of this two-bit meth fiend trying to rip off his business, and she hoped he wasn't rash enough to do anything stupid before she got this under control.

Allison slid a glance at the gunman. His attention bounced nervously between Sal and her, and she prayed he wouldn't notice the bulge beneath her blazer. She needed to get her hands free.

Sal took out another stack of bills, and his glare implored her to do something. The perp caught the look and thrust his gun at her.

"You! Over there!" He waved the pistol at the soft-drink station.

Damn it, she needed to get closer, not farther away. Her best chance was to disarm him at close range.

"Now, bitch!"

She took a baby step back.

"Now!" A burst of spittle accompanied the command.

Allison took several steps back, looking deep into those desperate eyes. It was the desperation that concerned her. He wasn't thinking logically. He was capable of anything. Those wild eyes told her he'd shoot her as soon as look at her, and the knowledge made her chest squeeze. She'd thought about being shot in the line of duty, but she'd never envisioned having her life ended by some tweeker with rotten teeth.

He turned and grabbed at the bills with his free hand as Sal stacked them on the counter.

"Faster!"

A flutter of movement in the convex mirror near the ceiling caught her eye. She tried not to call attention to it. Meth Man turned around again, and she glanced up to see someone slipping from the corridor at the back of the store into the aisle closest to the door, which led straight to the register. Tall and dark-haired, the man wore a charcoal suit and looked remarkably like the defense attorney Allison had gone to war with in court just last week. But it wasn't the attorney. This man was leaner and broad-shouldered and made a lot less noise.

"That's *it*? That's all you *got*?" Meth Man snatched up the pile of twenties and waved them at Sal. *"I want all of it!"*

Sal grumbled a response as Allison cut a glance to her left. The businessman hunched low now behind a beer display. His gaze locked with hers, and his hard expression commanded her to stay put. *Commanded,* as in, he was used to giving orders.

Crap, just her luck. *Don't try to be a hero,* she tried to tell him with her eyes, but his focus was on the confrontation now.

"Hand it over!" The perp was bobbing up and down on the balls of his feet—shrill and angry, but distracted.

Now was her chance.

She flung the pizza away like a Frisbee. In the next instant of confusion, she whipped out her gun and lunged for the man's weapon.

His pistol tracked her. She registered the black barrel

pointed at her face as a shoe came up and the gun cartwheeled out of the perp's hand.

Allison thrust a heel into the side of his knee. He howled and crumpled to the floor. The man who'd kicked the gun away shoved Allison aside and flipped the robber onto his stomach. A Glock appeared from nowhere, and he jabbed it against the perp's neck.

"Don't move!"

Allison's mouth fell open. The man turned and gave her a blistering look.

"Who the hell are you?" she demanded.

"You plan to arrest this guy?"

Her shock lasted maybe a second, and then she sprang into action, jerking a pair of handcuffs from her belt and elbowing the suit out of the way. "I got it," she said, taking control of the prisoner by dropping onto a knee on his back.

The robber squirmed and spewed obscenities as she yanked his wrists back and slapped on the cuffs. Allison's back felt damp. She took a steadying breath and tried to regain composure as she conducted the pat down.

"You're under arrest," she said, with much more bravado than she felt at the moment. Her lips were dry, her hands clammy. She glanced up at Sal, who was on the phone with a 911 dispatcher. "Tell them to send a cage car."

Sal nodded.

"You got any other weapons on you?" she asked the perp. "Knives, needles, drug paraphernalia?"

He didn't answer and she checked his pockets. When she was satisfied, she started to climb off him.

He exploded in a blur of movement. Pain stung her

cheek as she caught an elbow, and she had to sit on his butt to make him stop thrashing. The man in the suit pressed a shiny black wing tip between the prisoner's shoulders as Allison struggled with his legs. At eye level was a shelf of fishing supplies, and she grabbed a roll of twine. She ripped open the package with her teeth and lashed the binding around his ankles. The prisoner cursed and squirmed for a while, but finally the fight went out of him.

She tied the final knot. He was trussed like a turkey now, and she knew she was going to catch all kinds of S and M jokes from the guys at work.

Allison glanced up at the man now leaning against the checkout counter. His palms rested casually on the Formica, and the Glock had disappeared back beneath his suit jacket. He hadn't even broken a sweat.

He lifted a brow at her. "Not bad, Officer."

Okay, he was definitely a cop. DEA? Immigration? FBI? And suddenly it hit her. She knew exactly who he was and why he was here.

The corner of his mouth curved up, and she felt a surge of annoyance.

"You have a permit to carry a concealed handgun?" she asked, although she knew the answer.

He sighed and reached into his jacket. He pulled out a leather folio and flipped it open.

"Special Agent Mark Wolfe, FBI."

The legendary Mark Wolfe. Allison had heard he was coming to town, but she didn't say so. Better to save that little tidbit until after the tweeker was booked, and they could have a conversation about a *real* criminal. And maybe she'd finally get some answers.

• • •

Mark prowled the chat room, searching for any trace of Death Raven or one of his aliases. He hadn't found him yet, but it was still early, and many of these men were nocturnal. As he entered his second hour of searching, the sites started to blend together and the words became a blur. *Only this and nothing more.* The phrase echoed through his head. *Tapping at my chamber door.* His temples throbbed. He rubbed his eyes. *Tap-tap.*

Mark looked up.

Tap-tap-tap.

He crossed the room and checked the peephole, even though he already knew who he'd see standing on the other side.

He paused for a moment. Then he pulled open the door.

"Detective Doyle."

She nodded. "Special Agent."

She leaned a palm against the doorframe and looked him squarely in the eye. She wasn't intimidated by his federal badge or his height or the hard stare he used on vicious criminals. He knew why she'd come to see him.

Mark steeled himself. "What can I do for you, Detective?"

"You can talk," she said. "I want to hear about Stephanie Snow."

He weighed how much to tell her. It wasn't her case, yet she was interested—interested enough to come looking for him after an unusually difficult day to pump him for information. He could tell she was smart. Plus, she was young, which could mean open-minded. Maybe she'd listen.

Or maybe talking to her would put the freeze on his already cool relationship with the local police lieutenant overseeing the case—a guy who probably didn't want one of his people talking to the FBI behind his back.

But what the hell? What did he care about the politics of it? He'd be on a plane in the morning, and he hadn't managed to convince anyone who mattered to consider his theory.

Mark pulled the door open. She stepped past him into the room and glanced around. His laptop sat open on the rumpled bedspread, and he'd forgotten to clear the screen. She turned to look at him.

"I work for the Bureau's Behavioral Analysis Unit. You know what that does?"

"Profiling?"

"That's what gets most of the attention. We cover a lot of bases—counterterrorism, white-collar crime, crimes against children, kidnappings. Sometimes we get pulled in on homicide cases if the local police think they're dealing with a serial killer."

She looked at him expectantly.

"In the fall of 2000, I got a call about a murder out in Shasta County, California."

"That's north of Sacramento, right?"

He nodded. "This was near Redding. The year before, a woman went hiking in a park on October thirtieth, never came home. Her boyfriend reported her missing that same night. Her remains were discovered in a shallow creek east of the park a week later."

"Cause of death?"

"Sharp force trauma—her throat had been slashed."

"Sexual assault?"

"Too much water damage to know for sure."

"Lemme guess—boyfriend had an alibi?"

"Airtight," he confirmed. "November nineteenth that same year, another woman went missing, this time from a dog park. Same county. Her remains were discovered in a ravine six months later."

"Not a lot to work with by that point."

"You'd be surprised. A forensic anthropologist examined what was recovered. Marks on the bone indicated another throat cutting."

She propped a shoulder against the wall and folded her arms. "So the boyfriend's off the hook and now you're looking for a serial killer."

"*I* wasn't looking for anything yet. They didn't call me in until the next fall. Another missing woman, another body dumped in a remote area. Dara Langford. Twenty-three. She'd just graduated from college and found a job in Redding." He visualized Dara's smiling young face on all the fliers he'd seen tacked to lampposts and stoplights throughout the area. "She was living with her parents at the time. They reported her missing when she didn't come home from a jog on October thirtieth."

Allison tipped her head to the side. "So it's the dates that match up, not just the MO?"

"Looks that way. That same year, we had another disappearance on November nineteenth. Sheryl Fanning, a thirty-five-year-old mother of two. And another woman the following fall, Jillian Webb."

"October thirtieth?"

"Around there, yes."

Her brow furrowed. "What do the dates mean?"

"I wish I knew."

"Maybe some kind of Halloween connection? Day of the Dead, that sort of thing?"

"We looked into that. Came up with zip. Which isn't to say it isn't a factor, we just don't know how it fits." Mark swallowed his frustration. For years he'd studied this case, and still he hadn't put all the pieces together.

She was watching him closely. He doubted she missed much, which meant she'd sensed this was personal.

"With that last victim," he continued, "we can't pinpoint the date for certain because she was living alone. Her disappearance was reported after she didn't show up for work two days in a row."

"So five women." Her eyes had turned somber.

"That we know of."

Allison gazed away, looking pensive. "Stephanie Snow went missing October thirtieth."

The media hadn't connected Stephanie to the killings in California yet. Maybe they never would. Maybe nobody would, and Mark was spinning his wheels here.

But he didn't believe that. From the way Lieutenant Reynolds had reacted in their meeting today, he could tell there were some holes in the case against Stephanie's ex-boyfriend.

And besides that, Mark had a hunch. This murder *felt* connected, and his hunches about cases often turned out to be right—mainly because they weren't hunches, but predictions based on dozens of different factors, all viewed together through the lens of experience.

"So," Allison said. "Three years in a row you get these close together murders in northern California, and the dates match up."

"Also, the MO. The crimes are remarkably similar."

"How?"

"You haven't seen the case file?"

"It's not my case."

"Maybe it should be."

She looked uncomfortable now, and he could tell he was touching on something that was going to make her life complicated.

But she clearly didn't mind complicated, or she wouldn't be here.

"So, then what?" she asked.

"Then nothing. He's been inactive, as far as we know, for a decade. Now this."

"You're the expert, not me. But I didn't think serial killers just . . . stopped."

"They don't, usually. After about five years without anything similar popping up in ViCAP, we began to think he might be dead or in prison. By ten years, we were sure of it."

"But now he's at it again."

"Maybe. Depends who you want to believe—me or your lieutenant."

She eyed him silently. November nineteenth was two weeks away.

"I'd much rather believe Reynolds," she said. "I just don't think I do."

Fantasy.
Temptation.
Adventure.

Visit PocketAfterDark.com, an all-new website just for Urban Fantasy and Romance Readers!

- Exclusive access to the hottest urban fantasy and romance titles!

- Read and share reviews on the latest books!

- Live chats with your favorite romance authors!

- Vote in online polls!

www.PocketAfterDark.com

26119